CALAMITY

SAM WINTER

Calamity

ISBN: 978-1-954530-00-3

www.samwinterbooks.com

PROLOGUE

Officer Derrick Hart stared at the screen of his phone. His thumb hesitated above the name 'Janice' in his voicemail box. There was a twist of anxiety that knotted in his stomach as he heard the distant pops of gunshots and the pursuing police sirens that had become a banality in Birmingham. Law and order were the first to go after the news outlets began sensationalizing the deadly viral outbreak. The title of the last news article Derrick read was:

'Millions Suspected Dead in Florida—Is This the End of America?'

I don't have time for this crap, Derrick thought. *This city is about to burn.*

Derrick stuffed the phone back into the breast pocket of his uniform and went to step back inside the Judge's house but stopped at the doorway of the front porch. It was as if an invisible lasso had cinched around his hips and kept him from ignoring this part of his life he was so desperate to forget. Gritting his teeth, Derrick punched the splintering, brown wood of the door jamb and removed his phone from his pocket, clicking the voicemail.

"Hey Der– Derrick, it's Janice, um– it's Mom." Derrick pinched the bridge of his nose as he paced the front porch with the phone pressed to his ear. "I was just checking in on you. I tried calling a few times but I– they never made it through. I was just worried about you, you know... Maryland's not close to the outbreak down there, but they still have us all under martial law, just like everywhere else. All we can do is watch the news and all they ever talk about is you guys in the South. Every time they mention Birmingham or Alabama, I think about you. I guess I've been thinking about you a lot lately... I know we haven't talked much over the years, and that's my fault, but..."

Derrick could hear his mother move the phone away from her face so she could sniffle and clear the knot in her throat. "I just called to tell you that I am thinking of you, and praying for you, and– and... I really, really want to see you when this is all over."

The quiver in his mother's voice made Derrick clench his teeth.

This is her goodbye, he thought. *She knows that I'm next to die.*

"I'm just–I'm sorry. I needed to say– I've wanted to say it so many times, but– I'm sorry for everything. Everything I put you through... I can't fix what happened– what I did... I know sorry doesn't change anything but... I wanted to make sure you knew that I'm so sorry, and I love you and I always have loved you... um... just call me back when you can, okay? I'll talk to you soon, son... um, Goodbye."

Derrick chewed his lip. He hoped the pain from his teeth stabbing his fleshy cheek would remove his mind from the black hole of self-pity he spiraled into. Instead, the welcome distraction came in the form of a short scream of rubber tires chafing against the pavement followed by an abrupt crash.

From the front porch of the corner house where he stood, Derrick watched the beige minivan, already speckled in dents and scrapes from its recent wrecks of the past, skid around the backside of his parked patrol car and flatten the stop sign into the intersection. The violence and chaos that plagued downtown Birmingham were beginning to snake their tentacles into the affluent suburbs of this upper-class neighborhood.

The minivan driver– a middle-aged woman with stressed, unkempt hair, sat with panicked eyes that found Derrick glaring down on her. For a moment they stared at each other in silence. His eyes on her van idling in the middle of the intersection and her eyes on the oval, silver badge pinned on the chest of his uniform.

Derrick hadn't planned on charging onto the road in a cursing rage. He wasn't the type of person to lose his head. Over the past few days, since the outbreak began, he'd let worse crimes go unanswered than a hit and run. But when he saw a child's head pop up from the backseat of the minivan, a flash of anger boiled inside him. The little girl, no older than five years old, had tears in her eyes and appeared to have been unsecured by a seatbelt or a car seat. Leaping down the four steps leading to the porch in one stride, Derrick sprinted across the front lawn towards the intersection.

Perhaps it was his lack of sleep or even a trickery of the afternoon light, but as he ran the driver's face appeared to swap with his mother's likeness. But not the vibrant, middle-aged woman she was now. Not the woman who rebuilt her life after prison and began a new family. No, Derrick saw the pale, sunken-skinned Janice from his childhood with long, matted brown hair in need of a comb. He saw his mom as he imagined she looked after *her* car accident.

But it was this driver who moved in a frenzy. Lurching forward with acceleration, the wide-eyed woman fled the scene in a hurry sending the young child toppling over in the back of the minivan and disappearing from sight.

"Hey– hey, stop!" Derrick shouted at the taillights. "Stop! No, Mom sto–" Derrick bit down hard on his lower lip, stopping his pursuit as he looked around, with a flare of embarrassment.

"Wut the hell was that ruckus?" the familiar southern drawl of an old man's voice bellowed as he stomped outside. Judge Watkins was a barrel-chested man, with combed-over graying hair and a round face. Looking at the flattened 'Stop' sign in the middle of the road, he roared, "Goddamn lunatics!" the Judge beat his fist on the railing along his front porch as if his hand was his gavel.

Derrick rubbed his brow, centering his thoughts as he walked back to Judge Watkins' front porch. "Your honor, can you spare that minute now?" Derrick asked. Grumbling to himself, the Judge waddled back inside his house.

Following the Judge inside, Derrick walked through the open French doors into a long living room where the news played loudly on the TV mounted above a fireplace. The images being displayed on the screen were of aerial footage taken by a news helicopter in downtown Miami, Florida. Through smoky skies, the camera panned across a four-lane road tucked between buildings downtown. Hundreds of people ran through the narrowing street. From the elevated camera angle, the mass of panicked people looked like wildebeest fleeing a predator. The mere dots of people on the screen were chased by a handful of other dots–things that appeared to move faster than the fleeing dots; things that leaped onto the fleeing dots, tackling them violently into the pavement.

Derrick didn't need to watch the end of the news clip. It

had been recorded only a few days ago, but the video was already viral. It had been viewed hundreds of millions of times online and on the twenty-four-hour news networks now that the internet was beginning to lag across the nation. It was one of the few videos of the infected available to the public that hadn't been deemed too violent or gruesome for TV.

"That's right, David. We now have two senior officials inside the Pentagon confirming they have lost contact with the National Guard units deployed just days ago to restore order inside southern Florida. There's still no word from the White House–" The White House reporter's voice followed Derrick down the hall to the Judge's study.

"Alright, now. Let's have it." Judge Watkins huffed air in and out of his mouth as he side-stepped around his large mahogany desk in his study. The room looked more like a library with walls lined with bookshelves containing law textbooks and other historical books from around the world. Two leather couches that appeared to never have been used sat beside a small bar, which had more than a few emptied bottles on it.

Alyssa stood in front of the Judge's desk at the head of the room exactly where Derrick had left her to go outside to listen to his voicemail. She had a guilty look in her eyes, but the wavering line of her lips communicated her impatience as she chewed the corner of her thumbnail. Her blond hair was pulled back into a ponytail, and the t-shirt and jeans she wore revealed the collection of old and new tattoos she had on her forearms and chest.

Judge Watkins held out his hand expectantly to Alyssa, a layer of sweat forming on his brow as he waited. Fumbling with the stack of papers stapled together, she extended them to the Judge only for him to rip them out of her hands. Breathing loudly through his nose, he flipped through the pages in a rush, scribbling his name on empty lines and stamping his personalized red 'Judge Watkins' seal beneath each signature.

"What– is everything alright?" Alyssa whispered over her shoulder to Derrick. Derrick looked at the phone that was still in his hand and nodded as he put it away in his uniform's breast pocket.

"Yeah, it was Janice– it was my mom," he said. The word 'mom' always came out strange when he used it about his family. "She tried to get in touch to check on me. Damn phones keeps going in and out of service though."

"Heard on channel three it's them cell towers," Judge Watkins butted into the conversation without looking up from the papers he was signing. "Said they was overloaded er' some type of nonsense. Everybody in the country callin' at the same time to check on family in Florida... it'll only get worse. Soon they'll all be calling to check on us."

Derrick saw Alyssa flinch as her guilt worsened. "Is she doing alright? Janice?" Alyssa asked.

"They're fine," Derrick said, purposefully void of emotion. "Her new family's safe, too, it sounds like."

"Gawddang forms!" Judge Watkins snapped as he slammed his clubbed fist down on the desk hard enough to make an empty bottle of bourbon topple over and teeter on the edge before rolling off the tabletop. "I done signed that one twice already! Why do they need another?"

Derrick Hart had been in the Judge's courtroom enough over the years to know his question was rhetorical. Judge Watkins was known for his grandstanding whenever a defendant or lawyer made the unfortunate mistake to 'whine' about the proceedings in his orderly courtroom. Derrick had a good working relationship with the Judge as many of his cases over the years were overseen by him. In the private moments between hearings and motions, the judge and Derrick would poke fun of each other and exchange tales of their most recent fishing exploits.

"Now don't tell any them other police officers that I did this for ya, ya hear?" Judge Watkins glared over the top of his glasses at Derrick. "I'm serious. Don't have time for this. Got my brother, Eddie, waitin' for me up in Huntsville as it is..."

"Yes, your honor, thanks again–" Derrick started but the Judge waved away his thanks and went back to signing the last of the papers, finishing it off with a stamp.

"Nah, hush up with that now," the Judge said. "Don't know why y'all don't just fake my signature anyways. What're they gon' do? Arrest ya?"

"A few officers tried," Derrick admitted. "The army stopped giving out the Yellowband bracelets with just a signature. They need your stamp now, too." Judge Watkins nodded, as he, out of thirty-five years of habit, went through the stack of papers and double checked each page to cross the T's and dot the I's.

"Derrick... Derrick," Alyssa whispered until he looked at her. Despite the lack of sleep and stress that wore on her face, she still looked as beautiful as the first day Derrick met her. Rarely ever wearing makeup, Derrick always loved the natural look Alyssa had about herself. "You don't have to do this, you know."

"I know," he replied with a small, hopeful smile before looking away when he realized she had nothing else to say.

"Alright, all signed an' stamped an' all that nonsense," the Judge sighed as he tossed the stack of papers on the center of the desk. "Do y'all have rings?" he asked looking at Alyssa's empty ring finger on her left hand.

"Oh, um, no, we–" Alyssa started as a pink hue burned her cheeks.

They turned to Derrick as he dug into the cargo pocket of

his pants and removed a small gray box. The folded receipt from the jewelers was clenched in the case's mouth as he had intended on returning the ring before the outbreak put a halt to his life, like everyone else's.

Derrick saw the diamond, fourteen-karat white gold engagement ring staring up at him. Months ago, he had fretted over the ring for weeks, worrying if it was the right one for Alyssa. He used to look at the ring and feel anxious excitement over the possible future. Now he only felt foolish at its sight.

"Derrick..." Alyssa's voice was soft and full of pity. "I can't–"

Pinching it free from the jewelry box, Derrick dropped the ring in Alyssa's palm and put the box back into his pocket. "Just take it, it's outside the return policy anyway," he lied.

Reluctantly, Alyssa slid the ring down her left finger and stole the quickest of glances, admiring the look of her engaged hand. Taking off his reading glasses, the Judge used them to draw a lazy crucifix in the air as he said, "With the power vested in me I now pronounce you man an' wife, you can kiss the bride."

Alyssa looked around the room, fidgeting with her hands and feet, clearly uncomfortable, before turning to Derrick. Derrick circumvented the awkward moment by reaching across the desk and shaking the Judge's hand, ignoring the twisting feeling he felt in his chest. "Thank you, your honor. Good luck to you and your family."

"Son," Judge Watkins looked at Derrick and grasped his hand for a prolonged moment. "I'll pray for you and the other officers who stayed behind. Y'all are heroes and don't you forget that. And ma'am, best of luck to you."

Alyssa took the Judge's extended hand in a delicate shake before he snatched up a piece of empty luggage from behind his desk and waddled off to the bedroom through a side door.

Derrick and Alyssa hurried in a rush when the Judge left. Scooping the marriage certificate up along with the rest of the National Security Public Servant Act waiver paperwork, they made for the front door. Derrick hesitated for a moment in the hallway.

"Derrick, what is it?"

"Go ahead, I'll meet you at your car," Derrick said as he jogged back into the Judge's study. Pausing at the large desk his eyes jetted to the bedroom where the Judge packed his things. Gritting his teeth, he grabbed the small, wooden grip stamp of the Judge's name and the red ink pad beside it and slid them both in his pocket. Leaving the house, Officer Derrick Hart felt bile kiss the back of his throat as he rationalized committing petty theft in service to the greater good.

How many suspects have I arrested for crimes they thought were for the greater good? How many rationalized away their actions just like I am doing now. Derrick balked at his hypocrisy but did not turn around to return the stolen items.

I'll take being a hypocrite if it means this stamp saves other police officers' families.

From the passenger seat of his patrol car, Derrick grabbed a large yellow envelope and slid the marriage license inside with the rest of the paperwork. He took out a plastic card with his police academy picture on it. "Here take these documents; this is my Police Commission card." he handed the envelope and the card to Alyssa who stood beside her car parked ahead of his. "Go up 20th St. until Interstate 20– I'll radio ahead. All the road closures manned by police will wave you through."

Alyssa nodded, listening to instructions while balancing her car keys and the envelope in one hand and holding the Police Commission card in the other.

"Once you get to I-20, you won't find any police. That blockade is manned by the National Guard," Derrick continued and put a heavy hand on Alyssa's shoulder to emphasize his seriousness. "Drive slowly, follow commands, and keep your hands visible. Show them these papers and my ID. They'll give you a Yellowband bracelet," Derrick pointed to the metallic bracelet cinched securely on his right wrist.

The bracelet he had was thick with a red band around the center and a laser etched barcode in the middle. To receive the paperwork with the pre-authorized signatures for Alyssa to get her bracelet, Derrick had to allow himself to be Redbanded. It was his shackle to this city that would soon be his tomb.

There's a reason everyone calls these papers suicide contracts.

"...once you have the Yellowband they'll let you through to Georgia. If they don't, call me. If the phone isn't working, have one of the officers at the previous road closures radio me, okay?"

Alyssa nodded. Her starry eyes looked overwhelmed, lost in a sea of instructions and surmounting emotions.

"Are you sure you won't go to Tennessee?" Derrick asked one last time. "The infection will reach Georgia before Alabam–"

"My family's in Atlanta," Alyssa interrupted, already knowing where this conversation was headed. "They're all in Atlanta– I can't just leave them. I need to be– I need to be with my family."

Derrick nodded, accepting that echoing his opinion would be pointless. Alyssa set the papers down in the front passenger seat of her cherry-red Chevy Impala. Its flashy color stood as a shining example of their differences. While Alyssa was the bright, social butterfly, often getting lost in conversations with complete strangers at parties, Derrick was the quiet one who always seemed to be dragged to the party. She would congregate groups of friends and discuss her latest tattoo or lip piercing, and the clean-shaven Derrick would stand beside her and laugh along with her.

Derrick was a simple, plain spoken man who was more than content with the quiet life he had carved for himself over the years. Alyssa, on the other hand, had a destiny about her. Like she always believed she was meant for more in this world. An entrepreneur in the entertainment world, Alyssa's event planning business was just taking off when the outbreak began almost a week ago. Their contrasts grossly outnumbered their commonalities in every way, now that Derrick thought about it.

Why did I ever think someone like her would marry someone like me?

Derrick shook his head free of the past. He went to the rear passenger door of his cruiser and let out a long sigh, preparing himself for what lay behind it before opening the door. Immediately, a burst of energy and tail-wagging hit him.

"Hey– down. Down, boy," Derrick said on autopilot. Ginger, a middle-aged black lab, heeded the command and jumped onto the sidewalk, shook free the pent-up energy he had from being cooped up in the back of an air-conditioned police car for nearly an hour and began to hop around Derrick's legs, ready to play.

"Come here, good boy," Derrick said as he knelt and wrapped his arms around his dog and roughly rubbed the back of his neck just as he loved. He had found Ginger as a rescue pup from a dilapidated puppy mill that he helped shut down five years back and the dog had been his loyal friend ever since. Derrick nuzzled his face into the dog's neck and Ginger returned the gesture. "Good boy..."

Derrick's eyes stung and he felt a hitch at the back of his throat. He quickly straightened, giving his friend one last pat on the back. He walked Ginger to Alyssa's car and opened the rear door. He didn't ask for permission nor did he wait for a protest as he pushed a piece of luggage to the side and tapped the seat for him to hop in.

"I need you to take Ginger with you. I know he's not your dog, but I'm– I'm not going to be home for a while... days probably with the mandates at work. I know you'll take care of him," Derrick said, giving Ginger one last scratch under his chin before closing the door.

Alyssa pursed her lips and took a small step back, not meeting his eyes– a familiar gesture of annoyance that Derrick picked up on. Alyssa said nothing and simply nodded with a resigned smile, "Okay."

Derrick stood at arm's length from his 'wife' as they both struggled to make eye contact before parting ways. It was Alyssa who moved first. Wrapping her arms around Derrick's neck, she hugged him tightly. The feel of Alyssa's arms around him, the comforting smell of the moisturizer on her skin, the familiar way she nuzzled her lips into the crook of his neck... all of it, for the briefest of moments, made him believe the lie that she was really his wife. She hugged him like they were still together. She hugged him as if she loved him.

"Thank you," Alyssa whispered in his ear, letting out a wet sniffle. He was caught off guard when, as he began to pull away, Alyssa took his face in both hands and kissed him. It was not a stiff peck on the lips but a kiss that lingered. It was the kind of blissful kiss couples shared after being declared man and wife.

It was Derrick who pulled away from Alyssa. He wanted to believe her love for him, but the spell of the woman he cared for clouded the truth of the matter. It was a lie.

She isn't kissing me out of love. It is out of gratitude... charity... It's a kiss of pity.

Derrick nodded, gesturing to her car as he stepped away, even though his body clearly wanted to stay put. "Take care of

Ginger for me, okay?" his voice was thick with emotion as he tried to clear it away.

"I will, I promise." tears rolled down her cheeks as she opened her door. "And Derrick..." Alyssa paused, locking eyes with him. He could see the anguish as she fought to bring herself to speak the words she wanted to say. He saw her hesitation turn into resignation before she spoke. "Goodbye," she said and disappeared into the car.

Derrick watched her drive away with Ginger hopping around in the back seat. Even though, legally, he had just married her, Derrick felt as though Alyssa had broken up with him for a second time this month. His eyes were fixed on the folded stop sign that laid at the intersection a few yards ahead of him. Gunshots popped in the distance; their muted sounds were overrun by the roar of an army helicopter that passed overhead towards downtown.

Opening the front passenger door of his Dodge Charger, Derrick looked at his Colt AR-15 rifle locked in the gun rack between the two front seats then moved his gaze to the ballistic hard plate body armor that sat on the passenger seat laid atop of his duty bag. The bold white lettering on the back of the armored vest was chipped in some places and faded in others from years of use but the word was still readable.

"SWAT"

It's time to go to work.

PART I

Monday, April 29th

52 Hours, 14 Minutes Until Calamity Event

"Everything has a beginning… Even the end."

- Sharon Hill

ONE

Derrick Hart

Birmingham, Al

Nothing was as terrible as the sound of a man crying. It was like the sound of a lost child wailing in a park. It was the whimper of a wounded animal dying in the street. A man crying was an unpracticed and foreign sound that once heard could not be forgotten, even though all you wanted was for it to end. Especially when it came from one of these men. The sheepdogs who were meant to protect the sheep.

Officer Derrick Hart laid on his back in the dark roll call room, his fingers curled around the chain that held a pair of worn dog tags around his neck. He had never served in the military. The two pieces of metal were not to identify him as a soldier but instead were what tied him to his best friend. They were a cheap toy made of thin metal and meant to be snapped free from the chain and be lost days after a child received them for their birthday or a weekend trip to the toy store. The chain on Derrick's set had snapped on more than one occasion during his teenaged years, but he had the wherewithal to slip the tags down a stronger chain that would stand the test of time. He did the same for Brandon's matching set.

Derrick admired the drawings of two Viking warriors on one tag. Their tattooed, muscle-bound bodies strapped with heavy axes and broadswords looked nothing like his best friend nor himself, but Derrick had always pretended they did as a kid. Two brothers clasping arms before battle.

The second of the two tags read a quote Derrick had read and repeated with his friend a thousand times. '*Valhalla waits for no one...*' Of all the times he had read that, today was the first time Derrick's stomach had dropped as he weighed the meaning of those words. It was today he would see Valhalla.

Today is the day I die.

Dozens of police officers laid around him on the musky carpet and pretended to sleep; pretended not to hear the whimpering in the front of the room. It had been nine days since the outbreak in Miami, and Derrick questioned how many hours he had slept since then.

How much sleep has anyone gotten? How do you sleep when horror movies become a reality?

Sleep wasn't measured in days and nights for police officers anymore but in clumps of hours here or thirty minutes there, which made these precious minutes of peace all the more important.

The infected were coming. Thousands of them, millions, perhaps. The Army National Guard that was now in charge, refused to give estimates, but everyone knew the infected were running to Birmingham this very moment. They were coming to tear Derrick apart along with all those who remained in the city. The first of them were arriving today.

He twisted the bulky metallic Redband bracelet that had

been fastened on his right wrist for days now. His thumb rubbed across the barcode etchings along the side of the bracelet– the government imposed tether that he and all present in this room had agreed to wear for the sake of their loved ones.

Derrick felt the layer of dried sweat and grease coating his skin every time he moved. His auburn hair was the only thing greasier than his skin. He couldn't say when the last time he'd taken a shower was. The closest thing he had was pouring cold water over his neck from a hose behind the precinct yesterday.

At least I think it was yesterday.

He had stopped noticing his body odor last week and was getting better at not noticing others either. Derrick had an unassuming way about him. At twenty-nine years old, he was of an average height with plain looks and soft features. Few would guess he was a senior member of the Birmingham SWAT team.

The muffled cries that jabbed at the quiet room came from a young man who stood by himself near the whiteboard. The board behind him was covered in old messages from supervisors– 'OT Mandates,' 'found pair of handcuffs in sergeant's office,' along with an officer's hastily scribbled comment, 'also make sure all of the suspects cocaine is out of their pockets before booking them (Alex!).' Long gray tables and black wobbly chairs were shoved to the edge of the dim room and stacked on top of each other to make floor space.

Shrouded in the shadow of a stack of chairs taller than him, the young man held his face in the palms of his hands as he cried. Derrick could sense the old-timers beside him growing perturbed with these audible emotions.

Derrick did his best to ignore the messy sobs and focused on the other officers around him. Most tried to sleep but, like Derrick, they were too restless as they rolled about on the thin carpet that felt more like they laid on concrete slabs. Leaving on just their black work pants and black undershirts, officers had stacked their uniform shirts, body armor, and gun belts beside them.

Everyone dealt with the tense moments during downtime differently. Some men mumbled prayers to themselves–barely audible whispers filled with pleas for God's protection. Others stared at pictures of their loved ones under the glow of their cellphone screens. They twisted the Redband bracelets on their wrists. At some point, every police officer had doubts about signing the suicide contract so their loved ones could escape the city. Even Derrick.

No one talked to one another. He couldn't blame them. Just like he didn't blame the young patrol officer for crying. At some point today, every man and woman in this room would allow their tears to consume them in the privacy of a bathroom stall or patrol car. It was inevitable. There was only one thing on everyone's mind, and no one wanted to say it out loud. As if staying silent might keep death at bay.

Derrick took his phone out of his breast pocket hoping to see a green notification from her. A missed call or text message, some sign that Alyssa was alive. That she was safe.

That Alyssa is thinking of me, Derrick thought. He immediately hated himself for thinking it. But alas, the top of the screen showed the same symbol it always did. *No signal*. The only reason Derrick still charged the damn thing was for the few times it connected to a Wi-Fi signal, he'd receive sporadic data dumps of news updates, text messages, and voicemails that had been suspended in limbo for hours or days. But as 'America's Last Stand,' a term coined by news channels, approached, even the Wi-Fi seemed sluggish.

Instead, Derrick just stared at the photo on his home screen. It was a year-old picture of Alyssa on her tippy toes kissing a blurry-eyed Derrick on the cheek after a long night of drinking. The picture always made him smile, not just because of the moment, but what had occurred just after. His best friend, Brandon, had snapped the picture as they waited for their rideshare from downtown Birmingham back to Derrick's house. Not two seconds after taking it had Brandon vomited the pitcher of strawberry margarita he had inhaled an hour prior. The mess had covered the front of Brandon's cowboy boots that his wife had insisted he wear. Karen and Alyssa had spent the rest of the night chastising him for splattering on them, and Derrick couldn't stop himself from laughing. He was sure he still had a video of Brandon passed out in a bush in the backyard later that night.

Derrick's smile soured as the sobs of the patrolman grew louder. He was more than background noise at this point. The base in his voice rumbled, making officers who slept stir.

"Please god... Please..." The young officer's voice broke as he cried his prayer.

"Jesus Christ..." A heavyset officer to Derrick's right grumbled as he turned on his side. To be honest, Derrick didn't want to listen to this kid's tears, either. Deep down, he wanted this boy to man up and give everyone some much needed peace before they died. That was Derrick's exhaustion talking.

But how else should this patrolman act? The military that now fortified Birmingham with hardened defenses fit for a Russian invasion, gave the Birmingham Police updates on how far the infected swarms were from them. Three days. Two days. One... This rookie officer was tormented by videos of infected civilians tackling Florida police officers in fits of violence. Men and women stripped of their humanity as they growled and screamed like animals. An entire state lost in days.

Now, Birmingham was all that stood in the way of the infection spreading to the rest of the country. And the ETA of the amassing hordes of infected wasn't days anymore, but hours.

"Ah, for fuck's sake," Tommy spat. "Shut the fuck up!" Derrick couldn't see Tommy in the darkroom but knew his grating, Jersey-accented voice anywhere. It was ironic he was the one silencing another since Tommy had spent his whole career being told to shut his overactive mouth.

"Oh god..." The crying officer's voice broke. "I don't want to die..."

"Are you kidding me..." a deep voice groaned from the back of the room.

"Shut up!" another officer echoed as exasperated gripes joined in. Derrick felt a knot in his throat and another forming in his gut. He tried to ignore the heavy and obligatory pull he felt from within when duty called. It wasn't something Derrick could just turn off, no matter how much he wished he could. All he wanted to do was sleep, but he couldn't just sit back and listen to this rookie officer being berated.

"I'm sorry, I just– I can't," the young man tucked his arms into his chest. His hands covered his face as his cries turned to hysterical sobbing. The kind of crying he probably hadn't done in twenty years, since he was a little boy tucked in the safety of his mother's embrace.

"Look you fucking pussy," Tommy's voice boomed, again. This time he was up and lumbering toward the front of the room with heavy steps. Tommy was a giant to most. His six foot four, two-hundred and fifty-pound frame only amplified his broad shoulders and gaunt jaw. "I'll fuckn' kill you myself if you don't shut up." Tommy snatched the smaller officer up by his lapel making the boy's metal pins on his uniform clang against each other.

Tommy's voice was erratic and strained– a testament to the amount of stress they were all under after days of sleeplessness and nights of violent rioting. The infection might not have reached Birmingham yet, but the riots, looting, and surge in crime had plagued every major city in the United States for over a week now.

"In fact," Tommy pointed down to the young man's duty pistol in his holster, "why don't you take that gun into the men's room and fucking eat the muzzle like the rest of the pussy suicides, huh?"

"I-I'm, I just–" the boy stuttered.

Derrick scrambled to his feet, but his aching body didn't move nearly as fast as he thought it would. His feet were covered in blisters and sores from being on his feet for twenty hours a day for over a week, while his chest and arms were covered in undiscovered bruises from working the riot lines at night.

"Here, I'll fuckn' help you pull the trigger," Tommy spat, reaching for the boy's weapon. A small figure appeared behind Tommy before Derrick intervened. She was shorter than both of the men. When she came between Tommy and the crying officer, she looked like a child trying to hold back her dad from a fight. Both her hands propped against Tommy's chest, failing to hold him at bay. That's why it was to everyone's surprise when Tommy collapsed to the carpet like a chopped tree.

"I said, back the fuck off!" the woman shouted pointing her finger down at Tommy. Derrick recognized the voice and in the gray hue he was able to see Perry's familiar face.

Tommy writhed on the carpet. His hands clutched his groin, his knees pinched together like a cartoon character.

"You– bitch!" Tommy fumed through gritted teeth. Like an angry bear, he clamored to his feet marching towards Perry until he saw her Glock 19 half drawn out of the drop holster on her thigh. "Oh, you gonna shoot me now? Do it! Do me the favor, bitch!" Tommy held his arms wide open in a challenge as he stepped closer to her.

The room became icy cold as the two stared each other down. In that hair of a second, the room wasn't full of police officers, but just a group of people at their wits end. The anarchy that had spread through the country had finally found its way into the police precinct. Derrick broke from his trance long enough to muster as much of a commanding voice as he could despite his exhaustion. "Back off, Tommy!"

Tommy's eyes jolted over to Derrick, and he drew to a halt barely a yard from Perry. Tommy gave a measured snarl in Derrick's direction. Then, as if realizing where he was, did a brief survey of the dozens of officers staring at him.

With a final grunt Tommy relented, turning away from Perry and the cowering patrolman "Whatever... fucking cunt."

Perry's eyes didn't leave Tommy until he fell back to his spot on the floor. His hand rubbed his wounded crotch. Her hand seated her Glock back in the holster and she gave a brief nod to Derrick, which he returned. Derrick hadn't realized Perry was in the room until then. She was one of the few who still had her gear and uniform on, but unlike the patrolmen whose shirts and pants were black, Perry wore a baggy, forest green uniform that matched Derrick's. She also wore a heavy vest similar to the one Derrick had laid beside him. It was covered with filled magazine pouches across the chest and white lettering across the upper back panel that read, 'SWAT.'

"I'm sorry– I just, I need–" the young patrolman stuttered. His face was a mess of tears, snot, and shock from what had just happened.

"It's okay... it's okay... what's your name?" Officer Perry asked.

"Miles," he answered, wiping his nose with the back of his hand.

"Miles, my name is Perry," she said.

The barrel-chested patrolman beside Derrick rolled to his side with a labored sigh, "would you get that coward out of–"

Before Derrick could even speak Perry snapped at him, "Shut up you fat fuck and go back to sleep."

The man growled something to himself but did as he was told.

Perry turned back to Miles and pulled him down into an embrace, petting his hair as his mother might have. "It'll be alright, take a deep breath. In and out, come on."

The officer followed her instructions through wet sniffles. After a moment she pulled away but held Miles' shoulders as she looked at him.

"Listen Miles. I need you to suck it the fuck up, okay?" she said, pulling his six-foot frame down to her shorter self. "You're a fuckin' police officer. You're built for this shit, otherwise, you wouldn't have that badge on your chest. The rules are the same out there. Bad guys chase civilians, and we chase bad guys, okay? There's people out there who aren't as strong as you, who are counting on you right now. And more importantly, everyone in this room is counting on you, and I'm one of them. It's easy to be a cop when nothing bad is happening, but it's what you do now that matters most, okay?"

Miles nodded, taking a deep breath. He wiped his eyes on the back of his forearm.

"Okay. Now go outside, get some water on your face, and come back. Get some rest, alright?" Perry gave him a nod. Miles left the room quickly with his head tucked low. Derrick saw a brief glare of Miles' wedding band catching the light as he passed.

It's falling apart. Everything is about to fall apart.

Derrick laid back down beside his gear and rubbed his

greasy forehead. If the police were barely holding it together, the military couldn't be far behind.

And the virus isn't even in Birmingham, yet.

Derrick rolled to his side and tried to quiet his mind. With a deep breath, he allowed his body to release the tension and begin his fast descent into sleep. His fingers touched the rifle that laid beside him as the world faded into darkness as his muscles unclenched for the first time in days.

Before the warm embrace of sleep could envelop him, the hallway door smacked open against the wall, rattling the room to life. The cut of the bright setting sunlight from the summer day shone painfully across their eyes. The open door let the roar of thumping helicopter rotary blades fill the room.

"It's time. Everybody up!" Captain Elwood ordered. "They're here."

TWO

Rachel Anderson
I-65 N

Rachel Anderson pressed her hands against the dashboard as the Toyota 4runner barreled violently across the muddy terrain. Her butt jumped up the seat with every bump. The engine roared across a farm field that grew muddier the farther they drove away from the interstate. Rachel didn't know anything about cars, but she knew the sound the engine made meant their vehicle wasn't going to last much longer. The engine whined from the high RPMs as Sean turned the steering wheel side to side and pumped the gas pedal to escape from getting stuck in the thick cake of black sludge.

Come on, we're almost there.

They passed dozens of unoccupied cars, if not hundreds. Each with their tires half-buried in the muck and their sides splattered in a massacre of mud, evidence of the drivers' final attempts to free themselves from the clutch of the bog. The vehicles' occupants would be walking along the interstate with the others now. Their possessions abandoned along with their cars as they committed to the long walk north to safety, wherever that may be.

The forgotten vehicles extended to the left and right of the interstate for over a hundred yards in each direction. Rachel and the three men she rode with in the Toyota had been lucky so far. They had made it farther than most. The one good thing about being this far from Interstate 65 was they had distance between them and the tens of thousands who walked northbound along the road.

Rachel stared nervously at the endless procession of sweaty, worn down people who walked beside the traffic clogged road. She swore if she ever made it home to safety, she would lock herself in her bedroom with all her lights on and just be alone. For all her love of people and the years Rachel had dedicated to teaching the under privileged youth of America, the bleak chaos of the past days had caused her to question her core beliefs for the first time in her twenty-five years on this planet.

People were no longer an idealized vessel of hope to Rachel, they were unpredictable animals. Any group greater in number than their group made her wary. Staring out the window at the thousands across the field, her mind had violent recollections of being nearly trampled in panicked stampedes in Florida or bruised by muggers who swarmed her. Rachel had seen the dark side of humanity.

"Watch that bump there," Chris pointed from behind the driver's seat. Chris Carroll was a middle-aged man who was balding, though, as usual his head was covered in a Philadelphia Eagles ball cap that was worn and frayed at the edges. "Looks like a soft spot."

"They're all soft spots," Allen grumbled, the permanent

snarl fixed to his face beneath his hooked nose. "It's a goddamn muddy... trough."

Even though Allen sat behind her and she couldn't see him, Rachel had to literally bite her tongue to keep from cussing him out, again. The stress of survival had worn on everyone's nerves and regressed each person to their base personalities. The carefully crafted public identities displayed for the world to see had been stripped away days ago.

Rachel realized this about herself too. In the first moments following the massacre in Miami the outgoing, confident, and opinionated self she identified as had reverted back to the quiet, insecure teenager she had once been. The world she thought she knew was suddenly built on shifting sands. When the laws and rules of the land had been stripped away, Rachel had found herself timid and uncertain to speak. She hated herself for it. Sean was the only one who hadn't changed since the outbreak had collapsed Florida.

Sean ignored Chris and Allen's bickering behind them. His stoic gaze and square jaw was a constant poker face. Sean was not a boisterous person. A serious man with a calm demeanor, he maintained a focused exterior in every situation. While Chris's nerves sent him into a talking frenzy, and Allen's spiraled him into a moody pessimist who wasn't able to go two minutes without uttering a complaint, Sean Williams remained the rock that Rachel counted on to keep her centered. She had done her best not to demonstrate any affection towards Sean that Chris and Allen could pick up on over the past days as she knew it would only get Sean into trouble should they survive this ordeal. But sometimes just holding Sean's hand was enough. Like his calming aura transferred from him to her.

"Would you quit saying that?" Chris snapped at Allen.

"They're not going to let us cross the border into the city,

I'm telling you! We're walking into a death trap," Allen said. "And I'm–"

"You don't know that. You have no reason to think–"

"Why are they having us drive all the way to the border? Ignore signs?" Allen pointed to the blockade they approached a few hundred yards away. "Why didn't they send a helicopter to come to pick us up instead?"

"I don't know!" Chris yelled. "You can ask them when we're there."

"They're not going to let anyone who's seen this– this debacle live. Us included. The cover up starts at the border–"

Chris swiped at the air in frustration. "Would you shut up with your freaking conspiracy theory crap!"

"You don't–"

"Shut up! Shut up! Shut up!" Rachel whipped around in her seat. Her mind was ablaze from listening to these grown children bicker for too many days now. "Just shut up! I'm sick of both of your shit! Allen, if you have a better fucking idea– if you have an original thought for once in your life, then say it. Otherwise, shut up."

Allen covered the sour expression on his face with his fist as he pouted and fixed his gaze out the window. Chris simply sighed and mumbled to himself, finishing the argument under his breath while looking out his own window.

"Unbelievable..." Rachel shook her head.

The car rocked over a deep ridge in the muddy field and Rachel fell back into her seat at the impact with an especially cavernous bump. Despite the engine ramping up to a loud whine, the 4runner slowed and slowed before eventually gargling to a halt. Sean jerked the steering wheel trying to put the car in reverse, shifting into low gear and going forward but it wouldn't budge. He revved the engine until smoke spilled from the hood.

"We're stuck," Allen said as if it was everyone else's fault and he could have prevented it.

"Thanks captain obvious..." Chris murmured under his voice, and Allen turned on him.

Rachel whipped around in her seat to hurl more venom at the men behind her, but Sean's hard gaze caught hers and without saying a word Sean simply raised a hand to give her pause as if he advised her, *just let it go.*

"Grab your bag," Sean said. "We're walking."

Rachel hopped out of the car and immediately felt her feet sink ankle deep in the mud, the moisture seeping through every vent in her shoes and being absorbed into her socks within seconds. She felt the prickle of irritation travel up her spine to the back of her neck, threatening a mental breakdown if another line got crossed. Sean grabbed the dirty abused backpack that held the handful of refilled plastic water bottles and the little food they had left. Mostly energy drinks, a smashed bag of half-eaten chips, and two melted candy bars.

Rachel, Chris, and Allen followed Sean in a jog toward the interstate. They ran in a familiar formation that Rachel had come to be used to. Sean in the front, followed by Rachel and Chris and Allen behind her. They allowed no more than ten paces between she and them at any time. After days of running for their lives, Rachel's limbs ached. She tried not to think of the rescue site they neared. Doing so only led her down a path of imagining the safety of her father's arms.

Though Rachel was twenty-five years old and stood as tall as her dad, when he wrapped her arms around her, she still felt like a child. No matter how powerful of a political figure he had become, her dad was still the man who had called her every Sunday while she was away at college, traveled to every one of her volleyball games in high school, and he was still the man who had set aside work every evening to spend time with

Rachel when her mother had passed away from a heart condition as a child. Rachel's father was her best friend and biggest supporter, but nothing was more terrifying than surviving hell only to be on the brink of rescue. The closer her father's embrace became, the more panicked she felt. She worried it was all a mirage.

Sean had led them to I-65 and followed it north but kept them about twenty yards from the road until they reached the blockade. Rachel meandered along the outside of the crowd with the men surrounding her. They all wore battered clothes that smelled of body odor and dirt– same as everyone they walked beside. Rachel could see the outline of Sean's handgun in his waistband holster on his back right hip as she followed him.

A layer of sweat made Sean's dark skin glisten as the sun began to tip towards the horizon. Sean's eyes shifted from person to person as they walked past them, same as Chris and Allen from behind Rachel. To the outside world, the four of them looked just like a dysfunctional family. No one knew the three men that surrounded her every move were secret service agents. Loyal, highly trained, albeit annoying secret service agents.

It took several minutes before they reached a series of stanchions in the road–four-foot metal poles protruding from the concrete, spaced far enough apart to stop traffic from passing but leaving plenty of space for people to pass by.

Large signs guided civilians with arrows to the east of the road following a trail of muddy footprints along a ten-foot fence topped with razor wire.

'WARNING! WARNING! WARNING!
DO NOT PASS!
EXPLOSIVES/BOMBS AHEAD!

Follow arrows east to get to safety. Follow arrows to the right to safety.
You cannot pass going straight. You will be killed going straight.
Follow arrows east to get to safety. Follow arrows to the right to safety.'

The signs were written in five different languages and were posted along the border as far as the eye could see. The tired civilians followed the crowd, curving east without even stopping to look at the signs. Rachel guessed most of them were used to following the crowd at this point. Sean and the others paused, staring at the signs for a long moment. Even Sean's hard-set eyes betrayed him when he glanced at Rachel.

"Are you sure they were talking about these signs?" Chris asked. Allen snorted and shook his head but said nothing fearing Rachel's wrath.

Sean studied the border carefully before answering, "I do. You don't?"

Chris sighed, rubbing the back of his neck, "I don't know..."

Rachel saw Sean look at her for her input. "I think this is it."

"I– I don't think we should go that way," Allen said. "Not safe– it's not safe."

"Allen..." Rachel rested her hands on her hips.

"I'm just saying, I don't think it's safe. It doesn't make sense!" Allen said. "Why would they put a sign there if it's a lie? Why would they tell us to ignore it? It clearly says there's explosives–"

"What do you want to do instead, Allen? Suggest something, don't just–" Chris said.

"Let's just follow the crowd," Allen pointed along the fence. "The signs say it's safe that way. The signs say to go–"

A charge coursed through the solemn trail of refugees. Something stirred in the crowd. People hollered as others jogged with their bags and children in their arms. Rachel watched as two men shouldered past a woman knocking her to the ground as they scrambled to follow the arrows. *It's happening again. The panic. The stampede.* Without thought, Rachel stepped closer to Sean's broad shoulders and his soft but firm grip slipped around her wrist as he moved ahead of her. His right hand lingered closely to his hip where his duty weapon was concealed.

"Run, go! Hurry. They're coming!" a bug-eyed man with wild hair shouted as if someone had elected him to warn the others. His voice broke as he ran past Rachel. Instinctually, Rachel placed a guarded hand at her stomach as the man passed. "The rabid are behind– they're coming!"

Allen had already drawn his sidearm and kept it at his side. He was as panicked as any of them at the mention of the rabid. All of their eyes were locked on the worried faces that clamored by, looking for the red eyes or bared teeth. *They can't be here already. They're not that fast– they can't be...*

Three helicopters roared overhead. Their altitude was low enough that Rachel could read the words, 'United States Army' on the body as they flew south following the interstate. A flare of hope exploded inside Rachel as she uselessly waved at the helicopters with thousands of others. The sight made her believe they weren't alone. That up ahead there were protectors waiting for her. The loud roar of rotary blades waned as they flew south and became specks in the sky.

"We're going," Sean said with a finality in his voice. Rachel nodded and slipped her fingers into his hand.

"Okay," Chris adjusted his baseball cap.

Sean looked to Allen who grimaced, glancing back at the distant helicopters. "Alright, but let it be known, I said this was a bad idea."

Sean turned and, pulling gently on Rachel's wrist, jogged a dozen steps past the signs that warned of death for all who continued past. Allen had a brief moment of hesitation before he joined Chris, taking up their familiar formation as they separated from the procession of the thousands to continue north alone on I-65.

"And what haven't you thought was a bad idea, Allen?" Chris huffed as they jogged between the line of wrecked vehicles left abandon in the road.

"Has anything we've done over the past weeks been good?" Allen retorted.

"Touché."

Rachel smirked as she jogged behind Sean.

We can make it. We have to make it...

Screams began to flare behind them as they passed a traffic sign along the side of the road that read, 'Downtown Birmingham – 16 Miles.'

THREE

Derrick Hart

Birmingham, Al

"Everybody up, let's go!" Captain Elwood shouted.

He flipped on the lights in the roll call room and was greeted with a murmur of resentment as the officers stirred awake. They managed to get to their feet and began tossing their body armor over their shoulders and zipping up their patrol uniform. The captain's uniform was a wrinkled mess like he had bunched it up and used it as a pillow earlier in the day. Next to him was an Army Lieutenant in military fatigues, his sleeves neatly rolled up above his elbows. He was younger looking with a tight short fade, and unlike all the cops in the room his uniform looked pressed and neat as if the greatest trial he had faced today was sitting down and standing back up from an office chair.

"Alright, listen up," Captain Elwood began. "I'm going to assign intersections to everyone. You'll be in pairs. You are–"

"How far away are the infected?" an officer interrupted.

"How many are there?" another asked. The words spilled out of his mouth before he could stop them as if they had been gnawing at him in his sleep.

Captain Elwood's age was highlighted by the crow's feet beside his narrowed eyes. His bald head shifted from one insubordinate speaker to the next. Law enforcement wasn't nearly as strict as the army, but there was still a chain of command, and the brass were not used to being interrupted.

It's falling apart, the words repeated in Derrick's head.

"You are to report immediately to your post once assigned. Bring plenty of water and snacks. You could be out there for a while," the captain's voice boomed. Glancing at the Army Lt. to his side, the captain looked for permission to continue. When the iron-jawed Lt. said nothing, Elwood continued in a quieter tone. "The infected are expected to be at our perimeter within the hour, two at the max. I don't know how many, I don't know where..."

"I bet he does," Tommy's voice cut in. The room turned and saw Tommy, with harsh black bags under his eyes, pointing at the Army Lt. "Why don't you just tell us?"

"You don't need to know," the Lt. said flatly. "Your job is to support the military's supply lines and keep civilians out of the restricted area. Worry about that."

Tommy grumbled something to a man standing next to him but went silent when Captain Elwood continued. "Effective immediately," the police captain read from a piece of paper on his clipboard. He tried to keep his voice neutral, but an awkward twitch of his head gave away his displeasure. "We will no longer be taking anyone into custody." there was palpable dissent in the air as officers balked at the news. "No arrests. Booking is shut down. The jail is shut down until further notice."

"Why the fuck do I have handcuffs, then?" a voice hollered over the murmurs.

"What the hell do we do with people that refuse to stay out of the perimeter?"

"We can't risk any of our officers going hands on with a possible infected subject if they get into the city," Capt. Elwood said with a sigh, clearly annoyed by the situation himself. "And the sheriff's department refuses to risk letting Rhabdo-11 infection into the jail. Besides, there aren't enough deputies to safely staff the jail anymore. A handful of our most serious offenders, the military has transferred them north but most of the prisoners we booked over the last couple of weeks were just released this morning."

"Cause that makes a lot of sense," one voice grumbled, inviting a barrage of others to join in with their protests.

Even Derrick felt the urge to laugh at how absurd all of this was. He thought of all the arsonists they had arrested last week who had tried to burn the city down with Molotov cocktails and gas cans. How many men and women had been arrested for aggravated assault, homicide, and rape during the riots... as the infected neared, those crimes were the norm now. Theft and looting had become such commonalities that officers were forced to ignore them. Police had little time and even fewer resources to deal with non-life-threatening crimes. But now on the cusp of the chaos meeting its peak, the most terrible criminals in Birmingham had been released. *What are we even doing?*

"Quiet down... Quiet!" Capt. Elwood snapped. He fidgeted with his hands and again shot a look at the Army Lt. that went ignored. "Our only responsibility is dealing with our road closures and security details. As the National Guard begin their defense of the city, it's imperative their supply lines remain open, and civilians stay out of the hot zone. Under federal martial law, if any civilian violates your lawful orders and tries to cross into the restricted area, you have permission to use whatever force necessary to stop them... up to and including deadly force, effective immediately."

The room went silent. Every officer waited for the captain to explain more or qualify his statement. A few of the officers looked to one another trying to make sure they heard correctly.

"What the fuck?" Tommy bellowed.

"We're not soldiers!"

"Uh uh, nope, I'm not going to prison," an officer behind Derrick said to his friend.

"That's not legal," his friend replied.

"This is a signed directive from the President of the United States authorizing all federalized law enforcement officers, which all of the Metro Birmingham Police has previously been federalized, to enforce federal martial law and quarantine procedures with authority 'up to and including lethal force when necessary.'" Captain Elwood quoted the last of the sentence from a piece of paper buried on his clipboard.

The mood of the room shifted from exhaustion and self-pity to anger and mistrust. Derrick clasped his Redband bracelet and twisted it unconsciously. Every man and woman in that room was questioning what they were doing there. If staying had been worth signing their name on the suicide contracts earlier this week. It was hard for Derrick to imagine shooting a person for running past a barricade.

What if hundreds charge to get on the interstate? Are they going to have us shooting into the crowd? Killing hundreds of people just trying to save their own lives. In the chaos of it all, it was difficult to not have surreal moments when Derrick viewed himself as a page in a history book. *Fifty years from now will they say the government was tyrannical and criminal? Will the soldiers and police be blamed for excessive force, having only the flimsy shield of, 'I was following orders' to hide behind? Will history just see us as the twenty-first century Nazis?*

"Now listen up and write down your post and channel because I'm only going through this once," the Captain continued reading off his clipboard. "Traffic branch will be operating off radio channel P112. We don't have dispatchers anymore–they're all gone, too. It's just us. If you need backup, ask for Command. We only have two medics for the entire city. They're only here to respond for Police or military units injured, so don't bother asking for a medic for civilians." Derrick shook his head as he scribbled the radio channel down on the palm of his hand. "You and you," the Captain pointed at two patrolmen to Derrick's right.

"You'll be 6th Ave N and I 65 N entrance ramp. You and you," Elwood pointed at Derrick and the large-chested patrolman he stood in front of, "you both will be 6th ave N and–"

"Are you SWAT?" the Army Lt. interrupted, looking at Derrick. He eyed Derrick's green tactical uniform and the various weapons and equipment that laid by his feet. Captain Elwood's arms went to his side as he waited impatiently for the Army Lt. to finish.

Derrick gave a nod, "yes, sir." the Lt. flipped through his clipboard, looked at his watch, then made a face. He didn't look nearly as exhausted as the police officers did, but Derrick guessed he hadn't had to spend much time in the streets. The army didn't care about the riots; they had bigger fish to fry. The Police had been fighting their *war* for nine days now trying to keep the city from falling apart. The army's war was just about to begin.

The Army Lt. looked among the other officers in the room. "Any other SWAT in here?" he asked.

"Here," Perry, the young woman from before, called out.

Hidden behind the towering men in front of her, she stepped out into the open.

The Army Lt. gave her a measured but annoyed look and sighed. "Anyone else?" he surveyed the room, but when no one answered he looked to Captain Elwood. "These two are with me." his words weren't a request, but an order and he didn't linger for a response. "On me." The Lt. was already out the door as Derrick and Perry scrambled to get all their gear together. Perry left first with Derrick following after flinging his heavy vest and backpack over his shoulders with a *thud*.

"You and you, 6th ave N and 11th," Captain Elwood continued with the patrol officers. Derrick shouldered his AR-15 Colt rifle and jogged out the door not knowing what assignment he was just *volun-told* for. He was used to the chaos by now. The past week of every police officer's life had been in constant flux, with thinly stretched supervisors pointing them to complete tasks that had already been completed or already assigned. After seven years on the job, Derrick didn't fret over the assignment anymore. Cops were problem solvers. He was confident enough in his abilities to handle what came his way.

The hallways were alive with army officers and their staff hustling from one room to the next. The military had taken over control of the precinct, using it as one of their many operation centers. Derrick passed one conference room that had four men crowded around a TV in the corner. He could just make out a billowing cloud of smoke that rose from behind the Atlanta skyline. The banner along the bottom of the screen read 'Battle For Atlanta: End of America?'

Leave it to the media to care more about ratings than fueling panic– even now.

Information had been scarce the first few days after the outbreak was announced. The government had seemed more at a loss than anyone else. A sweaty infectious disease expert, Dr.

Ronald Towne, would stand in his business suit under hot camera lights and repeat White House fed lines for the public. "The CDC and USA MRIID are working hard and working well together– sharing information to figure out this infection. We do not yet have any factual, science-based data on this outbreak other than to tell you it is limited–contained to southern Florida where we expect it to remain. I caution any news reporter or online, you know, social media people, or what have you, from speculating on its origins or transmission as these guesses can be just as dangerous to society as this is a new infection."

But as the days had ticked by, the full weight of the internet and crowdsourced social media was unleashed on this outbreak. Every American had seen the bloody violence that once was only a thing of apocalypse movies come to life on their TVs, computers, tablets, and cellphones. #zombieaapocalypse and #shootheminthehead had trended number one and two in the first week, succeeded by '#bombflorida' during the next week.

There weren't many videos of the infected, but there were enough to see how surreal and violent those infected had become. It was easy to see how the general public could confuse the infected with *zombies*. Trembling videos of blood-soaked and wounded people who were sick with this unknown disease surfaced and showed them chasing civilians until the video cut. Body camera video of police firing on infected and them not reacting to the pain. The void of information created by the government didn't help and was quickly filled by the keyboard warriors on social media.

Alice Harris

'Omg! Why aren't the police or national guard in #Tampa

rn?! People are dying in the streets and the cops are running?!??!? What kind of President allows this! If you ask me, these people are just sick. Have you ever seen like a really violent schizophrenic or someone suffering from delusions?? They need doctors and medicine; they shouldn't be getting shot!! #miamiaoutbreak #impeachthepresident #standwith-florida'

Ross Clark

'Anyone else sees too many coincidences here? Like not to go tin foil here but outbreak hits Miami on April 20 (Hitler's birthday). Then I just checked and this 'unknown disease' started in one of the first places to just get the new bird flu vaccines. Hmm... #miamiaoutbreak #420conspiracy #blackflag #tellusthetruth'

Will 'SaVy' Williams

'Fam! Here me out FR! My bros in the army they strate up got there ass handed to them in #florida no lies! Armys going to #Birmingham and more goin fer #Atlanta They ready for a #zombiewar there FR FR! Shits crazy! Don't 4get u heard it here first. Follow my page 4more. #laststand #shoottheminthe-head #420conspiracy #miamiaoutbreak #willsavy'

By the time CDC officials had begun releasing information to the public no one trusted what the government was saying. What little Dr. Towne reported on the national address, had already been widely known. "The USA MRIID and CDC, who are working parallel with one another, have come to similar conclusions. This infection appears to be a radically new virus from the Rhabdoviridae family of viruses. We have assigned it the designation of Rhabdo-11 for common use," Dr. Towne had said in a nationwide press conference.

"For the public's understanding, I'd compare Rhabdo-11 to rabies. Um, it's similar in that it appears to be transmitted via infected saliva in contact with human mucosa or fresh flesh wounds. However, there are also reports that infected blood in open wounds can transmit the infection as well. It is not completely clear, yet. It causes extreme hyper aggression and confusion, much more so than the Rabies Lyssavirus. However, it deviates greatly from rabies when it comes to the incubation period." Dr. Towne adjusted his reading glasses as he glanced down at the notes on the podium.

"While rabies typically takes days, weeks, or longer for symptoms to develop, those infected with Rhabdo-11 appear to show symptoms within seconds, apparently. We have reports of infection outbreaks in southern Alabama, southern Georgia, and, yes, we can confirm there are a significant number of infected individuals, um, exiting Florida and going north. The President will talk more about that in his national address. State Governors will give more direction following that."

Derrick couldn't believe how unprepared the US government was for this infection. The response was knee jerk–the President trying to plug holes in a leaking dam, much like Derrick and the rest of the police in Birmingham were trying to keep law and order in the city. The National Guard had only been in Birmingham less than a week, but their presence had allowed the police department to regain a semblance of control of the rioting. However, Derrick had never directly participated in an assignment for the military before now.

"...simple escort mission. That's all," the Army Lieutenant said as Derrick jogged beside him and Perry. They stood in the entryway near the backdoor to the parking lot. The door pushed open every few seconds as army personnel hustled in and out of the police station. "You two will ride in convoy to checkpoint Alpha just south of the city. That'll be the I-459 overpass over I-65. There you will be meeting a Greenband and her secret service body men as they cross into Birmingham. Four people in total. There will be no quarantine for the Greenbands. They will receive an expedited decontamination protocol–should take about fifty minutes."

Perry and Derrick shared a puzzled look. Every other person who had been let in from the hot zone since the National Guard's arrival had been forced to comply with a six-hour decontamination process and a seventy-two-hour quarantine.

It was common knowledge, though, that Greenbands were treated as 'first class' citizens. These were civilians seen by the government as possessing specific, essential skills or assets that allowed them not only unrestricted travel nationally, but military logistical support to expedite their travel. Usually, they ended up being politicians. *Funny how that works. Politicians create Greenbands to protect politicians.*

The Army Lt. had seen their confusion and ignored it, continuing. "Once decontamination is completed, you two will escort the four Greenbands to your Birmingham Police Academy where the Greenbands will be extracted via choppers for Louisville. This was supposed to be a Tier One assignment, but our Tier One element was pulled. You will have a couple of army MPs driving you but besides that, you'll be on your own. Remember, lethal force is authorized on anyone who gets in the way; these Greenbands must be evac'ed at all costs. Once they lift off, you two will remain at the Police Academy gun range and provide security. We have civilians loading up the remaining ammo for transport."

"Sir, who's the Greenband?" Perry asked.

"Rachel Anderson, the Vice President's daughter," the Lt. replied. "Clearance only code name, 'Swan two.'"

"She's alive?" Derrick said surprised. One of the many early news stories in the outbreak that had been quickly buried was that the Vice President's daughter, who worked in Florida, was out of contact and presumed dead by many.

"As long as you guys do your job."

"When the civilians are done, are we escorting the ammo back to the front lines–checkpoint Alpha?" Perry asked.

"Negative," Lt. responded. "The ammo is being chopper'd and trained to Louisville for redistribution. You two will return here for further orders. You will not get on those helicopters, is that clear?" Derrick and Perry seemed to have the same question on their minds as they both started talking at the same time, but the Army Lieutenant only acknowledged Derrick.

"Why is the army taking all of our ammo?" Derrick raised an eyebrow. "Are you guys retreating? The infected aren't even in the city, yet."

A nasty scowl formed on the Lt.'s face at the accusation. He seemed to swallow whatever words he wanted to say. Instead, he clenched his teeth and enunciated each syllable as if he was lecturing a child. "It is not *your* ammo anymore, it's the military's. We aren't retreating. The army allocates its resources on a need basis, and we've decided Birmingham doesn't need it. Louisville is the staging point for all of our supplies and resources so that's where excess ammo goes."

In his anger, the Lt. lowered his arm that held a messy stack of papers in it. Derrick's eyes tracked to a sheet near the top that had a red 'TOP SECRET' watermark on it. The only words he could make out was 'Locke protocol.'

"Sir, is this part of the Locke protocol?" Derrick probed.

The Lt. revealed his true face of confused vulnerability for a moment as he was clearly caught off guard. It wasn't until he looked down at the papers exposed in his arm that the Lt. seemed to recompose himself. "That– that's on a need-to-know basis," he said. The Lt. must've deduced neither police officer was satisfied with the answer so before they could speak, again, he dismissed the conversation. "If you have any more burning questions, save it for someone in your own chain of command. Two Humvees are fueling out back and waiting on you two, so get moving."

The patrol officers from the roll call room had finished their briefing, received their assignments, and were filing into the hallway. The Army Lt. disappeared into one of the offices as Derrick and Perry put their backs against opposite walls to let the patrol officers pass. The officers' faces told each of their stories for the past weeks. Deep black grooves dug under their eyes from the sleepless nights. The nervous chatter and grinding of teeth as they mentally prepared to leave the safety of the precinct to face the civil unrest in the city. Derrick nodded at a few of his friends as they passed, and they nodded back or patted him on the shoulder in return.

After the last man had gone out the back door, Perry and Derrick approached one another, Perry gesturing at the room the Army Lt. walked into. "What a cock sucker," she said.

Derrick smiled, "I think he likes you."

"I think he'll like my foot up his ass," Perry said.

"He might," Derrick shrugged as he snapped his heavy vest in place and smelled the stale sweat-stained fabric. Derrick had always had a good working relationship with Jessica Perry ever since she had earned her SWAT pin a year ago. He had helped her prepare for the selection process by hitting the gym with her every morning for weeks beforehand. On more than one occasion she had asked if he wanted to go out for a beer, but Derrick had always politely declined. Though he didn't think Perry's intentions were anything but friendly, Derrick had been in a committed relationship, and he didn't like the optics of him having a drink with a single and attractive coworker.

Out of uniform, a person could be forgiven for thinking Perry was as soft as she appeared, with delicate features and an infectious giggle. Only the trail of black tribal tattoos down her right arm hinted at the hidden toughness that had carried her to become Birmingham's first female SWAT officer. Every patrol officer who had worked with Perry had the same response when they heard she earned her SWAT pin. 'Yeah, that sounds about right.' Perry was a cop's cop, through and through.

"I didn't even know you were still here," Perry smiled. "I was beginning to think I was the only one left."

"I think it's just you and me. Tom, Jeff... even Sergeant Bowers, all of them took their families and left town."

"Well, I'm glad I've still got you watching my back," Perry punched his shoulder.

Despite his exhaustion, Derrick could not help but feel a jolt of warmth surge through him at Perry's smile. "Yeah, me too," Derrick nodded back. He felt a vibration beneath his vest. Pulling his phone out from under his chest rig, he scrolled down past dozens of news updates and app notifications that had come in a data dump. Beneath it all there was a missed call from Brandon from two hours ago.

"You ready to go save the princess?" Perry said, grabbing her pack.

Derrick snickered and nodded to the door. "Yeah, I'm right behind you."

Brandon's contact name on his phone was surrounded by two middle finger emojis on either side. He dialed his friend's number and waited to hear the three familiar tones followed by "We're sorry your call cannot be connected at this time."

But to his surprise, he heard an unexpected ringing. Elation filled Derrick's chest. He heard something like less than three percent of phone calls were being connected nowadays, so this was a rarity.

He had so many questions about what was happening in Atlanta, but mostly he just wanted to hear his friend was still alive. It had been days since he last heard from Brandon. After several rings his call went to voicemail with a message after the beep– "The voicemail box you are trying to reach is full. Goodbye."

"Lazy... stupid, fucking... piece of shit..." Derrick gritted his teeth. "Can't even empty a damn voicemail box... Why do I have to have a freaking moron for a best friend..."

FOUR

Brandon Armstrong
Atlanta, Ga

The chorus of heavy automatic gunfire deafened Brandon leaving a permanent ringing in his ears. After so many hours even the chest thudding gunfire of the M249 light-machine guns positioned on either side of his fire team became background noise.

"Loading!" one of Brandon's men shouted in a hoarse voice. "Up!" he announced a few seconds later and continued firing.

"Loading!" another man yelled. "Up!" he said before letting loose his barrage of gunfire.

The quote of the battle, Brandon thought–*those two damn words*.

Sergeant Brandon Armstrong took cover behind an Atlanta city bus, its side plastered with an advertisement for Dumbo's Bail Bondsman service with a picture of two fat body gentlemen with their arms crossed. Despite the chaos of soldiers running back and forth on the overpass, Brandon's mind wandered. He wondered how much Dumbo paid for such a terrible looking ad as he grabbed a handful of loose 5.56mm rifle rounds from an overused plastic grocery bag. He thumbed them into an empty magazine leaving small, bloody thumbprints on the body of the casings.

"Son of a bitch!" Brandon cursed and threw a 9mm round he found in the bag on the pavement. It bounced across the road into a massive mound of empty shell casings that were being swept to the 'Atlanta side' of the overpass by a scrawny sunburnt face Private. The thousands of casings rained down into the dump truck bed waiting below.

Every time he threw a 9mm round, Brandon looked around for a runner to grab so he could beat the shit out of them. He took cover behind the bus out of habit from his training as an Army Ranger, but he knew there was no need for it. The rabid scurrying below the overpass wouldn't be shooting back. In truth, he was mostly just taking cover from the overpowering Atlanta sun. Its arc showed the sun was finally falling from the sky but even at night temperatures in Atlanta swelled and the humidity clung to each pore of his skin.

And it's not even May yet.

"Loading! Last mag!" Corporal Ryan shouted from the nearest side of the bus to Brandon. His voice was barely loud enough to pierce through the chorus of groans and screeches from below.

"Rabid climbing on the exit ramp! To the east! East!" another one of his men shouted.

Brandon took a deep breath, steadying himself, and keyed his radio mic attached to the ribs of his body armor. "2-7 to 2-5. 2-7 to 2-5."

"2-5, go ahead," a voice replied.

"Infected on the east exit ramp. Infected on the east exit ramp. How copy?"

"Good copy. On it," the voice on the radio answered. Brandon stood and saw another sergeant near the east flank of the overpass repositioning his men to address the issue.

"Ryan," Brandon said, holding his freshly loaded magazine out for him. Corporal Ryan took the magazine and Brandon noticed the bloody smear his thumb had left on the side of the magazine as he handed it off. Ryan shoved it into an empty pouch on his chest rig. Brandon examined the broken blister on the length of his thumb. He decided to switch hands and started loading with his left. His reload speed would be hampered dramatically, but at least he wouldn't run the risk of malfunctioning his men's rifles by getting blood on the primer.

"Sarge. Sarge! Runner to the west!" one of his men lying prone on top of the bus called out. He couldn't remember his name. Brandon was never good with names, and he had just been dropped in charge of this squad yesterday. It was a hodgepodge of Army Rangers, most of whom had left the army in the last year or two like Brandon and were stupid enough to enter into a suicide contract, also like Brandon.

Stupid fuckers like Brandon were easy to spot. They all had the same Redband bracelet on their right wrist–it was a halo to highlight idiots. Only Cpl. Ryan was still in active duty out of his team, so Brandon relied heavily on him for standards. While the overpass was the crux of the Atlanta defense it was also the simplest job. *Point and shoot.* It was the men on the border wall flanks that stretched east and west from Atlanta for hundreds of miles that required the sharp, critical thinking skills of the current active-duty Rangers, which was where they were deployed.

Brandon grunted to his feet and jogged to meet the runner halfway. The kid didn't have any ammo bags in his hands, which was odd, but he was wearing a backpack so it could be in there.

Almost immediately, from the moment the shooting had begun last night, everyone realized ammo was going to be the decider of the fight, especially after the President hog tied the military by not allowing any Air Force bombing runs, artillery deployments, or EOD explosives for what the politicians called 'indiscriminate killing on American soil.' Brandon had overheard the COs saying it was a legal thing. A loophole in posse comitatus.

Brandon hadn't understood it. As far as he saw, a predator drone launching missiles into a crowd of infected Americans was no different than eighty Army Rangers firing M2 .50 cal, M240s, and M4 rifles into a crowd of infected. But Brandon was a grunt. He wasn't paid to think. He was paid to pull a trigger.

The first wave of infected that had made it to their choke point last night were mowed to pieces. It was a sick game that only desensitized soldiers who were accustomed to violence could appreciate. The snipers and SAW gunners competed for the most and *best* kills as the slow trickle of the infected ran up I-75 north for Atlanta.

Private construction crews and the Army corps of Engineers had worked around the clock throughout the week, building blockades and digging trenches that extended east and west from Atlanta for hundreds of miles. Mounds of dirt piled high supported by ten-foot metal plating walled off the south. Trenches were carved eight feet deep to channel the infected. They had built a funnel that extended for miles meant to bottleneck the approaching infected into choke points as they chased the survivors from Florida. The soldiers' games and laughter gave way to silence when the trickle of infected turned into hundreds... and then thousands, culminating in the earth rattling feel of hundreds of infantrymen firing at monsters clamoring towards them.

'Runners' were selected to load sacks full of loaded magazines back at the forward operating base and bring them to the sergeants on the front line for distribution. But soon they didn't even have time to load the magazines. Runners began to only bring grocery bags full of free-floating ammo that had been haphazardly dumped together. Brandon begrudgingly moved from his position at the front lines of the fire fight to load magazines for his men.

"Give it here," Brandon yelled still a few yards from the runner. The boy looked exhausted, his face flush after a night and day of sprints.

"No, ammo, Sarge. Are you Sergeant Armstrong?" the private asked as he slowed to a jog and Brandon gave him a nod in reply. "Sir, Command's looking for you. They sent me to get you."

"No, they didn't. You're looking for Sergeant Major Wesley," Brandon shouted pointing his bloody thumb behind him farther down the overpass. Lt. Kendall was actually in charge of the overpass defense, but the Lt. had done little else over the past day other than sit in the Humvee and radio command. Sergeant Major didn't seem to mind nor did any of the other Rangers. As with everything in the military the enlisted men were the ones that got shit done, then waited for the brass to arrive to fuck it all up.

"No, sir," the private shook his head. "Colonel Holt asked for you by name. Wants you in the Command tent ASAP."

"That doesn't make sense," Brandon protested. The private could only respond with a confused shrug of his own.

If they wanted him, why waste a runner's time? Why not radio Lt. Kendall, God knows he's not doing shit. And why me? There were eleven other sergeants on the overpass with two more on the entrance and exit ramps. Not to mention First Sergeant and Sergeant Major.

"Take over for me. Load for my team," Brandon pointed at the bag of ammo on the ground. He stopped mid-turn and snatched the private's arm, scaring fear in his eyes. "And tell the other fuck-stick runners, if I find one more goddamn 9mm round mixed in with my 5.56, I'm throwing you all over the fucking bridge."

"Yes, sir," the runner shrunk back. Brandon jogged over to Ryan and tapped his shoulder. "Command needs me. You're in charge till I'm back!" Ryan gave a curt nod before returning to firing controlled bursts below the overpass. Brandon didn't get close enough to see below the bridge, but he knew the scene hadn't changed for the better in the last hour. He could hear the maddening screams and mashing of bodies coming from underneath the overpass, and he could imagine the blood bath as thousands of infected bodies were shot full of large caliber bullets.

Even for Brandon, who before this outbreak would watch videos of terrorists being blown to pieces by predator drones and laugh, the sight of this much gore was inhuman. He tried not to look at the faces of the infected when he was shooting. They were just targets. They weren't women and men. They weren't sick civilians who'd lost their minds. They were just interactive targets filled with red paint. At least that's what he told himself. If he had to do this in his head, Brandon couldn't imagine how Derrick was dealing with it in Birmingham. His best friend had always been a pussy about this kind of stuff. But even if he wasn't as hardened as Brandon, Derrick was still a tougher motherfucker than anyone else he knew.

Derrick'll be fine, he can take care of himself, Brandon assured himself.

It took a few minutes for Brandon to run back to the

Command tent with his rifle relaxed in his hands. The tents were set up across the black asphalt in the parking lot of a large business park beside the interstate. Military vehicles were scattered along the boundary of tent city with large construction equipment lining the building's sidewalk in the background. He didn't bother to compose himself before jogging inside the Command tent. He was taken aback when he felt the cool bite of air conditioning.

Fucking officers... There is a heat wave outside of ninety degrees with the humidity of April in Atlanta and the officer's tent has a goddamn AC.

The tent was long with several computers and monitors on one side and a smaller satellite tent set up on the other end. In the middle were several white, rectangle folding tables pushed together with stacks of paper spread across the top. No one was in the tent. Brandon used the time to catch his breath and walk over to the cluster of monitors at the far end. Two monitors on the top split a map of the United States.

Most of the country was colored green, but there was a rising red blur in the south that covered most of Mississippi, Alabama, Georgia, and South Carolina as well as all of Florida. The top portions of states below Tennessee were a yellow hue. It looked like a cancerous scan of the country with tumors sprouting out of each state, infecting the ones near it.

"Sergeant," Colonel Holt's voice startled Brandon. He had walked from the smaller satellite tent at the other end of the table.

"Sir," Sergeant Armstrong approached the Colonel and moved to attention.

"At ease," the Colonel waved him down as he stopped near the table. He picked up a green folder, glanced at the single paper inside it, and closed it again. Colonel Holt was a softer looking man. With a round face and thoughtful eyes. The

Colonel had a long cut on his forehead that was half covered in a white bandage and Brandon noted how familiar the man looked to him, which was strange, seeing as he didn't know any of the CO's. Hell, he didn't know any of the enlisted either besides Sergeant Major and a couple of guys in his squad.

Brandon Armstrong had been a retired Army Ranger up until last week. He had done his six years of active duty followed by two years of I.R.R. (Individual Ready Reserve) and had been enjoying being a civilian again, now that his contract was done. It had been a relaxing two years not having had to take orders and to grow a beard, until he signed his suicide contract last week. His wife, Karen, had made it out of Tennessee and to her grandparent's house in Kentucky because of that signature. One less thing for Brandon to worry about.

Karen had begged him not to join. She had even threatened him with divorce if he signed the suicide contract. He had been married to her for enough of his twenties to be used to her divorce bluffs by now. They had only worked in the initial years of their marriage; now he was wise enough not to care about her idle threats. The military had always been a point of contention in their relationship. Karen didn't like that there was another entity that existed in Brandon's life that could supersede her authority. But Brandon couldn't pass up this opportunity to be on the front lines of the mess. He wasn't about to let Derrick have all the badass stories while Brandon hid like a little bitch. He couldn't let Derrick hold that over him.

Rubbing his eyes, Colonel Holt sniffled and shook his head to compose himself. "Sorry, I just got off the phone with my wife and daughter. You were one of the Honor Bound signees, right?"

"Yes, sir," Brandon said with his hand resting on the butt of his rifle slung from his neck. Beads of sweat bulleted down his face. His body was still not acclimating to the air conditioning. Brandon refused to call it *honor bound* or whatever made up name politicians used to try and spin the draft that was loaded into the National Security Public Servant Act. Brandon knew what it was. Just another way for young men to die so rich men didn't have to. It's been the same story since the beginning of civilization.

It had taken a week for Florida to fall. But after twenty-four hours of news coverage of the outbreak, people had seen enough. Mass hoarding and migration had begun. Police, nurses, doctors, firefighters, even active-duty soldiers had quit in droves to flee with their families to the northern states. People weren't idiots. They'd seen the movies. They knew how this infection would end. Which was great. Because the number one thing you want to have happen after an outbreak of an unknown, deadly, and extremely infectious disease is uncontrolled, mass migration in every direction.

National Guard units had begun enforcing federal martial law measures such as mandatory shelter-in-place and state quarantine procedures. Most people could barely navigate the traffic jammed roads to leave their city, and the portions of civilians who made it to state lines were met with military roadblocks. Especially in the South and Midwest, traveling outside one's state was near impossible for most, at least by vehicle.

In an emergency session of the Congress, the government had created exceptions to the countrywide lockdown. Under the new National Security Public Servant Act, up to four members of any essential worker's family could be classified as a *Yellowband* and receive a government escort to one bordering state away from where they resided. The person's family could only flee if the essential worker signed the *Honor Bound* contract to remain behind and continue to work. Police officers, doctors, firefighters, and several other professionals in Alabama or Georgia with wives, husbands, children, siblings, or parents could have them sent to safety in Tennessee as long as the worker remained behind. Or a retired soldier living in Nashville could re-enlist and his perturbed wife could go to Kentucky while he got sent to the front lines in Atlanta. It hadn't taken long for *honor bound* signees to start calling the contracts what they really were–suicide contracts.

"Wife?" the Colonel asked pointing at the Redband bracelet Brandon wore. The Redband signified he was land-locked. It meant he was not allowed to leave the state.

Brandon nodded.

"Any kids?"

"No, sir," Brandon said, almost thankful.

Holt nodded. "Where is she, your wife?"

"Kentucky."

"Good, good..."

Brandon was getting annoyed with the pointless questions. The rumble of gunfire from the nearby overpass reminded him of his men standing out on in the baking sun. "Sir, do you need anything else? We are running low on ammo and–"

"We're out."

"I'm sorry, sir?"

"We're not low on ammunition, we're out of ammunition. Distributing the last of it as we speak."

The Colonel pointed to the men running past the entryway of the tent. Colonel Holt slumped into a folding chair and let loose a sigh meant for a man twice his age.

There was a long pause while Brandon digested this news. "When's the next shipment of supplies coming in?" he finally asked.

"We're not expecting any."

Brandon looked out the flap of the tent doorway and saw

men hustling from one tent to another. "What about air support? Are we preparing transport for evacuations?"

"I don't know if you remember or not. A lot has happened in the past twenty-four hours," the Colonel rubbed his forehead ignoring Brandon's question. "Early this morning just before daybreak, when the eastern wall caved in on the exit ramp?"

"Yes, sir, I was there."

"I know you were, son," the Colonel said. "You saved my life. I was the guy on the ground, beneath the fallen plate..."

Colonel Holt's face connected in Brandon's memories like the final puzzle piece sliding into place. It had been dark this morning as the sun had not risen, yet. A particularly large group of rabid had made it to the top of the exit ramp and collapsed a twelve-foot metal plate. It had been all hands on deck as the infection was the closest to spreading into Atlanta since the fight had begun. While they had been scrambling to slide more sheets of metal siding to plug the hole and fortify it, a soldier had backed an MRAP armored vehicle towards the hole created by the fallen piece of metal to temporarily secure the area.

"I remember," Brandon said after a moment. It was Brandon who had spotted the Colonel trapped under the collapsed metal plate. Holt had struggled to get free as the hulking sixteen-ton MRAP truck had been inches from backing over him in the darkness. This Colonel had no business being on the front lines. Whatever Lieutenant or Staff sergeant was supposed to be keeping an eye on him should've been fired this morning because they had nearly got him killed. With only seconds to spare, Brandon had snatched the Colonel's arm and dragged him out from under the plate before the MRAP had rolled its giant black tires over it.

The Colonel took a deep breath. "They rerouted all of our UAVs (Unmanned Aerial Vehicles) to the Tennessee border hours ago, then they took away our priority access to the satellites... compartmentalized communication to bordering units... General Rotoss informed me about fifteen minutes ago that the President has initiated the Locke protocol."

"What is it? Locke protocol?" Brandon asked.

"I think you have a pretty good guess," Colonel Holt held up the green folder then set it down on the edge of the table near Brandon. Before Brandon could pick it up, the Colonel removed a small black satellite phone from his cargo pocket. It had green electrical tape wrapped around the base of it. "You know what this is?"

"I've heard about them," he said.

"Every military command and high priority asset was issued these Greenband radios. The main channel communicates with others in the region. The secondary channel gives you priority access to satellite communication for phone calls. They're used mostly to coordinate the Greenbands and get them to safety." Colonel Holt stared at the table in front of him as he shook his head. "The things we give to protect... others... Greenbands get to travel anywhere in the country, meanwhile, Yellowbands like your wife can only get one state away to Kentucky. Then there's you." Colonel Holt pointed to Brandon's wrist where his Redband bracelet was secured. "And the men out there. Who run towards the danger so others may run away... I hope there's a heaven, Sergeant Armstrong. I hope there's a special reward for men like you."

He placed the satellite radio carefully on top of the green folder. "I used this to say goodbye to my wife and tell my daughter that I loved her." Holt was quiet for a moment while he stared at nothing on the ground. "Maybe give your wife a call. Maybe let the other men on the front lines call their wives and kids..."

Brandon nodded silently.

Colonel Holt stood up and moved to the small dark tent from where he had come. He stopped before going in and gave Brandon a final look. "Because of you, I was able to hear my daughter laugh one more time today. Thank you," he turned and disappeared inside the tent.

Brandon knocked the radio to the side and quickly seized the folder, opening it. He read the single sheet of paper watermarked 'Top Secret'. When he finished, he roughly flipped the sheet to the back to find it empty. He read the sheet, again and again, before letting the folder fall to the table.

Standing motionless for a long minute, his eyes stared at the monitors with the U.S. map on them. He watched the motion video of red blotches consuming the lower part of the country on repeat.

A loud bang of a gunshot from the small tent shattered the silence. Brandon reacted on instinct shouldering his rifle and entered the satellite tent with his weapon at the low ready. Colonel Holt's body was sprawled across his chair. His arms outstretched with his pistol dangling from his fingertips as blood dribbled from the exit wound in his temple.

FIVE

Rachel Anderson
I-65 N

Rachel gasped for air, leaning on the sizzling hood of one of the broken-down SUVs along the interstate before snapping her hand away with a shallow burn. The vehicles, like Rachel and her secret service agents, baked under the hot sun with little breeze to cool them.

"Come on," Sean panted, lightly pressing on the small of Rachel's back. "Keep moving... we're almost there."

Chris and Allen were falling behind as they neared the overpass ahead. The physical exhaustion of the past two weeks was colliding with the mental and emotional exhaustion of being so close to safety, true safety for the first time since the outbreak. Rachel limped ahead. Continuing her staggering jog maneuvering through the columns of hundreds of cars leading into Birmingham, Rachel kept her eyes low, staring at Sean's heels as he ran ahead. *Just follow his feet. One step at a time.*

Rachel was in great shape. An avid marathon runner and an obsessive CrossFit practitioner before the outbreak, she knew her limit and she could tell it was drawing close.

"Chris, Allen, come on!" Sean shouted over his shoulder as they struggled to catch up.

Once they were fifty yards out from the overpass, Rachel felt an eerie twist in her gut as she saw the hundreds of soldiers staring at her from atop. All she could hear were the sounds of their shoes clapping on the pavement and her own ragged breathing when suddenly, the roar of three helicopters flying overhead brought her back to reality. She looked over her shoulder and followed the three helicopters with her gaze until they stopped, hovering a mile behind them.

That's them. That's the infected. They're right behind us. They're coming. It was a terrifying reminder they were being pursued. *Who knows how many at this point? Hundred? Thousand? Ten thousand?* The number of people who fled north grew with every city the infection spread to as did the number of infected who gave chase. *We're not going to die. We've survived this long; we're not going to die here.*

Sean was the first one to reach the overpass and he was already shouting to one of the soldiers above who lowered an extended ladder. Beneath the overpass, I-65 was walled off with freshly laid concrete slabs that didn't leave even an inch of room to see through to the other side. Twelve-foot metal walls were erected on either side of the overpass that extended as far as the eye could see in both directions.

This was their wall. The line the army had drawn in the sand. No infected were to pass this parallel. Rachel couldn't help but think of the thousands of civilians who were being diverted east from the I-65 along the fence. *Were they even being brought to the border or just being led elsewhere to a more convenient place for them to die?*

"Go," Sean said as he held the base of the ladder. Rachel looked over her shoulder and watched Chris and Allen stop behind them. Both were close to collapsing where they stood as they sucked in air. Rachel put her hands on the ladder and looked at the crowd of hazmat suits that peered down at her from the top. "Come on... let's go!" Allen shouted between panted breaths.

"You guys go first," Rachel hesitated.

"Not happening," Sean said.

"We don't have time to waste," Allen looked over his shoulder at the three choppers that inched their direction.

"What if they only let me up and no one else?" Rachel speculated. Sean's eyes looked away as he considered the possibility. "Remember the helicopters that tried to pick me up back when this started? They're not letting anyone else cross the border. And I'm the Vice President's daughter..."

"They wouldn't do that," Chris shook his head. Rachel couldn't be sure, but she thought she felt the ground begin to tremble. *Is this the infected?*

"We'll be fine," Sean insisted as he pressed on Rachel's back to get her to move.

Rachel shrugged his hand off of her aggressively. "No, you all need to get up there first or I'm not going!"

Sean glared at her in silence, but his expression communicated his fury. His forehead glistened with a layer of sweat as she watched a drop fall from the bridge of his nose.

"Go, unless you think you're going to carry me up this rickety ladder without killing us both," Rachel crossed her arms defiantly.

"Goddammit," Allen grumbled as he pushed past her and started climbing, mumbling all the while, "...pain in my ass... damn woman..."

Chris sighed and followed. "You know we're not even

getting hazard pay to deal with your bullshit, right?" Chris said. He smirked down at her from the middle rung to let her know he was joking.

Rachel rolled her eyes and then looked expectantly at Sean who was glaring at her. "Go, come on. I'm waiting on you," Rachel said, but his looming expression was more intimidating.

Stepping into Rachel's personal space, Sean stared down at her, "wait all you like. My foot doesn't touch this ladder until you're up on it, Rach."

Rachel's gaze faltered and she knew her stubbornness had met his match. The child inside her took offense to the challenge but she knew this was no time to mess around. Rachel climbed the ladder and saw Sean follow once she was a few rungs ahead. At the top of the overpass, they were surrounded by a dozen orange hazmat suits and what looked like a few hundred marines lining the road. Massive turrets with powerful-looking machine guns were positioned over the edge of the overpass awaiting the rush of infected individuals.

"This way, ma'am. Follow him," one of the frontline workers in the orange hazmat suit said, pointing towards Chris' back as he was led in a single file line down the slope of the exit ramp to the other side of I-65. "Stay in line, don't talk, and don't spit or cough."

Rachel looked behind her to ensure Sean was there. A man in a hazmat suit wearing a large silver tank as a backpack held a nozzle attached to a tube that looked like a power washer hose. He followed behind Sean after he got off the ladder and sprayed every surface they touched and walked on. The liquid he sprayed grew into an orange foam on contact and hissed on the concrete. Like it was acid about to burn through the earth. Rachel wasn't told to keep her hands raised but she felt like she needed to as soldiers flanked their every step to the collection of tents below.

Over the next hour, Rachel and her three secret service agents were stripped of all clothes, weapons, and jewelry before being sprayed down with harsh chemicals, scrubbed with metal mesh brushes attached to yellow six-foot poles, then rinsed with scalding water. The rush of the process was evident the moment the three men and Rachel were told to strip naked in the same shower room.

"Fucking wonderful..." Allen muttered as he undid his jeans.

Rachel wasn't thrilled stripping nude in front of Allen and Chris either, but her exhaustion overrode any feeling of embarrassment. She gritted her teeth as scalding hot water rained on her from above and steel brushes raked over her back. Sean faced the same treatment as he pressed his hands against the wall and had two individuals scrubbing his muscled neck and shoulders. Their eyes met and held each other's gaze. They were weathering their final test before reaching safety.

The process was repeated three times inside the white hollow walls of shower trailers. Blood, hair, saliva, and skin cell samples were taken. Urine samples were asked for but none of them were hydrated enough to urinate an adequate amount.

While they were being sanitized, sporadic gunfire erupted outside–a cycle of pops and booms from various caliber weapons fired from the top of the overpass. But by the time their blood work came back, the gunfire had turned into a vibration of explosions that rattled the trailer walls. It was so loud that the doctor had to shout instructions to them as they exited the trailer.

"We know very little about this virus. Next to nothing," Dr. McGrath admitted as he guided Rachel and her agents over to a group of Army National Guard soldiers waiting for them. They had been given blue nursing scrubs to wear. Rachel's was two sizes too big for her and she had to tie a knot into her waistband to keep her pants up. Her already tan skin was now raw and red from the cleaning protocols. Her brown hair was tied back in a ponytail.

"You're sure we're not infected?" Rachel yelled over the barrage of gunfire, trying to keep up with the doctor.

"There are no indicators in your blood or skin cells. RT-PCR test on your saliva came back negative for any virus. You're the only people in the country who've been given permission for this truncated decontamination and quarantine timeline. They didn't give me time to do a spinal tap, so this is as sure as we're going to get."

"Where's my dad? Is he alright?" Rachel asked.

Dr. McGrath waved at an army officer as he handed the four of them off. "I'm sure he's fine. Here you go, good luck to you–"

"Wait, what about our stuff?" Sean touched the Doctor's shoulder. "Our guns, our... I had a watch. I... it was my father's..."

Dr. McGrath's eyes bounced between Sean and Rachel with a confused expression. "Everything you wore or brought across the border with you has been incinerated. It's gone," the doctor said with a callous shake of his head before continuing on his way.

"Ma'am, I need to see your wrist," the army officer said. Rachel's eyes lingered on Sean's sunken expression as she had never seen the man appear more broken in the eight months he had worked her detail. "Ma'am," the soldier repeated sternly.

"Yes, yeah," she said, lifting her hand to him. The soldier snapped a metallic green bracelet onto her right wrist then cinched it tight to her skin. Another soldier stepped up with a tablet and took her photo, her fingerprints, and a retina scan of her right eye, then scanned the barcode on her new bracelet.

This process was repeated for Sean, Chris, and Allen who also received barcoded green bracelets.

"What are these?" Rachel asked.

The army officer answered without looking at her. "Greenbands, ma'am," he sounded angry with her as if she had done something wrong by getting the bracelet. "It's going to get you across the country to safety."

Rachel looked around at the doctors walking from one tent to the other and the soldiers who jogged to and from the gunfire. Most of them did not wear anything but wristwatches, while a few wore metallic bracelets similar to Rachel's, only theirs were red in color.

"This way, ma'am, sirs," the army officer led them past several tents to a cleared lane along the interstate, obviously designated for vehicles. The camp was massive. Tents and trailers were laid out as far as Rachel could see up I-65 N. Construction cranes and equipment caked in mud and dirt after days of heavy use lined the grassy shoulder of the road. "You here for the Greens?" the army officers shouted to a man and a woman standing in front of two Humvees on the side of the road.

"Yes, sir," the man said. Unlike the army's digital camo uniforms, the two of them wore forest green uniforms with black armor vests that had large white lettering on the back of their body armor that read 'SWAT' Rachel immediately saw the same red bracelets on their right wrists; their army escorts seemed to notice as well.

"Your orders are to transport them to the Police Academy and no farther, understood?" the army officer said.

The male police officer's eyes narrowed as he nodded and said he understood. The female officer looked like she might punch the soldier at any moment. Without another word or a look, the soldiers turned and walked away with their tablets in hand.

"This way, guys," the male police officer said. "I'm Officer Derrick Hart and this is Officer Perry. We're escorting you to the Birmingham Police Academy where a helicopter will get you out of here."

"Out of here where?" Allen asked with the rumble of automatic gunfire in the background.

"I don't know, they didn't say," Derrick said over his shoulder. "I'd guess either Fort Campbell or Louisville where the military is staging. Two of you can ride in one Humvee with me and the other two can go with Officer Perry." Derrick opened the backdoor of the lead vehicle. Sean followed Rachel in without hesitation.

"We'll give you two love birds some alone time," Chris hollered as he went with Allen to the second Humvee. Rachel felt an icy sting go down her spine at Chris's overactive mouth. But after two weeks of being glued to each other's sides, Rachel wasn't surprised Chris and Allen had picked up on the tension between her and Sean.

"Perry, you good?" Derrick asked.

"I'll see you on the other side," Perry said, giving him a thumbs up.

Rachel walked beside Sean to their Humvee in front of Derrick. She was surprised when she felt Sean's fingertips interlace with hers as he took her hand for the first time since the outbreak.

SIX

Rachel Anderson

I-65 N

Even before they started driving, Rachel's mouth was watering as she stared at the grocery bag full of apples and water bottles on the bench across from them. Derrick's eyes followed Sean's gaze as he sat down beside the bag. The Humvee lurched forward once he slammed the door shut. Derrick grabbed the plastic bag and handed it to Rachel who jumped on it without a word.

"They didn't feed you guys or anything?" Derrick asked.

"No," said Sean, taking a large bite of a warm apple as Rachel guzzled half of a water bottle in one swig. The water was heavenly. It absorbed into every crevice of her parched cotton like tongue and soothed her dry throat. Finishing the bottle off in her second gulp, Rachel hid a burp, unsuccessfully, as her eyes met Derrick's who wore a half-smile.

"Thanks," Rachel wiped the stray drops of water from her

chin. Grabbing an apple from the bag, she took a bite, piercing into the soft, green skin. "We haven't had much to eat or drink over the past couple of weeks."

"Wish I would've known," Derrick said. "I would've grabbed more from the precinct before heading this way."

"No, this is great," Rachel said as she opened her mouth for another bite. Even though it was mushy and not the ripest, the explosion of flavor that came with the juices was something she wanted to savor but was too hungry to slow down.

Their Humvee slowed as it steered through a large crowd of people. Soldiers and police officers fought to push people back as hands and faces smacked against the vehicle's frame. A hand thudded against the window beside Rachel's head, making her jump. Sean's hand clapped over Rachel's thigh to pull her to him, but the vehicle slowly drove by the angry mob. Rachel saw Derrick's eyes take note of Sean's hand on her thigh before Sean removed it. She could see him piecing together the complicated relationship. *If only he knew just how complicated it really was,* Rachel thought.

"Is it like this everywhere?" Sean asked looking out the windows at the businesses they passed. Looted storefronts had the glass smashed in. Walls were covered in graffiti. A car in the street down the road was fully engulfed in flames and others were blackened from the previous night's fires.

"Some places are worse," Derrick said. "L.A., Chicago..."

"What about Texas?" Sean asked. "The Austin area?"

Rachel looked at Sean who had an uncharacteristic eagerness about him. He was from Texas, she knew, but Sean never spoke about his family or friends.

He must still have some in the area.

Derrick answered carefully, "I... don't know, sorry. The smaller cities seem to be doing better than larger ones. Less looting and riots..."

Sean nodded as he looked away and drank another sip of water. Rachel took a break from her second apple. The rush of sugar felt like her brain was waking up for the first time in days. The dehydration and malnourishment had become black clouds looming over her thoughts, which were finally starting to part.

"What's going on?" Rachel asked. "What's happening? Do we know who caused this?"

Derrick shook his head, adjusting his rifle between his legs. "They don't know much or if they do, they're not telling us. Richter & Allen is a pharmaceutical company whose name keeps coming up on the news–a lot of conspiracy theories about their new flu vaccine and an explosion in one of their buildings in Florida– but it exploded hours after the outbreak had already started."

"You don't believe it?" Sean asked.

Derrick shook his head. "When I see a mob with pitchforks going after someone, I do my best not to follow. Besides, there's so much bullshit being thrown around in the news right now. Some are saying it was a 'suicide infector' from North Korea, others are saying it's a naturally occurring virus; a dog with a mutated form of rabies. Who knows. The only consistent report is that the outbreak started somewhere just south of Miami ten days ago and it's spread like wildfire since then. Where were you guys when it happened?"

Rachel shared a silent look with Sean as she felt the memories she had locked away threaten to break free. "Miami," Sean answered.

"Oh..." Derrick went silent for a moment before asking. "What were you doing there?"

"I um..." Rachel cleared her throat as she set her half-eaten apple down on the bag beside her. The teenaged faces of two young men flashed before her eyes before disappearing just as quickly. "I taught underprivileged youth for a volunteer program. Mostly Spanish speakers who didn't speak any English."

Rachel looked out of the window for a distraction as they drove along the empty interstate through downtown Birmingham. Sean took her hand in his to comfort her, no doubt, but she pulled away, afraid the affection would break her. Derrick must have picked up on the tension because she heard a small murmur of an apology from his direction.

"How bad is it? The outbreak. Is it contained?" Sean asked.

Derrick stared at them for a long time as if deciding whether to lie or tell the truth. "The President sent in a National Guard unit last week, back when the infection was contained in Florida. They lost communication with them in forty-eight hours," Derrick sighed as he scratched his head. His light auburn hair was a greasy mess, and his gaunt face had a five o'clock shadow. His obvious exhaustion darkened his soft features. "The military scrambled after that. They set up defenses like you saw here. They have more in Atlanta and Charleston on the east coast to contain the infection in lower Alabama, Georgia, and Florida."

"Is it working?" Rachel asked, finishing the remains of the apple.

"If you believe the Pentagon briefings," Derrick shrugged. "The rabid have been attacking Atlanta since last night. Cellphones aren't working but I haven't heard the news say anything good about it. It... they say there are thousands of infected. Tens of thousands, but I don't know if I buy that."

"Jesus Christ..." Rachel whispered to herself.

"There's mass rioting in every city," Derrick said. "Last night alone thirty-one people were killed in Birmingham. Six police officers, two soldiers... the number is in the hundreds and thousands if you look at New York City or L.A."

"It's falling apart," Sean said.

"Six police officers?" Rachel repeated in astonishment. "Did you know any of them?"

"Yeah... all of them," Derrick said looking out the window.

"I'm sorry," Rachel whispered.

Sean stared at his hands as he picked at the dried apple juice on his skin. His focus narrowed in thought. Rachel processed the information she received differently than Sean. Sean was a secret service agent protecting the daughter of the Vice President of the United States, and before that he had been a marine. She could see him navigating this information like a battlefield and nothing more. He could turn off his emotions. Rachel not only felt every death and piece of destruction that Derrick told her about, but she held on to it too. She stored the pain inside her like it was her responsibility to carry it with her.

Derrick hesitated before asking, "How bad is it down there?" both Rachel and Sean looked up. "What are they like?"

Rachel's voice was hoarse as she spoke. "It's worse than anything you can imagine."

"They're fast. You can't outrun them," Sean adjusted in his seat, unnerved by the memory of the infected.

Rachel nodded her head in agreement. "And their scream–" she gritted her teeth as if she was reliving it. "That's how you know they're getting close. Their screams are nothing like you've ever heard before," Rachel continued. "They're like– like hyenas or something. Don't let them get close to you. No matter what."

Sean looked at the soldiers. They had turned off the interstate and turned down city streets. In a quiet voice, Sean leaned forward and said to Derrick, "you should get out while you can."

Derrick seemed to weigh Sean's words carefully like he had

been thinking the same thing himself for a time now. "Why didn't you leave?" Derrick asked. "The Vice President's Daughter? They had to have sent a plane or choppers for you guys, right?"

Sean pursed his lips and shot a side-eyed look at Rachel then looked away as if he knew his poker face was ruined. Rachel thumbed her palm in her lap as she felt herself shrink in her seat. Blurred faces of people she knew flashed before her eyes, her mind unlocking the door that contained all the images of the dead she tried so desperately to forget. *The children...*

"They sent a helicopter but..." Rachel's voice trailed off. "Out of my class of thirty kids, eleven couldn't find their parents and they were only fourteen years old. It was chaos in the streets, everywhere. Even before the virus reached where we were. The parents couldn't come and then the infected started attacking people..."

Rachel's voice shook as her eyes glazed over. "We got um– most of them there but I wouldn't get on the helicopter without the kids, and it couldn't fit them. It couldn't even fit the Sean and Chris and– they wanted my own fucking secret service agents to just fucking wait for another helicopter... Why didn't they send more fucking planes? They knew how many we had." Rachel was almost screaming and realized it. She swallowed and took a deep breath. "I refused to go. I wanted to save those kids..." Rachel mumbled and swiped hard at the tears falling down her face. "Lot of fucking good that did. I guided the kids... they trusted me and... and they died... Every one of them... they all died."

Sean looked out the window, his jaw clenched, as he listened to Rachel. Rachel wished she was like Sean in that moment. She envied his stoicism–he was an iron wall that could choose what to let in and what to keep out, and he kept Rachel miles away. The tears poured down her cheeks and she struggled to catch her breath as she silently wept. Desperate to stop herself from imagining each teenage face she had left behind–a part of her that she would never get back; a slice of her soul cut away and left to rot on the ground next to her abandoned student's bodies.

Derrick leaned forward and touched the top of Rachel's knee startling her from the dark place her mind circled. Behind Derrick's hard eyes there was a soft unsaid apology.

"I didn't mean... what could I have done?" Rachel's words spilled out before she could think not to say them. "I didn't know. I didn't know. I didn't– I tried to save them. I didn't know they would die if they came– what should I have done?"

Derrick silently retreated into his seat. He looked down at the rifle in his lap with solemn eyes.

"When that helicopter came to get you," Derrick said, "could you have lived with yourself?"

Rachel looked at him through red, tortured eyes.

"Leaving your secret service agents behind," Derrick nodded at Sean. "Leaving children behind to save yourself, would you be able to sleep at night? Had you done it, would you be able to live with yourself?"

"No, but maybe they'd–" Rachel started.

"There's no *maybe*, not anymore. There are only two kinds of people in the world. Those who do something and those who don't. *Maybe* is for those who don't. They have to say it to lie to themselves at night in order to sleep. 'Maybe I would have died if I had helped. Maybe more people would have died if I did something instead of run.' People die. You can't save everyone, no one can. All that matters when you're faced with life or death, is what kind of woman are you?" Derrick asked. "Will you step up and do something or not?"

Rachel looked back at him, willing herself to believe his words. She steadied her breathing with a deep breath. Derrick straightened and leaned back. "Every day, make the decision that allows you to sleep at night and you'll never go tired..." The Humvee turned up a steep hill with a blue sign on the side of the road that read 'Police Academy gun range.'

Derrick's eyes hardened. "You turned down a helicopter for those kids, because that's the kind of woman you are. And don't you fucking forget that."

Rachel looked down at her hands and digested Derrick's words. The pain of her students' death stung every bit as much as it did a minute ago or days ago. In truth, Rachel knew the pain was not something that would ever leave her. The screams they made as they were torn apart. The vicious wounds she saw the rabid open up in their teenaged bodies... that was what she would have to carry with her for the rest of her life. But the words Derrick had spoken to her made her believe that in that moment that she was the type of person who could shoulder this burden and keep moving forward despite it.

The Police Academy gun range was in a mountainous area surrounded by thick woods east of downtown Birmingham. Rachel knew this because she could see the setting sun dip behind downtown Birmingham. It created a mix of red and purples blurred across the sky. They drove up a hill that plateaued on a green field beside a gravel road. To the left was a large white trailer with a small, overworked AC unit that was sweating into the muddy dirt as the heat hung in the air despite the approaching night.

On the right, three large metal shipping containers were being unloaded by around twenty or so individuals drenched in sweat who carried heavy-looking boxes to the two transport helicopters stationed on the grassy field between the trailer and the shipping containers.

Derrick was the first one out the door once the Humvee stopped. Rachel took a deep breath and cleared her throat before following. Derrick's words had grounded her enough that she was able to put the memories of the past weeks back in the secluded part of her mind and focus on putting the next foot in front of her. *You can't save them all...* Derrick's words swirled in the back of her head.

The people who were loading boxes inside the helicopters slowed when they saw the four strangers wearing baggy nursing scrubs get out of the vehicles. One man, with a potbelly visible underneath a sweat-soaked polo shirt, made eye contact with Derrick and waved, prompting Derrick to wave back.

"Here," Sean handed the crumpled grocery bag to Chris. It still had two water bottles and a couple of apples in it.

"Holy shit!" a smile sprouted on Chris's face as he took an apple and water bottle out and handed the rest to Allen. Derrick made eye contact with Officer Perry and exchanged a nod as they began walking toward the trailers. While the two helicopters on the ground were being loaded with ammo, a third army chopper prepared to land. The thudding whip of its rotary blades grew louder as it neared the ground and finally descended.

There was a group of three soldiers supervising the loading. When the soldiers saw the Greenbands, they stood and greeted them.

"I'm Sergeant Shale, ma'am," one of the soldiers said to Rachel as he saluted her. He pointed to the third chopper and said, "This chopper is for you and your protective detail."

"Will it take us to where my dad is?" Rachel asked. The wind and noise picked up as their chopper landed and the rotary blades lifted dirt into the air.

Sergeant Shale nodded, squinting into the wind. "Yes, ma'am, the chopper will transport you to Louisville. It's the military's logistics hub right now. From there you'll be flown to a secure location," the Sergeant, who had ignored Derrick and

Perry until that moment, looked at them with an expression close to disdain. "You know you can't leave. You must stand by until the choppers are loaded and then report back to Command... Are you receiving me?"

Derrick only glared back in return, but it was Officer Perry who shouted back, "For the third fucking time, we know. Jesus..."

The Sergeant chewed on his tongue as he stewed on Perry's remarks. When the third helicopter landed, Derrick and Perry escorted the group to it. The blades on the two choppers haphazardly filled with boxes began to turn and quickly gain speed. Derrick put his hand out to stop the others and he saw the pilots radioing each other frantically. Their engines whining loudly as they powered up. Turning around, Rachel saw Sergeant Shale and his two corporals jumping inside the two Humvees that had just brought Rachel and the others there. The Humvees skidded in the gravel as they made a U-turn down the hill they had just come from.

"What's going on?" Sean yelled at Derrick over the whipping wind, but Derrick only shook his head with a bewildered look on his face. Rachel squinted into the wind as two of the three helicopters took off, spilling a half-loaded box of ammunition across the grass as it gained altitude with every passing second. The pilot on the last remaining helicopter aggressively waved at Rachel and the others to come over. He opened his door and stuck his head outside.

"Greenbands inside the chopper now for takeoff!" the pilot shouted; his voice barely audible over the speeding rotors.

"What's going on?" Rachel asked. Everyone seemed to know something that they did not.

The two helicopters that hovered overhead clicked on their spotlights. It shined massive rays of warm white light on Rachel's shoulders as she shielded her eyes. Sunlight had dipped below the horizon leaving slivers of magenta in the sky as the gray hue of night suffocated the ground. The spotlights zig-zagged one-hundred yards down the opposite end of the hill. Down below there was a field a hundred yards long with fifty shooting targets lined in front of a thick brush of woods that encompassed the gun range. The spotlights went past the shooting lanes and targets and hovered on the dark woods behind them, illuminating the brown tree trunks and the black spaces between them.

"Did they break through the barricades?" Perry asked, looking down the hill.

"Couldn't have," Derrick shook his head. "Not that fast, we're miles from the border."

The dozens of others who once were loading the choppers, now slowly gathered at the top of the hillcrest overlooking the gun range. Like moths moving towards the glow of the two choppers' spotlight, they inched closer in a silent stare. The rotors on the third helicopter were nearly at lift speed and the noise gobbled up whatever the pilot screamed.

Then, it was there. A single small figure pushed out of the woods between two targets downrange. The graying night made the figure impossible to discern when the roaming spotlight wasn't on it.

"Is that a..." Perry's voice trailed off.

It ran at full speed, but no one moved until the second spotlight shined on three more figures that bolted from the woods. Then five more figures. *They're here... they're here...* Rachel's mind screamed with the terror that she felt in her bones, paralyzing her in place.

Derrick turned and ran. Perry pushed Rachel, coaxing her to move her feet. The two helicopter spotlights blinded them briefly as they banked hard and flew away, leaving them in darkness.

The people who had been carrying supplies in boxes tossed them to the side and scattered in all directions. A handful tried to reach for the lone chopper, but Allen stopped them. He pointed them toward the trailer instead as he waved Rachel to hurry his way. Others ran for their cars but in their panic and exhaustion, many tripped and fell. Perry stopped short of the chopper and took a knee, covering them. Her short machine gun ready as she waited for threats to come over the hill.

"Go go go go!" Derrick yelled as he and Rachel rounded the front of the helicopter. "Get out of here."

"Wait!" Rachel pulled away from the aircraft after putting a foot inside. "Come with us," her eyes darted to Perry kneeling in the grass. "Both of you."

"We can't," Derrick shook his head. "We have to protect these civilians here," he pointed to the dozen people still running for cover.

Rachel held up her hand at Allen and Chris who shouted behind her. "We'll take them, too," Rachel blurted out. The panic and jitteriness were wild in her eyes.

"Fuck no, we're not," Allen yelled, pushing past Sean just far enough to wrap his arm around Rachel's belly and drag her onboard the helicopter. Rachel swatted and kicked at the air like a child being pulled away for a time out. Sean grasped Rachel's fingertips and managed to get his arm around her shoulders. In what felt like one move, Sean pulled Rachel from Allen's arms and kicked his legs from underneath him, shoving Allen to the grass.

"Touch her like that again and I'll fuck you up," Sean jabbed his finger down at Allen. He turned to Derrick as he righted Rachel to her feet. "We can't take the others, but if you two are coming, we gotta go now."

Allen had crawled onto the helicopter beside Chris, both of them yelling in panic for the others to get in.

A pull of guilt settled across Derrick's face as he looked back at Officer Perry just as she stole a glance at him. Rachel wanted to scream at them to get in the chopper. *They don't know. They don't understand. There's no surviving the infection. They're going to die. I can make this right. This can save your lives– let me save your life!*

Derrick looked at the people piling into the trailer and Rachel screamed his own words at him, "You can't save everyone." Derrick looked at her with softened eyes and a resigned smile as he nodded.

"I know... but I couldn't live with myself if I didn't try," Derrick nodded to Sean and backed away from the helicopter. Sean pulled Rachel inside the belly of the chopper as the pilot hastily lifted off. Rachel watched the ground grow smaller beneath them, listening to the roar of the rotating propellers, and saw dozens of infected that looked like speeding dots mount the hill before a burst of gunfire erupted from where Derrick and Perry stood.

SEVEN

Derrick Hart
Birmingham, Al

Perry snapped, "move your fucking asses!"

The six people scrambled to reach the gun vault trailer. Night might've fallen but the humidity of the south still choked the air. Derrick and Perry had sweat bulleting down their faces as they ran for the stragglers in the middle of the field. The first of the rabid crested the hill–a shadowed figure with features dulled in the low light, but it's scream triggered a jolt of terror inside Derrick. It was high pitched and ragged with breathy gasps. It was a maddening sound, vaguely human but stripped bare, with an animalistic aggression.

Derrick flipped on the light attachment on the barrel of his rifle and saw the figure's flush red face that matched the blood-stained whites of its eyes. It looked like he had been a young good-looking man, before the pandemic resulted in dirty clothes and torn flesh that hung untamed from his face. It closed the distance between itself and the last stragglers running for the trailer–an old man with a waddle in his step and a heavyset woman with glasses.

"Shit! Do we shoot?" Perry asked frantically.

Derrick's mind was inundated with information as it tried to process it all in a panic. *No gun, no weapon. Unarmed civilian. No shoot.* In a flash, his mind blurred, stretching back and forth between Alabama state law and gut instinct. The use-of-force policy he was taught in the academy almost a decade ago and the federal directive on deadly force read to him during roll call today. The red dot of his aimpoint pro reticle danced around the infected's figure as it ran. *He's infected. How do you know he's infected? Can you testify in court that he's infected?*

With a strained, choking grip of his rifle, Derrick shot the first round when the rabid was forty yards away from him. Perry, concurring with Derrick's decision, quickly took aim with her MP5 and joined the fight. They missed their first shots as the rabid neared its victims. It ran for the stairs of the trailer; Perry was the first to hit it, striking it in the hip but that didn't stop it.

Derrick got it in the thigh, but it didn't fall. Then Perry hit it in the same leg. They both were aiming low without having a solid backstop for their bullets. If any of their missed shots struck the siding of the trailer where the civilians hid, their rounds would pierce the flimsy trailer wall and anyone on the other side. But aiming low meant their hits were less lethal.

Derrick's peripherals picked up more dark figures coming over the hill. Five more ran toward him and Perry. Panic bubbled in Derrick's chest when he saw some of them scurrying on all fours like a pack of wolves. They screeched, causing the same horrific sound. It was wild and crazed. As if the infected themselves didn't understand what they were doing. They only knew rage. Bounding between confused screams and gurgling growls, Derrick felt a fear click inside him he didn't recognize.

"Perry, right! Right!" Derrick called out. Perry knew she was just given another sector of fire and adjusted ninety degrees to her right addressing the five new threats. A gray-haired man, wearing a flannel shirt tucked into his too high beige trousers, was almost at the trailer. A young woman held the door open, screaming for him to hurry. Derrick held his breath before he fired. His next shot hit the chasing rabid in the ribs, but the rabid collapsed on the old man. They both screamed as the pair fell at the doorway.

"Fuck!" Derrick shouted as he ran toward the trailer. The young woman who held the door desperately tried to slam it shut but the kicking bodies rolled in the doorway.

"Derrick!" Perry's voice cut through the gunfire. She was running his way with a pack of rabid sprinting in tow. He took aim, as if to lay down covering fire for her but realized they were far too fanned out to stop them all. He turned as she neared, and they both sprinted for the metal shipping containers that held the ammo.

There are so many of them, where did they all come from? About a quarter mile through the woods beyond the gun range was the I-459 interstate but Derrick had no idea how they made it past the army.

They ran between the shipping containers where there was a hollow gap barely wide enough for their shoulders and stopped at the other end.

"Hey," Derrick caught Perry's attention. "Here, here!"

She saw him bracing against the left corner of the shipping container and did the same on right side. He tried to calm his breathing as the red dot reticle of his optics sight bounced haywire with his quick breaths.

The first rabid appeared between the containers and

Derrick jerked his trigger back five times, each round striking the rabid's chest before it finally fell. More rabid joined the fray, bottlenecking as their shoulders bounced off one another and their faces slammed into the metal walls chaotically, trying to reach for them.

Perry fired her MP5 in quick succession and Derrick joined her. The infected didn't react to the hits. They didn't grab the wound or wince in pain. There was no sign of slowing down. The bullets only made them more ravenous. Perry and Derrick's overlapping fields of fire tore more holes in the rabid until their chests and heads were a gory mess of blood piled on top of another.

"Red!" Derrick shouted over Perry's gunfire. He ejected his rifle magazine and smacked a fresh one in, pressing the bolt catch shut, but when he came up on the target, the last of the rabid was shot to the ground. "Green," Derrick panted as he scanned.

Perry had slung her rifle and emptied her pistol into the now twitching rabid closest to them. As she reloaded her weapons, Derrick saw the pile of dead and dying bodies they had made. His ears rang and he felt dizzy for a second. The once white, mud-stained shipping containers were now splattered with blood. One of the infected in the pile of bodies was still fighting for a ragged and primal gasp of air. The delicate sound Derrick stilled to hear was quickly drowned out by the hard patter of footsteps behind him.

An infected leapt on her, slamming Perry into the container corner. She twisted free in one swift motion, the momentum throwing the rabid on the grass between them. Derrick shot at its thighs to avoid hitting Perry and then fired at its chest once Perry angled away. Perry alerted Derrick to more rabids scurrying like dogs behind her. "Run. Move, move, move!"

With little choice and no time to think, they sprinted back between the shipping containers. Derrick and Perry felt the squish of bodies under their feet. Twice Derrick nearly fell on a sunken body that shifted under his weight, but Perry grabbed his shoulder and righted him. He felt like a child sinking in a foam pit of flesh and blood.

"Tr– Trailer!" Perry spat out before she opened fire. Derrick looked up to face the direction they were running in and saw the infected pouring out of the gun vault trailer where the civilians had been hiding. They were easy to identify as the infected because they swarmed the door so much that they broke the flimsy wood off the hinges. Bodies poured over the railing and fell face first down the stairs. Derrick could only see the blood-red eyes when his flashlight waved across the clamoring swarm. The group behind Derrick bounced off the shipping container walls, their footsteps echoing loudly as they closed the distance.

Derrick stopped short to change directions. He used his free hand to catch himself from falling on the grass. They were caught in the middle of the field with no cover. In a panic, Derrick and Perry ran in opposite directions. The infected divided and chased after both.

By the time he realized Perry was not with him anymore, Derrick knew they were going to die. He turned the corner of the trailer and felt a hand claw his heavy vest from behind. He pivoted ninety degrees, firing his rifle from his hip, striking the stomach and chest of a large, barrel-chested rabid that had heaved itself on him. The bullets slowed it down but didn't stop it completely.

Derrick almost tripped, running sideways when he saw the line of rabid galloping on all fours for him. He looked for a place to hide but there was nothing. At the back of the trailer, there was a small clearing of mowed grass and beyond that were waist-high weeds that every officer in the department knew was riddled with venomous snakes.

In the summer, snake handlers were called three times a month to remove Copperheads and Cottonmouths from the range. Two detectives had been hospitalized last summer after being bitten during their annual firearm qualification. But venomous snakes were the least of his worries right now.

Derrick nearly tried to dive under the trailer itself, but it was a mere eighteen inches above the dirt. *Not enough room for a full-grown man to hide like a child.* Out of options, Derrick ran to the edge of the mowed grass and swiveled, his rifle raised and his teeth clenched. The trail of infected that followed him stretched around the corner from where he came, the closest swiped at his boots.

His firing was haphazard and chaotic. The bullets pounded into the rabid's upper back and immediately moved to the other rabid charging at him. He had to suppress the boiling panic that threatened to paralyze him when the rabid didn't fall after the first hits. The more he focused, the more his rifle sights centered the shots on their upper chest, neck, and head. The rabid fell faster.

He brought the reticle to his eye until it hovered over the next face and pulled the trigger. This time his shots were slow and smooth, his breathing controlled. The first target fell. He inhaled. Pulled the trigger. Exhaled. Pulled the trigger. Derrick's shooting became methodical. *Just like range day with paper targets. Chest-chest-head. Chest-chest-head. Reload.*

Derrick sidestepped as he smacked a fresh magazine into his rifle. The rabids closest to him were twitching in the dirt, giving him time to start picking off the farther ones as they rounded the corners of the trailer, attacking from both sides now.

They were too far away for headshots, but Derrick found

the upper chest wounds were doing the trick if he shot them enough times. Still, none of them fell instantly unless shot in the head. The last rabid in sight, took the corner and fell in a mess of mud and blood. Derrick gunned him into the ground until he stopped moving.

Releasing a breath he didn't know he was holding, Derrick swapped magazines in his rifle in a tactical reload and saw for the first time the sea of bodies around him. Over the dozen dead men and women he had killed. Then he saw their faces. They weren't just men and women. They were coworkers, friends... *Adam from records... Lisa from HR...*

A single gunshot startled him from his thought and Derrick remembered. *Perry.*

EIGHT

Brandon Armstrong
Atlanta, Ga

"Holy shit, did he just kill himself," one of the corporals said to his friend.

"I can't believe this shit," the heavier Corporal shook his head. They had run into the tent after they had heard the gunshot and froze at the sight of the Colonel's lifeless body. The corporals wore an army uniform that was clean and pressed and had obviously never seen combat before. "Hey, yo, Sarge," one of them called out to Brandon who was across the tent. "What'd he say to you? You know, before..."

Brandon ignored them just as he was ignoring the suicide. If the Colonel wanted to check out early, that was his prerogative. Brandon wasn't that guy. He held up a map he found, folded in the Colonel's tent beside one of the computer monitors, that displayed the southern United States. He used a pencil to mark all the red Xs he saw on the monitor.

"Hey, man, you hear me? What'd he say? It had to be bad, right?" the Corporal yelled just as the Captain walked inside the tent. Brandon had no idea who the captain was, only that he had been the Colonel's second-in-command lapdog all week. No one even pretended to salute him. The Captain saw the Colonel's body and took off his cover rubbing his forehead in a daze. The corporals only stared at him, waiting for a reaction of some kind.

Brandon was only half-finished updating the paper map, but it would have to do. He folded it messily and stuffed it in his pants pocket, then quickly put the Greenband radio in his cargo pocket, hoping no one had seen it. Brandon pulled at the loose siding of the tent and kicked a small carboard box beneath the fabric of the walls, hiding the box outside the tent.

"Okay..." The Captain said to himself. "Okay. Gather all support personnel by the west entrance ramp. Tell them to bring every bit of ammo and all the weapons they can find. W-we're making our stand."

Brandon imagined the Captain had thought it would sound more confident coming out of his mouth than it did. Instead, it sounded more like a child playing a war game. The corporals exchanged a brief look like they were insisting the other one say something. The Captain saw this and reminded them of their place. "*Now*, Corporals."

"Yes, sir," they said in unison and went outside.

"You too, Sergeant," the Captain nodded at Brandon. Brandon ignored the order but instead stared at the folder with the Top Secret piece of paper in it. "First Sergeant Dieves!" the Captain called out.

Sergeant Dieves ran into the tent like a dog who smelled treats in the captain's pocket. He was a square-jawed man with more bulk to his figure than an average human being. A sturdy specimen who seemed to be missing a neck. Brandon knew his type just from looking at the rigid way he carried himself. The army was full of sergeants who took themselves too seriously and would spend their leisure time holding their thumbs over the few they were in charge of. Brandon hated Dieves and he hadn't even heard him speak yet.

"Captain?" Sergeant Dieves said.

"The Colonel's dead," the Captain said as Brandon walked to them. "This changes nothing."

"You need to call the retreat," Brandon said. "All those men out there are about to die. We're out of ammo."

The Captain glared at Brandon, furious at him daring to give his superior officer orders. Brandon didn't really care anymore. The Colonel had done him the courtesy of explaining how fucked everything and everyone was, especially them. Respecting rank wasn't high on his priority list.

"No one is retreating," the Captain snapped. "We must hold the infected off so as many civilians as possible in Atlanta can escape."

"We're not evacuating the city," Brandon pointed to one of the monitors that had the local news on. Across the bottom of the monitor, a ticker read:

'ATLANTA. SHELTER IN PLACE. THE CITY IS UNDER MARTIAL LAW. ANYONE FOUND OUTSIDE WILL BE ARRESTED. REMAIN CALM.'

"We're just buying time so the fucking rich politicians and goddamn Greenbands can get to their bunkers while the rest of us die," Brandon said.

"Know your place, Sergeant!" Sergeant Dieves stepped forward. "We're soldiers." Brandon could tell this was a common move for Dieves–to square off with a subordinate and let his hulking frame intimidate a man into submission. Brandon looked down on him as Brandon's six-foot-three-inch frame had about four inches on him. "We follow orders. We don't get the luxury of always seeing the big picture."

Brandon pulled out the piece of paper on Locke protocol from the folder on the desk and stuffed it in the Captain's hand. "And sometimes we do," he said. The Captain's eyes lit up when he realized what the paper was, and he put it face down on the table beside him, obviously having already read it. The red watermark on the back of the paper said 'Top Secret,' repeatedly, at a forty-five degree angle.

"What is that, sir?" Dieves asked the Captain. He was irritated by the look of understanding that passed between Brandon and *his* commanding officer, but his curiosity got the better of him.

"Sergeant Dieves, go assist the corporals and make sure they're all heading in the right direction," the Captain said.

"Yes, sir," Sergeant Dieves said. He saluted the Captain and gave a final glare at Brandon before leaving.

"You too, Sergeant Armstrong," the Captain looked at the poorly stitched name on Brandon's fatigues. He pointed at the overpass. "The front is that way," his voice low and heavy as if he was suppressing his anger while pretending to be calm and in control.

Brandon felt the desire to strike the Captain in that moment, but he had bigger things to worry about than satisfying his urge.

Brandon left the tent. There were so many things on his mind that he nearly forgot to run around to the backside of the tent where he had hidden the small box with the Greenband bracelets. There were ten of them in the case. Each one was silver and metallic green with laser etchings along the outside.

Brandon had noticed the box sitting beside the Colonel's bloodied head. Grabbing the box was instinctual. At this point, these bracelets were worth more than gold.

He jogged to the overpass entrance ramp but stopped short after passing a few tents. Brandon ducked through an aisle between two rows of tents–some with tables and maps, others with cots and clothes. Distant gunfire still filled the air. The hundreds of support staff, most of whom hadn't seen combat outside of TV and video games, were running in all directions, looking for their flak jackets, trying to find the rally point. Brandon even saw one young boy crawling under a cot trying to hide. People saw the sergeant stripes on Brandon's uniform and ran to him looking for orders. He shut that shit down fast. "You're not my problem! Go fucking find your CO."

He didn't have time to deal with these eighteen-year-olds. If he was going to get out of here before this place was overrun by the infected, he had to act fast and go alone. He found an empty Humvee sitting idle next to the barracks tent. He took his chance and sped off in the vehicle despite a distant scream of protest from behind him. He circled the base to a supply tent at the back end that was hardly used due to it being far from the barracks, Command tents, and the front lines. *Which fucking genius picked this location?* Still, it worked out well for Brandon. There wasn't another person in sight.

It was true, the shelves that housed all their ammo cans near the front of the tent were empty. Brandon carried cases of water to the back of his Humvee.

What battle in U.S. history had ever been lost from a lack of ammunition? Ever.

There was no way to see what was happening at the overpass with night falling. It was nearly a mile away, and his sight was blocked by other tents, but Brandon could hear a change in the chorus of gunfire. The automatic gunfire was dying as the men ran out of ammo. Small arms fire popped at a slower cadence. He could see support personnel were peaking the overpass on foot with their M4s in hand. Their rifle safeties would be on and their hands trembling.

Hopefully, Sergeant Major Wesley would take the magazines right out of their weapons and hand them to the Rangers at the front lines.

Brandon shook his head free of any thoughts that would remind him of his men. He filled a small bag with a few Ready-to-Eat meals and went right for the large twenty-five-gallon diesel containers. He made three trips to his trunk and lugged five containers into the stolen Humvee. When Brandon went back for the last one, he noticed a large forgotten wooden box that was pushed into the back corner of the tent behind the diesel cans. He slid it out with both hands and read the half-peeled label: '30 Grenade Hand Delay M67.'

"Who the fuck..." Brandon let his voice trail off, wanting to beat the shit out of whatever moron stored a box of grenades behind diesel fuel. Opening the top of the crate, he saw the individually packed frag grenades divided into their slots.

Brandon shrugged. "Fuck it."

He grabbed both ends of the crate and carried it back to the vehicle. In his mind, he couldn't think of a specific instance in the future when he would need thirty grenades, but Brandon figured it couldn't hurt. As he had been loading for his men for the past few hours and not firing at the front lines himself, he was topped off on ammo for his M4 assault rifle, his Glock 19 side arm, and now, grenades. Brandon loaded the box in the rear and figured it was best to stop while he was ahead.

"Turn around, you piece of shit," a voice panted behind him. Brandon closed the door and turned. It was Sergeant Dieves. Out of breath, he pointed his M4 rifle at Brandon's chest.

Brandon instinctively raised his hands. "Whoa, bro, I was just loading up some supplies to bring to the front lines. Captain's orders."

"Yeah, and Captain ordered you to steal my Humvee, too?"

"My bad, I was just in a hurry, I didn't–"

"Save it. I knew you were deserting the second I walked out of that tent."

Brandon's soft smile disappeared as he gave up on his ruse. "They didn't *just* realize we were fucked down here, you know. That top secret memo? The Colonel's suicide? The military Command has been diverting ammo and supplies away from here, Birmingham, and every front line since this morning. They don't give a fuck about our lives or anyone else in this city."

Dieves seemed to consider this information, processing everything as if he had been given pieces of the puzzle throughout the day and was just now getting the last one to complete the picture. A soldier's mind is a confusing place for civilians to understand. Every person is born with self-preservation encoded in their DNA. It was the one basic animal instinct that is universal. Survival. Fight or flight. But soldiers are made to unlearn the flight instinct and instead taught to fight whenever possible; retreat only when necessary; die if need be. A civilian cannot comprehend dying for something bigger than themselves, but soldiers can. They are the ones who've built this country and won wars. Patriotism. Honor. Duty. These aren't just bumper stickers for a soldier just like the American flag isn't a decoration to them. A soldier's life and character is built upon these principles.

So, when Sergeant Dieves, after having a moment to digest this information, said, "I don't give a fuck about your life, you fucking coward," Brandon was not surprised.

"Now get walking," he jabbed his barrel at Brandon. "Go. The front is that way."

Brandon ground his teeth. He was sure if he made even the slightest of movements for his rifle, he would be shot to piss by Dieves. But he also knew there was only a difference of minutes at this point between dying here and now or on top of that overpass. "It's not going to happen, Dieves," Brandon finally said.

"I'm not fucking around," Dieves replied.

"Neither am I," Brandon shook his head. "Call me a bitch ass coward, but I got a wife to get to. So, if you think putting a bullet in my head is a good use of that bullet, then let's get it over with."

Dieves snarled at the challenge and raised his rifle. The moment lingered and the longer he struggled with the decision the more Brandon knew he wasn't going to be shot. Finally, Dieves lowered his rifle. "Get the fuck out of here," he said. "On foot."

"What?"

"I'm not wasting a Humvee on your ass. You're not taking anything with you. You want to leave? Then leave, but the Humvee and your weapons stay. I've got *real* soldiers up there who need your ammo."

Brandon knew he was as good as dead if he walked out of there unarmed. There was no way he could make it to safety in time. "That's not going to happen, either"

Dieves raised his rifle, again. "I'm not fucking around!" he shouted. "I'll waste a whole mag on you if it means keeping that truck."

Brandon believed him, too. The look in Dieves' eyes told him that he had found the excuse he could live with in order to gun Brandon down. Brandon rubbed his dirty, dry palms over his face and let out a long sigh. There was more shouting than gunfire coming from the overpass now and Dieves was getting antsy. "Now, motherfucker!"

No other way.

Slowly, Brandon unslung his rifle and handed it to Dieves. Pulling his six extra rifle magazines free from his chest rig, he dropped them at Dieves' feet. His Ka-Bar knife remained sheathed on the top left of his chest rig. Brandon unholstered and handed Dieves his pistol, casually, barrel forward. When Dieves grabbed the barrel of his handgun, Brandon slapped the muzzle of Dieves' rifle down and to the side as he drew the knife with his other hand.

In one swift tackling motion, he jumped on Dieves and plunged the knife into his neck just above his chest rig. Dieves squeezed the trigger releasing a barrage of automatic gunfire into the dirt as Brandon twisted the blade and stabbed again.

The First Sergeant's body was powerful as it curled and kicked at Brandon, nearly throwing him off. Dieves raised the rifle, awkwardly trying to point the muzzle at him with one hand. Brandon shifted his weight and flattened the firing weapon to the concrete, pressing the trigger. The bullets cut holes in the tent until the magazine clicked empty.

Sergeant Dieves cupped pointlessly at his neck. Brandon's mind was blank. It was as empty and black as the night. He stood back panting as the First Sergeant looked around panicked and wide eyed. Brandon looked down at the Ka-Bar knife that was sticky with the soldier's blood. Random thoughts flashed through his mind. *I've never stabbed someone before.* The red blood pooled on Dieves' chest and trickled down his left shoulder. *Massive bleeding wound.*

A few seconds passed and Sergeant Dieves stopped moving. His eyes lowered and eventually fixed in a forever stare at nothing. Brandon stood up staring at the body of the soldier he had just killed. *I've never seen a man die... not up close.*

Brandon focused at a spot above the body as if looking for the departing soul, floating away. Taking shallow breaths, he gathered his rifle and magazines and tossed them into the passenger seat. With one final look at the overpass, he saw soldiers starting to flee with no weapons in hand, the staccato of semi-auto handgun fire sounding like background music. Brandon entered the Humvee and accelerated away as the sound of the screaming men overtook the gunfire.

Brandon reached into his cargo pocket for his Greenband radio and saw the wet blood still dripping from his hand. He wiped his hand on his pants, drying it but doing nothing to dull the red stain on them. The hurried rubbing on his thigh and chest rig turned into an angry slapping, culminating in punching the steering wheel. "Goddamn it! Mother fuck! You didn't need to follow me! Let me go– you could've just let me fucking go!" Brandon shouted.

He removed a sandwich bag with folded and crumpled papers from a Velcro pocket in his chest rig while he zig-zagged between concrete traffic barriers, leaving the army base. Inside the bag, he had kept his passport, social security card, a cellphone with a long dead battery, a picture of his wife, and a scrap of paper with just two phone numbers written on it. One was his wife's.

Why call her, though? She's safe in Kentucky. She can't help me so there's no use in calling her.

It was the second number that he needed to call. He had to warn him. Brandon punched the number into the satellite phone, his eyes bounced between the phone, the paper, and the road. Speeding past a final roadblock, Brandon entered the interstate going north. Clicking 'send' Brandon let out a growl that ended with an exhausted breath.

Come on, you asshole. Pick up the damn phone, Derrick. You better still be alive.

NINE

Derrick Hart

Birmingham, Al

Derrick prowled around the corner of the trailer searching for threats on the other side–*none.* Then looked for movement–*none.* Night had choked the light from the open field. Black clouds shaded the sky from letting even the brightest of stars touch Derrick's path. Two porch lights attached to the sides of the trailer shined a stale light on the bodies spread across the field.

Running up the stairs and inside the trailer, Derrick could taste the copper tinge of blood before he saw it. The sight was a massacre. Splattered blood was sprayed across the far wall and torn bodies were piled on top of one another. He pointed his rifle light in every nook and crevice and saw no movement. Nothing was alive. He couldn't even recognize the body parts he saw.

"Perry?" Derrick whispered into the silence. Tables and

chairs lay flipped over and tossed about. The flimsy bathroom doors were bashed in and ripped off their hinges.

He let his gun relax as he stepped outside and saw the stack of bodies near the base of the trailer. The crickets and critters crawling through the tall grass and woods chirped and clicked, underlining Derrick's solitude.

"Perry!" Derrick yelled out. The silence of the night seemed to swallow his voice.

"Down here," a muffled voice said. Derrick looked at his feet and then to the stack of bodies by the trailer side beneath the AC window unit. Slinging his rifle, he pulled out a flashlight from his belt and saw mud-caked hands swipe out from underneath the trailer. Perry managed to extract her head out from under the trailer and gasped for air like she had just gotten out of water.

"Are they dead? Are they gone?" she asked.

Derrick breathed a sigh of relief and grabbed her hand to help her to her feet. "Fuckin' hell, Perry. You scared the shit out of me," Derrick said. "Careful, there's blood everywhere." Perry had to slide her heavy vest off to get out from under the trailer. "You're hurt," Derrick pointed to her forehead.

Perry ignored Derrick's observation as she stood and asked again. "Are these the last of them? They are gone?"

"Yeah. For now, I think."

Perry's hair and face were streaked with mud leaving more of her skin covered than not. The portion of her forehead that was visible had a nasty red gash several inches long oozing a stream of blood down her nose. Derrick reached into a small pack on the back of his hip and moved closer, cupping Perry's cheek to steady her and wiped blood away with a cloth.

"That explains why my head is throbbing," Perry mumbled, looking at the blood on the cloth. "Ouch," she sucked in air through her teeth when Derrick pressed on her wound.

"You're going to need stitches. Did they scratch you? Bite you? They said you're not supposed to get their blood or–"

"No, it wasn't them," Perry sounded more embarrassed than annoyed. There was a vulnerability in Perry's eyes that he had never seen before. She was usually such a walled-up person at work. It was the cross women in law enforcement were forced to bear. While men were encouraged more and more to open up about their feelings, female officers knew they had to be careful about how much they showed. Perry knew the trash officers would speak behind her back if she showed weakness, tenderness, or, God forbid, shed tears while on duty. There was a reason Perry was the first and only woman ever to be on Birmingham SWAT.

She was a tough motherfucker.

Derrick suddenly realized how close he stood to Perry when she looked up and her eyes met his. Feeling a surge of heat flare in his cheeks, he took a step back. Perry's eyes darted away, and her hands took over holding the cloth in place on her cut.

"I smacked my freaking head on this thing trying to get underneath it. I just flipped when they came out of the trailer and–" Perry straightened and looked around the muddy field. "Oh god... the civilians. Are they... did any of them–"

Derrick simply shook his head as he looked across the field of dead bodies–coworkers he had remained behind to protect. The innocents he had ended up killing. There were dozens of bodies. More than Derrick had ever seen at once. *You can't save them all,* his own words haunted him.

The moment clung to them both like a leach. It fed on Derrick's sorrow, leaving a gaping hole in his gut as he processed what they had done. What they had failed to do.

"How could this happen?" Perry spoke barely above a whisper. "We just left the border, how could the infected make it here already. We're ten miles from the front lines."

"I don't know."

Think. Can't change the past. Think. What's the next step.

Derrick switched on his radio that had turned off sometime during the fight. "We've gotta get with Command. Make sure everyone knows."

"Even if they broke through the army it still took us, what, fifteen minutes to drive here?" Perry's eyes were lost in thought as she touched her forehead. "You don't think they already spread to the city, do you?"

Derrick shared an icy stare with Perry as he keyed the mic on his chest rig. "4SAM86 to Command. 4SAM86 to Command," he checked his radio on his hip to make sure he was on the right channel.

Perry tried to brush the mud off her mic that bounced at her side. "Dammit," she cursed under her breath.

"4SAM86 to C–" Derrick heard a muffled chime from his chest that startled him. It had been days since he had heard a phone ring. Juggling his radio mic between his jaw and shoulder, he fished his phone out from his breast pocket beneath his vest and felt a wave of relief when he read the name on the screen. "Thank god..."

'Alyssa Calling...' his phone read.

"You got a call?" Perry asked, equally surprised as she tossed aside the piece of gauze that was now soaked in blood and mud. "You think the cell towers are coming back up?"

Derrick wore a smile when he looked up at Perry. She excitedly bent down to her own chest rig struggling to retrieve her phone from one of its pockets. Derrick saw it like slow motion. Hidden in Perry's hairline was a gob of wet mud that released a stream of crimson liquid down the top of her forehead. The line of the blood-like substance that almost perfectly divided her forehead slowed near the center as if deciding its fate, deciding Perry's fate. Derrick felt his stomach drop, he watched the droplet of blood curve alongside Perry's forehead arching to the side and merging with the gaping gash of a wound above her eye.

Derrick dropped his phone and radio like he was emptying his hands for a gunfight and ran to her. "No, stop– move your head back!" his words startled her. Perry looked behind her with a confused face and panic in her eyes.

"Move move!" Derrick said, shoving her hands to the side. He cupped her face and swiped precisely at the line of blood with another fistful of gauze he pulled from his medic pouch. He didn't know if it was her blood or infected blood mixed with the muddy earth, but he had to be careful. It was made very clear to them not to let infected blood in any wounds or orifices.

"Nng! No, no! Nnng..." Perry's legs gave out, collapsing her to the ground.

"Wait! Don't–" Derrick started but it was too late. She was on her knees, her fists filled with ripped grass and mud between her white knuckles. Her forehead dragged roughly against the earth as she flattened out. Derrick took a knee, putting a hand on her back but he didn't know what to do. "Perry, Perry! Stop don't–"

Perry let out an awful scream. It was a scream of pain, at first, but turned on a razor's edge. Cutting into Derrick's eardrums, the pitch switched as her vocal cords ripped. Her fingers tore at the earth. An involuntary spasm wracked Derrick's spine that straightened his back and made every hair on his neck stand on edge. His eyes went wide as his body backed away without thought.

It was a knee-jerk reaction of his nervous system. He felt as though a lion had just been released into a room with him. *That scream... that scream...* His survival instincts felt the presence of a predator.

She's infected!

Derrick couldn't get to his feet fast enough before Perry's blood shot eyes locked on his. Lunging on top of him, it was an explosion of strength he hadn't felt before. Perry's furious screams became lost in the thudding sounds as his body and head tumbled backward. Derrick shoved her away with the weight of her momentum, but Perry was on his back again like a blanket. Their rifles slung to their chest and clattered and smacked their bodies as she grabbed at his shoulders. His arms moved and Perry slammed them down. She was suffocating and violent.

Perry screamed while strings of saliva shot from her mouth attacking the back of Derrick's neck. He bucked his hips and put his back to the ground, trying to shake her off of him. But she scurried into the mounted position. His hands tried to press on her chest to keep her at bay, but the mud and blood covering her figure caused his hands to slip.

Her dirt covered face shot toward his. Her jaw wide open and slacking with every inch she got closer. Her wild, bloodshot eyes locked on him as she screamed. Derrick leaned left at the last moment and her bite missed his cheek.

Fight. Fight! Find a way to win!

Derrick screamed as he pushed with all his strength on Perry's throat. Her face lifted from Derrick and she immediately began to claw his arms. Derrick pushed his knee between them and kicked her to the side. He tried to stand, but the second Perry touched the ground her limbs clawed towards him. He made it to a knee before she was back at him. He managed to stave off her advance causing her to tumble in the dark grass as the momentum took her. It gave Derrick enough time to draw his pistol from his holster.

Firing wildly at the scrambling figure in the night, Derrick yanked the trigger again and again until his magazine emptied. Perry's limbs flailed on the ground like a dying spider.

Derrick snapped to his feet, backing away and nearly tripping as his trembling hands ejected his empty magazine and slammed a full mag into his pistol hard enough to run the slide forward in one swift motion. He turned on his pistol light attachment, shined it on Perry who was still twitching on the ground. Derrick did a fast, circling sweep through the dark with his pistol light. A sudden, choking fear overcame him as he expected more infected to appear behind him.

"Fuck," Derrick whispered to himself as he panted. The adrenaline rush shook his voice. "Fuck! Fuuck!"

His breathing was out of control. He closed his mouth to work some saliva into it, then gasped for another breath. Steadying his weapon light on Perry, he neared her. Several gunshot wounds dribbled carmine blood across her thighs, arms, and chest. Derrick looked at her face and then wished he hadn't. Her mouth was broken and wide, her jaw dislocated and teeth missing. And her eyes stretched out with crumbs of dirt and mud staining the pupils, which she didn't notice.

SWAT Officer Jessica Perry took a final gasping breath that ran like a shudder through her entire body before she went still. Her lifeless eyes remained open, gazing up at her killer.

There were a thousand things he knew he should be doing. They cycled through the back of his mind on autopilot.

Reload, rearm, check for survivors, radio command, head back to the precinct. The thoughts were on a continuous loop, yet his feet didn't move.

The familiar chime played again, causing him to find his way out of his stupor. Derrick's phone rang for some time before he realized what the sound was. Derrick palmed the breast of his uniform to find it empty, but his fingers closed around the pair of metal dog tags that had slipped from under his uniform in the fight and now dangled around his neck.

Valhalla waits for no one...

The words etched into the cheap piece of metal never seemed more appropriate.

Still in a daze, he walked to the grassy area where he recalled dropping his phone. Derrick would do anything to hear Alyssa's voice at that moment. All the time he spent worrying if he was coming on too strong or pushing her away seemed frivolous now. He didn't care if he looked desperate. He didn't realize how much he needed her until he saw it wasn't her calling.

'...Brandon Calling...'

Derrick shook his head, jarred from seeing his friend's name, and swiped at the screen, "Brandon?"

"I'm here, man," Brandon replied.

"Jesus, I thought– I didn't know if you made it."

"Lis–"

"Bran, the infected are here in Birmingham. We just killed– I just had to kill–"

"Derrick. Derrick! Shut the fuck up and listen," Brandon interrupted, his speech uncharacteristically panicked. Derrick had never heard him sound so jittery before. "That doesn't matter anymore. None of it does. You still in Birmingham?"

"Yeah, I'm here."

"Listen to me. You got to get out now. Like right fucking now. It's happening."

"What is?" Derrick asked. The urgency flooded his veins as if Brandon was sending it through the phone and Derrick understood what Brandon was talking about. It had only been a week since their last conversation, but a lifetime of events had occurred since then. Each horrible thing Derrick had seen and the countless times he had been forced to pull the trigger had left him a shell of the man he used to be.

Brandon had predicted this moment a week ago. Of course, he wasn't the only one. The millions of people who had abandoned their homes to flee with their families for safety knew the collapse was coming. The surge in suicides underscored the reality that most didn't want to admit. The end of the world was here.

"You mean now? Now, now?" Derrick looked around the field shadowed with bodies.

"I mean like right fucking now. As in we might already be too fucking late. The military is pulling back. They have been all day. They're letting the south go, leaving it to the rabid. Derrick, the infection is already in Atlanta. It overwhelmed the flanks on the sides of the city hours ago; probably did the same in Birmingham, too. Washington just didn't let the boots on the ground know so they would keep fighting. Give those pieces of shit longer to run and hide."

"What do you mean, *letting the south go?*" Derrick found life in his legs, again. Looking around, he started making his way to the shipping containers.

"I mean everything below Tennessee will be on fire soon. They're green lighting the Air Force to begin bombing raids. I'm talking cities, highways... they're carpet bombing it all."

"Jesus..." Derrick felt the weight of every person he cared about in Birmingham pressing down on him. His friends and coworkers, their kids... Derrick was going to have to abandon them all. "I'm leaving Atlanta now and you need to do the same, you hear me? Derrick?"

"I'm listening," Derrick said.

"You need to get the hell out now. No hero bullshit, you hear me? Meet me in..." There was shuffling papers in the background as he paused. "Rome, Georgia. There's a small airport on the east side of town. I'm headed there now. The army took over but it should be abandoned now–"

"No, wait!" Derrick said as the thought struck him suddenly like a bullet. "You need to get Alyssa. She's in Atlanta–"

"What? No," Brandon snapped.

"She's at her parent's place on um– uh– Sherbermen. 829 Sherbermen Ave. It's on the north side of–"

"I don't have time to save your fucking *girlfriend*. Are you kidding me?"

"Come on," Derrick said. He could almost feel Alyssa slipping through his fingers at that moment. Like she was dying before his eyes as he failed to convince his best friend to save her. Derrick knew Brandon better than anyone. He knew Brandon wouldn't risk his life for some girlfriend Derrick had dated for a couple years. In Brandon's eyes girlfriends were a dime a dozen. Trading cards you played with until you make it official with a legal marriage. *Marriage...* "She's not my *fucking girlfriend* she's my– my– she's my fiancé... Brandon?"

"Fiancé?"

"Yeah, fiancé," Derrick said with more conviction. He had to be careful with his words as Brandon wasn't a moron. If Derrick said Alyssa was his *legal* wife, which was technically true, Brandon would figure out Derrick rushed a marriage certificate to sign a suicide contract for her.

Stick with the fiction you wished was true.

"I proposed in Pigeon Forge in Tennessee before it all went to shit. Look, Brandon, please..." Derrick's voice was dangerously close to begging. He was desperate. If things were as dire as Brandon said, Alyssa would be long dead before Derrick could make it to Atlanta. Brandon was his only shot to save her.

Brandon was silent for a long moment as he weighed the tale Derrick had spun. "...Fuck," he finally said.

Derrick took that to mean a yes. "Thank you, Bran, 829 Sherbermen. 8 2 9. I owe–"

"I've got it. 8 2 9... Fuck off with that shit– I'll do what I can. No promises. You just get your ass to the airport in Rome. It's gunna be a nightmare to travel so get there by dawn, alright?"

"Dawn. I'll be there."

"I've got to sort this shit out now– but hey, don't get dead, okay, asshole?"

"10-4." Derrick hung up the phone and found himself in the dark, alone, and standing in front of Perry's body. The silence weighed heavy on his soul and threatened to sink him to the floor if he let it. Bowing his head briefly he whispered a small prayer before clearing his throat. "I'm sorry, Perry..."

He remembered the voicemail Alyssa had left him before Perry had turned.

Holding his breath, he tried calling her one more time. There was a long pause as the call attempted to connect, then he heard it. "We're sorry the number you're trying to reach can't be connected at this time," the operator repeated the message.

Derrick cursed to himself and clicked on 'Messages' and tapped her voicemail.

"Der– ick are you –ere!" the phone signal was broken but he could tell it was Alyssa's voice. It brought a faint smile to his lips. The message was left just minutes ago. *She's alive...* "Derrick– they're everywhere. They're pounding on the windows and– Eric get back!" Her voice was ragged and heavy with tears as she shouted at her little brother. He had never heard her like this before. She never cried like that before. "They're getting inside the houses. They're all around. You've got to come! Get here. Please! I didn't mean what I said before. The proposal just caught me by– I didn't want to break up! I was scared, I was– I'm just scared..." Alyssa was sobbing now. "Please, I don't want to die... I love you, I–"

Derrick gritted his teeth as the voicemail ended.

Just hold on, Alyssa. Please, God... just keep her safe a little longer...

TEN

Sharon Hill

Knoxville, Tn

"Uno!"

"Na, uh! That's not fair, she said it before the card was down."

"Did not!"

"Did too!"

"Shut up, idiot!"

"That's enough guys," Sharon warned. "We don't call each other idiots."

Her voice lost what little authority it had before she even finished the sentence. Even Sharon didn't take her own words seriously. She stared across the table at David who kept his eyes buried on the Uno cards in his lap. The flames of the dozen or so candles danced with every swipe of Annabelle's hand at Charlie's arm.

It was Sharon's idea to use all the candles tonight. Charlie, their eight-year-old boy, with a mess of moppy hair over his forehead and half his baby teeth missing, had been in a crying fit since the sun went down a few hours ago. His older sister, Annabelle, was starting to pick up on the silent tension Sharon and David had been emitting all day, so she wasn't far from tears either. The indefinite power outage added more than enough tension beyond the daily stress of marriage to Sharon's nerves. Dealing with a crying, unnerved Charlie was tough enough, if Annabelle started too, Sharon didn't think she could keep it together much longer. Especially with David having decided he would leave the parenting to her tonight.

She had already spent the previous night consoling David who had been on the verge of tears himself. It was a stressful situation, she knew, but there was a large part of her that wanted to tell David to get his shit together and man up.

That would definitely make him cry.

Sharon had known the type of man he was before she had married him; now ten years and two kids later she could tell exactly how he responded to any type of confrontation. Despite David's protests at burning all the candles tonight to comfort the children, Sharon had ignored his reasonable arguments that 'we should save some just in case' and had lit all fourteen of them scattering them across their dining room table and around the room before announcing the start of the latest nightly tradition of game night.

For the kids, the card games and added flicker of light seemed to have done the trick. Within a half hour, Charlie had relaxed, and his infectious giggle had returned. As her ever growing ten-year-old daughter swatted at her little brother, it at least sounded like a normal night at the Hill residence. Instead of the icy edge that was in everyone's voice after forty hours without electricity.

"Anna, stop," Sharon snapped. "Annabelle– Charlie! Sit

down, no punching your sister. David, are you going to say something?"

David was a wiry guy. He had broad shoulders and long limbs. A part of Sharon always had resentment inside her at how he was able to maintain his athleticism even ten years after college had come and gone. *If only it was men who had to give birth to children, maybe he would see how hard it was to stay in shape,* Sharon rationalized.

It was irrational anger, she knew, but it was easier than being pissed at herself for gaining a few pounds after each of the children were born. Sharon never obsessed much about her looks. Just like her mother, Sharon kept her black, naturally curly hair long and refused to cut it short like all her girlfriends were doing at this age. It wasn't until her roommate in college encouraged her that she started wearing makeup. But now that she was in her thirties and carried a bit softer hips and belly, she missed the confidence she used to exude as she walked out in the world. Her small amount of weight gain made her feel insignificant outside her home and jealous inside it. And Sharon couldn't stand looking weak. Even in front of her husband.

The candles between them did more to expose the dark crevasses in David's face rather than shine any light on the clean-shaven look that he presented. His gaunt angular face hid all expression.

"Kids, do what your mother tells you," David mumbled. The last of his words barely audible.

"Really? That's all you're going to say?" Sharon crossed her arms. The boiling anger must have been clear in her voice, because rather than engage in the brewing argument, David retreated. He tossed his cards on the table, pushed his chair back, and stormed into the kitchen.

It is like I am the single parent of three fucking kids, I swear...

It had been more manageable when the power outages had been on a cycle. Knoxville, like many other cities in the south, had been on rotating brown outs to conserve power. From 10 pm to 8 am, the power would be cut from the city with a handful of exceptions for emergency services. Sharon had made her peace with it. She had come to schedule her life around it. It had become a daily routine this past week–starting the coffee maker at 8 am, emptying and refilling the bathtub with water, and turning on the TV for the governor's daily morning address.

As simple as the sacrifice was, it made her feel like she was doing her part to help those frontline workers. She wanted to do more. She wasn't proud of it nor did she admit it to anyone, but the lure of a life free from the responsibilities of marriage and motherhood was at the center of most of her wild dreams. The adventurous fantasies she had as she sipped her morning coffee had her enlisting in the army and being deployed in Atlanta or Birmingham.

That was all the news covered–*America's Last Stand.* Before the infected had reached Atlanta, the news channels would flip flop between experts discussing Rhabdo-11 and the coverage of rioting in the city and the police brutality in response. The kids weren't allowed to watch TV. Sharon was forced to dig in the closet for the kids' old DVDs and had them watch those during the day while she snuck away to the bedroom to watch the news. She figured if the news terrified her, it would petrify her children. The kids couldn't know that monsters were real.

Sharon still didn't want to believe it. She lied to herself saying it's not as bad as the news said it was, that the government had it under control. She kept herself busy by reading articles online, when the Wi-Fi cooperated, about this infection being a black flag operation for the deep state to take over. Conspiracy theories of the pharmaceutical companies' involvement went wild when news broke of some of the executives receiving Greenbands and priority transportation into government protective bunkers. It was all garbage, but it kept her mind occupied as the nerve-racking days passed.

Things had become serious for David and Sharon the previous morning when the power hadn't turned on. 8:15 am, 9:30 am, 4:00 pm... Sharon had sat, dabbing her sweaty forehead with paper towels, and stared at their one battery-operated clock that hung on the wall and just listened for the AC to kick on with the power. It never had.

"I bet it's just routine, maybe they just forgot to tell us, you know?" David had said. "Governor Nickels said the Atlanta defenses were going to start tonight, remember? It's nothing. It's going to be fine. The power outage is only for the troops. For the military to move protective supplies, you know. Power will be back on tonight, just watch." David had been talkative, which meant he was nervous. Sharon had tried to convince herself he was right. This was all part of the army's plan. This was normal. Things were fine. *But if they weren't fine, how would we even know? There's no mail. Cell phones are basically useless. We don't have a internet...*

Sharon had checked the radio in David's car he kept parked on the street in front of the house. She was able to pick up a couple stations playing music, which made her relax some and believe, even if for a few minutes, that everything was okay. They lived in a quiet suburb north of downtown Knoxville. It was strange there–kids played outside while their parents sat on the porches enjoying what little breeze there was during the day. They drank and grilled out. It was like people chose to forget the outbreak was ravaging millions of people in the south.

Staring at the candles flickering between her and David, Sharon wished she could forget the outbreak. The tension between David and Sharon was palpable enough to stop the bickering between the two actual kids. The cards they played with had made a mess in the center of the table. Charlie and Annabelle stood silently beside each other waiting to figure out how this argument would turn.

"Alright, guys, bedtime!" Sharon said with a forced smile. Charlie looked as though he was about to break into tears again, so Sharon quickly put an end to that. "Come here my airplane– whoa, my super-duper airplane!" Sharon snatched Charlie up by under his arms and twisted him around in the air. Once in the hallway near the stairs she blew fishes into his exposed belly, which effectively took away all indications of a wailing, and the house was filled with Charlie-giggles. Sharon set him down and told Annabelle to take the battery-operated lantern upstairs and to brush their teeth. They raced upstairs and Sharon felt her smile disappear with them.

"So, are you done pouting like a child?" Sharon asked from the kitchen entryway. David was leaning over the sink staring out the window. She didn't want to argue. To be honest, she didn't even want to talk right now. But she was sick of his shit. "I'm serious David, I need you to– I can't keep doing this by myself."

"How are you doing this by yourself?" David turned. The glow of moonlight hitting his back through the window darkened his face. "I'm right here, aren't I?"

"Sitting in a fucking chair and being a fucking father isn't the same thing," Sharon pointed to the dining room.

"What d'you want me to do? I told you we shouldn't light all the candles and you did."

"Candles, of course, it's about the fucking candles," Sharon rolled her eyes. "So, then you just pout because I didn't do what you said? What are you, five?"

David rubbed his hands over his face, gnashing his teeth as he did. "I don't need this right now, Sharon. I'm not– I can't... I can't handle this," his voice broke as he started to sniffle.

"Jesus..." Sharon sighed as she paced in the kitchen.

"Fuck you!" David snapped as tears fell from the corners of his eyes. "You don't know what it's like to have the kids and you looking at me to fix something that I can't fix!"

Sharon was taken aback by David's cursing. He had never been a fan of swearing and rarely did it. This might have been the first time she had ever heard him curse at her or anyone for that matter. "I don't look to you for anything. Not since your last greatest idea," she said, putting her hands to her side. "Look how well that worked out for us."

"You think we would be better off out there? That we should have left our home?" David pointed to the door. "We would be like everyone else you hear about on the radio. Just walking along the interstate. At least we're safe at home!"

"Safe! This is safe?" Sharon jabbed her finger at the window and cut her voice lower to keep it from the kids. "We've been without power for two nights now. The National Guard has been gone for two days! The radio in the car said Atlanta is on the verge–"

"Stop! Stop fighting!" a voice startled Sharon. It was Annabelle. She was half hidden by the stairs, but she bounced on her feet, balled up fists at her sides, shouting at her arguing parents. "All you guys do is fight, then you pretend to be happy. I'm sick of it!"

"It's okay, it's okay, honey," Sharon said, kneeling in front of her. She made a quick swipe at her eyes when she felt tears forming. "I'm sorry, we weren't fighting, we were just–"

"Come here, it's alright," David scooped Anna up into a hug. "Mommy and Daddy are just tired. Here come on. Let's go to bed." David walked her up the stairs with Anna's arms clenched around his neck.

Sharon sighed and felt a rush of heat to her face as she was left alone downstairs. She had to look at the ceiling for a minute to keep the tears from spilling down her cheeks. Her inability to argue without crying was something she hated about herself. It made her appear weak. Even when she was winning an argument, the second she wiped free a tear she felt like the loser.

Not today, bitch. Not today, bitch. Not today, she repeated to herself. *No crying today...*

Sharon went back into the kitchen and pulled a half empty bottle of vodka out from under the sink. She unscrewed the cap and poured a mouthful down her throat. She winced at the bite of the after taste and then drank another mouthful. Sharon wasn't proud of her secret evening ritual of shooting three shots of vodka, but it had seemed to be the only way she could sleep the past week. The liquor stung sliding down her throat but once it settled in her belly it felt as though her shoulders fell and relaxed a foot lower than their strained position.

Staring out the window, her eyes traversed the length of Burkitt Road until it crested on a hill several blocks up. The National Guard's empty storage containers and concrete pylons were still strewed in the middle of the road–the remnants of a day and a half of looting. The neighbors in the area had taken their turn to run out in the intersection during the black of the night just to grab a handful of whatever supplies remained.

Within thirty-six hours of the President declaring a National State of Emergency last week and announcing martial law, most major cities had been sent a portion of the National Guard units. Tennessee especially had a heavy military presence as it was a way point for military supplies to go south. If Louisville was the official military hub, Tennessee was the gatekeeper. Every police department and military personnel guarded the train tracks and interstates with routes from Louisville to Florida.

Sharon and David had watched the looting and rioting on TV. In the bigger cities–New York, Chicago, Los Angeles–the violence was surreal. Entire city blocks downtown had been ablaze and hundreds had been murdered each day. It had made the National Guard's presence in Knoxville all the more welcome. Though they had had some looting downtown, Sharon and David knew their neighborhood well enough to feel safe as far north of downtown as they were.

It was last night when the power had remained off for over twenty-four hours that Sharon had watched a convoy of National Guard Humvees and other vehicles leave under the cover of darkness. "M-maybe they're just repositioning? Like going to a worse-off area?" David had speculated. "Do you think they're coming back?"

Sharon had said nothing out of fear she might break down in front of the kids. She had wanted to run outside as they passed to scream at them, "Stop you fucking cowards! Don't leave us!" some of her neighbors had tried to wave them down but the engine had roared past all the same.

They hadn't slept well last night. Every bump and noise that had come from outside had caused one of them to jump to their feet to have a look out the window. Sharon had nearly been brought to tears when Charlie had broken out into a scream in the middle of the night. Her mind had raced to every possibility. *Had the infected made it to Knoxville? Were looters here? Was someone robbing them? Breaking into their house?* The way she and David had charged into Charlie's room had only made Annabelle join in the crying from her room. She was too smart not to know something was wrong for how they were acting for just another one of Charlie's weekly nightmares.

Laying in her bed last night, the most terrifying thought had been how exposed they were. They had no means to get help. They could not call for an ambulance if there was a medical emergency. There was no way to call the police. In the middle of last night, Sharon had felt how truly alone they really were in their house.

Sharon swallowed a fourth gulp of vodka quickly as if she was hiding it from herself, then screwed the cap back on.

"I'm sorry, Shar," David started. Sharon hadn't heard him come downstairs because of the sound outside. She should have been trying to hide the bottle in her hand, but she heard the noise, again. "I don't mean to be a jerk–"

"Listen," Sharon interrupted. David stood beside Sharon and looked out the window where Sharon stared. At first Sharon thought she was hearing things, just the kids upstairs horsing around, but then she heard the noise a third time.

"Is that..." David started, then paused as they heard it, again. "Is that someone screaming?"

The sound was muted and distant but getting louder. David went to another window to look. A popping sound came from a different direction. It sounded like firecrackers... maybe gunshots. *What do gunshots sound like? Maybe it was fireworks.*

A silhouette of a figure appeared up the road at the crest of the hill. There were no streetlights or house lights, just the motion of the black figure as it caught the moonlight. *The government would've told us if the infected were here,* Sharon assured herself as her imagination wandered.

How would they tell us without electricity? They can't call or make announcements.

"There," was all Sharon said. David returned to her

window to see the figure trip and fall over a concrete pilon. It was a woman. Her screams matched her pained movements.

"She's hurt," David commented as she struggled and failed to get back to her feet. Two more figures appeared behind her. Bigger. Masculine in size. They stood over her for a minute. *Talking maybe?*

Sharon shook her head, "do you think they're police?"

"Why aren' they–"

A flash of light ignited from one of the broad-shouldered figures followed by a louder *pop!* The gunshot made Sharon jump. The girl's gut-wrenching scream cut into Sharon's heart. Sharon's hand caught onto David's shoulder. Then the man fired, again, and the woman went silent and still.

"Oh my god," David covered his mouth. "He just– did he just shoot her? We need to call the– is there a way to... I don't know, radio the police. We need the army back–"

"Get the blinds," Sharon said. "We– we need to– make sure the doors are locked and the blinds–"

There was a crash of shattering glass behind the house. Sharon went as still as ice, feeling exposed in her own kitchen. It was close but it didn't sound like it came from inside their house. Sharon wanted David to go see what the noise was. The thought of looking out their back window terrified her. She didn't want to see what was there. But David remained firmly behind their counter island.

Sharon tiptoed into the living room and nearly tripped on one of Charlie's plastic figurines. At the corner window, she carefully peeled back the long drape curtain and saw the edge of their fence in backyard. She saw multiple houses on the next block on fire. Some were just starting with small licks of flames while others were fully engulfed.

The movement in the neighbor's backyard caught her eye before she heard the next glass break. There were people in

Mrs. Daniels' backyard. Four of them. They threw rocks through her back windows and were scrambling to climb inside. More quick pops came from the front of the house along with David's whispered voice, "Sharon!" he ran from the kitchen. "Sharon! There's people in front of the house. They're breaking in. They're coming up the street!"

"They're behind the house, too," Sharon said.

ELEVEN

Brandon Armstrong

Atlanta, Ga

"Come on you piece of shit," Brandon growled under his breath. "Load up so I can go save someone else's fucking *fiancé*."

The roadblocks were beginning to collapse. The major thoroughfares the police and military closed off from civilian use were beginning to fill with pedestrians charging the streets and a few honking cars bulldozing through the crowds. Brandon jerked the wheel of his Humvee around a skinny guy soaked in sweat trying to wave him down and roared past the crowds as they hurled objects at his vehicle.

If I lose this ride, I'm dead. I cannot stop.

'Acquiring signal..." the soothing British accent voice on the GPS said. Brandon twitched his eyes over to the device he had stolen from his wife's car before leaving. 'Acquiring signal..." The GPS repeated.

"Mother fuck! You said that already, bitch," Brandon had been receiving an on and off signal for the past five minutes. He knew he was going the right way, but he also knew there was a turn coming up in the next couple miles.

The final defensive point will collapse any minute and when it does, anything left in this city is as good as dead, including me. The infected will flood the city like a tsunami.

With how tightly packed the city was with people–hiding in their houses, running in the streets to escape, or the morons looting–the infection would spread like wildfire.

I could just lie to Derrick; Brandon gripped the steering wheel harder. *I tried to save her, but the house was overrun. I tried to save her, but she was already dead when I got there,* Brandon rehearsed the lie in his mind. He tasted the sourness in his mouth. *I tried to save her but... it was too late...* Brandon chewed on those words for a mile before he shook them out from his head. *Fuck.* He couldn't do that. He couldn't lie to his best friend like that. Anyone else, *who gives a shit,* but not Derrick. Brandon had grown up with him like a brother. If the roles were reversed, he knew Derrick would risk his life to rescue Karen, so Brandon must, too.

It wasn't that he didn't like Alyssa. She and Karen loved each other, and the couple dozen times Brandon had hung out with Derrick and Alyssa over the past years he had gotten along with her. Alyssa was a woman who knew how to party, had a nice body, and she wasn't a bitch. Checked all the boxes as far as Brandon was concerned. But with the state of things now and where they were going to be in a month, there was no time for generosity. Brandon had a lot of friends and extended family he liked, too, but not enough to risk his life for. Everyone was on their own.

Brandon's thoughts dragged to Corporal Ryan on the front lines and the rest of his men he had abandoned on top of the overpass. They would be shrouded in darkness as they reached for another magazine of ammo that wasn't there, he imagined. They'd look for orders from a sergeant that wasn't there, because he had run. *Because I ran, I abandoned them, I left my fucking men.*

It was a decision that came easily to Brandon but not without a cost. Brandon wasn't a coward. He knew how to die a soldier's death, if need be, but he wasn't stupid either. There's a difference between dying on principle and dying to make a difference. Him running face first into the rabid without ammo wasn't going to help anyone except the coward ass President who apparently was fine with letting an entire battalion be slaughtered.

As if his mind wasn't torturing him enough, his thoughts jumped to replaying the last seconds of Sergeant Dieves life as he had gargled blood, gasping for air. *I did that. I killed him.* Brandon bit down on his tongue hard as he felt the salty tears fill in his eyes. *Kill or be killed.* He'd brought himself to the brink, but he held his breath as he flexed every muscle in his body. Smacking his face until the sting overtook him, he stopped the tears from falling. *Crying was not what men do, you pussy.*

"Signal acquired... Calculating... Estimating eight minutes until you arrive at your destination." Brandon took a deep breath as he crossed into the north side of town.

The city was a mess with looting. There were no police to enforce laws. It was a scene out of a dystopian movie. The strong survived while the weak were trampled. When Brandon was forced to cut off of the interstate and hit the city streets it was pure chaos. Ramming through the yards and fence, Brandon navigated around gridlocked streets. He ran over bushes and cut through a school's playground, but the farther northwest he drove, the fewer people he saw.

At first, he welcomed the abandoned streets and not having punk teenagers pelting his Humvee with rocks. But then the empty streets turned to streets filled with mutilated bodies. That was his first sign something was wrong. As the GPS called out the final turns to Alyssa's house, Brandon saw people running across the street. *They're being chased.*

He heard the maniacal screams and watched the group of rabid appear almost out of nowhere as they poured between the houses. They swarmed a young couple who ran. Like locusts, they buzzed about the roads and front lawns until something garnered their attention and pulled them to the next street over. What remained in the street of their victims were piles of mangled limbs and torsos. There wasn't enough flesh and bone to call them bodies. *The infection is in the city. The rabid are here.*

Brandon stopped in the front lawn across the street from 829 Sherbermen Rd. The roads weren't jammed with cars here, but the subdivision was in ruins. His vehicle's headlights revealed blood smeared siding on the houses along with broken windows and kicked-in doors. If this was Alyssa's house, there were no signs of life. The front door of her house was broken in with no lights on or movement.

Brandon had a mind to leave, to put the Humvee in drive and flee. Even if he did, survival was no guarantee. The infected had flanked the military's defense somehow. *Either the Colonel didn't tell me they had circumvented our defenses or Washington never told the Colonel that the infection was already in the city.* There was no telling how far it had already reached. *Maybe it's already in Tennessee?*

Brandon looked out from the window of his car and saw no movement. Gritting his teeth, he let out a long sigh as he thought about his best friend, "Fuck you, Derrick..."

Carefully, he climbed out of the vehicle after shutting the

engine off, quietly latching the cumbersome door. His M4 rifle shouldered, his finger extended above the trigger guard as he scanned for threats. There were screams coming from every direction, though distant. Glass broke. Footsteps pounded the ground. Brandon didn't see any of the infected until he heard the familiar *booms* of what sounded like a 12-gauge shotgun down the road. He froze, crouching to the side of the engine block as the infected swarmed around the street corners. Rabid fell out of the shattered windows of houses along the street and scrambled towards the gunshots.

The man who fired wore a blood-stained, white button-up shirt and ran across the street. The man clearly realized he had made a mistake. The charge of rabid sprinted after him and disappeared around the block. The man fired one more shot before Brandon heard his agonizing screams.

When the coast was clear and the screams were a block away, Brandon shook his head, whispering to himself, "well, this was a good idea..." Circling around the rear of his car he clenched his teeth as he sprinted across the street as fast as he could but also as quietly as he could. Moving up the wooden porch, he put his back against the siding beside the gaping front door. Above his shoulder were the house numbers *829* in bold, black italics. The eight had faded red marks inside the circles where someone had drawn in smiley faces years ago. A memory of a time before fourteen million Americans had died within two weeks.

The front door was completely smashed off its hinges and there were smears of dried blood on the door jamb. Brandon shouldered his rifle and took a final deep breath. After an all-clear glance inside the doorway, he cleared the living room area from corner to corner as he moved deeper inside Alyssa's home. There was no electricity, and the house was steeped in darkness. He flicked the light attachment on and off as he went. A light gray sofa lay flipped backward in the middle of the living room. Blood stains were smeared along the cream-colored walls. Windows were half boarded up with lopsided pieces of wood nailed into place. The back door in the kitchen had a refrigerator pushed in front of it. Brandon had to loosen his grip on the support hand of his rifle as his fingers were going numb. It had been a while since he had done room clearing, and never by himself.

As he neared the hallway to his right, there were muted sounds that became louder. Brandon slowly peered down the dark hall and saw three figures pressed against a door at the far end. In the darkness, he could see a light begin to crack through the top edge of the bedroom door as it bowed with each bang of the rabids' shoulders. Their backs were all to him but Brandon knew he had to mind his fire. Any missed bullets would chew through that door and every person behind it.

Brandon pivoted out in the open and flipped his rifle light on. The red dot reticle fell on the first head. *Fire.* He moved to the next skull as the first dropped. *Fire.* As they collapsed against the door the third turned in a sprint toward him. His next five shots populated over the rabid man's chest. As it lunged, Brandon retreated and fired two more bullets into the back of its skull where it fell for good measure. He checked the collapsed rabids for movement. An easy clearing, but Brandon knew that the gun blast had started the countdown for more to arrive.

"U.S. forces! U.S. forces!" Brandon shouted out of habit as he ran to and pounded on the bedroom door. "Alyssa, open up! It's Brandon!" he heard movement inside the room like furniture being dragged across the floor and tried the door again. "We're on the clock, let's go!"

Another few seconds passed before the door finally swung open, and Brandon nearly shot a furry creature that leapt on him. Ginger's powerful tail whipped back and forth as he leapt up on Brandon's side with his front paws, the black lab's nose bumping into Brandon's arm as he instantly recognized Brandon's scent. "Down. Ginger, down! Good boy," Brandon patted the top of his head. *Derrick better not have sent me here to save his damn dog.*

A gray-haired man was in the doorway with a pot belly and thick-rimmed glasses. "Thank god," the man panted as he looked over Brandon's army uniform. "Are you the army's evacuation?" His hand touched the shoulder of a skinny teenage boy who wore a pair of thinner glasses.

Brandon looked past them and saw Alyssa standing behind her dad and little brother, he assumed. She was sweaty and disheveled with her blond hair tied back in a ponytail. Her colorful but faded tattoo sprawled across her chest–the thing that had made her the easiest to spot.

"Let's go, come on!" Brandon pulled on the man's shirt, nodding at Alyssa. If the others wanted to cram into the Humvee they were welcome to. Brandon didn't care as long as they stayed out of his way, but he was only here for Alyssa.

"Is the army here? Is Derrick?" Alyssa moved to the door as her dad pulled away.

Brandon looked down the hall where just a pinch of ambient light shined at the mouth of the hallway. *Still clear.* "No, it's just me. Derrick's fine, he called me to get you. We gotta move, more are coming," Brandon said.

"Ginger, no!" the teenage boy said to the dog who was in the hallway licking at the dead rabid.

"How many of you are there? Is there an ambulance?" the old man asked. He was standing beside a large green lazy boy chair. He and his teenage son started to wrap a blanket around a pale skinned woman who trembled in the seat. She had dark hair and stressed skin that made her look twice her real age.

Medical equipment stood on one side and an IV bag hung on the other. Brandon remembered a distant conversation buried in mind. Brandon had walked in on a drunken conversation between his wife and Alyssa when Alyssa had talked about her sick mother. *Cancer*. Alyssa's mother looked so frail he would've thought she was dead if it wasn't for the weak murmurs escaping her lips as her husband tried to move her.

There was a pounding sound that came from outside the house, then quickly sounded inside the house. "Hey! The dog!" the teenager yelled.

"Ginger, stop!" Alyssa yelled as the black lab bounced past Brandon's legs to the noise coming from the front of the house. The patter of hard footsteps became rabid growls and then high-pitched screams. The yelp that came from Ginger was barely audible as the infected smashed into the hallway. Brandon shoved past Alyssa and braced against the doorjamb as he took aim. Two rabid slammed into the hallway wall hard enough to dislocate shoulders and shatter jaws but not sufficient to slow them down. Brandon squeezed the trigger and watched the burst of bullets shred their chest, hips, and legs. It took an extra second, but they fell in the hallway on top of the other three.

Each shot was like a homing beacon just beckoning more rabid to their position. "We're going, now!" Brandon grabbed Alyssa's shoulder and pulled her into the hallway.

"No no! Mom! Dad, get mom!" Alyssa cried, pushing back into the room.

Her father tried to lift her mother from the chair, but the groaning scream she made forced him to set her down.

"Eric, grab her– grab that side!" Alyssa's father yelled in panicked. His son was on the verge of tears. They tried lifting the dying woman again, but this time she squirmed in pain, falling back into the chair. Alyssa cried and struggled to get to her mother, but Brandon stayed in the doorway keeping her from re-entering. The windows at the side of the house shattered and more gruesome figures appeared in the hallway.

Brandon flattened Alyssa against the wall and emptied his magazine shooting in their direction. One fell but the second sprinted ahead with no signs of slowing. The rifle went dry and Brandon transitioned to his sidearm, firing until the slide locked and emptied. The last rabid dropped at Alyssa and his feet; neither of his weapons had a single bullet left in them. *If there was one more rabid, we'd all be fucking dead,* Brandon thought as he reloaded his pistol and holstered it.

"Move move move!" Brandon pulled Alyssa to her feet and pushed her down the hallway. They stepped on and over rabid bodies. She shook and squirmed under Brandon's arm. "Goddammit."

"Mom!" Alyssa cried running back into the room. Brandon smacked another magazine into his rifle. His mind was bouncing between the idea of knocking Alyssa unconscious and carrying her out or just saying *fuck it* and leaving her. *If she doesn't want to save herself, it's her choice. I fucking tried!*

"Okay... okay..." Her father stared wide eyed at his wife. His shaky hands held the top of his head as if it was breaking into a thousand pieces and he did all that he could do to keep his thoughts together. "Okay, go. Just go. It's okay, just go," he palmed Eric's shoulder and guided him to the door. Eric protested as he pulled his father into a hug that Eric refused to let go of.

"What?" Eric's voice cracked. "Dad. No, no, no."

"Alyssa– it's okay. Take your brother and go," her father said. He was sweating profusely and was on the verge of tears himself. "We'll be fine. Your mother and I– we'll be fine."

"No, we're not leaving," Eric cried as his father shoved him away.

Brandon sprinted down the hall to the front door of the house from where he had entered. Ginger was lying outside the front door, blood leaking out of a wound on his chest as life slipped away. If it was any other animal, Brandon would have run by it without a care, but Ginger was Derrick's dog. *He was a loyal dog.* Ginger lifted his head with hopeful recognition in his eyes at the sight of Brandon. He gave the dog a final pat on the head and ended its suffering quickly with a single gunshot.

He barely had time to get his rifle up to address the rabid that leapt up the stairs on all fours. His rounds cut up the rabid's center from hips to shoulders until it dropped. Blood spattered his neck and arm. Brandon froze. For the briefest of moments, Brandon panicked. *What if the infected blood had splattered in his eyes or mouth?* But his thoughts were overrun by the incoming thirty or more rabid running across the lawns in his direction. They ran in a large horde with a single, vicious purpose.

Brandon took a step outside. His body wanted to run for his Humvee but he doubted he could even get inside before they swarmed him. *Great fucking job, Brandon.*

"Please, stop– stop saying–" Alyssa pleaded with her father. The old man half-heartedly pushed her and Eric outside the bedroom. Brandon ran into the room and took over. With the side of his rifle, he roughly shoved Alyssa and Eric off balance and to the floor.

"Get them out of here!" Alyssa's father yelled in a trembling voice. He returned to his wife and knelt beside her, pressing his head into her shoulder as they held another, weeping.

"No, no!" Alyssa shouted, scrambling to her feet. Brandon had her by the arm but she spun out of his hold running back for her parents. "We're all going or none of–"

Brandon gnashed his teeth and fired a loud automatic burst

of gunfire into Alyssa's father and mother. The bullets speckled bloody patches across both their chests and faces as they collapsed into a limp pile of limbs instantly. The screams that Alyssa made didn't sound human, they sounded animalistic. She screeched then broke into indiscernible cries. The last look Ginger gave him before he ended his suffering assaulted Brandon's thoughts. The image of his wide, innocent eyes looking up at him for help as he whined.

Brandon shoved Eric into the hallway and grabbed Alyssa by her hair, dragging her with him. Alyssa screamed and her arms smacked at Brandon as they went into the kitchen. Alyssa was attacking and grabbing at Brandon until she heard the collective screams hounding towards the front door. *Good,* Brandon thought, *pissed off is better than crying.*

He let the sling around his neck catch his rifle and ran to the refrigerator pushing it away from the back door. Alyssa and Eric helped pull it as the infected topped the front porch stairs. Shoving them through the back door as soon as enough space opened up, Brandon leapt outside, closing the door as the riot of bodies smashed through the front doorway and windows, the rabids tumbling forward into the living room.

It was hard to see in the dark. There was a ten-foot privacy fence surrounding the backyard that was filled with high grown grass and weeds barely visible in the moon lit sky. Brandon ran for the nearest fence and looked at Eric. "Climb!" he ordered.

Eric rushed to him and Brandon shoved on the boy's feet and butt to toss him over the fence. Alyssa did the same and made a hard *thud* when she fell. Brandon clamored over the fence behind Alyssa as the back door exploded off its hinges. The neighbor had a shared fence with a black metal gate latch that led to the front yard. Alyssa was already busy opening it.

Brandon's fingers gripped under Eric's armpit and pulled him to his feet. "Get to the Humvee– across the street,"

Brandon huffed, trying to gather a breath after the fall knocked it out of him.

They sprinted out the gate and into the street. There were rabid bottlenecked on the front porch of the house. Brandon emptied his magazine at the doorway as they ran. While Eric and Alyssa climbed into the vehicle, Brandon yanked the pin on a frag grenade and threw it at the porch. The blast rocked a dozen rabid off of their feet, stunning them long enough to let Brandon get inside the Humvee.

Accelerating hard, Brandon heard the engine whine and roar before it finally lurched forward. The waves of rabid were flooding the dark streets from every direction. Their headlights shined on sprinting bodies circling houses, bursting out of windows, and falling down the porch steps. Most of them barely wore any clothes as they sprinted for the living. Brandon skidded off the road and cut through a hilly park where he nearly crashed into a tree evoking screams from Alyssa and Eric in the back.

He jumped a curb back to the road and made two more turns before the sea of infected that chased them disappeared. For a long moment the only sound in the car was the hard panting as the three desperately tried to catch their breath. Brandon felt a wave of lightheadedness wash over him as the adrenaline began to subside and he struggled to get his bearings.

"Y– you... you," Eric's broken voice mumbled between breaths. "You killed my mom n' dad..."

TWELVE

Sharon Hill

Knoxville, Tn

The crash of drawers being ripped open and flung about in the kitchen downstairs was the only thing Sharon could hear over the thudding beat of her own heart. She cupped her hands over Charlie's ears as he sat in her lap hugging her with all his strength. It was better than him crying. Annabelle's fingers dug into Sharon's right arm. She was getting so strong as she was growing up, but with the manic laughter downstairs she had begun to revert into a shrunken form of herself. Her tender hands trembled while she fought back tears. The four of them cowered on one side of the carpet in Sharon and David's bedroom. Tucked between the nightstand and a tall dresser, David squished against Sharon.

"Mmm!" Annabelle protested, flattening against the wall. Sharon had to push her husband back to keep from squishing Annabelle into the wall.

The violent destruction of their house downstairs halted and a rush of footsteps came up the stairs. Annabelle's room was the first on the landing and they could hear its door bang against the wall as it was slammed open. A moment later the footsteps were right outside the master bedroom, and Annabelle let out a small yelp when the door was flung open. With no lights in the house, Sharon could only see the shadow of a man. He froze when he saw the family hidden in the corner. The shadowed figure stared at them and they stared back. Charlie fought to turn his head to see, but Sharon maneuvered her hand to keep his face buried against her chest.

Slowly, the figure approached, stepping into the room carefully, like he was walking into a minefield. A touch of moonlight from the crack of their windows showed the man's bald head and the contours of his angled nose, just as two more men burst into the room and appeared behind him, faltering at the sight of Sharon and her family. A fourth figure, barely discernible, held back in the doorway. The young man in front had a sleeve of tattoos down one of his arms and a heavy-looking backpack strapped to his back.

With his hands raised between them he said softly, "We're not going to hurt you. Just– just give us your money."

Our money? Our money? He says they're not going to hurt us but wants our money!?

Sharon felt herself stirring on the inside. She was sick of this. Sick of all of it. She wanted to tell these teenagers to go fuck themselves. Sharon squeezed the grip of the steak knife she kept hidden against the carpet to her side. The thought of using it, cutting or stabbing at one of these guys nearly made her puke. *What if they have guns? What if they have their own knives? What if they overpower her and David?* The tattooed man saw their hesitation and must've read the defiance in Sharon's eyes because in a sudden fit of rage he lashed out, smashing his fist into the door and making a terrible crash. “Your fucking money! Now!” he shouted.

“O– okay– okay!” David said. He took out his black leather wallet. It shook in his outstretched hand as he crouched forward. “Just take it, just– I don’t– that’s all we have.”

The man snatched the wallet from his hand and scooted back quickly as if it was a trap. “Your food,” a woman blurted out from the hallway. She was hidden behind the men. “Where’s your food?”

“I– it is all in the kitchen. In the cabinets,” David shook his head.

“Bullshit!” the woman shouted. “There’s nothing there.”

“Others robbed us before you,” Sharon spat through gritted teeth. “They must’ve taken everything already.”

The tattooed man recoiled at her words. Like he was about to apologize or explain their actions. He seemed offended at the notion that they were robbers. He remained where he was for a minute before his friend called out to him. With the wallet in hand, he followed the others downstairs and moved on to the next house.

This was the third group that had hit their house in the twenty minutes since the rioters had overtaken their street. The first one didn’t even bother coming upstairs. Sharon and her family listened to them ransacking their kitchen and running out the front door in flat three minutes. Once a few windows had been shattered and the front door kicked in, the second and third group of looters had come much quicker in succession. Sharon and David had argued silently over leaving the house and driving away.

“And go where? And do what?” David had whispered. “No, someone will come– the police are... the army’s coming back.”

It felt impossible to argue or convince David of their helplessness. When the neighbor's houses had been broken into, Sharon had become desperate for a weapon. It was the only time in her life she had felt foolish for not owning a gun. The boom of gunshots had echoed throughout the neighborhood, and there she was digging through the silverware drawer for steak knives to defend her family. Her point had only been accented when a second looter had made his way to their bedroom.

It had been a skinny man with a shotgun. He had barged into the room with a white knuckled grip on his weapon that had made the barrel shake as it passed over David, Sharon, and then the kids. Sharon had held her breath the entire time he had stood in the doorway. Her chest had clenched as hard as her teeth like waiting for a bomb to go off. In her mind she had prayed to a God she didn't believe in that her kids wouldn't suffer.

Let them die quick– please... Do what you want with me. Send me to hell, but don't let them suffer.

When the gunman had lowered his weapon, he had simply said *sorry* in a weak and meandering voice, and run back downstairs. It was in that blunt, visceral moment that Sharon had realized the obvious truth. The person with the gun decided who lived.

Our kids are only alive right now because the intruder allowed them to live.

After the third group of looters fled their house, Sharon worked to her feet. Little Charlie's hands and face only dug harder into her body as she stood. "It's okay, honey. I'm not going anywhere," Sharon whispered. She looked at David more sternly, "David, come on."

She wasn't going to debate this anymore. They were leaving and that was final.

"We can't leave!" David protested. His was voice erratic

and panicked. "It's not safe. There's nowhere to go. We– we– we can block the doorway here. Put furniture in front–"

"Enough!" Sharon snapped. She tried to restrain herself from boiling over, but she could barely keep her voice stable. "The kids and I are going, with or without you."

"Mom!" Annabelle started crying as she scooted to her father's side.

There was a loud boom of a gunshot nearby, so close it rattled the bedroom windows. Sharon felt it in her chest. The clinking sound of wrecked glass raining into an already ankle deep pile downstairs meant another person had clamored inside their house.

"Help!" a strange voice • screamed through panicked breaths. "Somebody– please!" Sharon and David froze with their eyes locked on one another. The man ran erratically through the house until more voices boomed below. Two of them laughed and spoke casually. The bass of their voices carried up the stairs. It sounded like they were in the living room.

Sharon looked to her husband. He was crouching in the middle of the room, unable to turn or move his limbs. It was as if he had transformed from a thirty-year-old man into a frail child staring at the dark, scary doorway. The ominous dark void of the ajar door became a tormented presence in the room, a threatening beast without form that embodied childhood fears brought to life.

"Please, don't– don't kill me!" the man begged below. "Don't! I don't want to–"

Sharon's whole body jolted with the gunshot. The house went still as though the blast had silenced the world and stopped it from spinning.

Sharon's mind awoke when David started running. She reached out to stop him but only brushed his shirt as he darted for the door. She wanted to yell for him, but she knew if his running didn't alert the men downstairs then her shouts would. David swung the door closed and at the last minute tried to shut it quietly, but in the excitement of his movement, ended up latching the door with a thud that filled the house.

For the briefest of moments, their home was silent. David stared at the door and Sharon stared at David's back. The kids must have gathered this was serious, because they didn't make a peep. There was not a cry from Charlie or a complaint from Annabelle, their eyes transfixed on their father in the center of the room.

The first of the footsteps thudded on the stairs. They were slow and heavy, like they belonged to a giant. Each nearing step embedded the terror deeper inside Sharon's hard exterior. She pressed her back against the wall hard enough to form bruises beside her children. David tried to block the door with a dresser that was too heavy for him to move. Sharon's knuckles hardened around the steak knife held to her side.

The door handle shook. It had a thumb lock on the door handle, but Sharon knew it wasn't even strong enough to stop her. Sharon pulled Charlie off of her, but his fingers clawed desperately at her skin.

"Help!" David yelled at the closed window. The dresser he pulled at was only a few feet away from the wall it used to be. David abandoned the dresser to try and open the window. "Help us! Somebody!"

The door shook furiously.

Annabelle squeezed Sharon's arm tight enough to cut circulation to her fingers. She screamed in Sharon's ear, "Mommy! Mommy!" Sharon thought this must be what hell is like. Listening to her children cry, terrorized and helpless. With a powerful impact of force, the door crashed open and a thin piece of wood smacked Sharon on the forehead.

Two men spilled into the bedroom. The one with the gun had a large stomach with a sweaty white undershirt stretched across it and a flannel button up, with three buttons on the top open. He charged at David with his pistol aimed at him. David collapsed to the ground; hands raised.

"Don't move, don't fuckin' move, motherfucker!" the gunman yelled.

"I'm sorry I'm not– we're not! Take what you want," David cried out.

"Take what I want? You telln' me to do somethin'?" the man spat through clenched teeth. He swung the butt of his pistol and struck the top of David's head with it. He fell to the ground recoiling in the fetal position.

Sharon didn't move from her children hoping the stillness would keep them from being noticed. Her eyes flickered between the gunman and his friend, who just stood in the doorway staring at her. The friend didn't have a gun but something in the way he stared at her terrified her more. He walked toward her with heavy work boots thumping the floor with each step. The boots were outlined with dried crusted concrete and mud. He was balding and had a gut that was hidden by the baggy gray shirt, almost soaked through with sweat. David cried as he was kicked again and again but Sharon stayed silent. She didn't think words could form if she tried to speak.

The advancing man stood over her watching her with an intense interest. There was a murky shadow that concealed his eyes. When Sharon saw him reach down to touch her face, her body moved without her even registering it. Blood splattered on the floor from the wound she opened on his hand. She swiped the knife again and missed.

Her element of surprise gone, Sharon dove at the man and tried to stab at his face. She swung with reckless abandon to stop him– kill him if she could. The large man, now distraught and yelling, turned and caught her wrist. She kept him pressed against the bookshelf. Snow globes, statues, and books poured from the shelves as she screamed and pushed with all her might to put the dull knife tip through the back of his skull. But with his hand around her wrist and the other gripping her throat, Sharon felt foolish trying. His strength was enormous compared to her.

The stinging pain that struck the back of her head made her arms go numb and her legs limp. The blackness of sleep consumed the edge of her vision leaving just the slightest view of her two attackers looking down on her where she had collapsed.

Have I been shot? Is this what dying feels like?

"Fucking bitch," someone said. His voice echoed and felt distant despite his feet touching her side. The balding man wrapped a small piece of cloth from a drawer around his bleeding hand while he shouted curse words at her.

No, I didn't hear a gunshot. I'm not dead. I'm not dead...

The world above her began to move. She felt her hair getting pulled on the carpet and felt a tight squeeze around her left ankle. But her tunnel vision was focused on the gun in the man's hand as he dragged her. Sharon was in the hallway and she thought she could hear her son crying. She moved her lips but no sound came.

She didn't care what happened to her. But Sharon needed to know what was happening to her son. Her daughter. *Why were they crying?* Her gut twisted as she lost sight of them.

When she was lifted up to her feet, she felt some strength return to her legs, like someone turned the power back on inside her. They were in Annabelle's room. The yellow wallpapered walls closed in on her making her feel like she was in a child's jail cell. The dark room gave the brightly colored cartoon posters along the walls an ominous look–an audience of cartoon characters leering at her. With a hard thud on an unforgiving mattress, Sharon was shoved onto Annabelle's twin bed. The short desk to the right had a small vanity mirror that Sharon could see herself in. She remembered Annabelle begging for one like mommy's for months leading up to Christmas last year. And the excitement when she finally got it Christmas morning–she couldn't wait to put on makeup just like mommy did.

Sharon could feel hands pulling at the buttons of her jeans. The man was on top of her. She looked down at his hair, at his flannel shirt, and her eyes immediately came alive. The mess of cobwebs that clogged her mind were gone in an instant and terror shot through her like a bullet.

Her hands pushed at the top of the man's head. Then she smacked and swung her small fists downward on his ears and cheeks. He barely seemed to notice. She snaked her hips back away from the man and felt her pants slide down her thighs.

"No no no," Sharon's voice was more of a cry than the scream she intended. Panic coursed through her as she felt the man's hand pull hard at her pants. An unrelenting gravity was sucking her deeper into despair. She was falling into the darkness of the ocean, watching the last of her air bubbles float away. Sharon's hair glued to her sweaty forehead as she kicked, hit, and scratched at the man. The moment seemed bigger than her. This couldn't happen so fast. She wasn't ready. She didn't know. There was no warning.

The heavy man laid on top of her like a wet blanket and smothered her movements. Sharon felt trapped. She couldn't breathe. Her pants hung on by one leg and she couldn't even strike her attacker anymore because his hands pressed down on her wrists like cinder blocks. She wanted to scream but she was afraid she'd start to cry. She wanted to cry but she couldn't let her kids hear her tears from the other room.

The man shoved his mouth in the crook of her neck beneath her chin and ignited a flame inside her. The feeling of his sweaty face pressed against hers jammed against the thought of her kids crying helplessly in her room. The cool terror that consumed her waned for a rage that boiled inside her at the thought of her frightened children.

Sharon's teeth and stomach clenched. Her whole body went rigid. She seized her body from side to side and when the man was distracted, she shot her right hand out of his grip. Smacking the side of his face, she clawed down the center of his face with her nails. For the first time she felt him retreat.

"I said no, you fucking piece of–" Sharon growled at him through gritted teeth. The crook of her thumbnail found the man's nose and hooked it inside his nostril, raking outward. When her thumb broke free, it slid to the side and felt the fleshy sensitive skin of his eyelid. She pushed on it as hard as she could, making the man howl. She kept pressing forward until he was almost falling backward and she was sitting up. His painful cries excited her–a feeling she had always known lurked inside her. She was going to rip his face off. *I'm going to kill this piece of shit!*

Then her head was knocked back down to the bed.

She hadn't seen the punch before it struck her face. The left side of her face was hot and numb with a tingling sensation at the same time. She questioned where she was for a second, but when the muzzle of the handgun pressed to her forehead she remembered instantly. Sharon gripped the gun with both hands and pulled it away from her head. The ringing in her ear wouldn't stop and neither would she.

He grabbed her hair and she swiped at his face. He twisted and threw her off with such force, her whole body smacked into Annabelle's headboard, snapping the wood, but she held onto the muzzle. Sharon felt the man's grip on the pistol falter for a moment and she had it all but free from his hand when a second punch hit her head like a cinder block and her arms fell away like they no longer existed. The final punch struck her behind the ear and Sharon lost feeling in her body and her world went black.

I'm coming home, mom.

THIRTEEN

Derrick Hart
Birmingham, Al

Derrick veered down a side road bouncing violently over a curb, his body going airborne with the jeep. The tires squealed when he dropped back to the road and skidded around a wrecked-out sedan. The keys to the jeep he drove were taken from one of the dead human resource staffers he left behind at the academy. Ben was his name, but Derrick couldn't be sure. He played pickup basketball games at the gym with him and a few other officers and knew Ben drove a white jeep. Derrick didn't say a prayer over Ben's body or any of the other civilians who perished at the gun range. No tears fell either. There was no time. Like Perry's death and every other awful thing he had to deal with in the last ten days, Derrick just had to bury it all deep inside himself where no one could see it.

Turning up his police radio, Derrick hurled the jeep through a series of backyards to cut through a subdivision. He held the mic to his mouth. "4SAM86 to Command. 4SAM86 to Command."

There was a long pause and another officer keyed up. "Command's not responding. Hasn't been for a while."

"Fucking assholes," Derrick cursed to himself before depressing the receiver on the mic, again. "4SAM86 to all units monitoring. The infected are in the city. The infected are in the city."

There was a silent pause, and then a cluster of officers all tried to radio in at once.

"What's their 20?"

"How many?"

"What's their direction of travel?"

"Is the army direct?"

"I spotted them at the academy twenty minutes ago. They're probably elsewhere too..." Derrick kept the mic depressed so as not to lose the air as he struggled to think of what to say.

I'm a coward and leaving you guys. That's what I should say. The truth. I'm abandoning you.

"I'm leaving– I'm leaving the city. Get to your families, protect yourselves. Run. The city is falling."

Derrick tossed the radio into the passenger seat as he jerked the jeep sideways through a small gap between a line of cars, scraping the sides of his vehicle as he did. The outskirts of Birmingham were thick with traffic. By now, every street that existed had multiple car accidents, with no one obeying traffic lights. Police were not directing traffic and car towing services weren't clearing wrecked vehicles from blocked roads. Houses and cars had caught fire that burned and spread unabated until there was only ash without a fire department.

How did this happen so fast?

Speeding through the north-west side of town where the

traffic was lighter, he found mostly large land plots and small subdivisions. There were still groups of panicked people running through the streets–those who had chosen to hunker down in their homes rather than weather the risk and uncertainty of trying to flee for the northern states. The dark road opened up into blocks of neighborhoods. He was a few miles outside of the city limits, but Derrick knew this area. A few officers lived out here. It was a middle-class neighborhood with one and two-story houses and white picket fences. It was the kind of place Derrick had imagined him and Alyssa starting a family in, had she said yes.

It was my fault. I should've known she wasn't ready, Derrick cursed himself.

He had planned his proposal to Alyssa for months. They had been dating for over two years, and he couldn't imagine being with anyone else. Alyssa had been casually talking of vacation plans for years– backpacking in Europe, climbing Kilimanjaro in Africa, cruising to Alaska–trips that Derrick had had no desire to take, but he would have gladly accompanied his free-spirited girlfriend anywhere. Travel, tattoos, and adventure were her thing while Derrick was content in the small life he had carved out for himself in Birmingham. Pigeon Forge was Derrick's idea for a first trip they could take together. The secluded mountains of Tennessee where it was just the two of them was much more his speed, but he had promised Alyssa the next trip would be hers to choose.

"You know, when I said I liked hiking when we first met..." Alyssa had stopped walking along the trail that snaked up the Smokey Mountain. She had been panting and had swiped at a mosquito that never seemed to land but refused to leave her be. "I think what I meant was, I like the idea of hiking. Not that I wanted to go trekking into the wilderness."

"The wilderness..." Derrick had scoffed as he had stopped

ahead of her and taken out a water bottle from his pack. "We just passed a bathroom and bench along the trail ten minutes ago, I don't think this counts as wilderness." Derrick had smirked as he took a gulp of water and handed the bottle to Alyssa. It had been the first day of the five-day trip they had planned.

"Well, my idea of hiking involves more, you know... wine and, like, I don't know. Someone to do my walking for me," Alyssa had giggled and taken a drink.

Derrick shook his head as he laughed. "This coming from the girl who wants to climb Mount Kilimanjaro on a path to Mordor to destroy the ring."

Alyssa had furrowed her brow, "ring? What ring? What's Mordor?"

Panic had struck Derrick as he had thought he had just let slip his intentions to propose in just a few short days. The ring, kept in his cargo pocket just in case the right moment arose naturally, had felt like it was burning a bright flame into his thigh. "You know, one ring to rule them all..." Derrick had said with reddening cheeks.

"Oh, why can't you just quote comic book movies like a normal guy?" Alyssa had rolled her eyes.

"Do you want to go back to the days of quoting Anchorman back and forth to each other for hours on end?"

"You know I always win in that game." Derrick had said putting the water bottle back in his bag, "you only win 60% of the time..."

"Every time..." Derrick and Alyssa had said simultaneously then laughed.

"Come on, hot stuff. I think we're almost to the end of the trail," Derrick had said taking Alyssa's hand in his. She had slumped her shoulders and let out a groan before meandering up the trail with heavy feet.

Derrick was glad he had waited till the last day of their trip to propose. He recalled the moment he had opened the small jeweler's box and held the diamond ring out to Alyssa. They had been lying half naked in the bed together. Sheets had been snaked around Alyssa's shoulders as she had curled into Derrick's side. The cop in Derrick had seen her answer to the question before she had even spoken. The stiffness of her upper body followed by the shifting panic in her eyes. His stomach had dropped when she sat up right, putting distance between Derrick and her as she gathered her words. When she had refused, Derrick's ears had lost focus of the litany of reasons why she couldn't get married.

Derrick had felt his heart retracting and hardening to protect itself. Suddenly, they were dressed, and Alyssa had still been talking. Her words had shifted from explaining why she'd said 'no' to suggesting it was a good idea to take a break while they 'got on the same page.' The more she'd spoken the more it had sounded as though she had been contemplating this 'break' for some time. They had driven home a day early in a mostly silent car. He had wanted to know what she didn't like about him but hadn't wanted to hear her say it, so he hadn't asked. *What's wrong with me?*

Alyssa's rejection had felt like he'd been discarded. It still ached like... abandonment. The black hole of his past swallowed his present. He felt like he was twelve years old, sitting on the living room floor of his dark apartment, and waiting for his mother to come home. *Always alone.*

Derrick entered the subdivision as headlights lit up in driveways and garage doors opened. Families that had abided the lawful command to shelter in place and respected the strict curfew, now loaded their possessions and families into vehicles in the dead of night.

Derrick slowed as cars and pedestrians cut in front of him

haphazardly. News of the infection spreading through Birmingham must have hit the internet and cable channels. These families were, however, too far removed from the violence of downtown; they didn't realize how much time they'd wasted boarding up windows, loading luggage and valuables into their vehicles.

I was just scared... I was just scared... Derrick recalled Alyssa's tearful words on his voicemail. As soon as he'd heard her cry those words Derrick knew them to be true. He could see it in her face that night he'd proposed. *She was just overwhelmed. Taken by surprise is all,* he realized. *Alyssa is a wild spirit who wants to see the world and she saw marriage as a shackle that tethered her to the ground. But it doesn't have to be.* There was an exhilaration inside Derrick as he nodded to himself. *She knows that now. She knows that...*

Derrick slowed and saw the faces of each passerby who ran across the street or along the sidewalk beside him to discern if they were infected or not. There was a restrained panic in everyone's eyes. He kept his right palm resting on the grip of his rifle in the seat beside him. On the floorboards was a backpack he had repurposed from the gun range and filled with 5.56mm and 9mm ammo boxes along with a couple bottles of water and extra magazines for his weapon systems. He also had two stun grenades and two smoke grenades remaining on his chest rig. *God, I hope it's enough.*

"Ahhh! Help! Help!" Derrick heard a woman scream. It was distant. Derrick knew he couldn't stop, but out of instinct he still slowed to a crawl and looked in all directions as if he was still in a patrol car and on duty. The streets were black except for the yellow glow from dimly lit streetlamps and the bright lights from the garages and houses nearby.

As he neared the flashing red light of an intersection, commotion caught his eye to his right. Three women. They screamed and ran in a panic. From the shadows behind them a man gave chase. Under the streetlamp, he watched him move in an all-out sprint. The streetlamps he ran beneath shone light over the bloody flap of torn skin on his cheek and the glaring wide eyes. *The rabid are here.*

There was a sudden *click* that blackened the subdivision instantly. Streetlamps, house lights, traffic signals... they all went dark. Derrick turned to look back at the Birmingham skyline and saw the lights shut off one block at a time as the wave neared downtown. God seemed to be turning off the power. Birmingham and the world, as far as Derrick could see, went dark.

He realized too late that his foot had lifted off the brake and he had idled into the intersection. A pickup truck smashed the side of Derrick's jeep, spinning the vehicle violently. The impact jarred Derrick's head into his window. The wreck was forceful and narrowed Derrick's vision as he slipped into unconsciousness.

FOURTEEN

Derrick Hart
Birmingham, Al

The pool of black haze slowly parted as Derrick's consciousness resurfaced. Sight was the first to return, it was always the first thing to return. Derrick had been knocked unconscious four times in his life, though all the other times he had been doing something childish and stupid with Brandon, each time equally as disorienting when he awoke. Nothing made sense as he turned his head, studying the shattered windshield or the passenger seat headrest penetrating the side window. Sounds came next but they were even harder to place. Ragged growls and screams accompanied by chips of glass chiming as they rained down somewhere. He tried to move but his deaf limbs were numb and pinned in the compacted jeep.

By the time Derrick's pain sensors flared throughout his body, the world started to move in full speed. Smoke billowed from the engine of the pickup truck that had T-boned the passenger side of Derrick's jeep. The night outside his jeep was dark and full of screams. The sound of glass snapping and breaking piece by piece was eclipsed by the breathy screeches of the rabid pickup driver as it forced its face through the windshield. The jagged edges of glass tore at its lips and cheeks peeling them from its gums. Its red, bloodshot eyes locked on Derrick and with no care for self-preservation it jammed its upper torso through the tiny glass hole in the truck's windshield.

Derrick rammed his shoulder into the door, forcing the handle and popping it open, spilling onto the asphalt. Moving his arms and legs he took a mental note of no debilitating injuries from the crash besides a throbbing headache and a sore shoulder. While the rabid was still stuck in his windshield, Derrick gathered his backpack and rifle that had lodged in the floorboards only to feel a hand grab at his shoulder.

Derrick whipped around, shouldered his rifle at the target, and flipped the safety off. He went to pull the trigger and quickly thumbed the light attachment. *STOP!* His finger froze at the trigger guard. The face he saw was of a pudgy man with eyes full of worry.

"Don't– don't shoot!" the man yelled in a high-pitched voice, his hands shielding his face. "Help me! Help– my wife!"

Derrick stared at him unsure what to say in the moment. *No hero bullshit...* Brandon's words weighed heavy on him but the pull he felt in his gut was too strong. Shaking his head, he lowered the rifle, the cop inside overpowering his friend's warning. "Where is she? What's wrong?" Derrick asked.

"She was attacked! She–" The pudgy man's eyes snapped above Derrick as he stumbled backwards. Derrick turned around just in time to see the rabid pickup truck driver leap from the hood of the car. Derrick ducked on instinct and had a fast enough reaction time to get out of the way. Agility that the heavier husband did not possess. The rabid latched onto him like a leech. Its arms and legs wrapped around his side and dug into his shoulder as they tumbled to the pavement.

"Shit!" Derrick snapped as he aimed his rifle at the rolling target, but he couldn't get a clear shot.

"Help– get it off! Get it–" the poor man cried as the rabid clawed and ripped layers of his flesh away with its teeth. Derrick slung his rifle tried to grab the rabid but it was coated in blood. Derrick maneuvered to grab the husband to pull him away. Hooking his hands under the man's armpits, he yanked on the man's torso when his pleas turned from words to a high-pitched scream. The hairs on the back of his neck stood tall and Derrick backed away shouldering his rifle, fumbling the light attachment on. The heavyset civilian was now stretched prostrate as every muscle flexed and the blood vessels in his eyes blew.

Derrick snapped the trigger back after the large man swiped at his boot despite being getting mauled by the other rabid. He fired twice into the crown of the man's forehead then pivoted to the rabid truck driver who scurried like a spider for its prey. His rifle rounds painted a line up its spine with Derrick's last round entering the base of its skull.

"Dammit!" Derrick cursed over the dead bodies. Quickly scanning the perimeter with his rifle light, all he could see were mothers and fathers pulling luggage and running with children in their arms. *They're all running in the same direction.* Horrid screeches pierced the air behind him, and Derrick pivoted. The smoke from the pickup truck had turned black as flames licked up from the engine and transferred over to the jeep.

Derrick didn't see the infected female in her blood-stained night gown through the smoke until she slammed into the other side of the hood. She reached uselessly over the hood and through the flames for Derrick. Her arms burned, long drapes of matted hair caught fire, and her screams intensified. Derrick backed away; slack jawed. His mind unable to comprehend the primal rage as her flesh burned black.

Gunfire exploded from a house's windows behind the rabid. The shots sounded like those of a shotgun or hunting rifle. A domesticated weapon that civilians kept around the house with no real intention of ever using for their survival.

They don't feel pain... They fear nothing... Derrick thought as he stumbled backwards, nearly tripping over two dead rabids, while watching the flaming woman turn and sprint to the house diving inside one of the black windows. But Derrick was quickly shaken from his trance by the wall of screams that ran his way.

Dozens of rabid charged towards Derrick, their feet pattering on the road. He didn't have time to think, only run. Heaving the backpack onto his shoulders he sprinted ahead of men and women whose voices called to his backside as he passed them. Their screams replaced their cries for help as the rabid tackled them to the pavement.

Run. Run. Freaking run, Derrick!

Derrick cut between houses and leapt over bushes to make it to the next block. He needed a replacement car, but first he needed safety. Flattening his back as best he could to the side of a house, Derrick hid behind a tall bush as six rabids that hunted him scurried by. Derrick held his breath as they growled and fanned out acquiring new victims in this neighborhood.

The screams for help were everywhere now. People scampered out of their houses and tried to make it to their cars, while others beat on locked doors searching for refuge. The infected had plenty of easy targets to choose from.

Amidst this chaos Derrick saw the headlights of a car back into a nearby driveway. He sprinted to the car, rounded the back of the trunk of the black Impala, and scooted between the closed garage and the taillights. Inside, a man was bent over the front seat and appeared to be loading something into the vehicle.

"Sir! Sir, Metro Police, Metro–" Derrick whispered as he neared the gray-haired man. His shirt and hands were stained in blood and he was strangling the limp body of a woman with dead gray eyes in the driver's seat. She too had short gray hair and very well could have been his wife before the infection had taken him.

The man growled and screamed at Derrick whose feet skidded out from underneath him at the shocking sight. In a panic, Derrick fired a dozen rounds cutting across the rabid's chest and throat. It collapsed but Derrick didn't have time to relax. Five shadows that had been running elsewhere stopped abruptly, falling over themselves as they now clamored to get to Derrick. *Shit, the gunfire!*

Clicking on his light attachment, he acquired his targets from the middle out. Firing rounds into the chest, arms, and head, he succeeded in dropping three of them. Their faces skidded across the pavement from their momentous speeds. Derrick wounded the next one, jerking its shoulder backwards, but his rifle locked back empty.

The rabids pounded up the driveway causing Derrick to retreat behind the vehicle. His rifle clattered behind him as he drew his pistol and alternatingly fired into the two rabids' chests until they too fell. The rabids rolled over themselves, smacking face first into the garage door and leaving a bloody smear where struck. *It's sound! The noise is what keys them up. Noise is what gets the rabids' attention.*

Hiding behind the trunk of the car, Derrick reloaded his weapons and caught his breath. His gunfire had brought more rabid to the streets, but they quickly divided into packs towards every new scream they heard. Derrick approached the driver's seat of the Impala more carefully. The unresponsive woman in the car was ghostly white with dark, black bruising around her throat, clearly deceased. *Who knows how long it had been strangling her.* The interior of the car was speckled with wet blood, either from the woman or the rabid Derrick had shot.

With any cuts I might have from the wreck and the infected blood dripping inside; I can't take the risk. Perry gave her life showing me how easy it is to get infected.

Derrick ran to the other side of the house and crouched in the darkness. *Focus. Breathe. Prioritize. What do you need?*

I need a car.

I need to get out of this area.

I need to get to Georgia.

Brandon is counting on me... Alyssa is waiting...

The ground shook and a rumbling roar erupted from the black sky. The houses rattled as a low flying plane buzzed overhead. Derrick sunk to the ground and covered one of his ears with his free hand. It was barely visible with the black underbelly. More aircrafts jetted south following the first. *Military planes.* Dozens of them. Hundreds, maybe. The jet streams shook parked cars and rattled windowpanes.

The shaken ground sounded the car alarm of the blood-soaked Impala, and its lights flashed even after the rumble of jets had passed. Derrick stood when he saw the horde of infected figures converging on his location. *How are there so many?*

Derrick nearly fell running through a series of front lawns and cutting between houses. With a labored breath, he scaled a ten-foot wood fence ahead of him. The soles of his boots scraped on the splintering wood as fingers swiped at his heels. With a heavy *thud,* Derrick hit the ground and felt a sting in his shoulder. A woman screamed from inside the house he was in front of and Derrick angled his rifle to its glass door. He saw fast moving shadows ripping at an elderly lady from all sides.

No time, move!

He heard infected scaling the fence behind him as Derrick leapt into another backyard. Crumpling to his knees as he fell, with a pain in his ankle, he found three rabid in the yard he had just entered. Scrambling to his feet, Derrick fired blindly behind him as he circled the backyard and found a broken wooden gate.

Turning on a razor's edge, he bottlenecked the three rabid as they approached the gate. At a close range he fired in rapid succession into the rabids' chest and head dropping them. Lost and running on fumes, Derrick ran for the road knowing more rabid would be closing in on the sound of his gunfire.

"Help! Help– help me!" A young woman screamed as she zig-zagged running ahead of Derrick. Two rabids gave chase and were quickly closing the distance, their fingertips swiped at the strands of black hair in her ponytail.

Stopping just long enough to exhale, his eye focused on his rifle's optic, he tracked the zig zagging rabid left and right and squeezed the trigger with surgical precision. The second rabid trailing behind fell after taking two shots in the back, but the lead rabid closed the distance.

The woman ran to the right at a distance upwards of seventy yards– a difficult shot. The rabid had caught a hold of her shirt. Salty sweat poured down Derrick's nose and lips as he gasped for air. His tracked the lead rabid and squeezed the trigger before it could maul her.

Lifting his eyes from his optic, Derrick felt his stomach drop and color leave his face. *No...*

The woman collapsed to the pavement with a gunshot in her lower back. The rabid tripped over itself as it stopped to pounce on the woman. The woman's screams, as the rabid tore into her back with its teeth, were like poison to Derrick's ears. Gritting his teeth so as not to let a tear fall, he ran to the two flailing bodies; Derrick felt the trembling twist of uncertainty fill him. He fired two rounds into the rabid's head then another two into the woman's just as the pitch of her scream scraped the high, rabid octave.

The world became numb to him. As he ran, he passed packs of rabid attacking innocent and helpless victims. Mothers were being chased around corners away from their children's dead bodies. People pounding on front doors to be let in only to be tackled violently from behind. A young man's fingernails ripped at the grass as a rabid dragged him screaming into the shadows, and still Derrick ran.

You're letting them die. You're doing nothing. You're damning these civilians to the most torturous death because you're a coward!

Derrick's hands didn't feel the splintering wood of the series of backyard privacy fences he scaled to avoid the increasing number of infected that angled for him. He ran and ran until his lungs burned and vision blurred. Stumbling around a corner, Derrick saw the darkness that suffocated the world was being burned away by orange flames in the sky. A dozen houses had fire leaping out of the windows and incinerating the structures. The red hue the fire shot across the intersection revealed dozens of bodies and streaks of blood across the road. The rabid screams from blocks away that filled the air were the only signs of life as everything on this road was dead.

The bushes to his side shook and Derrick broke from his hazy stare to fumble his rifle in that direction. His finger closed on the trigger as he faltered on unsteady feet. Snaking his finger around the trigger, Derrick fired blindly. His finger loosened when he saw a small hand reach out from the bushes. Two teenaged girls peeked out from behind the green leaves. A tall, lanky girl and a slightly shorter version of her clinging desperately to her side. *Sisters...*

Derrick glared, pointing his rifle at them longer than he liked. The orange flames lit their faces and he stared at their eyes, half believing they were infected. Part of him thought of shooting them even though they weren't infected.

Wouldn't it be kinder to kill them now? Stop the suffering before it begins?

Derrick felt a twitch of shock jolt through him as if he had just woken up to his thoughts and he quickly took his finger off the trigger and lowered his rifle. His mind wasn't right. His moral compass was gone. Lost somewhere in the tall grass of the gun range where he had left Perry's body.

The older girl continued to stare at him with fear and uncertainty clouding her eyes while the younger one, perhaps fourteen or fifteen years old, remained hidden behind her elder sister. Derrick scanned his surroundings.

There was a charred, white jeep and the skeleton of a pickup truck that smoldered with dwindling flames. *I'm back where I started.*

"Please–" a quiet voice spoke. "Please... Hhh-h-h-h help us." Derrick turned and watched older girl look up at him, struggling to stutter out the words.

He sneered, his back toward the two teenagers. He thought about the dozens who had begged for help that he had refused, then of the woman he had tried to aid and ended up murdering. *Someone else will come.* They weren't his kids, and he wasn't the police anymore. He made the decision and left the girls behind. *No hero bullshit*, Derrick recalled Brandon's words.

Derrick jogged fifteen yards before saliva pooled in his mouth and he felt his knees give out. His stomach went dystonic, puking acid in the street surrounded by the dead. The world spun and he found himself unable to concentrate.

Perhaps it was from the smoke that clouded his lungs. It could be dehydration, as the droplets of sweat rained from his brow to the road. His tongue was a dry sponge that crusted into the back of his throat. Derrick pressed his forehead on the stony asphalt as he failed to steady himself.

"Zoe..." a voice whispered behind him before there was a tap on his shoulder. His adrenaline was spent, he barely reacted to see if it was a threat. The younger of the two teenagers held a half full bottle of soda towards Derrick.

He took it in his trembling hand and drank a large gulp from it. He groaned as he thought he might puke it back up. The flat soft drink filled his mouth with flavor and silenced his rumbling stomach. He swallowed another gulp and gave it back to the girl who then zipped it inside a small, blue backpack with horses running across the front. The world began to show contrast after a moment as Derrick's vision cleared. The sugar rush gave his mind focus.

"Okay..." Derrick said softly and rose to a knee, looking back at the two girls. Waving them over, he said, "okay, come on."

FIFTEEN

Sharon Hill
Knoxville, Tn

The black sludge occupying her mind was viscous and deep. It consumed her whole and she wondered if this was death, if it was her afterlife. Sharon never believed in God or heaven, but as silly as it sounded, she prayed for an afterlife. What she would give to see her mother again. It had been so long since she had seen her. If it wasn't for the old photographs she had of her, she didn't know if she would even remember what her mother had looked like at all. Sharon wanted to ask her so many things.

Was she disappointed that I never traveled the world? Was she sad that I married so young just like she did? Did I make her proud at being a mother?

The answer was the same, always–disappointment. Sharon didn't know why she thought that of her mother. She had been the most supportive person she had ever had in her life. Anna,

Sharon's mother, had never been a woman who minced her words. She'd been the most capable woman Sharon had ever known. A single mother who had juggled three jobs and spent most of her off –time cuddled up on the couch of their studio apartment with her little Share-Share.

As a child, Sharon and her mother would fall asleep watching the history channel or the Discovery channel together under forts of pillows, blankets, and couch cushions. They would pretend to be in the African Serengeti, an igloo in Antarctica, or a high-speed train passing through the green plains of Ireland. Sharon would force herself to stay up late just so she could be awake for her mom to come home from her bartending job. She had never missed her father who had abandoned the two of them before she had even been born. Her mother's love had been more than enough for her.

Anna had filled Sharon's curtained-off section of the room with posters of African elephants, Australian crocodiles, and every magazine page of the setting sun she could find. Just lying in her bed at night, Sharon would feel like she was on the other side of the world by looking at her walls. She wasn't a ten-year-old in a studio apartment in the Bronx. At night, she was a safarist, a photographer, a marine biologist. And her mother had loved it. She had encouraged every dream and every passion Sharon had ever had. Anna Hill had been a woman who had set very few rules for Sharon. In fact, as she had entered her teenage years, she could only recall her mother repeating three rules to her constantly.

You can't have kids until you're married.

You can't get married until you're thirty.

Go see the fucking world!

The last rule had almost been an inside joke. When she got to it, Sharon would echo them as they laughed. The times she remembered these moments always hurt Sharon. They reminded her of her betrayal. Sharon and David had had their daughter when Sharon was twenty-four years old, eighteen months after her mother had passed away unexpectedly from a stroke. *A stroke... at forty years old...* Sharon and David had married a year later. And with every passing year, the lie that *next year will be the year that she starts her travels to see the world,* became more difficult to believe. Facing the possibility that this blackness was death, a small part of Sharon hoped that she would not see her mother so she would not have to see the disappointment in her eyes.

I broke all three of our promises.

In the nothingness of the dark, sounds began to form. Crying. Creaking sounds, like that of stressed wood begging to snap. More crying. Sharon's eyes opened just enough for her to see from under her eyelids. She saw something shiny beside her face that glinted in the moonlight coming in from the window. She tried to move her arms, but she couldn't feel them, nor could she see if they were even moving. The world came back to her slowly. She felt dirty. She felt exposed and sweaty. Something trickled down her forehead, beaded at her left eyebrow, then circled down the corner of her eye. Sharon turned her head instinctively to keep any more liquid seeping into her eye.

How long have I been unconscious? She wondered as thoughts came back to her one at a time.

The man was there. He was on his feet and slid his underwear on clumsily one foot at a time. The left side of his face was scratched and showed signs of small smears of blood. Sharon realized she was naked. Her shirt and bra were pushed up to her chin and her jeans and underwear clung to her right ankle. Every instinct told her to close her legs and cover herself. To curl up in a ball or runaway, but she fought it. In the darkness of the room, the man hadn't noticed her move, yet. He was too distracted by the leg hole in his jeans to see her turn her head slowly back to the side. A different set of instincts turned on inside her then, telling her to not to run and hide, but to lay and wait. To look for a weapon. *The bedside lamp? The nightstand?* They told her to leave herself exposed, for now, so she could have the advantage later. She would be the prey no more.

Sharon heard the man hopping on one foot as he tried to get his leg into his pants. Her eye caught the reflection of the object laying by her head again. She focused this time and realized the man's silver handgun was sitting on the pillow beside her head. Her body tensed. Sharon's heart thudded her chest. She felt her fingertips become slick with sweat and her mouth go dry. She wanted to lunge for the gun immediately, but it seemed too easy.

What if the gun is empty? What if it has the safety on?

Sharon had never held a gun before; she only knew of them from what she saw in the movies. She knew you held the handle with two hands, pointed, and pulled the trigger.

What if– was it a trick? Maybe he was baiting her to see if she's awake.

The longer she waited the faster her breathing became. She was starting to pant through her mouth in anticipation, which was starting to turn to worry. She contracted her fingertips slowly to test if they worked. *They did.* A heavy bulge of fear grew in her stomach that threatened to consume her entirely. She thought of the gun *clicking* instead of firing. She thought of him beating her to death.

I'm going die, I'm going to die, I'm going to die. The mantra repeated in the shallows of her mind without her even realizing it. The man brought his zipper up and Sharon knew this was her only chance.

Her whole upper body twisted for the gun. The man shouted something and moved for it too. The pain on the side of her head was dizzying. The world blurred as soon as she lifted her head from the pillow and suddenly, she questioned how far away the handgun truly was. The man was at the foot of the bed charging for the gun, but her hands were already closed around the handle.

Sharon swung the pistol downward and thought she might throw up from the spinning in her head. The man swiped at the gun but Sharon pulled it out of his reach. She couldn't see his face. She clenched her hands around the handle and squeezed the trigger. The loud bang of the shot and the sudden recoil startled her and struck terror in the man's face. She saw him backing away with his hands raised now. She had missed.

"Okay, okay!" he yelled with his hands trembling and covering his face. "Don't shoot! Don't–"

Sharon steadied the pistol over the silhouette of his figure and squeezed the trigger twice. The recoil surprised her less with each explosion. The man fell to the ground groaning. There was a commotion in the next room; she could hear her children's terror through the walls.

"Mom!" said Charlie, his voice muffled. The other man barged through the door, and without hesitation Sharon fired into his chest and stomach. She didn't know how many times she squeezed the trigger, only that she kept squeezing until there were no more bullets in the gun and it would only *click*. The second man dropped to the ground quicker. For the briefest moment, she worried it was David she had shot and scrambled to her knees in the middle of the bed. But when she did, she saw the bald head and gray shirt of the intruder on the ground. The two men laid on the floor moaning and cursing, while Sharon kept the empty gun in her trembling hands raised. Some loose piece inside the gun rattled in the eerily quiet room as her hands shook.

"You fuckn...you stupid fuckn bi..." One of the men

mumbled. The other couldn't talk anymore, gasping for air every few seconds. "You... you..."

After a few minutes passed the men stopped moving. Sharon let the heavy gun fall to the mattress in front of her. A mental light switch flicked off and her senses turned back on. She felt wet sticky blood matting the side of her hair. The pain was excruciating, and it was universal; she felt it course through her entire body.

She wrapped herself in Annabelle's light blue comforter that was stained with her own thick blood that now looked black, and she felt the tears swell up in her eyes. Her arms, her throat, a large scratch down the back of her left thigh–she felt the agony everywhere. Sharon held it in as long as she could, but when the tears fell, she couldn't control herself as a messy wail escaped her lips. She gasped for air and coughed as the tears and snot clogged her airways; then she cried more.

"Mom!" Annabelle rushed inside the room and Charlie tried to follow.

"Charlie! Come bac– Oh my god..." David scooped up Charlie and they both stopped at the sight of the two men's bodies in the doorway. Annabelle barely looked down as she leapt into bed to hug her mother. Sharon clutched the comforter tight around her body and covered her face with her hands. She didn't want her children to see her like this. But she wanted nothing more than to squeeze Anna tightly in her arms. Anna nuzzled her nose into the crook of Sharon's neck. The tears poured down Sharon's cheeks and disappeared into the back of Annabelle's shirt as they rocked back and forth in each other's arms.

SIXTEEN

Derrick Hart
Birmingham, Al

Valhalla waits for no one...

Something about him crouching in the dark made those words always float to the surface of Derrick's mind. Touching the dog tags that dangled beneath his body armor, Derrick thought of his friend waiting for him in Georgia.

"Brandon's going to kill me..." Derrick mumbled to himself as he led the two teenagers over to one of the few houses not on fire. "What's your name?" Derrick asked, taking a knee and porting his slung rifle to the behind him.

"J-j-Jessica," she stuttered, closing her eyes to focus. "This i-is Zoe," she nodded down to the skinny girl by her side. "S-s-sorry, I stutter when I'm n-n-nervous."

"That's okay," Derrick smiled. "Jessica and Zoe, nice to meet you. I'm Derrick. You– um, you guys sisters?"

Jessica nodded. An uncomfortable knot formed in his gut as

Derrick struggled to learn how to parent surrounded by mutilated bodies and an entire neighborhood of houses ablaze. He was out of his depth. *Maybe this is why Janice stopped mothering me as a kid, it's too fucking hard,* Derrick joked darkly.

"Are your parents 'round here? You live here?" Derrick asked and immediately regretted doing so.

Jessica shrunk into a slouch as tears welled up in her eyes. "No, m-m-m-my Dad was taking us o-o-out of town. We crashed."

She pointed to the truck that had T-boned him earlier in the night. His eyes fell to the pile of three rabid he had killed and left to rot beside the burning vehicles. *The rabid truck driver– he was their father,* Derrick pieced together. *I didn't even see kids in the truck...*

Derrick felt his stomach flip upside down when he looked back at the girls, wondering if they had seen him kill their father.

"C-c-c-could you take us back to our Mom?" Jessica asked. "She's in H-h-h-hoover."

Derrick knew that was impossible. Hoover was on the exact opposite part of town– the south side. Likely, their mom was already dead. "Jessica, I can't– I can't do that right now, it's not safe to go that way. It's not safe to stay here. Will you, um– you see this?" Derrick said, pointing to his police patch. Zoe turned her head from under Jessica's shoulder to look as well. "I'm a police officer. My job is to take care of you guys, okay? Will you come with me? I can get you some where safe?"

Jessica immediately nodded her head as she pulled the straps of her book bag tighter on her shoulders. Derrick recognized the look of relief on her face, like she was glad she wasn't hiding in a bush with the weight of her silent sister clutched to her side. Perhaps it was because of Jessica's stutter but he found himself treating her like a child even though she looked to be sixteen or seventeen years old. She was nearly as tall as Derrick and her long brown hair draped down her back. Zoe hovered just over five feet tall. Her black hair was pulled back in a short ponytail that left a fray of hair sticking from the back of her head.

"Okay," Derrick maneuvered his rifle around and was careful not to laser the girls with the muzzle barrel. He swapped out the almost empty magazine for a full one. "We're going to walk down the road a bit. I want you two to stay together and stay behind me. If I hold up my hand like this, stop where you are and don't move. Now this is most important. No matter what, don't scream or make any noises, okay?"

Jessica nodded and Zoe did the same.

"Hey, Zoe," Derrick said, trying to sound as non-threatening as possible. "It's– um... look it's okay to be scared. I'm scared, too." Derrick half laughed at the words that sounded like the understatement of the century. "But just stay with your sister, and I'll keep you guys safe, okay?" Derrick lied, knowing he couldn't possibly guarantee the promise. He gave Zoe a half-smile and to his surprise she returned it. The girls kept up with his slow jog as they stayed in the front lawns of the houses. They passed a few vehicles and Derrick checked the doors as they did.

Locked. Locked. Locked.

He knew eventually the rabid that had chased survivors to new neighborhoods would circle back their way. Even the smallest of sounds would attract them and he assumed light would too. And in the dead of night, with no city lights in sight, nothing was brighter than an entire block of houses on fire. They left the fiery streets behind and stepped into the darkness. They stopped at the first untouched house with a vehicle parked in the driveway. The car was locked. Derrick rang the doorbell to the house several times and removed his flashlight from his belt and flashed it inside the window. The house was quiet. Still. Derrick checked the handle*, it was locked.*

No answer. No movement.

Derrick moved the girls to hide between the garage and the car parked in the driveway. "Stay here," Derrick whispered to Jessica who showed she understood with a nod. Derrick did a quick look around the street. He could hear the rabids' faint growl; they were probably a few blocks away. He didn't think he heard any nearby. *I'm about to find out if there are...*

Derrick took a stance in front of the door and with a snarl he raised his right foot and slammed his boot squarely beside the handle. There was a loud crack as the door bowed and partially broke. Glancing behind him, his ears perked up for the screams of any alerted rabid. He struck the door again. The second kick caused wood to splinter and the door swung open. A long piece of wood from the door jamb spiraled into the house. Derrick raised his rifle and cleared the doorway, his mind feeling more at home doing something he was used to.

"Birmingham Police. Come out with your hands up," Derrick yelled just loud enough to permeate through the one-story house. His rifle trained, he flicked on his light attachment and cleared the downstairs area. The house seemed to have been abandoned for days with dusty but clean rooms and a kitchen void of dishes. Derrick returned to the entryway and noticed the tray on the table beside the door. On it there was an old leather wallet that looked discarded and a set of keys. Derrick pocketed the keys and slowly backed out of the house.

Thumbing the key fob, Derrick released a sigh of relief when the lights flashed on the SUV in the driveway. The children climbed into the back and Derrick watched Jessica buckle Zoe and herself in as they scooted side by side. Derrick got in and drove to the edge of the neighborhood to get the farthest from infected blocks as possible. After making several turns, he found his bearings and sped away. He did a quick inventory check after a minute on the road.

Two and a half magazines filled. Five hours until sunrise. Two-thirds of a gas tank left... God, I hope that is enough.

Derrick angled the rearview mirror to look at himself and didn't recognize the face that stared back at him. The right side of his face was a series of scrapes and bruises. Blood dripped from his forehead, drying and crusting in places down his cheek. He hoped it was his blood, unadulterated with infection, but at this point he wouldn't be able to do anything even if some of it was infected. The dark circles under his eyes made his face look sunken and gaunt. Jessica held Zoe tightly in her arms as she stared suspiciously at Derrick. But perhaps that was just his imagination. Or maybe not. Derrick didn't know if the silent judgement he read into her expression in the dark backseat was real or not. *I was the man who tried to leave them to die.*

The drive was quiet. Derrick felt his white knuckled grip on the steering wheel loosen as his heart rate slowed. Relaxation traveled down his body without his say. And as he felt his muscles weaken, Derrick's control over his emotions did as well. He stared at the road ahead, wide eyed to keep from falling asleep, but it didn't take too much effort to stay alert. The cuts on his cheeks had begun to sting and burn, then his nose started to run, tears fell from his eyes like spent bullet casings falling to the ground. This was all the distraction he needed to not fall asleep at the wheel. He wiped his face, sniffled, and tried to sit up straighter, surprised at the unexpected leak of emotion.

Stop crying– stop fucking crying you piece of shit.

Derrick bit his lip hard until it hurt, but it wasn't enough. Regret filled Derrick's mind as a flutter of images stampeded his thoughts.

The woman who had begged for help whom he had shot...

He imagined his friends who took their duty as officers more seriously than he did. They'd be alone downtown, still trying to keep the peace while he fled the city.

The old woman he watched being torn to bits in the shadows of her own home...

Derrick recalled the smile on Perry's lips as they had joked before and her eyes when she had looked up to him. The memory was overtaken by the sight of Perry slamming her forehead in the dirt and dragging it violently across the grass. The wretched scream that had torn at her vocal chords.

Why didn't I just get in the helicopter with Rachel? Perry would be alive right now if...

Derrick covered his mouth, trying to stifle any sobs that slipped out, but none did. Tears streamed down the back of his hand as he panted out of his mouth in silence, so the girls didn't hear him sniffling. His eyes bounced periodically to his rearview mirror to make sure the girls weren't watching him. Zoe dug inside her backpack while Jessica looked down at her.

You're not the bad guy, Derrick...

A montage of images flashed behind his eyes, of all the civilians dragged away by rabid as he had run. The image of his pistol firing into Perry's stomach assaulted in his thoughts. The look of her rabid eyes as life had slipped out of her was a frozen still plastered across the back of his eyelids–an image he could see every time his eyes closed.

You're not the fucking bad guy...

A tap on his shoulder startled him. Zoe extended a clump of tissues in her hand to Derrick. Her eyes were soft and free of judgement as Derrick took the tissues without a word. Derrick wiped his eyes and blew his nose before tossing the tissues aside along with his emotions.

The sun was pushing to rise by the time they had reached

Rome. The kids had fallen asleep, and Derrick was fighting with all his might to stay awake. The road into Georgia was filled with roadblocks. Every few minutes he had to double back and cut through farmlands and lawns. In the glove box of the car he had found an old paper map of the United States. It didn't help much from how large it was, but it got him going in the right direction.

As the sun parted the horizon, Derrick began to panic looking for the airport. He knew he was in Rome; the signs told him as much, but he was driving on fumes up and down the same back roads over and over finding nothing. Finally, he caught sight of a small sign with an arrow that read *airport.*

As Derrick entered the abandoned gated area of a single runway, he spotted the Humvee backed up to the sole hangar. Relief flooded his body as he realized Brandon had made it. He was sitting on the roof of the vehicle keeping a lookout. Derrick didn't dwell on him though, as his eyes searched for her before he parked. When he didn't locate her immediately, his eyes went back to Brandon. He had an orange, drawstring bag in his hand that he fiddled with.

No Alyssa... No Alyssa... Brandon's alone.

The airfield itself was a mess of abandoned equipment and boxes. Civilian vehicles were parked off to the side of the hangar and thousands of loose papers blew about; most had become stuck in the chain link fence that surrounded the perimeter. Two small, single propeller planes remained tucked in the hangar. *If only we knew how to fly.*

Derrick parked near the main entrance facing the Humvee and got out of the car with an ache in his heart as he prepared for bad news. Brandon hopped down from the Humvee with a wide welcoming grin on his face. It was then a teenage boy, Alyssa's younger brother, walked out from the shade of the hanger.

"Eric?" Derrick said, surprised.

The only response Eric gave was a glare from behind his red puffy eyes that cut as deep as one could. That's when he saw her. Alyssa walked out of the building drinking from a bottle of water and froze at the sight of Derrick. A strand of her blond hair caught in her lips.

Brandon went still beside the Humvee. His wide eyes switched from Derrick to Alyssa to Derrick. Tears quickly filled Alyssa's eyes as she dropped the water bottle and ran to Derrick. Derrick slung his rifle behind his back and jogged to her.

She's alive. She's alive!

"Shit," Brandon placed the orange bag inside the Humvee carefully. "Der– Derrick, wait."

Alyssa's look turned to one of rage as she neared. "You fucking–" Alyssa screamed as she shoved Derrick's chest. "You sent him!? You sent– Why didn't you come? Why'd you send–" Alyssa cried. Her cheeks were pale and clammy, and her nose was red and raw from what looked like hours of crying.

"Alyssa, wha–"

"They're dead!" she lashed out. "They're all dead!"

"Whoa, whoa," Brandon stepped between them.

"Don't fucking touch me!" Alyssa screamed at Brandon as she shoved him away.

"Okay.... Okay..." Brandon held his hands up. "My bad."

"I'm sorry..." Derrick said in a confused daze. He wasn't sure what he was sorry for but it felt good to apologize. It felt right to be blamed. *I left those officers behind.* "I'm sorry!" Derrick stepped forward and pictured Perry dying. "I'm sorry!" *I killed that woman.* "I'm fucking sorry!" he felt his cheeks flare as the guilty rage boiled inside him.

"I tried." Derrick shook his head as Alyssa shrunk away. "I couldn't– I couldn't save... I tried!"

Alyssa's expression broke as she unfolded her arms and buried her face in her hands.

Derrick moved toward her cautiously. As if the strength had left her, she fell into Derrick's arms burying her face in his shoulder. He felt the soft skin of her cheek on his fingers and smelled her comforting scent. They hugged for a long time, whispering apologies to one another.

"Hey," Brandon blurted out. "Who the fuck is that?"

Derrick separated from Alyssa, rubbing his coarse knuckles across her wet cheek, and looked back where Brandon pointed. Jessica had woken up and stood beside the ajar door with Zoe at her side.

Brandon turned to Derrick with a look of disbelief. "You've gotta be freaking kidding me, Derri–"

A deafening *crack* exploded in the air and sent Derrick to his knees with everyone else. The ground shook and the blast pierced with a high-pitched ring. Flames clouded over the air strip as military jets banked over the top of the airfield.

Derrick saw Alyssa on all fours clutching Eric as she screamed. He stumbled to her on shaky legs and pulled them to Brandon's Humvee.

"Move your asses!" Brandon shouted and struggled to remain standing.

The whip of jets speeding overhead was disorienting, causing a feeling of lack of control. Every whisp overhead could be the sound of an incoming bomb that would be their end. Clouds of smoke grew hundreds of feet into the air. Derrick pushed Alyssa and Eric into the backseat. Brandon was already starting the engine.

"Derrick! Get in!" Brandon shouted.

In the fear of the moment, Derrick nearly hopped inside on top of Alyssa and Eric, but then he remembered. Jessica and

Zoe had dived inside the car they had arrived in, their skinny legs dangling out the open door as they recoiled.

Derrick couldn't think. He didn't have time. He just ran.

"Derrick! No– Son of a bitch!" Brandon growled, when Derrick ran back for the girls.

The roar of a missile overtook the air as Derrick watched the object blur through the sky and strike the terminal building across the strip. The loud explosion caved in the tall concrete walls and ignited the air with rock and flying debris that rained down on him.

Jessica had Zoe clenched to her chest as they screamed wordlessly and laid across the back seat. Derrick shouted at them to move but the explosions sucked away his voice. He pulled on their stiff shoulders that were paralyzed with fear. Derrick heard Brandon's shouts. He had pulled up the Humvee beside Derrick's car as he struggled with the girls.

"Fucking leave them!" Brandon hollered.

Derrick wrapped his arms around Jessica's waist and pulled hard, dragging her to her feet, then lifting her in the air while her legs and arms flailed for her little sister.

"No! Wait n–" Jessica panicked as she was separated from her sister. "No!"

Another explosion grayed the air and sent scratching concrete particles across Derrick's face as he fell with Jessica inside the back of the Humvee. Brandon lurched the vehicle forward even with Derrick's legs still dragging on the pavement.

"Jessica!" Zoe's high-pitched voice cried as she ran for the fleeing Humvee.

"Brandon– stop stop!" Derrick shouted, but Brandon only accelerated, and Derrick could barely hang onto the adjar door flapping in the wind.

Alyssa grabbed at Derrick's vest trying to pull him inside. "Derrick– in! Close the door!"

Over his shoulder, Derrick saw Zoe's thin legs running for the Humvee as it drove away, her wide eyes full of fear as she begged for her older sister to come back. The child growing smaller than farther they drove away. With the roar of another missile whistling overhead, Derrick let go of the door, and fell to the rubble covered concrete as Brandon drove away.

PART II

Tuesday, April 30th

41 Hours, 33 Minutes Until Calamity Event

"When you choose the lesser of two evils, always remember that it is still an evil."

- Max Lerner

SEVENTEEN

Derrick Hart

Crystal Springs, Ga

"I can't... How can they– thousands of people... Jesus, millions of people just... gone," Derrick crouched with his head between his knees. "Brandon, the United States is bombing its own cities. Its own people!" Derrick's eyes tracked overhead at the clear morning sky.

The light blues mixed with the warm yellows on the horizon where the sun rose in an open view free of clouds. The only thing that marked the sky were dozens of chemical trails that traced behind the fighter jets and bombers. The planes would pass each other going north to rearm and then south to drop their payloads on the next target in the south.

"You think Washington was just gonna lie down and give up?" Brandon said. "The rich and powerful will slaughter whoever they need to stay alive– we are nothing to them. The Washington elites are doing what they need to in order to survive and that's exactly what we need to do. We can't do shit about them bombs. But what the fuck are you doing?" Brandon shook his head as he crossed his arms beside his friend. "I mean, what the fuck are you doing, Derrick?"

Derrick tipped a crinkled bottle of water down his head, letting the drops fall down his neck and face. The humidity was already thick in the air. It was going to be another hot one.

"You save everyone now? What are you? Jesus?" Brandon threw a hand up in the air. "I told you it was over. That was the plan. Whoever found out first that it's time to stop following orders and start running tells the other one. And I freakn' told you to cut and go. That means stop being a cop and start saving yourself."

"I did, didn't I?" Derrick stood. "I left. I left my friends behind! You know how many officers I left to die? How many were still blocking streets and protecting the city while I ran? I came here. We made it here. What's the problem?"

"You don't know them, those kids that you jumped out of a moving vehicle for. The ones that almost got me killed. They're not even yours. They weren't your responsibility!"

Twenty minutes north of the now demolished airport they had stopped on a side of a road deserted of traffic. Zoe was a jittery mess. Still shaken from the bombing, Zoe, who had ceased crying hysterically, now rocked back and forth in Jessica's arms as she dry heaved. Alyssa tended to them both with bottles of water. Derrick and Brandon had walked out of earshot of the Humvee, while Eric emptied a can of diesel into the gas tank like Brandon had shown him.

Derrick had somersaulted hard when he had fallen from the back of the vehicle on the airstrip. He'd got to his feet just as Zoe had caught up to him; he breathed a sigh of relief when he saw brake lights in the clouds of smoke ahead. *Brandon had actually stopped.* Derrick knew Brandon would have never stopped the Humvee for only the girl. Falling from the Humvee had been the only way to save Zoe.

"I know they're not mine, I know that. But they're teenagers. They're fuckn' kids! What was I supposed to do?"

"Leave them!" Brandon shouted as if it was the most obvious thing to do.

"Oh, fuck off!"

"Look–" Brandon started.

"Who the fuck are you?" Derrick turned on Brandon. "You're a soldier, huh? Whatever happened to never leave a soldier behind? Or– or putting your life in front– stepping forward to save an innocent?"

"They're not soldiers," Brandon pointed toward the Humvee. "They're not yours. They're sure as hell not mine, but you just made them our problem. What happens when we're being chased by a hundred infected and one of them breaks their leg? Huh? You gonna stop for them then? You already nearly got us all killed when you jumped out for that kid."

"But I didn't! I got them both in the car. We all made it."

Alyssa snapped her head in their direction. Their voices had reached a point of no return.

"Barely! Tell me somethin," Brandon stepped closer to Derrick, their shoulders squared. "If the crying chick– Zoe? If she didn't run to the Humvee just as we were pulling away, would you still have gotten out to get her? You make that call, to go back to pull her out the car, and we all are blasted body parts right now. One hundred percent. And that's now– when all we have is the military to deal with. Wait until the rabid are here. You stop for her, I'll stop for you, and the whole group goes down."

Brandon's finger jabbed Derrick's chest. Anger flared from Derrick with every thrust into his chest. Like a repressed inferno inside him that had been stewing for days was leaking free with every jab.

"But you and I?" Brandon continued, "We don't die– not at first. We're trained so we fight just long enough so you get to watch Alyssa get torn apart. Then when we get to my wife, I'll get a front row seat to watching her get ripped apart. Along with the two girls you just adopted. *Then* you and I die, after watching everyone else go."

Derrick tasted acid burning his tongue. He quickly steadied his breathing and focused his thoughts before his mind was lost down the rabbit hole of the nightmare Brandon had created. He knew Brandon was right on some level. Brandon's obtuse view of reality was always right to an extent. If Derrick could turn his emotions off and think with only selfish logic, he could understand where Brandon was coming from. Brandon made smart decisions, but not always right ones.

Derrick didn't want to think about the dark corners of life. The harsh truths that poisoned the reality of human existence and boiled life down to a simple math equation. He wanted to believe if they did the right thing, good things would happen to them.

That's how it worked in the movies, right? The hero always wins?

"That's now a possibility," Brandon said. "Because you brought us two more liabilities to care for..."

"That's not going to happen..."

"It already has! These minutes we're wasting here while the chick pukes everywhere– these might be the difference between life and death. You don't understand, this is fucking war. You're not a cop anymore. You're in a warzone. In war you either live or die. You kill or be killed."

"You don't know what the fuck you're talking about," Derrick shook his head. "Stop talking like you know the way, like you got a fuckn' map. This isn't Iraq or Afghanistan. Look around!"

"That's just it," Brandon said almost in mock laughter. "That's the problem. You're still seeing the world as it is now or how it'll be in a week. You're seeing cars and roads and fucking laws. What laws give the President the right to napalm Miami? Birmingham? Go back to Atlanta and check out the bombed skyline and tell me this isn't as much of a war zone as Afghanistan." Brandon motioned to the sky with his hand. "You've seen some shit? That's just a taste. Wait till you see a wall of fucking thousands of infected running for your men and you. Wait till you shoot so many that the blood forms a river coming down the interstate."

Derrick hung his hands on his hips and took a breath. He let the heat from his face dissipate as he let out a long sigh.

"...I get it," Derrick said after a pause. "I get it... You're right– I know you're right in my head, but..." Derrick's shoulders softened as he conceited to Brandon's points. Brandon took a deep breath as if calming himself down.

"Listen to me," Derrick continued. "And I know it's hard for you to hear me because you're a piece of shit and all..." Brandon snorted a chuckle and shook his head. "But there's got to be more than just survival. I'm not going to kill little–" Derrick scratched his forehead as he tried to think of what he was trying to say. "A line still exists. Survival isn't enough. Just the last man standing isn't enough."

Brandon's square jaw flexed as he silently brooded on his words. Derrick knew Brandon well enough to know that his friend wasn't actually hearing him, but he was done arguing, for now. Derrick's eyes lit up when a sudden thought struck him.

"Ginger– did you see what happened to Ginger?" Derrick looked back at the Humvee half hoping the clumsy dog would fall out one of the open doors. That he had been scared and hiding in the trunk this whole time, even though Derrick knew the dog would've bounced to him the moment he heard Derrick's voice. "Alyssa had taken him..." but when Derrick looked back at Brandon, he could already see the apology in his friend's face as he shook his head.

"I'm sorry, brother," Brandon said. Derrick clenched his jaw as he stared hard at the sun climbing the sky. He tried to distract himself, forcing his eyes to stay open so as not to tear up. "He got hurt when they came. I made sure he didn't suffer, though."

Derrick nodded and tried to think of anything to change the subject so his mind wouldn't linger on his dog, but nothing came to mind except the last scratch he gave his pup behind the ears. The last look back out the rear window of the car Ginger had given him as Alyssa had driven away.

Derrick sniffled and heard how wet and runny his nose was, then felt tears pool in the corner of his eyes. Quickly, he swiped at them with the back of his hand, then under his nose, stealing a glance at Brandon to see if he was being watched. Brandon, with his hands on his hips, looked away at nothing in particular in the road ahead, giving Derrick privacy.

Derrick sniffled again and cleared his throat, "Damn dogs..."

"Yeah, I hear ya," after another moment Brandon added, "Alyssa's pissed at me."

"About leaving their parents behind? I know– it's my fault," Derrick spoke, glad of the change in topic. "I forgot about her mom being sick. I should have–"

"I killed them," Brandon said flatly, his shaken eyes leveling with Derrick. "Her mother couldn't move and her father wouldn't leave. The infected were everywhere. A hundred of them chased us out the backdoor."

Derrick was able to stop the shock from showing on his face but could not think of anything to say that wouldn't make Brandon irate. Instead, Derrick let the silence hang between them as he processed the information. Derrick tried to imagine the chaos of the house being overrun and Brandon fighting the infected off by himself. Derrick knew how Alyssa was, how close she was with her mother. She wouldn't have left her parents behind.

After a moment, an irritated Brandon added, "I could've left your fiancé's little brother to die or gotten killed myself trying to drag the mom–"

"No..." Derrick finally said. "No, you did the right thing. You did the right thing..." Derrick's eyes found Brandon and he nodded to him. "Thank you. I would've gone for her myself if I was there..."

Brandon shook his head with a shrug. "She's your fiancé, what else would I do? Besides, I know you'd do the same for Karen." Derrick felt the twist of guilt at the mention of Alyssa being his fiancé. A lie that grew more poisonous the longer he let it fester, uncured by the truth. "I just can't believe you finally had the balls to ask her. And you didn't tell me. You propose over that trip you guys did to the Smoky Mountains?"

Derrick nodded with a sour smile. He didn't know which hurt worse, the lie to his best friend or the truth that he had proposed, and she said no. Brandon sighed, scrubbing his eyes with the corner of his palm. "I suppose the apocalypse put a damper on your announcement plans."

"The world coming to an end tends to do that."

After a few silent seconds, Derrick asked, "You think we're going to make it?"

To Derrick's surprise, Brandon laughed. "Do you?"

Derrick looked back at Alyssa who was shielding her eyes from the sun as she looked his way. "Yeah, I do."

With a hint of a smirk in the corner of his lips, Brandon said, "Jesus Christ, man, you never change. Not even during a freaking zombie apocalypse."

"Yeah, and you're a changed man. Full of cotton candy and rainbows now, huh?" Derrick shouldered Brandon who stumbled back a step.

"I do love cotton candy... I never asked– hadn't had the time," Brandon said. "The cuts on your face... you've been through some shit getting here. Did you make it outta Birmingham before the infected got there?"

"Almost."

"That rabid infection jumps person to person fuckn' fast. You get hurt anywhere?"

"Everywhere," Derrick smiled despite his exhaustion. "Na, nothing major. Cuts and bruises."

Brandon nodded. "I've got a kit. We need to cover any open wounds." Brandon removed the small phone with green electrical tape from his cargo pocket and checked something on it before he dropped it back in his pocket.

Derrick nodded in agreement. "We need to stay ahead of the infected. Miles ahead. States ahead, if we can. Start thinking about the endgame. Figure out where we're going. Back home to Maine, Canada, out in the country somewhere..." Derrick said as they slowly walked back to the Humvee.

"I agree. We got a lot of shit to sort out, but look," Brandon said, touching Derrick's shoulder, "you know me, I'll have your back no matter what. But when the moment comes, I'm not choosing those kids over my wife, and you shouldn't choose them over your fiancé either. You get me?"

Fiancé. Every time Brandon said the word, Derrick felt a new pang of guilt in his gut, a knot forming in his intestines that only grew tighter. *I need to tell him the truth.* Derrick was afraid to find out how mad Brandon would be to learn that

Alyssa had rejected his proposal only to have a sham marriage certificate signed by a judge so she could be with her family in Atlanta. Brandon had nearly bitten Derrick's head off just for saving two girls.

This was no time to have that fight. I'll tell him once we are out of this mess.

"Yeah, I do..." Derrick said.

"Hmm. You're so full of shit." Brandon shoved Derrick's back.

"Hey, Valhalla waits for no one," Derrick grinned.

Brandon shook his head with a smirk, "Valhalla waits for no one..."

EIGHTEEN

Rachel Anderson
Louisville, Ky

"Ma'am, Ma'am?"

"Rachel..." Sean's low voice seeped into the recesses of Rachel's mind. "Rachel."

Rachel's eyes shot open as she startled awake and jolted upright. Tucking her arms into her chest, she sucked in air as she measured her surroundings.

"It's okay, it's okay," Sean showed her his palms. "You're safe." Rachel's eyes ached as the sun's bright, yellow rays blinded her. Despite the roar and the vibrations of the helicopter they rode in, Rachel's exhaustion had overpowered her into a deep sleep. She wasn't sure how long she had been out, but they now sat in an open runway with the helicopter's propellers making their final rotations before stopping completely. Allen and Chris stood outside the chopper with impatient looks on their faces as Sean and another soldier hovered over Rachel.

"I'm– I'm awake," Rachel cleared her throat with the grogginess of sleep still clinging to her.

"Come on, we're here," Sean said, stepping off the chopper.

Rachel followed suit, refusing the soldier's helping hand. "Where's here?"

"MOB Louisville, Ma'am," the young soldier answered.

"MOB?"

"Main Operating Base, Ma'am. This was Louisville's International Airport until the army took it over."

Their journey over the past night slowly came back to her as she limped behind Allen and Chris toward the airport building. After fleeing Birmingham, they had flown all night to Fort Campbell where they had waited for a couple of hours for a second helicopter to transport them to Louisville. They had been stuffed inside some kind of conference room and given unlimited MRE rations and bottles of water. They'd stuffed their faces with the food. When Rachel had found a small M&M package in her second meal, she had been tempted to open all the meal boxes provided to them to find all the candies, but she'd managed to find the self-control to stop herself. Instead, she had savored the chocolate sweets, eating each piece individually and chewing thoroughly.

Food had been a rarity in the final days before they had reached Birmingham. Southern Alabama had been picked dry of every bit of food by the procession of thousands who walked before them. The handfuls of half-eaten bags of chips, stale slices of bread, and canned cheese whiz that they had looted from houses they'd broken into was all they had had to share for the last three days.

The chopper to Louisville had been much more comfortable.

The army had found clothes–camo pants, dark green t-shirts, and combat boots–that actually fit them. On top of that, the second helicopter appeared more civilian in its purpose with cloth seats for them to sit in. Rachel had put on her earmuffs so she could talk to the others over the roar of the helicopter engine if she wished, but none of them had been in the mood to talk. Instead, Rachel had leaned her head against the window as they had lifted off and thought about the two officers they had left behind.

Derrick Hart and Officer Perry. I never got Perry's first name.

She'd thought about them refusing to get on the helicopter even after all they had told them about the infection. Rachel didn't want to forget their names. In the back of her mind, she knew they were already dead. The infected weren't something you could fight and survive. The infection meant death. *You can't fight death.* Rachel had dozed off to sleep with the thought of a dozen speeding gray dots clamoring toward the two bursts of light from Perry's and Derrick's rifles.

"In here," the soldier said. He had led the four of them up a set of stairs and sat them down in the boarding area of Terminal V22. The airport was a ghost of what it once had been. Across the hall was a bar & grill that was closed and beside it was a coffee shop with all its lights off and café chairs flipped upside down on the tables. Rachel found herself staring at a picture of a steaming cup of coffee and her mouth watered at the thought of making herself a warm cup. The massive airport was void of people completely except the lone private that stood over them, nervously shifting his weight as they waited.

"Are you going to tell them?" Sean whispered over his shoulder. Allen and Chris sat in the next row of seats ahead of them, out of earshot.

"Tell them, what?" Rachel raised an eyebrow.

Sean's eyes flattened, underscoring his annoyance. "You know."

Rachel's eyes bounced from his powerful gaze to her feet as a flare of anger and fear kissed her cheeks. So much had happened that she had been able to push personal matters to the back of her thoughts for weeks now, but with survival not at the forefront anymore, topics that shouldn't be ignored, couldn't be ignored, rose to the top.

"You don't have to tell everyone," Sean continued. "But you should tell someone. Ask to talk to a corpsman or a doctor in private. Someone who–"

"This really isn't your problem anymore, now, is it?" Rachel shot back loud enough to get inquisitive glances from the others. Sean looked away in silence. The prospect of safety was a foreign feeling after the past weeks, but with it came the ordinary problems they were facing before the world began to end. Rachel couldn't help but wonder about the future. About *their* future. She questioned the memory of the forgotten argument between the Sean and her. All the things that were left unsaid between them and appeared to continue to go unsaid.

Rachel mimicked his actions, pretending to be unphased by the silence. *I'm not going to feel bad. He doesn't get to make me feel guilty.* But in truth, Rachel hated how quickly the *trivial* problems from before had returned. The one and only good thing that had come out of the outbreak and the following days of running for the lives, was the focusing of priorities. When a violent death was constantly chasing you, there was no time for grudges or arguments. For concern over careers or worries about the future. You can't think about the future when you have to live in the moment to survive.

Rachel thought back to the first few nights of the outbreak when they had been forced to hide in the dark conference room of an empty business. She recalled the screams and gunfire that had come from outside as they had laid still on the gray carpet, and the safety she had felt with Sean spooned behind her with his palm resting on her belly. She missed the simplicity of the moment.

Soldiers and doctors arrived in airport buggies that looked like extended golf carts with flashing lights in the back. The dozen soldiers appeared bored and disinterested as they hung back while the doctors wearing white coats approached.

"Ms. Anderson? I'm Colonel Fields. I'm the ranking doctor at this base," Col. Fields spoke on autopilot as he read through a navy blue medical file in his hands. Fields was an older man with a deceptively young face. If it wasn't for his gray hair, he could pass for someone in his thirties. Though, his youthful face didn't contain a hint of tenderness or warmth. "I was instructed to welcome you to the base. But I have a lot on my plate, so I won't be the one conducting your second set of tests."

"Tests?" Rachel asked as she stood to face Fields.

"Yes, you all will be undergoing a second battery of blood and saliva tests similar to the ones you went through during quarantine."

"Sir, I'm Agent Sean Williams with the Secret Service. I was under the impression that Ms. Anderson was to report directly to her father, the Vice President of the United States, without delay."

"Yes, agent, I know who you are, and I know who her father is," Colonel Fields' tone darkened beyond annoyance as he turned to Sean. "That is the only reason why I'm even allowing myself to be bothered right now and the bottom line is, I don't care. I'm in charge of making sure this infection doesn't spread to this base, and more importantly, this country. So, I don't care about your impression or the President's for that matter. As far as I'm concerned, my job is the most important there is. So, we won't be skipping one step of protocol. We won't be taking any shortcuts, do you understand?"

Sean stared at Colonel Fields and with a set jaw replied, "Yes, sir."

"Good," Fields said and turned back to Rachel. "Should everything come back normal, you will be on your way by tonight. Major Benning, they're all yours."

Fields smacked the navy blue medical chart into Major Benning's chest who scrambled to keep it from falling to the ground. Major Benning was a bald man with glasses who unlike Colonel Fields seemed to have a perpetual smile on his face. He looked over his shoulder to make sure Fields was out of earshot before mouthing *sorry* to Rachel.

Rachel smiled for the first time in a while, already feeling a level of comfort with this new doctor. Benning looked at Sean, Allen, and Chris with a shrug. "It really shouldn't be that bad. Nothing like you had to endure during your quarantine. We'll do the tests, complete physicals, and make you comfortable while we wait for the results. Sound good?"

"Anything with rest in the description sounds great," Chris added, lightening the tension.

"Right?" Benning smiled. "Now, I do need to know if you guys have had direct contact or been within twenty yards of any infected person, or infected blood or any suspected infected fluids?"

"Yes," Sean said.

"You have?" Benning said with an edge to his voice. "Just you or–"

"All of us," Rachel clarified.

"Okay..." Major Benning adjusted his glasses. "How many days ago was your last exposure?"

Sean and Rachel both looked at another as they tried to

separate the days from another, but it was Allen who spoke up. "The day before last."

Major Benning furrowed his brow. "Two days ago? Wait, you mean two days before yesterday or like including today– this morning?"

Rachel didn't like the panic she was starting to detect in the Major's voice. She was quickly wondering if they should have lied to him. But Chris obviously didn't share the same sentiment. Shaking his head, Chris stepped to the front of the group.

"No, no. Not yesterday, but the day before that. There was this infected person that chased us into a gas station that we had to take down."

Sean shot Chris a look that told him to shut up, which he did. Sean seemed to be thinking along the same lines as Rachel. Major Benning backtracked slowly as he flipped through each of the medical folders in his hands and shook his head.

"Colonel. Colonel!" Major Benning shouted just as Fields was about to be driven away. The Major ran to exchange words with the Colonel who seemed more annoyed than usual.

"You idiot," Rachel whispered at Chris who shrugged, confused.

"What?" Allen said.

"Just let me talk from now on," Sean said with a small sigh.

"You know, all the bullshit from before aside, we both outrank you?" Allen said.

Rachel waited for Sean to tell Allen off but, as always, he didn't. She couldn't take it and rounded on Allen. "*All the bullshit from before*– you mean when we were running for our lives in Florida, Allen. You were happy to let Sean make the decisions then, weren't you?" If Allen was about to square off with Rachel in one of their many shouting matches, they never would know, because it was Colonel Fields' voice that boomed through the terminal.

"Are you kidding me!" he shouted at Benning. "Call Fort Benning! Take care of it! Now! That's an order!"

It was the soldiers who ran for them now. Their boots thundered and surrounded them. Sean pulled on Rachel's arm moving in front of her as the soldiers cornered them against the back row of seats.

"The hell is this?" Allen shouted as the soldier's rifles were half raised in their direction.

"Umm... uh, step outside, please," Major Benning stuttered, rubbing the back of his bald head.

"What's going on?" Rachel shouted as she took a step around Sean's side with anger threatening to explode.

"On the ground now!" the nearest soldier shouted as he shoved the muzzle of his rifle in Rachel's face. Her eyes focused on the barrel and imagined the bullet shooting out to strike her in the head.

Killed by the U.S. Army.

"Hey– Hey!" Colonel Fields yelled from beside the buggy with a satellite phone to his ear and pointed out the large window that overlooked the runway and watched the helicopter that had brought them here beginning to ascend. "Get that damn chopper on the ground either by radio or by force, now! I don't give a shit if you got to shoot it down!"

NINETEEN

Brandon Armstrong
Crystal Springs, Ga

Brandon fetched the paper map from the passenger side of his Humvee. After Brandon's rough handling of it for the past few hours, it was now a wrinkled mess with a long tear cutting through North Carolina and ripping into east Tennessee. *If only it was that simple for Washington D.C. to rip the southern states off the map and be done with them.* The B-52 bomber whipped overhead as it flew south to its predetermined target to drop its payload. Alyssa shielded her eyes from the sun as she followed it with her gaze.

I guess they'll have to settle with just blowing it off the face of the earth.

Derrick whispered to Zoe as he kneeled in front of her. She sat with her knees to her chest in the shade near the wheel well of the Humvee. Alyssa knelt down and made Zoe take another sip of water. She had taken quickly to mothering the two sisters, which was good. *Having a job to do will distract her and keep her off my ass.* Eric still sulked at the rear of the vehicle and shot under-eyed glares at Brandon to make sure he knew his anger.

The boy can walk to Tennessee for all I care.

Brandon was glad Derrick was here. There weren't many people in this world he could say he trusted with his life both in and out of combat. It felt as though he had been running around with a coiled spring in his gut, ready to pop at any moment until now. Having Derrick here allowed him to let his guard down. To slowly release the tension in the coil, enough so that Brandon could breathe again.

Brandon loved his wife, of course. She was most important in the hierarchy. Brandon had a signed marriage certificate with Karen, which meant she took his last name and in return Brandon was responsible for her safety. That's what marriage meant. She took care of his needs and he protected her. Maybe Brandon was a little old fashioned, but it worked for him. He wasn't happy about having two more liabilities with them, Alyssa and Eric, but Brandon was glad his friend had finally decided to grow up and get engaged. Marriage was an important part of being an adult.

Brandon and Derrick were different in many ways, but similar in that they were both stubborn and iron-willed. Derrick had always been a bleeding heart for those in need–the weak, the helpless, the victims... His concern made Brandon laugh or at least it used to. They'd go out for beers every couple of months when one was in the other's town, and by the fourth or fifth round Brandon would be busting his friend's balls about the calls Derrick answered. The *victims* he saved while they attacked him for arresting their abusers, or the homeless people he was transporting to a shelter, crapping in the back of his patrol car.

The thing Derrick could not see but Brandon could, was

that they were not victims searching for help, they were suspects waiting for their opportunity. It wasn't Derrick's fault for not seeing it. He just hadn't seen the world as Brandon had. If three deployments during his time as a ranger had taught him anything, it was the truth about humanity. People were only as good as they needed to be. Without a military to protect the borders, without police to enforce laws, there wasn't a need to be good. People could become the animals their instincts told them to be.

The roar of a low flying jet shook the ground and casted a blur of a shadow overhead. Everyone ducked their heads in anticipation for the impending explosion that never came.

"Jesus!" Alyssa yelled.

"Are they g-going to bomb us again?" Jessica asked.

"No, no. We're fine," Derrick reassured her, then turned to Brandon with a look that asked the same question in silence.

"I mean, they probably won't," Brandon clarified.

Derrick glared at Brandon who replied with a small shrug.

"Why is this happening to us?" Eric asked from the backside of the trunk. He looked overwhelmed by the situation. He was a skinny boy who kept his hands tucked inside the sleeves of the dark long sleeved t-shirt he was wearing. His glasses sat on his crooked nose. "The– the freaking infection things were in the city before we knew. There was no warning, no nothing! I thought the army was protecting us. I thought you were supposed to protect us!"

Alyssa held a hand up to her little brother's chest, trying to calm his anger at Brandon before speaking. "Why'd they bomb us?" her voice was focused and void of emotion. "We weren't infected. Back at that airport, there wasn't even any infected nearby. We were alone."

Brandon could see Alyssa's restraint in her eyes. She was much farther along in processing her parent's death than Eric who was stewing behind her. *How long does it take to get over mercy killing someone's parents?*

"They weren't bombing *us*, they were destroying the airport," Brandon said as he unfolded the map on the hood of the Humvee, the same map he had stolen from Colonel Holt's Command tent and marked up. "The military doesn't care about us or any single person in the south right now. What matters to them is containment."

"C-c-containing who?" Jessica said, peering out from behind Derrick with Zoe following her like a shadow.

"Everyone." Brandon shot her a look to scare the two girls into staying quiet.

"What's the X's?" Alyssa asked. Before fleeing the Command tent Brandon had taken a black pen and transposed as many X's as he could from the digital map without being caught. The X's covered the map near the Alabama–Georgia border and between Atlanta and Tennessee border.

"They're bombing targets," Brandon said as everyone crowded the map. "It's called Locke Protocol. Among other fucked up things, they're protocols sanctioned by the President to allow the U.S. military to bomb its own soil. The X's are on train stations, port harbors, interstates, major population centers, airports–any place with high concentration of civilians, or places that give civilians the ability to flee the containment zone."

"Atlanta? They're going to drop bombs on Atlanta?" Alyssa pointed at the X on Atlanta on the map and shook her head in disbelief.

"Atlanta was probably the first place hit," Brandon said. "You saw it when we left. How many rabid there were. Go back now and you'll see the charred houses and bombed out buildings."

"They're only bombing here? Why not Florida? That's

where this all started. Why not Miami? They did this!" Eric whined jabbing his finger at Florida on the map that had no X's on it.

"Oh, they definitely are leveling Florida," Brandon said. "I didn't have time to mark all the target sites down. I only marked the ones between us and Tennessee, that's where safety is."

"But there's no X on Rome's airport?" Eric said. "You said you put X's on–"

"Yeah, yeah, I know. I'm not perfect, kid. I missed putting a mark on Rome's airport. I was kinda in a hurry because my friend needed me to go save your ass–"

"Bran..." Derrick warned him, and Alyssa put her hand on Eric's trembling shoulders, keeping the peace.

"They're blowing up all of the south, so does that mean they really don't have a cure for this thing, or a vaccine, or *something*?" Alyssa asked.

"The government doesn't have shit. They're scrambling. They can't even safely experiment on the infection. I've heard stories from guys in my unit of crazy experiments being done in prisons and on soldiers. People being infected with rabid. Being tortured. No idea if it's true, but I wouldn't doubt it is considering what's going on."

"Jesus..." Alyssa cursed.

Derrick crossed his arms looking at the map. "You said Tennessee is safe?"

"For now, yeah." Brandon dragged his finger, blackened with dirt, across the Tennessee–Georgia border. "Locke Protocol calls for all the available units, weapons, and ammo to be pulled back to the nearest securable border to fortify and hold while the Air Force carpet bombs the hot zone and that's south of North Carolina and Tennessee, from Mississippi to the god damn Atlantic Ocean." Brandon drew a circle with his finger around the bottom right section of the United States where they were trapped. "We're in the kill zone right now. But eighty miles north is the Tennessee border. If we can get into Tennessee, we'd be safe and one of the good guys again."

"What do you mean one of the good guys?" Alyssa asked. "You're army and you– you're a police officer they have to let us through."

"We're not supposed to be alive right now," Derrick said. "Think about it, Lyss. I'm supposed to be in Birmingham blocking a road while its being bombed. Brandon and the rest of his unit were left to die on the front lines in Atlanta."

"The Atlanta news was advising people to shelter in place even as the city was being overrun with infected," Brandon added. "We're all supposed to be killed in the bombing runs. They stopped letting soldiers across the border at midnight last night– per Locke Protocol."

"This isn't happening, this isn't happening..." Eric mumbled to himself as he paced on the gravel on the side of the road.

"Can we sneak in?" Derrick asked, hovering over the map. "I mean, look how much border they have to guard. That's got to be four or five-hundred miles just across Tennessee. The military will have a strong presence on I-75 and I-59, sure, but there has to be some podonk, swamp trail, or dirt road that gets us north, right?"

"Maybe... probably," Brandon agreed. "Which is why this plan of theirs will never work. Some hillbilly who's lived near the Tennessee border his whole life and knows these woods and mountains is going to bring infected blood or tie up their infected child and drive them into Tennessee looking for a hospital. Like you said, the border's too big to patrol, but we're not going to be able to sneak in. We don't know our way around the backroads at the border and I don't know if you noticed, but the roads are near impossible to drive as is. We'd waste all our time fighting traffic looking for a way in. And on top of all that, Locke Protocol calls for predator drones to patrol the border. They can't stop everyone from crossing, but a hellfire missile can stop a lot."

"So– so, what?" Eric's voice broke as he came to a sudden stop with his hands hanging off his head. "We just stay here then? On the side of the road?"

"Why not?" Alyssa furrowed her brow as she chewed on her lip. "You said it yourself, they're blowing up all the infected and major population centers and we have a map of where they're going to bomb, right? We go to a small town that's not marked and gather enough supplies to last a few weeks and we find a building or a house with a basement."

"Gun store or a grocery store," Eric added. Brandon could almost see Eric's mind connecting the dots between their current situation and whatever video game he played instead of getting laid.

"Yeah, something like that. We stay quiet and give military time to figure this out," Alyssa said.

Brandon scratched his head and tempered his irritable senses before he spoke. "There's nothing to figure out. Locke Protocol is not a game-winning play, it's a Hail Mary pass... do you know what that means?"

"You don't have to be such a condescending prick," Alyssa snapped. "I know what it means!"

"Wake up, then, both of you!" Brandon yelled. "This isn't some game. This isn't a movie where everything works out just cause you want it to. Locke Protocol was initiated the second Washington D.C. realized Birmingham was going to fall–population 150,000. Charleston and Savannah fell–300,000. Atlanta fell, population five million. The media has been saying it all week, if one of these major cities fell, the whole south would fall. If all of these cities fell, the country would collapse." Brandon eyed the icy stare everyone was giving him as they processed what he was saying.

"You guys need to understand here and now that the world you knew is gone. This Locke Protocol and Tennessee border bullshit is not going to work and the military, the White House, congress, everyone knows it's not going to work. Today or tomorrow, it's going to collapse, and one person is going to get through because that's all it takes. One infected person. One drop of infected blood and the entire border comes crashing down. All D.C. is trying to do is buy as much time as they can to get as many Greenbands–the rich and powerful fuckers into as many bunkers as they can before the country collapses. Then, the continent."

Brandon saw the realization dawning on Derrick as well as the others. The sobering reality that their lives were never going to be the same. That TV, restaurants, Christmas, and careers were a thing of the past. The only thing that mattered now was survival.

"We can't stay here," Derrick finally spoke, looking at Alyssa. "I don't know what you saw... what you had to deal with in Atlanta. I'm sure it was terrible, but the rabid when they overtook Birmingham–the speed, the sheer number... we wouldn't survive trapped in some city surrounded by them. And maybe the bombing runs killed most of the infected in Atlanta but that still means hundreds of thousands, maybe millions of rabid are still chasing those who survived north, right behind us."

"What's the alternative then?" Alyssa spoke with a flustered panic in her voice. "Brandon said they won't let him cross the border even with the Humvee and he says we'd get killed if we tried to sneak around the army. You say we can't stay here because a million infected are coming to kill us, so what? What's a better option?"

Brandon walked around the Humvee and grabbed a small box from the passenger floorboard that rattled as he carried it. He set it down on top of the map. It was the metallic Greenband bracelets he had commandeered.

TWENTY

Sharon Hill
I-75 North

"Annabelle, don't look at it, just keep walking," David said. Sharon could see Annabelle fighting to keep her head forward, but her eyes were locked on the corner at the old man who laid limp along the road. He wore black pants with his checkered gray flannel shirt tucked inside the waistband. The pockets on his pants were inside– out, a sign that people had already searched the corpse for food and water. The skin on his arms and face was a grayish white.

He has been dead for a while, Sharon guessed. He wasn't decayed or picked at by the birds yet. But the way his face was pressed to the concrete and his belly stuck out, he seemed less human and more like an object.

"Share," David said, "let me take him." Sharon turned to David and handed an exhausted Charlie to him. Ever since they had abandoned their car hours earlier on the interstate, they had taken turns carrying Charlie to give him a rest from the walk. Annabelle had been a trooper so far, letting out barely a peep, but now with the southern sun beating down on her, she was starting to get cranky.

"How much farther, Dad?" Annabelle sighed letting her arms hang in front of her. Sharon saw that the exposed white of her arms was starting to show hues of red as the sunburn was setting in. *It's not even noon.*

"I don't know, hun," David said, bouncing Charlie into a more comfortable position on his shoulder. "Stay close to Mom."

Sharon kept Anna close so that no others would walk between them. The entire shoulder of the interstate on both sides and the median were inundated with thousands of people all migrating north. Both sides of the I-75 had bumper to bumper northbound traffic. There were several head-on collisions that could be seen as they walked. A few of the cars had human remains inside. The car accidents along with the heat, and animals pecking at the bodies, had turned the human forms into haunting skeletons with chunks of withering meat.

Nearly every abandoned car had signs of damage on it. The drivers' last-ditch effort before leaving the safety of the vehicle was to try and ram their way out of being blocked in by four lanes of traffic and three more makeshift lanes of traffic on the shoulders.

David had been smart enough to keep to the breakdown lane for most of the drive north. In fact, they were only able to move more than a couple feet at a time when they drove around vehicles on the grassy right shoulder. In many ways, they were lucky to have gotten as far as they had. They had taken Sharon's jeep instead of David's Lexus, which had saved them from the clutches of the mud when it had rained briefly in the middle of the night. Cars had kept trying to drive on the grass around abandoned vehicles only to get stuck in the muddy ditch, which had lead other cars to try and drive in the ditch to get around that vehicle. And so on. And so on, until it was David roaring the jeep's engine through a farmer's muddy field thirty yards from the road just to get around stuck traffic.

The process took hours just to travel a few miles, and the farther they went the more people there were who attacked their SUV. It started with glares. Walkers alongside the road staring angrily at them as if it was Sharon's fault they had gotten out of their cars and started walking. Like she and David were the assholes for not pulling over and letting the thousands of people invade their car. Some of the parents had tried to plead to let their children in the car. Others had let loose profanity as they had driven by.

Sharon had just stared blankly at them. It didn't feel like this was real life. Everything had happened so fast. An endless trail of stalled cars surrounded by an endless trail of exhausted people. When people had started chasing their jeep and throwing rocks, David had accelerated and ventured farther from the road, chancing getting stuck each time. David hadn't said a word, but Sharon had seen his white knuckles clenched around the steering wheel and more than once he had nearly hit the men who had charged at them. That's how she knew David was scared. He hadn't even tried to brake when someone had been in front of their vehicle.

They had ultimately got stuck just like everyone else. Luckily for them, their jeep had been nearly fifty yards from the road, in a grassy field. Far from the masses of migrants who would've surely swamped them the moment they had stalled. In the early hours just before dawn, they had sat in silence watching the gas gauge flirt with the empty line. Getting out of the car to join the others walking was the hardest decision that they'd made in silence. There had been nothing to consider, nothing to discuss, and no alternate option. There had been no one to call. They didn't have enough gas to turn around and help was not coming. If they wanted to get to safety, if that existed, they were going to have to walk there.

The rain had turned to sprinkles and finally quit after a while. They'd loaded up the sleepy children, leaving the last shelter they had, and joined the thousands of others walking north with the only possessions they owned in their backpacks.

The morning in Tennessee was hot and muggy thanks to the overnight rain showers. It was mid-morning according to her cellphone, but temperatures must've been close to eighty degrees. It was going to be a hot day. Sharon's head had been spinning for over an hour now. The stinging pain from the contusion behind her ear, hidden in her hair line, had turned into a throbbing headache.

After hours of walking, Sharon's shield of toughness she wore in silence was beginning to crack. Her feet felt like they had anvils strapped to them. They barely cleared the grass as they dragged along to find the next step. The bruises along her thighs, hips, and ribs flared with every movement. They were a nauseating reminder of every place she was touched while unconscious.

The looting in their neighborhood back home had become a full-on riot in only an hour. Hundreds of people had filled the streets and run from house to house taking whatever they could. Sharon didn't know who they were or where they'd come from, but more people had arrived by the minute from the direction of downtown Knoxville. The social contract had been broken. It wasn't just criminals anymore, it was everyone. David had taken the kids back to the other bedroom so Sharon could get dressed and clean up. The gun on the bed was out of bullets. With tears still in her eyes, she'd picked it up and watched the two dead men near the doorway carefully as she'd stepped over their bodies.

Sharon had gone into the kids' bathroom in the hallway and out of habit flipped the light switch. "Fuck!" She'd screamed when the room stayed dark. The spark of anger had felt good in her throat. She'd slammed the handgun down on the counter. "Fuck!"

Sharon had sat on the toilet through clenched teeth and felt a tenseness in her shoulders that wouldn't relent. She'd wanted to rip the walls down and use them for tinder to burn the world to ashes. Every time she'd winced or moved her face, she had felt the dried blood pull on her cheek. David had avoided Sharon, she thought. Either because he hadn't known what to say or because he had been afraid of her. He'd kept the kids busy packing backpacks so that she could use the water that remained in the clogged bathtub to clean her wounds and the dried blood from her face.

Leaving the house had been a blur and Sharon recalled it more like she watched someone else do it. The neighbor's house beside them had caught fire, which had caused a foggy smoke in their house that had hastened Sharon into changing her clothes. What little canned food and bottled water they had in their kitchen had gone now. Using the inches of remaining bathtub water, they had found three soda bottles to fill up. Even as they had run to her jeep in the driveway, Sharon had known as she saw the hundreds of people running in the streets, *we stayed behind too long*. Before leaving, she'd zipped the empty handgun into her backpack.

Sharon touched the wound in her hairline and felt a sting, but she saw no blood when she pulled her hand away. Her head pounded with the memories of the past twenty-four hours, but she couldn't think about it. She would never think about it, she decided. Sharon wouldn't talk about it and eventually her injuries would heal. There would be no sign that anything had happened, and she and her family could move on. *We'll just forget.*

"Dad..." Annabelle said quietly as if she was embarrassed. Anna had saved all her complaints and questions for David since they left the house. The young girl obviously knew something terrible had happened to her mother, but Sharon hoped that she didn't understand what it was. "Can I have a drink of water?"

David turned back and looked at Sharon with broken eyes– a lost look that she returned.

"Honey," Sharon said. "We don't have any more right now. Once we get to the next town, we'll get you some, okay?"

"Oh, sorry, mom," Anna said looking down at her feet.

"No, don't be sorry, you're doing great, hun," Sharon replied feeling heartbroken that she couldn't even give her daughter a sip of water. In the monotony of shuffling along the road in the body odor ridden crowds, her mind constantly reassessed their decision of leaving the house and heading north. *Should we have stayed? How could anyone expect me to stay after... Where else should we have gone?*

Sharon heard the argument and women screaming before she saw the scuffle that broke out on the other side of the interstate. Over the roofs of the cars that littered the interstate between them, she could see large, bodied men smashing into one another as their fat fingers yanked at a small bag. Fists swung, knocking each other and those standing nearby, down. Sharon held Annabelle closer and pushed her up the road. Fights and robberies became common the hotter the day became. People were getting desperate as resources grew scarce.

Sharon's mind flashed back to the sprint for their lives through Carryville just two hours prior. It was a nice enough looking town built around the interstate. A truck stop stood across the street from a greasy-spoon diner where truckers and the few old locals would go for eggs and corn beef hash before the pandemic. The dollar shop and local grocery store looked as though it had once been a peaceful place for local farmers to shop, but not anymore.

The glass on every storefront had been shattered and the brick siding of the 'downtown' road had been tagged in red spray paint that read, "end as we know it." Sharon and David should have known it was going to be bad as soon as they had seen the black smoke while entering the town.

Locals had lined the grassy hills that flanked the interstate. Dark, exhausted circles underscored their eyes and heavy hunting rifles and shotguns were clutched tightly in their hands. The look on their faces had revealed a worn town that had been through hell these past days and still they refused to abandon their homes. Whatever relief Sharon had felt as she approached the town for refuge and shelter had quickly evaporated as the dozens of men in tractor baseball caps and flannel shirts had glared down at her. *And not a police officer or soldier in sight.*

The shooting had started as it always did, with one man. A lone man who had been walking twenty-five yards ahead of Sharon's family had veered off road and trudged up the damp embankment for the restaurant with the crooked sign overhead that read "Meg's Diner & More!"

A boy had shouted at him from the top of the hill and the man had shouted back as he'd continued to go toward the diner. The silence that had settled over the thousands of people who had watched this happen was eerie. It was a restrained stress buried in everyone that had quickly simmered to a boil. Sharon hadn't seen who fired the first gunshot, but before the man had fallen down on the grass and rolled back down into the ditch, more gunfire had erupted. Scattered amongst the procession of migrants along the interstate, others with guns had fired back as more of them had tried to make a break for downtown Carryville. Hundreds had run up the grassy hills on both sides, while Sharon, like most others, had just tried to survive passing through the town.

Sharon shoved Anna's upper back and the girl ran with her onto the interstate beside the cars, ducking behind them as bullets hissed and snapped nearby. David had dived between the front and back bumper of a pair of SUVs with Charlie cradled under his arms. Sharon's fingers had raked the old backpack David wore before finding her grip to pull David to his feet.

She hadn't known what the right thing to do was, but she'd known they couldn't just lay there and wait to die. It had taken a few tugs on the backpack for David to get the message and he had stumbled to his feet following Sharon who had scooped up Anna by her waist. It wouldn't be until after they had run the gauntlet through the town that they would stop and realize Sharon had inadvertently pulled open David's backpack, spilling their three bottles of water on the road behind them as they ran.

The world was different now, Sharon knew. If the riots in her neighborhood didn't communicate that, the lawlessness she had witnessed in Carryville did. *Laws didn't matter anymore.*

Now as Sharon and her family approached the next town, Pioneer, they did so with caution this time and not the naive optimism from before. She could already hear and see the large crowds forming alongside the interstate before entering the short stretch of the town. Dead bodies trailed the ditch beside them with the bloody streaks in the grass. Sharon looked up and saw the sunken faces of soldiers along the tree line of woods that led to Pioneer. They were looking down on the procession of people with exhausted eyes and sweaty faces. The expression being given was hard and void of compassion.

"Just give us some water!"

"You're the army for God's sake!"

"You're just going to let us die!?"

"Help us, please!"

"Fuck y'alls!"

At the cusp of the town, two sheriff deputies stood atop an entrance ramp with a dozen soldiers standing behind them. The road was blocked with concrete pylons and some sort of home-made razor wire. Crude two by four planks of building wood were nailed together with a mess of metal wires attached. Each wire had had razors threaded through it. The mob was in the hundreds and growing as handfuls of passerbys stopped to join the crowd.

Sharon approached from the back, the crowd that swarmed the barriers. She couldn't help but feel relieved to see the army convoy of vehicles parked in the gas station parking lot behind the soldiers. The uniformed men and women, the American flag... in truth, before all this, Sharon didn't think much of those things. Patriotism. The military. Law enforcement. It was something that had barely been a part of her. But now, that flag and those soldiers meant law and order. They meant safety. Looking down at her daughter, Sharon had a glimmer of hope for the first time that day.

"Should we tell them about the people?" David asked. "Back in Carryville? Maybe they can go back there or–"

"I'm sure they already know."

One of the deputies, who was older and more rounded around the waist than his partner, pointed to a large, printed sign that read:

'TOWN CLOSED TO ADMITTANCE. TRESPASSERS WILL BE ARRESTED. FORCE WILL BE USED AGAINST ANY VIOLENCE'

Then a smaller sign was attached to the bottom with handwritten words painted on, almost as an afterthought

'CONTINUE WALKING, REFUGEE CAMPS AVAILABLE IN THE NEXT TOWN'

Sharon doubted this was true, but it was a good ploy to keep people walking past their town and most did. Thousands of migrants didn't even try to stop in Pioneer. With their heads hung low, they trudged past Sharon and continued on. Even if the sign was true, what it didn't say was that the next town was thirty miles away. Since the internet and GPS on people's cell phones weren't working, most people had no idea where they were at any given time. In fact, Sharon bet most people didn't even know which way they were going if it wasn't early morning or late afternoon, and they could see where the sun rose or set. They were just following the crowd.

"Dad, I'm thirsty..." Charlie whined as he began to struggle in David's arms. The heat and dehydration were clearly beginning to fluster the boy.

"I know, me too, son," David said, letting Charlie down but guiding him by his hand.

"Come on, let's go over here." Sharon led her family to the opposite side of the road away from the crowds of people and under the shade by the woods. The kids instantly plopped down on the grass, happy to be away from the baking sun. Sharon could see Annabelle's flush cheeks and clammy skin.

She knew how dry her own tongue felt. She thought if she had water to drink, it would all be absorbed by her tongue before reaching her belly. *These poor kids...* David sat down with a pained face as he rubbed one of his calves.

"We could, I don't know, maybe talk to them," David said after a minute, gesturing to the two deputies. "Maybe they'll give us something because we've got kids, you know. Or maybe even let us in, or the kids at least."

Sharon didn't want to sit. She was afraid to sit. She feared that if she sat, the worry that weighed on her shoulders might crush her into the ground. Then the tears would be squeezed out of her like the last pinch of water in her body. If she started to cry again it would all be over. There would be no coming back from it. She would stay on the ground, with her kids at her side, helpless and waiting to be just another body to be passed by others.

"The kids don't leave our side," Sharon shook her head, staring at the military vehicles being loaded across the interstate. It was hard to see from their downward angle, but it looked like the soldiers were loading supplies from the gas stations into their vehicles–pallets and boxes of food and water.

"It's worth a try, Share," David said. "We... you know, we have to do something." David's voice faded.

"Half the people up there have kids. Do you see any of them getting anything? That woman in the front there... you see her? She has a baby. Are they giving her anything?" Sharon said with more anger in her voice than she intended.

"Mom!" Charlie yelled and Sharon sighed, swiping at her sweaty brow.

"Shut up, Charlie!" Annabelle defended her mom.

"No, I'm sorry, guys, I'm just tired," Sharon rubbed a drop of sweat from her upper lip. "Do you... do you have any other ideas?" Sharon looked at David who, with defeated eyes, only shook his head.

From their frequent road trips up north, Sharon knew the next town was too far to walk to. She also knew there were several lakes, ponds, and streams in the surrounding woods in this area, but she didn't know where or how far.

The only thing that could make things worse right now is being lost in the woods looking for water. It's not even dark yet but it will be.

Three times while walking along the road, David had tried to ask other families for water or food for their kids. Most people had avoided them as soon as he had opened his mouth. They had ignored the question and maneuvered their own kids to the other side of the crowd. Gangs of men had formed in the crowds and shouldered for dominance. No one with any supplies had been able to drink their water or eat their food without being swarmed, beaten, and robbed. If someone had walked off the road to the woods, everyone knew it was to take a drink of hidden water or quickly eat food. Sometimes a group of men had walked after them and screams had erupted from the woods before complete silence.

What have we done? We should have never left Knoxville. At least there we knew where to find fucking water. We can't keep walking. We'd never make it another thirty miles. We can't turn back, there's no way we can walk back through Carryville, again.

"No one's going to help us," Sharon mumbled to herself, lost in a daze looking at the increasingly volatile crowd.

"What?" David asked.

"No one's going to help us," Sharon repeated with more surety in her voice. She became more confident as she talked it through. "We can't go forward. We can't go back..."

"Share, what are you–"

"No one's going to give us water. No one's giving us anything," Sharon glared at a tall pallet of water bottles being taken out of the gas station front door with soldiers on both sides. "If we want something, if we need water, we have to take it."

TWENTY-ONE

Derrick Hart
Near GA–TN Border

"Are you sure you're okay?" Alyssa asked.

"I'm fine," Derrick half laughed as he reassured her a third time. "Just go slow with that thing."

Alyssa held the large pair of bolt cutters wide, taking up much of the free space in the back of the Humvee. The teeth of the cutters pinched between the skin of his wrist and the Redband bracelet he wore. Derrick had already cut Alyssa's Yellowband free despite Brandon swerving left then right around a column of stopped traffic had which jostled Alyssa into almost falling over. Jessica and Zoe had kept their hands to her back, steadying her.

Pursing her lips together, Alyssa pulled the arms of the bolt cutters together and Derrick heard the crunching sound of severing metal until the final *snap* sounded as his metal bracelet was cut free. Derrick pulled the cut Redband free and rubbed his wrist for a few seconds. The skin covered by the bracelet was moist and tender, having not felt fresh air in days.

Alyssa set the bolt cutters down on the floorboard between them. They were a lucky find of Brandon's in the abandoned airport hangar back in Rome where Brandon had cut his Redband free, making it possible for his plan to work. Alyssa picked up one of the few remaining Greenband bracelets from the box and slid it onto Derrick's wrist. Derrick begrudgingly allowed her to fasten the metal straps over the skin they had just freed from the shackles of government tagging, the moment lasting only a few short seconds. His thumb brushed over the etched-in barcode and serial number on the face of the bracelet. Everyone else already had their Greenbands strapped on.

God, I hope this works.

Traveling to the border was maddening. A constant feeling of driving ten miles forward only to backtrack five miles to circle around a small bridge or overpass clogged with abandoned cars. Everywhere they drove, there was always a crowd. Most walked along the sides of the road in a long procession. They carried their things in backpacks and luggage that they wheeled behind them like they were in an airport searching for their terminal to catch a plane that would fly them to a tropical paradise. Only now they would be happy with shelter; the Hawaii and Bora Bora dream vacation had been replaced by the simple desire for basic food and water.

A few cars followed behind them–trucks, jeeps, and four-wheeled SUVs that could handle the off-road terrain. Derrick had kept a close eye on the bony faces of those who followed. It was an understatement to say the anti-government movement was beyond popular right now. News stations across the country had turned against the police days ago after the many questionable shootings had been videoed in every major city around the country. Martial law had only exacerbated an already volatile situation.

By now the news had spread videos and reports of the military's bombing runs on American cities in the south. The radio reported on potentially hundreds or thousands who had already died from thirst and heat exhaustion migrating north on foot. All the while sightings of military stock piling of food and water were happening across the nation. These government actions would only bolster support for anti-government and Alt-Right militias that resisted the military's authority. Ironically, local and federal attempts to quell the riots and keep the peace had seemed to unite the far-left extremists with the far-right in their mutual anger towards the government.

Derrick stared down any driver who wandered too close to their bumper. A simple purposeful grip of the large turret gun that protruded from the Humvee roof sent any pursuers braking to create space from their lone military vehicle. Not that Derrick even knew how to fire the turret if he wanted to, but the threat seemed to be enough.

"Thanks," Derrick smiled at Alyssa who returned the look, brushing the loose strands of her blond hair behind her ear. She looked tired and distracted. Her eyes shifted and refocused as if there was something on her mind that she didn't know how to say–a common enough tell that Derrick was able to spot after she had broken up with him. During the awkward days after she had turned down his proposal, while he had held on to the hopeful strands of reconciliation, Derrick would lay awake at night thinking about every *almost* fight they had ever had. They had never got to the real fights because Derrick realized every disagreement had ended with Alyssa's eyes bouncing back and forth as if struggling to say, "you're wrong. I disagree."

Instead, she would remain silent and stew on her unvoiced disagreement, or so Derrick surmised. He could see that look in her eyes now. The same look she had when he had talked about buying a house together or having children together. The same look she had when he had proposed.

"What is it?" Derrick asked.

"Hm? Oh, nothing," Alyssa said which only highlighted her tell more so, like an amateur poker player with pocket aces.

Derrick bit his tongue while glancing at Jessica and Zoe who were distracted by the people outside the window. Eric sat up front beside Brandon and they seemed preoccupied with where they were driving. Derrick reached out and gently took one of Alyssa's hands in his. "What is it?" Derrick whispered more sternly–an action that earned him a peculiar reaction from Alyssa as his insistence was out of character.

Pursing her lips and looking around at their limited privacy, Alyssa relented, whispering a reply, "I don't want to... I don't think the story is good. We need a better story or– I don't think the army's going to buy it. I just– I don't know. I'm scared."

Derrick nodded and felt Alyssa squeeze his hand back, making his heartbeat quicken.

"Do you think the Greenbands are going to work?" Alyssa continued. "I mean, do you think Brandon's plan will actually get us across into Tennessee? Because part of me thinks that maybe just holding up somewhere safe, somewhere we can make safe, maybe that would be better than..."

"Then what?"

Alyssa leaned closer to conceal her voice. "What if you have to kill, you know, soldiers or just people– regular people at the border? And not to mention willfully creating a *total loss* thing which..." Alyssa shook her head in disbelief, "I mean, if the bracelets don't work, that's the back-up plan, right? You'd have to kill people protecting the border? I mean those guys could be you or Brandon just doing your job... cops... soldiers..."

Her eyes searched Derrick's with a terrified curiosity. "Could you do that?"

The image of Perry's blood shot eyes looking up at him as the life was drained from them flashed behind his eyes. The image wouldn't leave him. It lived beneath his skin. Like an infection of its own kind. It was a part of him. Derrick thought about Alyssa's simple question, *could you do that?* His mind cycled through every person he had killed in the last week. People he had killed in the riots over the past week. The faces of agonized infected, of civilians he could have saved, or who had died in the crossfire of his escape. It wasn't Alyssa's question that bothered him, it was his answer.

Derrick didn't feel well about a single trigger press he had done. He knew each press had been necessary. He understood, logically, it was life or death, but under the concrete floor of reason, a minutia emotional conflict picked apart every decision. Yet, he continued to move forward, pressing towards the next objective. It was in the moments between fighting when his thoughts and soul questioned his actions most. In the heat of the moment, Derrick almost felt like a different person.

Combat was a skill. And despite his conflicted emotions, there was no denying Derrick's combat abilities were improving exponentially. He had never fired his weapon in anger before this week, however, now he could not count the number shots he had fired in life-or-death scenarios. Every trigger press was smoother, his movement more fluid, and his mind worked the problem before him quicker. His adrenaline didn't surge uncontrollably when attacked which mean greater clarity in the moment. Glancing over his shoulder at Brandon as he drove, Derrick didn't question if he could kill soldiers that stood between them and safety... he worried that he would have to.

In truth, if the bracelets failed, they would all be long dead before he could even lift a finger to take a soldier's life. Derrick stared at his hands as Brandon hit a bump that bounced them in their seats. Derrick's skin was visible for the first time after days of being covered under the grime and dirt. Before starting the drive, they had used bottled water and alcohol wipes for any dirt buildup on their bodies and a bleach-based spray that burned on contact, for any splattered blood stains on their skin or uniforms. Brandon passed around a used tube of crazy glue and roll of duct tape to seal any open wounds to prevent exposure to infected blood.

This plan felt more like they were choosing their way to die rather than finding a way to survive. Derrick's instincts were to lie to Alyssa. An innocent lie to give her comfort. *Tell her everything will be fine. What good will come from saying we're all about to die?* But that was what the *old* Derrick would do. The Derrick that Alyssa had dumped.

"I... will do what it takes to keep us alive," Derrick said and let his mind wander. "To be honest, I can barely believe I survived getting out of Birmingham. Every second my mind wanders, it goes back to that city. Thinking about the chaos, the infected... how isolated I felt. The things I had to do to get out... the officers I left behind..."

Alyssa's palm, soft and gentle, cupped Derrick's hand. His eyes couldn't help but fall on the diamond ring she wore on her ring finger. Looking up, he recognized the pity in her eyes and quickly tried to wrap up his thoughts, "I can't tell you how many people I've killed in the past week. Not just people infected with the virus, either..." Derrick glanced at Alyssa's expression to see if there was disgust in her eyes but all he saw was sympathy. "I don't know if this is the right thing to do. There's no map. There's no one we can call for help or advice. All I know is Brandon's plan gives us the best chance of survival, not just surviving a day or two but real survival. And even though I'm scared as shit right now, I'd rather be here with you than back in Birmingham, alone."

Alyssa's lips broke into a tender smile. When Alyssa brought Derrick's hand to her mouth and gave the back of his hand a kiss, he felt a surge of warmth fill his chest. He couldn't help but still feel connected to her as if they were still together. *Funny, we are now legally married and yet so far apart.*

Before beginning their long drive this morning, Brandon was distracted reloading the medical supplies back in the Humvee when Derrick had pulled Alyssa aside. He had to tell her... he had to tell someone.

He didn't want to widen the scope of his deceit into a conspiracy by involving Alyssa, but Derrick didn't want Brandon finding out about it either during such a volatile time. Like when they were about to cross into Tennessee, the most heavily armed border in the world.

"Listen," Derrick had said as he had walked Alyssa a dozen yards down the road. Brandon had been heaving a large diesel fuel tank into the trunk of the Humvee. "I don't want to make you feel... I have to tell you something so we don't distract Brandon right now, I mean, that's why I'm bringing it up. Not because–"

"Derrick, what are you talking about?" Alyssa had asked.

Derrick had sighed and hung his hands on his hips as he'd struggled to find the words. It had felt as though he was apologizing to Alyssa for her dumping him. Derrick had gritted his teeth to push the weakness out of his voice. "I lied to Brandon... for you," Derrick said, sounding more righteous than he meant. "Brandon called and told me he was leaving Atlanta and I knew I couldn't be there in time to get you, so I asked him to get you. He wouldn't do it for just my girlfriend," Derrick had seen Alyssa shrink backward at the mention of *girlfriend.* The guilt of the situation weighed on her heavily.

"And I knew he'd be pissed if I told him of our fake marriage for the suicide contract, because you know how seriously Brandon takes marriage," Derrick had continued. "I told him... we were engaged. That I proposed in Pigeon Forge and– and you said, yes."

Alyssa's wide eyes had trembled in surprise. "You... you never told him that I... that we–"

Derrick had shaken his head. "No, I thought I'd wait and see– no, I never got around to it."

There had been a long pause that had been filled with slamming doors and the trunk as Brandon had started the engine. Alyssa had hung her head and when she'd raised it, Derrick had seen the tears that filled her eyes. "Derrick, I'm sorry..."

"No, I didn't– I don't want you to feel bad," Derrick had raised his hand between them, trying to hold back her tears. "It's fine, it's just– don't tell him the truth. Not yet. Once we pass the border and are safe, I'll tell him the truth." Derrick had said, swiping sweat from his brow as he had glanced down at her empty ring finger. "If Brandon asks about the ring, just tell him you didn't want to lose it so you took it off and left it in a drawer back in Atl–"

Alyssa's hand had dug in her jeans pocket and pulled out a small plastic baggy. Opening it, she had pulled out the familiar looking diamond ring. The ring Derrick had researched and obsessed over for months before emptying a savings account to purchase.

"I didn't know... I didn't think you held on to it," Derrick had said.

"I..." Alyssa hesitated, struggling to find her words as she looked away from Derrick's eyes. After a moment of searching for words that weren't there, Alyssa had said, "I couldn't let it go."

Alyssa had sniffled a wet breath as she'd slid the ring onto her left ring finger. "Derrick," Alyssa had spoken barely above a whisper. "I should have never–"

"Derrick!" Brandon's shout had cut through the moment. He had half leaned out the open driver's door. "Your *kids* are all buckled in. Let's go."

"Yeah..." Derrick had called back. His hand taking Alyssa's as his thumb had brushed over her engagement ring. He had given her a small smile that she had returned before they walked back to the Humvee.

The shouts of the hundreds of southerners migrating north filled the Humvee as they neared the border. It had been a long drive north, and they were cutting it close. It was almost noon.

"We're almost there," Brandon hollered into the back of the vehicle. "Are we set?"

"Yeah, I'm going to dump the stuff then," Derrick replied. He tossed his severed Redband bracelet into the box with the few remaining Greenband bracelets and Alyssa's Yellowband. He found an empty stretch of land, devoid of people, and opened the door, tossing the box in a grass ditch. Brandon wasn't specific about what would happen if they didn't make to the Tennessee border by noon, he only said it 'wouldn't be good.' Derrick checked his watch. *11:37am.*

"It's still there?" Brandon looked at Eric who was in a daze, staring at the thousands of people they passed. "Eric! You still got the bag?"

Eric straightened after hearing his name. "Yeah, yeah, sure, it's right here." Eric bent over and felt the orange drawstring bag stuffed beneath his seat.

"Pay attention, man. There can't be any hesitation. What's the word you're listening for?"

"*Bag*," Eric answered, adjusting nervously in his seat as they passed a road sign welcoming them to Rossville, Ga.

"Alyssa, you copy that?" Brandon glanced back at her. Alyssa only nodded with trepidation in her eyes.

"You have them ready if we need them?" Derrick asked her. Alyssa only nodded and kicked the backpack between her feet. Derrick saw the worry in her eyes and added, "We won't need them."

Because if the bracelets don't work, we're as good as dead.

"Shit," Brandon cursed. "I don't know how much farther we can go this way."

Derrick could see the cars and mobs growing thicker by the moment as they entered Rossville. It was a small town on the Tennessee border. The kind of town with a few thousand people living in subdivisions on the outskirts. They drove past restaurants and super centers with boarded up doors and windows. Thousands of people were walking down highway-27 leading north, their suspicious and desperate eyes glaring at the Humvee.

Brandon dug into his pants' cargo pocket and removed the small radio with the worn and frayed green electrical tape on its bottom. Brandon checked the screen before keying the radio button along the side.

"Army Rangers 2-7 to Tennessee Border Command..." Brandon said and received only silence in return. This was the first step in several steps that needed to work for their plan to succeed. If they couldn't even receive communication from Border Command, they were already dead. "Army Rangers 2-7 to Tennessee Border Command, do you copy?"

"This is Border Command, identify yourself," a stern voice replied.

"This is Sergeant Armstrong out of FOB-Atlanta. I'm in possession of four Greenbands with orders to escort them to MOB Louisville."

There was a long silence on the radio. Derrick and Brandon exchanged looks of trepidation.

"Border Command to 2-7, how many are you, total?" the voice asked.

"Four Greenbands and two escorts– that also have Greenbands." Brandon made a face that said he didn't like how that sounded.

There was an eerie silence in the Humvee as everyone held their breath waiting for a reply.

"Confirm location, Rossville, Georgia, highway-27 passing Park City Rd., single Humvee. Confirm?" the voice asked.

Instinctively, both Derrick and Alyssa looked out of opposite windows for watchful eyes they couldn't see.

"Confirm. That's us," Brandon radioed back.

"Divert to Battlefield Parkway, proceed West to MacFarland Ave."

"Copy."

Eric pointed to a sign indicating Battlefield Parkway one mile ahead. Brandon set the radio down on the center console. Everyone seemed to release the breath they were holding.

"How do they know our location? They know where we are down to the road? I don't see any army watching us," Alyssa said.

Brandon looked back with a stern warning in his eyes. "Predator drones."

TWENTY-TWO

Sharon Hill
Pioneer, TN

Sharon dumped her backpack behind David so that his body blocked most of its contents from the crowds of people continuing to walk down the road. Not that anyone cared about a laptop, external hard drive, photobook, first-aid kit, and a bunch of clothes anymore. Hell, Sharon could have poured hundred-dollar bills across the grass and most people wouldn't have made a move for it. Everyone needed the same things now. Food, water, and safety, and money couldn't buy those things anymore.

"What are you doing?" David looked back at the pile of junk. Sharon leaned forward and spoke in a quieter voice so that the kids wouldn't hear.

"We need water and food. It's as simple as that, David," she said. "We can't just keep walking down this road hoping for someone to help us."

David interjected, "The sign says there's FEMA camps in the next–"

"No one's helping us!" Sharon whispered more aggressively than she meant to and quickly softened her tone. "It's a lie, David. We have to do something now or we're going to be just more bodies on the side of the road."

A hollowness came over David's eyes as if the thought of them dying had never occurred to him.

How nice it must be to live in his fantasy world.

"No one will give it to us," Sharon chewed on her lip as the thrill of fear bubbled inside her. "So, you're going to wait here with the kids, and... and I'm going to go get us some water." She kissed the top of Charlie's head. "You guys stay here with Dad, alright?"

"Where are you going?" Anna asked in a panic.

"Oh, not far, sweetheart, not far at all," Sharon said, rubbing her fingertips across her daughter's back. "I'm going to talk to some people across the street there, that's all. Going to see if I can get us something to drink and eat."

Watching Anna's eyes light up at the prospect of water broke Sharon's heart and only hardened her resolve. *I have to do this. I won't let my kids go thirsty a moment longer.*

With her empty backpack on her shoulders, Sharon looked at David for a brief second and bit her lip before turning to cross the road. David caught up with Sharon a few paces from the kids and pulled her arm. "Share, wait. They're not going to just give you stuff, you know."

"I'm going to do something."

"Something? Something, like what?"

"I don't know... I don't know, something. Someone has to do something. I'm not going to let our kids die of fucking thirst," Sharon's voice broke as she said it. David's eyes were wide and lost in response. She could see he was searching for an alternative. To tell her not to do anything because he would... because he knew... but there was nothing. There was no one. David wasn't going to do anything. They were alone with their kids and if they were to stay alive, someone had to do something. The resolved look in David's eyes as his shoulders recessed and his expression sank, showed his recognition of their new reality. The actuality he had hidden from himself but could no longer hide. David would wait with the kids because that's where he needed to be. Sharon was going to do something because that is who she was.

Sharon pressed her hand against David's chest gently and nodded. Their eyes met in a moment of acceptance as she spoke gently. "I need you to stay with the kids, okay? No matter what, you need to stay there for them, okay?"

David nodded and looked down as he rubbed a tear from the corner of his eye. Sharon felt a sudden urge to hug her husband, but she knew she'd start crying the second she felt his embrace. If she hugged him, this would be a goodbye. *This isn't goodbye. This isn't goodbye.*

Holding her breath so as not to let a single tear leak free, Sharon turned and walked casually to the edge of the crowd across the street. She watched speculatively at the scene before her, as she stepped around the cluster of sweaty men and women.

Sharon looked up the hill that led to the convenience store and saw the line of soldiers that stood behind the barrier. There was no way through. Sharon could see the soldiers nearest to the mob of people tightening the grips on their rifles and eyeing the chaos. They were an inch away from shooting into the crowd, it seemed. The sight of the pallets of water being loaded into the semi-truck under guard was like a bad tease. It was only fifty yards away. Sharon's mouth salivated just looking at it.

Near the backside of the gas station, from where they were carting the supplies, there were several bushes and a few yards of grass. Before that was the edge of the woods, much of which had makeshift barbed wires that ran across the outer tree line. It was possible to crawl underneath the wire but doing so would get her arrested or shot for sure. Every twenty yards, two soldiers stood sentry behind the barbed wire along the woods.

Standing on the outskirts, watching more and more people crowd and overwhelm the soldiers, Sharon imagined different routes she would run through the woods to go undetected. She thought of places she could hide and things she might say if she was caught. She stood there for twenty minutes, watching the crowd simmer to a boil until it happened. A pair of chubby men with wild eyes, dissatisfied with shouting, pulled one of the signs from the ground and used it as a shield to ram into the nearest barbed wire at the top of the exit ramp. The surging crowd ignited by the forward motion, cheered.

Soldiers ran from the parking lot where the water was and shoved the men back. A younger woman shouted, "Fuck you, you Nazi fuck!" the woman was slender with thick-rimmed glasses, dark hair, and a black tank top. She appeared to have several supporters in the crowd as they followed her. "They can't do this to us! They can't deny us access to public property, public roads, public water! They can't stop us all!" the crowd roared in agreement, and the two deputies leveled their shotguns at the approaching mob.

"Oh, what! You're going to shoot me? Hands up, don't shoot!" the young lady yelled as she stepped forward with her hands raised. "You going to shoot an unarmed girl?"

Sharon had been edging toward the tree line that led up to the town. When Sharon looked back at the troublemaker woman, she saw that four soldiers had come to the front and were wrestling with the skinny woman. Each soldier grabbed an arm while the others fastened zip ties on her wrists. She refused to walk so the soldiers carried her, her feet dragging behind her, as the crowd roared behind her. Everyone seemed to move forward up the hill leaving Sharon behind.

The two soldiers in the woods closest to the action ran to help their friends quell the disturbance slowly turning into a riot, leaving an opening in the woods–an unwatched section of barbed wire. Sharon didn't have time to wait and see if the advancing crowd would win. She sprinted up the hill on her hands and knees like an animal towards the woods and dove under the barbed wire, her heart thudding in her chest so hard she could feel her pulse in her ears. *What are you doing, Sharon? You're going to get caught.*

Gunshots cracked over the sound of hundreds of shouts and Sharon waited for the pain of the bullets to pierce her body. When it didn't come, she kicked her legs under the barbed wire and ran to the tree line.

The twigs and sticks scraped at her forearms and knees as she scrambled to her feet. Staying low, she ran far enough so that the returning soldiers would not see her. More gunshots rang out. Sharon hid behind a thick tree and saw one of the soldiers firing their pistol above their head to silence the crowd. The gunfire seemed to slow down the raging crowd, but it paralyzed Sharon.

Her eyes pinched shut and she tried with all her being not to see the stocky man's silhouette in front of Annabelle's yellow walls. The moment replayed in her mind. No sound. Sharon clapped her hands over her ears. She could see the man begging her not to shoot him with his hands up just before she pulled the trigger and watched him fall. The moment kept on repeating like a computer gif. A cold sweat coated her neck and palms, and her hands moved to her face as she tried not to make noise.

Make it stop.

The man pinned her arms to the bed. *Make it stop!* The widening pool of black blood around his body as he gargled his last breaths. She couldn't take a breath. Her chest felt tight and sunken in. Like she couldn't make room for even air. Collapsing to her knees, Sharon's hand clawed at the tree she hid behind and her palm felt the rough scratches from the bark she tore free. The pain helped her escape from the maddening loop of images as she gasped for air, tears streaming down her cheeks against her will. *What the fuck is wrong with me?*

Sharon clenched her teeth and felt a flare of heat in her cheeks at the weakness she had just felt. The weakness she had just showed. Sharon took deep breaths and made sure no one was near her before her eyes focused back on the convenience store.

The backdoor was propped open with a large rock. The dozen yards between the tree line and the door looked terrifying. The chaos by the road was returning to normal levels of shouting. Soon the soldiers by the road would return back up here. Sharon couldn't wait any longer. Biting her lower lip, she ran out into the open and sprinted into the back of the gas station.

The air inside was stale resembling the inside of a thawed freezer. She took off her empty backpack and walked down the narrow hallway and passed the open loading doors for the beer cave that was empty like most of the store. She looked inside the main lobby of the gas station from the back-room doorway and saw no one. Most of the store shelves had already been emptied. There were a few items left on the shelves to the left, though.

Sharon ducked inside quickly but quietly. Her backpack already open, she filled it with whatever she could find. She grabbed two whole racks of beef jerky, a dozen bags of pretzels, and candy to fill the bag to the brim. Zipping the bag shut and putting it on her back, she saw a pallet of bottled water in the next aisle near the front door. It was staged to be loaded into the truck.

There wasn't an exact escape plan she had but she figured she could carry the supplies out and maybe hide it in the woods down the road, then circle back around the way she came to pick them up.

The difficult part is not being seen by the crowd. If the army sees me, they'll what? Arrest me? Kill me? But if the crowd see me with supplies, they'll mob me and take everything I have.

Gnawing her lip, she tried to decide if it was better to just grab a couple of bottles and make a run for it. It would be easier to conceal and transport, but it wouldn't last the four of them long. She picked up two large cases of bottled water and struggled to stand with it. She tested carrying three cases, but it was heavier than she thought, and the cases stood taller than her head. *Two cases it is.*

Tiptoeing back to the door she had entered from; Sharon wore a small smile for the first time in days. In her excitement, it would've been easy to sprint through the doorway, but the sound of a shotgun made her freeze. Sharon turned around slowly and saw an old woman with sweaty gray hair pulled back in a loose ponytail, pointing a black and brown pump shotgun at her.

"Put it down, lady," the old woman growled. She accented the word *lady* as if it was an insult. She said it in such a nasty tone that Sharon found herself more annoyed by her voice than having a shotgun pointed at her. The woman had a heavy build that was hugged by a too small t-shirt with a picture of a wolf on the front.

"Okay," Sharon said carefully as if her voice was tiptoeing

over a minefield. She set the water down on the floor in front of her and stood back up just as slowly.

"If you move before the soldiers get back in here, I will shoot a hole in you, I promise you that," the woman said with narrowed eyes that made Sharon believe she would actually do it.

"Okay, but just wait," Sharon held up her open hands as non-threateningly as possible. "Just wait... I'm not trying to rob you or steal or–"

"Looks exactly like that's what you're doin.'"

"I know, I know. I-I– I've never done anything like this before. I don't steal, I don't sneak into places. I go to church," Sharon said, wondering if the woman could tell she was lying. It's true it had been a long time since she'd stolen anything, but her adolescent years were filled with instances of shoplifting and stealing from the church's donation bin. In fact, the last time Sharon was in church, she had most likely been a teenager and she had probably just stolen from the collection tray. But for some reason, when trying to sell yourself as a good person to a stranger, church was the first thing that came to her mind.

"My son and daughter are eight and ten years old and are outside starving and haven't had a thing to drink in days. No one is selling us anything and the– the army's not giving us anything. Not even water for my eight-year-old son, Charlie" Sharon felt a hook in his name that almost pulled tears from her. She quickly stifled the tears out of habit, but then regretted doing so. *If there ever was a time to cry...*

The woman continued to listen though her face was hard as stone, but Sharon noticed the muzzle of the shotgun had lowered a bit and took that as a good sign.

"I'm not trying to take much, but please, please God, please," Sharon begged as best as she could manage in a whisper. "Let me take something back to my children. Please. Just a couple bottles of water."

"You know what?" the old lady said after a short pause. "We had a single mother came in here last week, before the army got here. Power was out then, too. She cried about her two babies in the car and just needn' some food. My husband tried to get help to her, told her we closed, but would get her directions to the town supermarket, which ain't far. Then while George was writing them directions down and getn' her kids snacks, her boyfriend hit 'em in the back of the head with a baseball bat. They took the till and twenty cartons of cigarettes." the woman kept the shotgun pointed at Sharon. "Tommy, over at the oil change cross the street said he saw the pair fly off in their car. No kids in sight," she said.

Sharon's hands shook. "Ma'am, I promise you. Right outside–"

"Help! In here!" the old woman shouted. "I got a burglar. Help!"

Sharon could hear the movement outside the store front. She ducked and sprinted behind a shelf and heard the loud *boom* of the shotgun followed by the exploding display glass behind her. She didn't know if she had been shot but her legs still worked so she kept moving toward the back door. She heard the rack of the shotgun and boots run inside the store behind her. She ran so fast that when she hit the turn in the storage room, she had to push off a wall to keep from face planting into it.

I'm not shot. I'm not shot, Sharon finally realized.

Down the narrow hallway and past the loading bay for the beer cave, she ran out the open backdoor and was immediately lunged upon. The set of arms were long and lanky but strong as they pinned her down to the hot asphalt of the parking lot.

"Give me– give me your hands!" the soldier yelled as he

grabbed for her wrists. Another soldier stood over both of them with the muzzle of his rifle inches from Sharon's cheek. Sharon's mind went black as she could think of nothing else but Annabelle's bedroom. The soldier held her wrists down on the pavement and she could smell the body odor of the man from last night. Other soldiers arrived and helped rip the backpack off her shoulders. She remembered how naked she felt last night laying in her daughter's bed. The feel of his sweat-soaked shirt pressed to her face.

They tried to pull her hands behind her back. Sharon twisted sharply. She swung her elbow blindly and surprised the first soldier as she connected flush with the young man's jaw. The boy fell unconscious to the pavement beside her and Sharon's eyes opened wide as if she had just awoken from a nightmare. The men in army uniforms tried to grab her as she struggled to get up, crab-walking backwards. It was the one female soldier who stabbed the butt of her rifle down on Sharon's mouth, hard enough to make her lose feeling in her face.

"Fucking handcuff her already!" she heard the echo of the woman's voice. The next thing Sharon remembered was licking the blood from her lower lip and the stinging pain that throbbed from her jawline. Her eyes blinked as she regained her awareness, and her feet were hovering over long untrimmed grass, soldiers on either side of her.

Where are we going?

"Get them back!" the same woman's voice bellowed behind her. Sharon saw the crowd of thousands pressed against another, edging closer to the imaginary boundary for the town. She looked forward and saw she was being brought to a police patrol car and it all came back to her then. She started to struggle against the grip of the soldiers. *What have I done? Oh, God, what have I done!*

"Wait, wait," Sharon said in a panic. "I'm sorry I didn't mean to hit him I– my kids didn't have water. I just tried to get some for–" they started pushing her down inside the back door of the patrol car, its seats covered in plastic. Fear took a hold of her.

David and the kids!

"Wait! Please! My kids are here. I'm not a criminal. I can go. I can just go, please don't!" She stiffened so they couldn't sit her down. "David! David!" tears streamed down her face now as she looked desperately in the crowd for her family but couldn't find them. "David!" she screamed, before being violently shoved inside the car and the door was slammed shut.

"Get off me, bitch!" a woman she had landed on, bucked her shoulders. Sharon strained against the zip ties on her wrists and righted herself beside the younger woman. It was the girl with the black-rimmed glasses from before. The troublemaker that they had hauled away out of the crowd. Sharon ignored the girl as she spat at her own window and cursed at the soldiers as they walked by.

"No no no no no no..." Sharon whispered to herself between sniffles. Her eyes darted over the crowd out the back window, but she couldn't locate the faces of her family. "I'm sorry, I'm so sorry."

Two sheriff deputies, one bigger than the other, sat down in the front of the patrol car. The younger deputy in the driver's seat sighed, turning the car on.

"Fucking pigs!" the woman shouted.

Sharon pressed her face up to the plastic divider between the front and back seats. "Sir. Sirs. Okay I-I'm sorry. I didn't mean–"

"Now hold on, miss," the older deputy said in his drawn Tennessee accent. "We'll be right with you."

Sharon caught her breath and nodded. The young deputy

put the vehicle in gear. "We are taking them back to the station then?"

"They emptied our cell this mornin'," the older, rounder deputy shook his head.

"Good, it needed it. Where then?"

"A sergeant said they got a bus over at Charlotte Ave and 22nd Street."

"A bus?" the deputy started to drive away. "The heck they goin' with all these prisoners?"

Gunshots rang out behind them and Sharon turned to see several people in the crowd fall to the ground and the rest scatter backward.

"Jesus Mary 'en Joseph!" the young officer hollered as he looked behind him at the interstate. "I think they just shot into the crowd."

"The way those animals were acting, it was bound to happen," the old deputy said looking in his sideview mirror. Sharon couldn't think of what to say but scanned the faces in the crowd. A tall man stood up from his knees on the left side of the crowd. It was David, it had to be. His hair and shirt match, but they were too far away now, and Sharon couldn't see the kids.

The girl on Sharon's side kicked at the divider. "Call us animals? Fuck you!"

"Stop, stop the car!" Sharon yelled as the patrol car lurched forward, but her voice was drowned out by the screaming curses of the girl beside her. "Please! My kids are back there."

The deputies said nothing. Sharon couldn't think of anything she wanted more than to see her children's faces one more time. "Please, somebody listen– please, just...help me..." Sharon cried to no one.

TWENTY-THREE

Derrick Hart
GA–TN Border

"What's your father's name?" Derrick asked.

"Adam– Adam Westfield. He's a researcher with Richter & Allen Pharmaceuticals," Eric said.

Derrick looked at Alyssa beside him, "What's his date of birth?"

"1/8/68," Alyssa closed her eyes to remember.

"Jessica," Derrick looked at the two girls who admired and twisted their Greenband bracelets. "Where do you guys live?"

"M-m-m-m-miami, Florida." Jessica stuttered.

"Good... good," Derrick turned and locked eyes with Brandon in the rearview mirror.

Brandon shook his head, unconvinced. "We're all going to fucking die."

"Shut up, Brandon," Derrick snapped. "This was your freaking plan."

"Well, it sounded a lot better in theory," Brandon mumbled as he took a turn onto MacFarland Ave.

"Who is Adam Westfield?" Alyssa asked.

"He is a manager or researcher with Richter & Allen Pharmaceuticals," Derrick said.

"That's the Pharmaceutical company they think caused all this?" Eric asked. "Then why would they let him– or us through?"

"Early in the outbreak," Derrick continued. "Just when they were rolling out the Greenbands, me and a few other SWAT guys were to supply logistical support to some Navy Seals who were extracting Westfield, but they never made it out of Florida. I looked him up later. He was among the first on the list of Greenbands after politicians. He should be an unknown on their list. Not confirmed dead and not confirmed in custody and safe."

"I still think there are too many holes in that story," Alyssa said. "We should stick with the CDC story."

"Jesus Christ..." Brandon groaned.

"What if they ask us about our mom, our address? What if these bracelets are blank and they make us fill it with our info and all four of us have different stories?" Alyssa argued.

"Look up there," Eric pointed to the right. "There."

The outpost was on a side road between a gas station building and a grocery store. There were fifty soldiers behind concrete barriers that Brandon had to drive zigzag through to get to the checkpoint.

"It's too late to change it, Alyssa," Derrick whispered. "Don't mention CDC. All you have to say– all any of you say is, 'my dad is Adam Westfield, he's a researcher for Richter & Allen Pharmaceuticals. That's all."

Derrick looked over at Alyssa who sighed with a defiant look in her eyes but nodded in agreement. Sentries were on the roof of the two buildings that overlooked the road, but they didn't seem particularly interested in their Humvee. Their rifles were trained on the civilian masses as they walked by towards the border. A Corporal came out from behind the concrete barriers to Brandon's side of the vehicle as they slowed at the checkpoint.

"Where you coming from, Sarge?" the Corporal said, his voice barely audible through the hazmat gas mask. Every soldier wore a military chemical suit with a gas mask that hid their faces. Duct tape was wrapped around their wrist and ankles. No skin showed on their person. Derrick couldn't imagine how miserable the soldiers must have been considering the temperature was nearing ninety.

"Atlanta FOB. Got four Greenbands heading to Louisville for evac," Brandon thumbed at the boy sitting next to him. The Corporal looked past Brandon at Eric and nodded. Derrick sat frozen, listening for more questions and unfriendly commands, or any sign that this charade was falling apart. The Corporal surveyed the others in the back, seeing each of their Greenbands.

"No chem suit?" he asked.

"We left the hot zone in a rush, left them behind in Atlanta..."

"The entire south is the hot zone now, Sarge."

Soldiers circled the Humvee looking in the windows and used an extendable mirror to look at the undercarriage.

When Brandon didn't respond, the Corporal sighed and let them through. "Roads blocked up that way. We stopped using the main gate days ago. Too many civilians." the Corporal nodded down McFarland Ave, then thumbed behind him. "Follow this Chickam road for a few miles; it'll get you to the sally port gate."

"Copy," Brandon said, putting the vehicle into gear. Two

other soldiers moved a long concertina wire barrier to the side and Brandon slowly drove past them.

Derrick set his rifle down behind him casually but kept the safety off and made sure the sling was to the side where it wouldn't get in the way if he had to shoulder the weapon quickly. But Derrick knew if he had to use the rifle, he would likely be already filled with holes before he even got on sights.

"Oh my god, oh my god..." Eric said to himself as they drove up the road.

"Hey, Eric?" Brandon asked calmly. "Can you do me a favor and shut the fuck up now?"

Alyssa looked at Brandon, "Don't fucking talk to him like that."

Air Force jets roared overhead, leaving a long chem trail behind them and rattling the Humvee as they drove down Chickamauga Ave, a two-lane road with thick woods on either side.

"I can't do this. I can't do this!" Eric panicked. "I can't–why do I have to be up front?"

"Eric!" Alyssa snapped. "Shut the fuck up! All you have to do is sit there and be quiet."

Brandon eyed Alyssa as if to ask, *why can you say that but I can't?* He hesitated before adding, "And give me the orange bag when I ask for it."

"*If* he asks for it," Derrick corrected his best friend. Brandon responded to Derrick's optimism with a shake of his head.

The plan was as simple as it could be, which is why Derrick thought it might actually work. Locke protocol shut the Tennessee border to all personnel including soldiers not already there, but everyone knew Greenbands were getting special treatment. These highly rare bracelets were put on the select few meant for survival in government bunkers. Derrick had seen them on the Vice President's daughter that even allowed her to basically skip the three-day quarantine and decontamination procedures, which was unheard of. Brandon stumbling across a box of the bracelets was like finding winning lottery tickets; they couldn't throw away this opportunity.

The problem was each of the bracelets had etched-in barcodes that were supposed to correspond to the wearers. Derrick had seen the barcodes scanned on Yellowbanded individuals. On the tablet screens, a picture of the bracelet owner appeared as did all the identifying information for them. Height, weight, family, social security number...

Brandon didn't know if these Greenband bracelets had other people's information programmed on them. Maybe they were each blank of information or maybe they were pre-filled out with specific civilians destined to be saved. If they were pre-programed, they would probably be accused of stealing the Greenbands and shot on sight after the first one was scanned.

Brandon guessed, and Derrick agreed, that the bracelets were probably blank. They were meant to be programmed on a case-by-case basis. If that was true, they had a chance. Besides, Brandon and Derrick both admitted that almost no one scanned the Greenband bracelets. Soldiers just took them at face value because they were so hard to come by.

Please, God. Let this work.

They drove for a mile down the street slowly. The road was lined with concrete barriers and soldiers standing guard. To their left, between the buildings, Derrick saw tens of thousands of people packed together as they jostled to get through the massive crowd. Hundreds stood on cars and hopped from one to another trying to get closer to the border. A tall steel reinforced fence with soldiers standing guard kept stragglers from entering Chickamauga Ave. Derrick looked at the time. *11:52am.*

"Everyone just stay cool and remember the plan," Derrick said. They drove around a bend in the road and saw a sally port in a large fifteen-foot fence. Two Humvees sat on both sides of the gate with soldiers manning railgun turrets whose barrels tracked their approach. Derrick felt a cold stillness of fear clutch his insides as he imagined the damage those turrets could do to their bodies.

"Fuck!" Brandon cursed.

"What?" Alyssa sat straight.

"There's no civilians at this gate, fucking not one."

"We're–" Derrick started.

"Derrick, if our Greenbands don't work, our backup plan relies on civilians–"

"Just be cool, Bran," but Derrick felt the panic racing through his heart. "We're committed now."

At the sight of them approaching, soldiers fanned out from the checkpoint and made a perimeter. Derrick felt a jittery, panic boiling in his stomach when he saw the line of rifles pointed in their direction. The world he was trained in, anyone who leveled a gun at him was fired upon, immediately. There was no negotiating or talking when someone pointed a gun at a police officer, that happened before they took aim.

Regret and second thoughts filled his mind. *Maybe we should have found a building to hide in Georgia. If we died in a few days, that's still living a few days more than today. Or trying to cross the border somewhere else. Sneaking across? At least if we died by a hellfire missile, I wouldn't see it coming...*

When they pulled up to the gate, a soldier approached Brandon's door. Derrick imagined a suspicious look on the soldier's face under the visor of his gas mask. He opened the rear passenger door and inspected everyone's Greenband visually. Then, one by one, he shined a flashlight in each person's face, instructing them to open their eyes wide. He did the same with Brandon and Eric while other soldiers investigated the undercarriage and trunk, again. Derrick felt streams of sweat pour down the back of his neck when one of the soldiers did a double take at Derrick's SWAT uniform, obviously different from the military uniforms. Derrick waited for bullets to start chewing him to bits at any moment.

Brandon and Derrick had concocted a story that mirrored the truth close enough to spin to anyone that interrogated them. Derrick assisted in escorting a supply convoy from Birmingham to Atlanta for pickup. Once there, Atlanta couldn't spare any soldiers for an unexpected Greenband escort. Under the supervision of Sergeant Armstrong, Derrick was selected to bring the Greenbands to Louisville. *Only now it sounds completely made up.*

The moment seemed to hang in the air forever before it passed with a wave of the soldier's hand as he backed away and shut Derrick's door. He watched a soldier inside the gated area go to a small metal box and press a large green button. The gate rumbled and buzzed as its motor roared and the gate opened, retracting to the right. Derrick noted there was another silver box with a green button on the inside of the fence, as well.

"You see it, Derrick," Brandon mumbled under his breath.

"I see it," Derrick said.

"Silver box. Green button," Brandon reiterated. Derrick exhaled a small sigh of relief as they pulled past the second checkpoint but knew this was when the real test began.

The border was a fifteen-foot fence lined with spiraling razor wires along the top. Large, armored tanks stood guard outside and a busy swarm of soldiers moved on the other side of the fence. They drove slowly past the first fence to find themselves caged by another fence thirty yards ahead that ran parallel to the first. Brandon was directed to drive down a winding path in between the two fences. The army had cut trees down and cleared part of the woods for their border. The 'lane' they drove in was marked with white spray paint on the grass and muddy tire tracks. Soldiers jogged in both directions in their chem suits while civilian employees stood out as they wore traditional orange hazmat suits.

Brandon was directed to turn and stop at a large open area surrounded by white trailers on either side. In front of them, just beyond the steel reinforced fence, was Tennessee. And directly behind them were twenty or thirty thousand civilians screaming and pushing to get through the main gate on MacFarland Ave. Derrick felt as though he sat in the lion's den as he was enclosed by a dozen army soldiers. The chain link fence rattled harshly behind Derrick. Women screamed for safe passage through, while a man cursed the soldiers for doing nothing.

"No NBC suits?" a female Lieutenant said, approaching Brandon's rolled down window. Her eyes locked on the clipboard she scribbled on. The army officers still wore hazmat suits inside the fenced-in path, but their masks were different. Their faces were visible under a clear glass shield and appeared much more comfortable.

"No, ma'am," Brandon replied.

"ID?"

Brandon produced his army credentials from a breast pocket and the Lieutenant continued her questioning without looking up from her scribbling on the clipboard. "Anyone infected or possible exposures?"

"No, ma'am."

"Been in contact with or within fifty yards of infected?"

There was a rigidness that Derrick felt in the air. Eric didn't move. He just stared forward in his seat. A tremble was sent through Jessica's body as she turned at every noise around the vehicle.

"No, ma'am."

Derrick slowly looked over his shoulder as casually as he could manage and saw the thousands of people pressed against the reinforced gate. A few yards behind their vehicle on their side of the fence was a small silver box like the control box that opened the sally port gate to let them in. This one though had a single piece of duct tape that held the silver box closed so as not to accidentally lift and press the green button.

"Your Greenbands, four of them? Where are they going?"

"Command just said they were expecting them in Louisville ASAP," Brandon shrugged.

"Why are they Greenbands?" she asked, looking in the back of the Humvee. Without waiting for a response from Brandon, the Lieutenant pointed at Alyssa. "You, how did you get your Greenband?"

"Me? ...Oh, I don't know," Alyssa shrugged with a high-pitched voice.

"You don't know?" the Lt. pressed. Derrick immediately felt his gut twist. All the blood in his body surged to his face and adrenaline spiked at her deviation from their agreed upon lie.

Alyssa continued, "this doctor at this CDC tent hospital thing put it on us and said there was something special about our blood or something." Alyssa's voice was airy in a way that Derrick had never heard before. It made her sound more clueless the longer she spoke, which is why she probably kept talking. "Like, I didn't even know my blood type, but I guess it was a special kind–"

"Our, you said. They're your family?" the Lieutenant said pointing at Zoe and Jessica. Derrick sat frozen staring at the back of Brandon's head. They were completely reliant on Alyssa's tale as she spun it. Both waited for the sign to come for them to start shooting.

"Um– yes– I mean no or– Sorry, I'm new to the military and stuff," Alyssa giggled as she spoke. Derrick could see the annoyance building in the Lieutenant's eyes as her face shield fogged in front of her mouth. Alyssa continued. "That's my little brother up front, his name's Eric. These two girls here, they're not my family, but the doctors said they had good blood too, I guess... ma'am," Alyssa bounced as she shrugged.

"And what about you, back there? You family, too?" She eyed Derrick over her clipboard.

Derrick shook his head. "No ma'am. SWAT Officer Derrick Hart, assigned to assist Sgt. Armstrong with the escort mission."

The officer gave Derrick a hard stare then pulled back to look at Brandon who only gave a nod confirming Derrick's story. She gestured to someone by the gate and circled something on her clipboard.

"You all will complete a preliminary ninety-minute decontamination program on-site, then you all will be transported to an offsite quarantine," the Lieutenant said. Derrick did his best not to show the relief he felt seep through his body. Alyssa's hand slid a few inches to the side to touch Derrick's hand and give it a squeeze of restrained excitement.

"Once scanned in," the Lieutenant continued, "you're going to pull the Humvee around the back of this trailer. This vehicle along with your clothes and weapons all have to be decon'd and sterilized..."

A soldier surprised Derrick when he opened his passenger side door. Derrick let out a shallow breath as he calmed himself. *Relax. Everything is going to plan.*

"Your wrist," the soldier said. He was older sounding with a harshness in his eyes. Derrick could see a tablet in his hand. "Name and date of birth?"

"Derrick Hart. 5/16/95." Derrick held his arm up, and the

soldier turned his Greenband around to get an angle on his barcode. Still listening to instructions by the Lieutenant, Brandon stole a look back at Derrick.

Derrick turned back to watch the soldier's face as he scanned his bracelet. He paused, scrolling through his tablet device before furrowing his brow and scanning it again. Alyssa's fingers were clammy and clenched on his other forearm behind his back.

Derrick absorbed everyone's stress like a sponge. It twisted and knotted in his gut. He watched the soldier's face change when he scanned Derrick's bracelet a second time. The color left his skin and his jaw went rigid. The idiocy of hoping this plan would lead anywhere but here became perfectly clear to Derrick at that moment. Whatever lies Derrick held onto to spin upon interrogation slipped away when he saw the man's eyes raise to meet his.

The soldier's hand lowered to his rifle as he dropped the tablet. The white screen of the falling tablet was a blur of text except for the square profile picture of a much older bald man with a thick, gray beard, and glasses.

The soldier brought his rifle up as Derrick gave a warning, "Brandon..."

Plan B.

Derrick pulled his arm away from Alyssa's grasp and swiped down at the soldier's rifle with milliseconds to spare as the barrel exploded a burst of fire meant for Derrick's chest. The bullets rattled off the floorboards making the women behind him scream. Holding the barrel down, Derrick pulled the tanto blade from his chest rig and plunged the knife into the soldier's throat.

He withdrew the knife and plunged the blade above the soldier's clavicle again before the soldier's hand could reach for his neck. Blood spewed and soaked the front of the soldier's chem suit as his body went limp and fell into the Humvee as he tried to scream but could only push out a wheeze. His windpipe was punctured and the jugular severed. For the briefest of moments, the soldier's wide, begging eyes came into focus from beneath his hollow gas mask. His ragged breaths raked across Derrick's ear drums for an agonizing moment that refused to end.

What have I done?

And then the shooting started.

TWENTY-FOUR

Derrick Hart
GA–TN Border

Brandon's automatic gunfire thundered from the opposite side of the Humvee deafening Derrick's world. Everything suddenly moved in fast forward. Derrick drew his pistol from the drop holster on his thigh with the bled-out soldier sprawled across his lap. Derrick fired at the two soldiers that stood closest to him. The 9mm rounds his Glock fired couldn't penetrate the heavy body armor they wore so he aimed for their gas masks, using up half his magazine to drop them before the stunned sentries could shoulder their rifles.

"Bag! Bag! Bag! Eric, fucking bag!" Brandon shouted over his gunfire. Eric had dived to the floorboards of his seat.

Alyssa's hands fell from cupping her ears to reaching for the two smoke grenades stuffed in Derrick's backpack at her feet. She ripped the pins out, like Derrick had showed her, and tossed them out Derrick's door just as they had discussed.

Gunfire was returned at the Humvee as the soldiers began turning their attention from the border to the shooting.

Derrick didn't even bother to holster his side arm. There was no time. He tossed it to the seat behind him, shoved the limp body off his lap, and shouldered his rifle. Derrick stepped out into the open as the grenades bellowed smoke to conceal him. Brandon had gotten the jump on most of the sentries that overlooked their position. On the opposite side of the Humvee, Brandon's rifle fired hard bursts of bullets into every soldier in sight manning a turret.

Derrick held his breath and watched the red dot of his rifle optic bounce as he swept his rifle across the soldiers nearest him, fast walking as he fired, switching from target to target as bullets snapped and whizzed around him. Derrick felt a noticeable calm and focus while acquiring his targets. Like the last twenty-four hours of combat had been preparing him for this moment.

The gunfire was focused on Derrick–the loud, moving target, which gave Brandon time to pick his shots as he dropped the remaining shooters who manned the .50 caliber turrets. Derrick rammed into a small box that stood about waist high behind their Humvee. The pillows of smoke shrouded everything now, but not for long. He couldn't see the box, but he felt the duct tape on it and yanked it free. Bullets pelted the ground around him. A stab of pain punched the air from his lungs as Derrick felt two punches impact his back armor plate as he smacked his palm down on what he hoped was the green button.

Derrick didn't wait to see as he ran back for the Humvee. The roar of gunfire came from every direction now. By the time he felt the door of the Humvee, a bullet bit into his left thigh and another cut into his shoulder.

Reinforcements.

Derrick dove inside and slammed the door behind him. He was on top of Alyssa who laid on the floorboard as their armored vehicle thudded with bullets from all sides. Brandon snatched the orange drawstrings bag from Eric's hand and jerked the black paracord from the small opening at the top. With the door cracked open, Brandon flung the bag forward against the front gate ahead of them.

"Fuck!" Brandon slammed the door as the barrage of bullets pounded the Humvee violently. The windshield splintered and spat shards of glass into Brandon's face. The metal doors bent and bowed, and the glass cracked, chipped, and broke open.

Derrick heard screams, he didn't know whose, as bullets pierced the windows and ricocheted inside the vehicle. His eyes were focused on the bloody paracord Brandon tossed in the back and the dozen grenade pins tied along the rope that were no longer connected to grenades.

The explosion sent a shockwave that shook the Humvee violently. It tossed Derrick off of Alyssa and he landed on the seat behind him. The explosion from the grenades ignited the diesel filled water bottles stuffed in the same bag to create bright orange flames that flashed outside the windows. The attacking gunfire stopped. Derrick could hear nothing except an incessant ringing. He felt Brandon shifting into gear as he gassed the vehicle and rammed over what remained of the toppled and destroyed gate. The vehicle bounced and roared as it dragged on the concertina wire then jolted free into Tennessee.

"Help! No, no, someone– no, please–" Jessica screamed.

"Brandon! Oh my god, I'm shot– I think I'm shot!" Eric cried.

"Eric!" Alyssa yelled.

The world tumbled around Derrick as he slid on his back

from one side of the floorboard to the other with the violent turns of the Humvee. Derrick felt a sting in his shoulder when he hit the door; then saw a smear of blood when he rolled away from it.

Brandon jerked the steering wheel to the side and the vehicle skidded off road sending everyone tumbling to one side. With a loud thud, Derrick was launched in the air and landed hard on his butt like everyone else.

"Fuck!" Brandon cursed through a curtain of blood covering his face. "Can't see shit."

They were in Tennessee, but the terrain had become hilly and full of unexpected turns as they raced away from the border.

Derrick gnashed his teeth as he held his wounded shoulder. The vehicle accelerated over the bumpy grass and onto the paved road. Zoe was on the floorboard beside him with blood oozing from a wound in her stomach.

"It's okay, it's okay!" Alyssa said in a frenzy while holding Zoe by her arms. Jessica bled from a superficial cut on her forehead but clutched her little sister's wound instead of her own.

"Brandon, I'm shot– I'm shot, Brandon," Eric said again, clutching his thigh and writhing in the front seat. "Fuck. It hurts, Brandon. What do I do!?"

"Shut the fuck up, Eric! Everyone's shot!" Brandon snapped as he swiped blood from his brow with the back of his arm.

"Eric! Are you okay?" Alyssa asked.

"Move your hand– let me see. Move–" Brandon said, glancing over to his lap. The rearview mirror caught Brandon's eye. "Fuck. Derrick! You good? Come on, I need you, buddy. They're coming up behind us! Eric, you're fine– it's not bleeding much, kid. Pressure, keep pressu– Derrick!"

"Yeah... yeah," Derrick said, not entirely sure of his voice.

He had hit his head hard on the side of the Humvee and the world was moving slow. His mind felt stalled, stuck in neutral, revving to go but unable to start.

Derrick ripped open the collar of his shirt beneath his heavy vest and felt a small pool of blood. It was warm and slick. One of the bullets fired at him had gone over his heavy vest and penetrated into his collar near his shoulder. As best he knew, the injury was survivable. He could still move the arm despite intense pain.

"Fuck, Derrick!" Brandon shouted

"I'm– I'm here," Derrick shook the cobwebs from his mind and struggled to his knees. "I'm good."

"Did– Did it work?" Derrick struggled to sit upright. "Did the civilians make it through?" as he spoke, he tried to look out the back, but every window was tainted with blood, filled with a spider web of cracked glass, or caked with mud.

Plan B was a Hail Mary pass in its own right. They couldn't simply ram the gate and flee if the Greenbands failed. What would keep them from routing a predator drone or Apache helicopter from gunning them down? If you couldn't beat your opponent, then you have to take the fight out of them. Make them not want to attack you.

"We need to cause a total loss scenario," Brandon had said while they stood on the side of the road earlier that morning. "If one or five civilians make it through the border, they'll hunt them down and kill 'em. If a hundred or a thousand civilians get through, the Pentagon could consider this defensive position a total loss. They wouldn't waste air support on a lost cause."

"That makes sense," Derrick had agreed, perhaps lying to himself as much as the others. "They'll retract their resources to the next defensible point which could be hundreds of miles north of–"

"So, you guys want to *intentionally* let people, some of whom could be infected, north of the Tennessee border?" Alyssa had asked.

"Yeah, pretty much," Brandon had answered with a shrug.

"We want to give the civilians at the border a fair shot at survival. Same as us," Derrick rephrased. "They're fleeing the infected and the military bombings just like we are."

Alyssa had looked at Derrick and Brandon in disbelief. "And you're capable of killing a bunch of soldiers just doing their jobs to do that?"

Derrick hadn't responded this time, but Brandon had. "There are no soldiers anymore. There's no cops and robbers, civilians and military, men and women. None of that matters anymore. All that matters is there are people who want you dead and there are people who don't... and you don't want to be someone who wants me dead."

"She's dying, help her–" Jessica pleaded, clutching her kid sister. The Humvee bounced down a steep Tennessee hill, which Brandon sunk into rather than rolling the vehicle.

"I don't know if it worked," Brandon said. "But–"

Almost as if answering the question themselves, bullets hissed by their vehicle. A large caliber weapon roared behind them. It was gunfire like nothing Derrick had ever heard before.

"Drive, drive! Drive faster!" Alyssa yelled.

"Drive faster?" Brandon yelled as he angled back onto the road. "Like I'm choosing to go slow! Derrick, get up on that .50!"

Derrick balanced himself against the radio box between the front seats and stuck his head out the turret port hole in the roof. The wind chopped at his face as the sunlight cut into his vision. Past the tree line behind them, missiles from unseen planes strafed the clear sky. They impacted the ground miles behind them at the border, exploding reverberations through the ground.

It wasn't until Derrick was in position that he saw the tan Humvee that was pursuing them. The roads were isolated and empty except for the two Humvees, surrounded by thick woods that bent the road left then right. This was the only thing that was keeping them alive, as the Humvee that followed let loose a burst of gunfire every time the road straightened, and the gunner caught sight of them. Derrick ducked his head inside when a bullet skipped across the roof near his head.

"Fuck!" Derrick cursed. *This was not a part of the plan.* "This was not a part of the plan!"

"No shit!" Brandon cursed back.

Derrick stood again and gripped the gun tight as the g-force pulled on him with every sharp turn. He tried to swivel the turret that was locked in one position but it wouldn't budge. "Brandon! The fucking gun won't move!" Derrick shouted trying to be heard over the whipping wind.

Brandon cursed out loud, then reached to the side of the port hole where a rotary crank lever was located and pulled something up. Instantly, Derrick felt the swivel on the .50 caliber machine gun break loose. It was still sluggish to turn just by holding the weapon. There were two Humvees now in pursuit. The second was much farther back and couldn't fire as the first swerved in and out of its sights between them.

Derrick ducked his head behind the large piece of steel shield at the front of the turret as the first Humvee chugged bullets at him. They pinged and slammed into the shield and Derrick felt a vicious rattle in his grip.

"Shoot, motherfucker, shoot!" Bandon shouted from below. There were two handlebars at the back of the gun that Derrick gripped with both hands and his index fingers reached uselessly for a trigger.

Nothing. Fuck!

Derrick turned the gun to the side and looked for a trigger that wasn't there.

Nothing. I never fired a .50 cal! When would a cop use a fucking .50 cal machine gun?

"Fuck!" Derrick squatted down and looked under his arm. "It's not firing! Brandon, where's–"

A barrage of bullets chewed through the glass and ricocheted over Eric's head. The violent clatter of the enormous projectiles striking the armored metal stung Derrick's ears.

"No! Please, no! No! No!" Eric screamed as he balled himself up on the floor of the passenger seat.

"Shit!" Brandon swore. The car jerked in all directions. He slammed on the brakes then jolted forward in acceleration. "Son of a– Shoot them, fire at–"

"I can't. Where's the fucking trigger?" if his adrenaline wasn't so high, Derrick was sure he'd feel like an idiot for asking but he didn't care. He didn't want to die. He could already imagine the bullets obliterating his body if they struck him.

Brandon shouted the instructions, but Derrick could hardly hear between the barrage of gunfire behind him and the roar of the wind.

"What!?" Derrick yelled, kicking at Brandon.

"Thumbs! Thumbs! Thumbs! Fucking thumbs!" Brandon screamed as his head hunched behind the steering wheel, hiding from another burst of attacking gunfire.

Derrick raised up and gripped the machine gun again with both hands on the grips and his thumbs naturally found a flat pedal on the rear of the gun. He depressed the pedal with both thumbs and the gun jumped, recoiling from the shot of gunfire.

Derrick's eyes lit up and he felt the wind whip his face. He grunted and swiveled the barrel of the turret towards the pursuing Humvee. The machine gun chugged hard in

Derrick's grip as he depressed the pedal for several seconds. The attacking Humvee was close enough that Derrick saw the shock in the gunner's eyes when Derrick started firing at him.

The spray of bullets pounded the hood of the army vehicle. The barrel danced around, pounding bullets into the front and side of the pursuing Humvee. Derrick's ears rang as he struggled to keep the sights centered on the enemy gunner. Bullets pierced through the windows and thudded against the armor siding.

They returned fire and Derrick heard the snap of bullets torpedo by his ears. Watching the muzzle fire in his direction from the enemy weapon made Derrick cringe as he anticipated the burst of pain from a hit.

He instinctively lowered and gained a better grip as he aimed the muzzle toward the gunner. Releasing the trigger, he realized how hard the recoil was on the gun and began firing in shorter bursts. The gunner of the other Humvee tucked behind his shield. To account for the high speeds they traveled at, Derrick began leading the enemy Humvee with his barrel.

Derrick snarled as he fired in continuous short, hard bursts.

"Aahhh!" Bullets thudded all around him, but Derrick stayed behind the sights firing until one of the bullets he fired exploded the enemy gunner's chest. Blood misted over the back of the roof of the attacking Humvee and another round dislodged the gunner's arm at the shoulder.

Derrick took his time and lowered his barrel over the windshield of the pursuing Humvee. He saw another soldier climbing in the turret position. Derrick depressed the trigger letting loose a flood of .50 cal bullets that sprayed the hood and windshield of the vehicle. Most of the bullets probably missed the soldiers driving but it shattered the glass and sent projectiles bouncing around inside the cab. Brandon must have gotten a sense of Derrick's firing cadence because Derrick noticed his

Humvee straightening and idling, giving him the opportunity to aim. Gritting his teeth, Derrick fired a long burst of rounds, pelting the windshield to end the fight.

Either from the chaos created inside or because a bullet had struck the driver, the pursuing Humvee jerked and veered off-road to the left. The vehicle came to a sudden halt when it struck a wide stump of a tree and entered into a barrel roll. Derrick watched the soldier who was replacing the dead gunner launch forty yards into the thick woods

Derrick gasped, releasing a breath he didn't know he had been holding. He felt a smack on his calves. Celebration of his 'good hit' from Brandon, no doubt. Releasing his grip off the turret, he watched the distance grow between them and the mangled Humvee. But the second Humvee still approached, too far away to have a clean shot, yet. Every few hundred yards they'd take another turn and Derrick would lose sight of it. He took deep breaths trying to center himself and rest his arms before the next fight. They were on a straight path now and their pursuer wasn't far behind. Derrick mentally prepared for the second round of this onslaught.

However, he didn't have to. The other Humvee stopped abruptly and turned, making a U-turn. Derrick stared for several seconds looking for it to reappear in pursuit, but it never did. "Brandon," Derrick said in a crouch. "You see this? They just stopped."

"What?" Brandon said.

"There was a second Humvee chasing us," Derrick said. "They just turned back."

Brandon looked over his shoulder at Derrick and shared the same confused expression. They drove for another few seconds before Brandon slammed on the brake. Derrick nearly tumbled into the front as the girls in the back screamed.

"Shit," Brandon snapped. Brandon took a hard turn right into an open field and powered into a wide patch of tall grass.

"What– What!" Derrick yelled, holding his head.

Brandon hit the brakes again as the Humvee skidded to a dead stop in the dirt. He flung his door open. "Everyone out! Now! Run in opposite directions– go!"

"Brandon– wha–" Derrick shouted.

"Drone! That's why they pulled back!" Brandon screamed. "Predator drone!"

TWENTY-FIVE

Rachel Anderson
Louisville, Ky

Rachel sat with her head against the glass wall, defeated. She had spent most of the morning screaming and beating her fists sore on the glass. The box they had put her in was big enough to stand and sit cross legged in but that was it. She and her three secret service agents had each been shoved into their own glass *cube,* as Rachel heard one of the soldiers call them, and after several hours of waiting had been carted around to a semi-truck where they were loaded into the back as if they were food supplies heading out for delivery.

Colonel Fields and Major Benning had disappeared almost as soon as Rachel and the others had marched back outside onto the runway and forced to sit surrounded by thirty or more soldiers. The army had become their God–when to sit, where to move, when to stop–a sergeant wearing a full hazmat suit, had been guiding all their movements. That should have been the first of many clues that something had gone wrong. The ten soldiers who had previously guarded them had been swapped out for thirty soldiers in camo hazmat suits without an inch of skin showing.

By the time their cubes had arrived, Rachel had gone through every cuss word in her arsenal for the mute soldiers guarding them as well as for Sean who had tried to hush her one too many times. The cubes had clearly been designed by the CDC for easy transport of highly contagious and infectious patients. They had been driven around on the semi-truck for about half an hour before arriving at their destination.

There was a sudden sound of rushing air and Rachel's ears popped as she heard three beeps in succession from her cube. Rachel's cube had been carted into a larger CDC holding room. It was a ten-by-fifteen-foot glass cell, which shared a glass wall with another room that mirrored hers.

"Ms. Anderson? Your cube is unlocked. You can step outside now," Major Benning's voice came through a metallic speaker box that was built into the glass wall of her new home. Rachel stepped out of her small glass cell into her larger glass cell. It looked like a brightly lit hospital room with a single bed, medical monitors, and a couple of dressers.

"What is this?" Rachel asked.

On the other side of the large wall of glass, she saw Colonel Fields standing over Benning's shoulder. "These are our mobile BSL-4 quarantine cells, they're meant–"

"Why am I in here?" Rachel interrupted. "Why did I have a gun stuck in my face!"

Colonel Fields pressed Major Benning to the side. "It was unfortunate how the situation was handled, but this is the first major breach we have had in our security. We had to deal with it swiftly."

"Breach? How did we–"

"You skipped your mandatory quarantine period once crossing in from the hot zone, Ms. Anderson," Fields said incredulously. "You received improper decontamination..."

"What do you mean? We were scrubbed, hosed down, tested up and down–"

"You were given an abridged decontamination," Fields' voice boomed with annoyance. "One that is not certified by the CDC, WHO, or any infectious diseases specialist worth their salt. Which is why we are going to complete the *entire* decontamination process, again, just in case the White House deemed you worthy of skipping certain steps."

"Ma'am," Benning spoke up in his understanding tone. "You were supposed to be quarantined for seventy-two hours after crossing from the hot zone into the green zone. You and your men weren't quarantined for even an hour. Proper decontamination takes at least four hours..."

Rachel was realizing the implications of their words and what they meant for her. "I can't stay here for three days, I can't. Did you hear what happened in Birmingham? The infection is there, it's already spread into the city. I can't be here when–"

"The White House has already moved the green zone border to Tennessee," Benning said. "Trust me, you're safe here in Louisville. The military has this under control."

"Under control? If I had done the quarantine in Birmingham I'd be dead right now." Rachel snapped. "Does my father know about this?" she hated playing the *daddy* card but as she looked around her room and saw she had no control over anything in this sterile environment, she was strapped for options.

"Ms. Anderson," Fields sighed. "I assure you; the White House will know you are safe and cared for, but I will not allow anyone to compromise the safety of this base or this country.

Roll your eyes all you like, but these quarantine protocols exist for a reason. We are dealing with a virus that is more contagious than anything this planet has ever seen. A spontaneously occurring virus that is still evolving, for all we know. So, unless the President of the United States himself orders me to breach protocol, this is your home for the next seventy-two hours."

Fields stormed away from the speaker box and toward the door that had two soldiers standing sentry at it. Benning pointed to the dresser at the side of the room. "There are blankets and a change of clothes in there for you. I'll be back in an hour, and we'll get this decontamination process completed."

Lost in thought as she processed her new situation, Rachel only nodded.

How fast could the infection spread? It took ten days for it to get from Miami to Birmingham. Surely it couldn't make it to Louisville in three days.

The large doors the two sentries were guarding slid open, and Rachel saw three towering cubes being wheeled into the room. Allen, Chris, and finally Sean, all gave Rachel solemn expressions as they were carted into the BSL-4 room beside her own.

TWENTY-SIX

SHARON HILL
Undisclosed Location

"SIR," Sharon said as non-threateningly as she could. "Sir, I–"

"Shut the fuck up and keep moving," the soldier's voice boomed through his gas mask. He shoved her off the school bus into a parking lot. It must have been noon or nearing noon judging by how hot the sun felt on Sharon's skin. The small elementary school she stood outside of was located in the hills of eastern Kentucky. She had no idea where in Kentucky she was. According to the road signs she had been watching religiously throughout their drive, the next biggest city was Lexington, forty or so miles away.

"Get your fucking hands off me, you dickless fuck!" Tabitha shouted as she was pushed off the bus behind Sharon. Tabitha was a tough girl, defiant, and hostile towards authority from the moment she had been put into the back of the police car with Sharon at the town of Pioneer. Sharon and Tabitha had been driven to a pair of school buses quickly and loaded on board with several other 'prisoners.' Sharon had become a mess of emotions. The farther she had been driven from her children, the worse the pain she felt in her chest had gotten. Like a shard of broken glass had been twisted into her flesh until it had chewed into her heart. Dried snot and tears had crusted on her face as she had been dragged to her seat on the back half of the bus. They weren't meant to talk, but Sharon had overheard whispers from the men behind them as they were being driven. She had heard them say that they had been taken from Johnson City and Bowling Green.

It had been infuriating for Sharon to watch the miles tick by as the bus had taken her farther from her family. She had lost herself staring at the back of the brown bus seat cushion, at the faded penned in stick figures, and hearts drawn around kids' names. The farther they'd traveled, the more she had wondered if the hug she had given her children before leaving to get supplies would be their last hug from their mother.

Everything changed once they arrived at the elementary school. The ties that bound their wrists were cut loose, which might've been a good thing except the soldiers who received them were all wearing full camouflage hazmat protection equipment. The black bug eyes underneath their masks leered down at Sharon as she, along with the other prisoners, were shoved into two lines in the parking lot–the look the soldiers gave them was intimidating enough to briefly silence even Tabitha as they marched forward.

The elementary school was colorful and warm in its appearance. A large wooden banner near the front door had an oblong earth painted on it with stick figure children holding hands around it. The military had dissolved the school's hospitality with ease. In the corner of the parking lot was a pile of children's desks, chairs, and cubbies stacked ten feet high.

Barbed wire with razor blades on the wiring lined both sides of the front door creating a five-yard-wide alley. Choppers were landing and taking off constantly on a flat patch of the field behind the school. The entire school was encircled by a valley of hills with overgrown tall grass that swayed with the blowing wind. Flood lights were stationed at the four corners of the school with two soldiers manning large machine guns at each corner.

They filed into the alley of razor wires at a pace of a few steps every minute. Sharon saw large glass boxes on wheels being pushed out the back of a white CDC tent attached to the side of the school. Two people in hazmat suits pushed the glass cube with wet stained walls inside a side door.

Sharon read the large white sign nailed over the main entrance as she slouched underneath it.

DETAINEE RULES.

1. LISTEN AND FOLLOW COMMANDS OF ALL PERSONNEL

2. NO TALKING UNLESS SPOKEN TO

3. DO NOT TOUCH ANYONE ELSE

4. REPORT ALL CURRENT ILLNESSES AND PREVIOUS MEDICAL CONDITIONS TO INTAKE STAFF.

Sharon stepped into the double-door entry hallway. Soldiers lined the walls on either side. The only sounds were the patter of the procession of prisoners and the murmur of talking ahead. The two lines of prisoners made their way to a long stretch of tables, manned by what appeared to be doctors in more traditional yellow hazmat suits that Sharon had seen the CDC wearing on TV. Four stations total. Peering over the man who stood in front of her, Sharon saw the doctors drawing blood and filling out questionnaires on a laptop.

"Someone needs to explain what's going on to us," Tabitha shouted. "You can't treat us like ani–"

"Quiet!" a soldier stepped away from the wall and pointed his gun in her direction.

"Go head, shoot me for fucking talking! What is this Nazi America?" the soldier said nothing and neither did Tabitha. The silence hung in the air as the line moved forward until Sharon was up next. There were two soldiers standing behind each station. A third stood on the other side of the desk where the prisoners sat. The soldier nearest to Sharon went behind her and pressed on her shoulder to sit her down. She complied, keeping her chin high and was careful not to show her trembling hands, hiding them in her lap.

"What's your social security number, first and last name, and date of birth?" the yellow CDC suit asked. She was a female, but the mask she wore deepened her voice to an almost male-like quality.

Sharon hesitated for a moment then gave her identification information.

"Are you sick or injured?"

Sharon looked back at Tabitha; she was causing a scene refusing to go to the next available station.

"Ma'am," the doctor spoke louder. "Sick or injured?"

Her head throbbed where she was cut and her body ached all over, but she doubted if she answered *yes,* she would receive any treatment. "No," Sharon said. "Who are you?" she asked, glancing back at the soldier that stood over her shoulder.

The yellow suit sized her up, then grabbing her hand she looked at her fingers, finally returning to her laptop. "I'm Dr.

Ellis. When was the last time you had anything to eat or drink?"

"Couple days... What is this place?" Sharon asked.

"Are you allergic to any medications, have been diagnosed with any disease, or currently have any STDs?" Dr. Ellis persisted. The mention of STD stung Sharon's ears. It was like opening a door she had previously thought was locked.

Sharon cleared her throat. "No."

"Give me your arm," Dr. Ellis said, pushing her laptop to the side and setting a pre-prepped tray down between them. The tray had vials, swabs, and a blood drawing needle. Dr. Ellis tied Sharon's arm, swabbed the crook of her elbow in alcohol, and plunged the needle in, drawing several vials of blood.

"I'm not infected," Sharon said softly. When she received no reply from Dr. Ellis, she continued. "I'm from Knoxville and my family and I were trying to get to safety. I have two kids. My son's eight–"

Dr. Ellis looked up at her. "You'll be safe here," she filled the seventh vial of blood.

"Why do you need that? No, I'm not giving you my social; that's my personal information," Tabitha ignited beside Sharon. The soldier by her side had already shoved her back down into the seat twice.

"No, this isn't correct," Dr. Ellis said to an assistant wearing an orange hazmat suit behind the doctor. Sharon looked down and realized the needle and tie were off her arm. "We're doing compound series one-hundred right now. I don't want this." Dr. Ellis handed a plastic container with two capped syringes back to her assistant.

"It's from Washington," the assistant said and shrugged. "Said highest priority."

Dr. Ellis sighed and shook her head. She took out the syringes and grabbed hold of Sharon's wrist. Without a word she pulled her arm over the table and injected her in the meat of her shoulder. "Other arm." Dr. Ellis motioned for Sharon's right arm.

"What is it?" Sharon asked. Dr. Ellis sighed again as she stabbed an injection into Sharon's left arm. The injection burned as it went in and the sting seemed to last even after the needle was out of her arm.

"No, you're not taking my blood. I have rights; my blood is my property!" Tabitha screamed as she stood up. "I want my lawyer!" the girl began to walk away but was grabbed by a soldier for the third time. "Get off of me! I want my lawyer!" the girl smacked and pushed the soldier in his gas mask, struggling to get away.

The gunshot that rang out caused a ringing in Sharon's ear. Blood splattered across the floor and Tabitha's body collapsed lifelessly on the ground beside Sharon's feet with a bullet wound to the back of her skull. The soldier behind Sharon holstered his pistol. The prisoners waiting in lines cowered to the ground and retreated, while some yelled at the soldiers.

"What the fuck?"

"What did she do?"

"You can't do that!"

Shouts erupted from among the lines, but the soldiers lining the walls quieted them with their raised rifles. Slowly the disrupters were shoved back into terrified lines of silence.

Sharon was frozen. Her eyes locked with the young girl's now dead eyes staring up at her.

"I'm done with this one," Dr. Ellis said, throwing all of Sharon's blood and needles into a plastic container. "Dr. Schafer, take my place."

"Next! Come on, step around her," the Dr. Schafer said, gesturing at the dead girl, waving over the next person in line as if they hadn't just witnessed an execution.

"Let's go," a soldier said to Sharon. He grabbed her arm hard and lifted her from the seat. Sharon's knees quaked and her arms shook. *What the fuck is this place? What did she do? What is happening?*

"Wait, wait, I didn't do anything," Sharon cried. "Please no, don't!"

"Move!" the soldier dragged her into an adjoining classroom. Sharon screamed as her feet crinkled against the plastic covered floor before the door slam shut behind her.

TWENTY-SEVEN

Brandon Armstrong

Chattanooga, Tn

The base of the tall grass that choked Brandon on all sides was moist and sticky. He brushed his palm on the butt of his pants where he crouched, not wanting to know the source of the stickiness while in the Tennessee countryside. Nature's sounds hummed, rustled, and ticked around him.

As he ran fifty yards from their Humvee, he had seen movement in the grass ahead of him. Small animals, maybe foxes and prairie dogs, he hoped, darting out of his way as he stomped deep into the chest high weeds and bushes, fleeing for his life. He had separated himself from the others so if a hellfire missile did strike the car or one of them it wouldn't necessarily kill them all.

Hopefully, it bombs someone other than me, but if it's my time to go, take me before a damn snake or brown recluse does it first.

He had been in the marshes long enough that his breathing was finally beginning to normalize and the blood from the cuts on his forehead had stopped trickling down the rest of his face. Brandon looked overhead and listened. No explosions yet. No thudding propeller blades of an approaching Black Hawk or Apache Helicopter. In fact, it was getting to the point that the ticking rattle and rustling bushes surrounding him were becoming more worrisome. It was becoming increasingly difficult to convince himself it wasn't a snake lining up his ass cheek for a strike.

Just as Brandon went to stand, he heard the sound of an approaching engine. Several engines, but they weren't the heavy diesel engines like those of an Army MRAP or Humvee. Readying his rifle, Brandon peaked his head over the grass tips and saw a trail of vehicles speeding down the winding road. Each one nearly skidded off the road as they whipped around the bend. The cars were civilian and looked as though they were filled with families. Slowly, Brandon straightened as the last one drove out of sight.

"Bran? Brandon..." Derrick's voice called out.

"Yeah," he replied.

"You see that?"

"Yeah, guess there's no damn drone. I'm heading back to the car," he stomped through the weeds, back the way he came.

To his right, about thirty yards away, he saw Derrick's head appear above the grass, the others behind him. Jessica sprinted back to the Humvee ahead of the rest. Her little sister still lay in the vehicle, dead or dying. The civilian cars came from the Tennessee border just like they had, which meant more civilians must've busted through the perimeter.

"Oh my god, Zoe. Zoe!" Jessica cried over her sister's body.

"You got him?" Derrick asked Alyssa, who took over shouldering Eric's arm as he limped, clutching his wounded leg.

Derrick gently put a hand on Jessica's back and moved her to the side as he looked over Zoe. "Bran, you got that med bag? She's alive."

Jessica was already scrambling in the back of the vehicle looking for the bag they had used earlier. Brandon stood behind Derrick and looked over his shoulder at Zoe. Her skin was ghostly white and clammy. One of Derrick's palms pressed on her wound and the other clapped against her back as he held the entry and exit wounds. She was whimpering, barely awake. Brandon hadn't seen any kids wounded in his tours overseas; they were already dead by the time his unit arrived at the scene of an IED detention or execution. It was strange how quiet Zoe was being. Her teeth clenched and her eyes showed her slipping in and out of consciousness. *Tough young lady.*

"We need to get to a hospital," Alyssa said as she heaved her little brother up against the hood.

"Ahh, ahh, it hurts," Eric cried as he hopped on his good leg.

"I know, I– he's still bleeding. It won't stop–" Alyssa panted.

"Cause your tourniquet's not tight enough," Brandon said. He walked to the boy and undid the crude knot that had been hastily applied in the tall grass. Wrenching the windlass several more times, he ignored Eric's yelping and protests until the small drip of blood from Eric's wound ceased, and he properly velcro'd the tourniquet in place. Derrick and Jessica had packed Zoe's wound with gauze from the med-kit and were wrapping her waist with bandages that were becoming stained in blood as they pulled tight around her abdomen.

"She needs a hospital fast," Derrick said over his shoulder. Brandon assessed the wounds of each individual before saying something that was sure to ignite a fight. Everyone seemed to be bleeding from somewhere. Brandon had been shot in his left arm, but it was just a flesh wound, he was sure. Alyssa bled from her nose, Eric was shot in his thigh, Zoe was... *goddamn civilians... bleeding heart just had to rescue them.*

Assuming a drone didn't kill them in the next few minutes, the last thing they had was time. If the military wasn't hunting for them, the infected would be soon. Not to mention the hundreds of thousands of refugees that could be pouring across the border right now. They had to stay ahead; if they got too far surrounded by the masses, they'd be as good as dead. Brandon's eyes found the blood-soaked shoulder of Derrick.

"Hey, you hit?" Brandon stepped to Derrick's side and pulled him back from Zoe. The wound on Derrick's collar had drenched the sleeve of his left arm in blood. "Fuck, man, you're bleeding, a lot," Brandon said.

"Oh my god," Alyssa said when she saw the wound.

Derrick winced as he moved his arm. "Forgot about it till now. Doesn't hurt too bad."

A worry awoke inside Brandon like a jolt of adrenaline. He didn't know if Derrick had internal bleeding. Not knowing how many more gunfights were between here and Louisville, Brandon knew he wouldn't make it without Derrick by his side. "Shit, alright let's go; we'll see if there's a working hospital in the next town. Maybe rioting in Chattanooga hasn't destroyed everything, yet."

Alyssa and Brandon covered Derrick's wound with whatever gauze and wraps they had left.

"What about the army?" Eric asked. "Did it work? Are they still after us?"

Brandon grunted as his body screamed in pain when he attempted to sit in the driver's seat. "If we die in a ball fire in the next five minutes, that'll be the answer to your question."

Alyssa sat in the back, pressing into Derrick's wounded

collar when the realization seemed to strike her. "Does that mean we collapsed the border?"

Brandon looked at Derrick. Alyssa's question was left unanswered as the Humvee lurched from park and accelerated out of the tall grass.

It took ten minutes of driving through the suburbs to come upon any signs for a hospital. The drive through the quiet neighborhoods was strange. Kids who were playing basketball at the open courts of a park stopped when they saw the battered and damaged Humvee drive by. They passed restaurants with couples and families eating on outside patios and others leaving stores with bags filled with their purchases. A woman walking her obese poodle scowled at Brandon as he sped through a stop sign, causing her to stop in the crosswalk, though the poodle seemed happy for the rest.

"Are you kidding me?" Alyssa whispered incredulously to no one. The sight of normalcy was alien after the disaster they had experienced. Chattanooga looked as though it was in a bubble. Protected from the chaos in the south.

Nurses on their smoke break stood in the shade on the side of the hospital when they pulled into the parking lot. Staff gave their dilapidated Humvee confused stares as they walked inside the ER carrying their packed lunches.

Brandon jogged to the ER entrance as soon as he parked. When the motion activated doors opened, he immediately felt the kiss of the extra cool AC. The quiet waiting room had a handful of people spread throughout. "I need some help outside. Now!"

The two nurses behind the reception desk in the ER lobby stared in shock at Brandon as if his appearance was alien. He remembered the dried blood smeared across his face. Their eyes moved to the M4 rifle slung to his side. "Hey... gunshot wounds. Move. Now, you fucks!"

The two nurses finally got out of their reveries. One stuck her head through a door behind her and shouted something while the other quick stepped her way around the desk following Brandon outside to his nearly demolished Humvee. Not a single window remained intact and the doors on the passenger's side couldn't even open; they were dented so badly from the gunfire. Two Chattanooga police officers had pulled their patrol cars into the parking lot behind the Humvee and were now out and helping Zoe's fragile body out of the back. One held her arms and the other grabbed her feet.

"Eric, just stay seated," Alyssa comforted him. "Don't move your leg."

"It hurts so bad," Eric whined.

"How many are there?" one of the officers asked. He was skinny, with a smooth baby-like face. He looked like he couldn't grow a stubble even if he tried. The concern was palpable in his frantic movements.

"Hm?" Brandon's eyes widened when he realized the officer was talking to him. His thoughts were barely coherent. Brandon found himself getting lost more often as the lack of sleep and food took its toll on him.

"In the ambush, could you see how many there were? Or which way they went?" the officer asked with a southern twang in his voice.

"Uh, fifteen to twenty, I think. They came out of nowhere," Derrick interjected. He limped around the front of the Humvee gripping his shoulder. "The Sons of Liberty– those militia guys all over the news," Derrick answered for Brandon while giving him a knowing stare. "There was like twenty of them when they ambushed us, you think?"

Brandon caught the hint and nodded, "Something like that, yeah. Not sure which way they went."

"I-i-is she gonna be a-a-a-a-alright?" Jessica asked. The

nurses struggled to get around Jessica as the officers met them halfway with a wheelchair and sat Zoe's limp body in it.

"Let us take a look at her," one of the nurses said, pushing Jessica to the side. "Gunshot wound to the stomach. No exit wound."

The nurses pushed Zoe away hurriedly. The two officers helped walk Eric through the front doors right behind her.

An older nurse that the others seemed to respond to stepped up separating her staff from the wounded in the front lobby. "Wait, wait!" she looked at Brandon. "My name's Nurse Stevens, this is my ER." Nurse Stevens was a shorter woman with short black hair and some heft to her waistline. "Have any of you had *any* contact with anyone infected with Rhabdo-11? Did you get within twenty feet of any infected blood?"

Derrick stepped forward and shook his head. "No, none."

"Weren't even south of the border," Brandon lied more convincingly than Derrick.

Nurse Stevens gave them a hard skeptical glance before finally seeing something in Brandon's demeanor that convinced her to lower her arms and let loose the half dozen nurses that had gathered behind her. They swarmed Jessica and Eric.

"I'll be right behind you, Eric," Alyssa called after him. No one else seemed to notice Derrick was shot as well, but he, like Brandon, was in his own world. A trance of sorts. Alyssa was at his side, guiding him towards the ER. "I can get another wheelchair for you."

Derrick waved her words off as he limped on, with Brandon walking beside them. "The cops said the crazy militia guys have been ambushing police and military sites all over Kentucky and Tennessee," Derrick whispered to Brandon. "Told him they hit us while we were transporting Greenbands."

"Smart," Brandon murmured.

"I have my moments."

Alyssa looked back at Brandon. "Are we safe here?"

"Who knows," Brandon spoke honestly. Alyssa shot him a dirty look and Brandon just shrugged. "What? You want me to lie to you? We're great. Take a load off. I only thought about getting across the border. Can't fucking believe we made it this far."

"How much time do you think we got?" Derrick asked, his eyes caught the images on the TV in the corner of the room. Explosions of fireballs bursting up from the Atlanta skyline from amateur video recordings.

Brandon considered the question, half lost in a stupor. "If the border has fallen, the army won't be targeting us, not anymore. The civilians will be flooding across the Tennessee border, mostly on foot, I'd guess. Which means we've as much time as we want to waste."

Derrick nodded and stopped so he could lean against the front desk that was now empty. "We'll stay here long enough to get stabilized. Disinfect our wounds, clothes, get antibiotics... Then we'll keep moving."

Brandon nodded in agreement. A nurse came out of the double ER doors with a wheelchair. Derrick gave the chair a measured look then eyed Brandon "You want it?"

"Na, I'm not a little bitch," Brandon joked in a monotone voice.

Derrick slumped hard into the wheelchair making it creak and rattle as if it was about to crumble into pieces. "Good, cause I am."

"We always knew."

Brandon began to trail behind Alyssa as the nurse wheeled Derrick into the ER. To Brandon's surprise, the halls were bustling with doctors and nurses. Dozens of them. They switched rooms and radioed each other to ready imaging equipment. Jessica cried in exam room one as they wheeled her little sister away for a CT-scan. A group of four doctors stood outside of exam room three, talking, while Eric sat inside writhing in pain as a team of nurses examined him with another doctor.

One of the many nurses who trolled the hallways stopped and pointed at Brandon's face. "Sir, you want me to look at that?" she was a younger woman in her early twenties with long blond hair.

Brandon had nearly forgotten about the cuts on his forehead from the crushed windshield. They had stopped bleeding on the drive here. Now his face was stiff and didn't want to move when he lifted his eyebrows. He shook his head at the nurse. "Just give me a minute."

Retreating to the corner of a dead-end hallway, Brandon lost sight of the others as he put his head and arms against the wall, leaning forward, to rest his eyes. Almost immediately, Brandon started to collapse as he fell asleep standing. Being in such a calm environment after spending days in combat felt surreal. Being alive in Tennessee was not a reality Brandon actually thought would come to fruition. He had done his best to keep his doubts to himself, but after seeing the hordes of infected invading Atlanta, he had been sure they all were going to die. Brandon figured dying trying to get to his wife was better than dying being ripped apart by the rabid.

Now that he was north of the border, there was something more terrifying about all the possibilities before them.

We should be able to make it to Louisville to get Karen. Then what? Try for Maine? Keep going north to Canada? Where do we go? Where do we stop?

Brandon didn't like the direction his thoughts took. They were lies. False hope. The more he tried to deliberate upon the places to stay long term, the more he thought about the life they were running towards. A post-apocalyptic future like a scene out of the movies. With the rich and powerful cowering in bunkers while the few who survived extinction earned the right to live in fear. Existing in a world without electricity, running water, or a steady food supply, survivors would be on the move constantly to find food or to avoid the infected. *This is what I'm rushing towards...*

"I got some coffee for ya, sarge. Looks like you need it," the deputy said, handing him a warm Styrofoam cup. Brandon took it with an appreciative nod. The deputy was in his fifties and based on how he talked and carried himself, Brandon guessed he had enlisted at some point. *A Marine, maybe.* "It's a damn mess out there, I hear," the deputy continued. "I know you can't tell me about it– I know how it is. Just want to say I appreciate your service."

"Thanks," Brandon sipped his steaming black coffee and felt the tingling burn on his tongue.

"Truth be told I'm surprised to see y'all back here."

"Back?" Brandon raised an eyebrow.

"Yeah, the army unit that was here packed up and tore outta here like fifteen to twenty minutes ago," the deputy said, sipping his own coffee. "You didn't know about that?"

Brandon didn't like the deputy's question. It felt like he was still being interrogated. "I'm not stationed over here. Just came down from Louisville to pick these Greenbands up when we got hit."

The deputy nodded, pursing his lips. "You know, if y'all are coming back for your doctors?"

"I don't know shit except what they tell me," Brandon shrugged.

"I get it. This was a military collection point for those hurt in riots and militia attacks," the deputy said. "A good chunk of the doctors n' nurses from the surrounding hospitals– all them that signed those *honor bound* contracts were sent here, from what I'm told. The rest I heard were sent to

Louisville. That's why we got more doctors than we know what to do with."

Brandon shook his head. "I guess the doctors are yours to keep for now."

Alyssa had moved to Eric's room. He was the one making the most noise and obviously required the most attention. Brandon knew he had to get far away from him. The deputy had gone to the CT room to check on Zoe and offered to show Brandon the way. Brandon ignored him. He went down the hall checking every empty room until he saw Derrick lying in one near the ambulance bay. He was as unconscious as unconscious could be. His gun belt, rifle, and body armor were piled in the corner of the room and Brandon made a mental note to keep an eye on it. The doctor that stood above Derrick and checked his head wounds before examined the gunshot wound on his shoulder all without Derrick even flinching.

"He sedated?" Brandon asked.

The doctor half laughed, shaking her head. She was a middle-aged Indian woman with kind eyes and a round face. "He's just *out,*" she said. "Poor thing hasn't slept for days, I bet. You either, from the looks of it. Thanks for your service," the doctor gave him a small genuine smile that Brandon returned with a tilt of his head.

"Is he gonna be alright?" Brandon asked.

"We'll take him for a CT-scan after the child is done," the doctor said. "I'll know more then, but I don't see anything too worrisome, yet."

"Thanks."

"When I'm done with him, I'll take a look at your–"

"Oh my god! Oh my– is this real? Is this real!" a woman shouted down the hall. More shouts came from the nurse's station and Brandon entered combat mode instantly. His rifle half raised as he dropped his coffee to spill on the floor, he sprinted down the hallway shouldering past nurses. The crowd of people gathered around the TV hung on the wall behind the nurse's station.

A salt and pepper haired man stared into the camera as he reported the news. "-again, if you're just tuning in, we're receiving breaking news from the White House that the President of the United States is dead," the news broadcaster announced. "This is shocking information. Really, terribly sad. We're being told President Walker died in his sleep from a heart attack. White House staff says he did not suffer and was discovered by his wife at approximately 5:30 am eastern time."

"Jesus Mary n' Joseph..." one of the nurses whispered.

"Vice President Anderson was sworn in as President a short while ago from an undisclosed location and will be addressing the nation in just a minute. Wow, it's a um... it's a lot to take in, especially in these, um, tumultuous times. Let's bring in our panel here in D.C. while we wait for the new President Anderson's address. Sydney Davis, a professor in public policy from Harvard University, Vice Presid– well, now, President Anderson has been a much softer touch in the administration over the years than the former President Walker, how will this new President change the United States' approach in handling the Rhabdo-11 outbreak?"

"I think we should pray," a nurse suggested. The southern drawl in her voice was thicker than others.

"I agree," another nurse added.

"Come on let's hold hands."

The dozens of the nurses and doctors stepped back to form a circle and clasp hands around the desk. One of the nurses tried to start and said, "Dear Lord..." but was interrupted by a sound. Brandon couldn't stop himself. He stared at the TV and couldn't stop the chuckle that was growing inside him. He shook his head and covered his mouth, but it only made it worse. The circle of men and women broke as they stared in offended disbelief when Brandon's slap-happy chuckle became teary eyed laughter.

Brandon couldn't believe everyone was staring at him.

Why wasn't anyone else laughing, he wondered. *This was all too fucking funny.*

TWENTY-EIGHT

Sharon Hill
Undisclosed Location

Sharon glided across the floor in her cube. The glass box they had thrown her in had an overpowering smell of cleaning chemicals. It stung her throat more than it burned her nose. After a pair of soldiers forcefully stripped her of her clothes and jewelry, they shoved her naked body into the glass box and tossed her a set of loose-fitting purple scrubs. When the soldier latched the door shut, Sharon was already in the midst of a coughing fit, trying to exhale the bleached air that poisoned her lungs.

Panic set in as she thought she might choke to death on the toxic fumes. But a rush of cool air shot from the floorboards below as a suctioning sound made the glass walls bow. Sharon clapped her hands over her ears. The pressure built until there was a *pop* in her ear canal that was followed by comfort. The circulating air was a relief that allowed Sharon to breathe normally. It brought the stench of bleach down to a manageable level.

She was being carted around like a caged animal in a circus. Only instead of a metal cage it was a glass *cube.* Sharon remained still, kneeling in the corner as her cube led the line of ten or more cubes being pushed down the school hallway past the thin gray lockers that lined the walls on either side. The walls were covered with colorful but rudimentary drawings by children too young for this school–drawings of colonial houses and stick figure families. Bright colors and rainbows decorated the background. Sharon crossed her arms to cover herself as she was carted away. She had pulled her paper scrubs on, but they were too baggy for her comfort without undergarments.

The floor, the walls, and ceiling of where she was carted to were coated in a tunnel of opaque plastic sheets that blotted out whatever familiarity the school offered. Thin, yellow poles of white medical lights stood in the major hallway intersection and blinded Sharon when she was rolled by them. Orange and yellow suited workers scooted past. Panic thumped at Sharon's chest the more foreign this world appeared.

I was just at my house. Last night. I was with my family this morning. This is some mistake. This can't be happening.

At the end of the hall a soldier was carefully rolling a cube out of a dark room. The cube was barely narrow enough to pull through the doorway. Once out, he and four more soldiers pushed more down the hallway toward Sharon on a collision course.

"What the fuck, man?"

Sharon stopped abruptly with a light tree on her left and a short, wide hallway to her right at this T-intersection. The soldier that pushed Sharon's cube poked his head around the side and yelled at the ones approaching. "Hurry the fuck up!"

Sharon's escort shouted in the muffled tone from under his mask.

"Go fuck yourself, Nickels," the approaching soldier said as he turned his line of cubes down the wide hallway to Sharon's right. Sharon saw *her* soldier, Nickels, cross one foot behind the other tapping his boot toes on the taut plastic floor impatiently. It was such a casual move, Sharon thought Nickels could have been waiting in line at the grocery store.

"I would, but I'm tired from fuckin' your mom," Nickels shouted. Sharon watched the line of five cubes get pushed past her into what looked like a gymnasium. The individuals inside all pressed their palms and faces to the glass making desperate but muted pleas for help. Anxious nerves caused Sharon to bite her lower lip until blood was drawn.

They were rolled into the same classroom the others had been rolled out of. The desks and furniture had been removed from the classroom leaving only a series of cubes that had been haphazardly rolled into the room in no particular formation. Sharon cried silently on the floor. She had given up begging for help long ago. Help didn't exist anymore.

She could hear Nickel laughing down the hallway. "It's like Tetris. You fill a line, and the blocks disappear."

The plastic on the floor crinkled as he forced the classroom door shut with a thud and Sharon was left alone with two dozen other prisoners, each fighting an internal battle.

The windows had their shades drawn with plastic covering them. The little daylight that made it through the barriers created a gray, murky hue in the dark room.

Sharon looked down on the floor and saw a clear plastic baggie with two bottles of water and two dark red apples inside. Her stomach was stressed into knots of uncertainty, so she left the apples and cracked open one of the water bottles. In all the chaos, she had forgotten how thirsty she was. She gulped down most of the bottle and released an audible sigh of momentary physical relief. Her throat was so dry it felt as though it absorbed all the water, leaving none of it to reach her stomach, despite her wet belch when she finished her drink.

"No shit. They forget to turn yours off, too?" a voice from an unknown direction spoke.

Sharon looked about at the many shadowed faces that stared at her, unsure of who had spoken. "What? Can you hear me?"

A balding man with glasses in the center of the room stood up and looked her way when she spoke; another figure near the wall waved her hand. "Yeah, I can hear ya. Hey, over here."

The woman by the wall looked to be in her twenties. In the darkness all Sharon could make out was her outline, which gave her an athletic look. "These cubes are airtight. They got their own air systems, speakers, and everything. Someone forgot to mute our speakers, I guess," she said.

"What is this place? Where are we?" Sharon asked.

"I don't know. North Kentucky, maybe," the woman said. "I was in f–"

"Hey!" the bald man shouted. The speaker in his cube crackled from the sudden burst of noise. "They tell you why we're here? What they're going to do to us?"

Sharon shook her head then realized he probably couldn't see her through the other cubes. "No, no, nothing. They wouldn't even talk to me. They just put me on a school bus and brought me here. They took my blood and– and–" the image of Tabitha's body going limp from the gunshot wound replayed in her mind but to her surprise she felt little emotion. She was numb to the violence

"Yeah, yeah..." the man growled. "I don't need your life fuckn' story. You coulda just said, 'no.'" He punched the glass wall and the sound reverberated like plastic being bent.

"Don't mind him," the woman said. "He's just naturally a dick. Trust me, I've had more than enough time to find out."

"Fuck off," the man grouched.

"What's your name?" the woman asked.

"Sharon– how long have you guys been in here?" Sharon held her breath for the answer, feeling a strange, illogical worry in her chest, expecting the answer to be in months or years. Her hands flattened against the glass, and she wondered if the rest of her life would be locked away in here for trying to steal water and pretzels.

"Sharon. Sharon..." the woman tasted her name on her tongue looking around the room. "You look too young to be a Sharon. Too nice sounding, too." she waited as if Sharon was going to respond, but Sharon wasn't in the mood for banter. "Carl, when you say you got put in here?"

Carl was silent, pouting in the corner on his haunches, but eventually said, "Last night."

"I made it here early this morning before daybreak, but our bus took forever coming from Charlotte," the woman said leaning against the glass.

Sharon sighed, relieved it had only been a few hours.

A few hours was good. My kids would be safe for a few more hours, she thought.

"So, what'd you do to get in here?" the woman asked. The question seemed so surreal to Sharon. Like she was sharing a prison cell with an inmate.

I'm not a criminal. I was trying to keep my fucking kids alive!

"I-I didn't do anything," Sharon said exasperated. "I tried to get food and water for my kids. How can that be wrong? How can I be in the fucking wrong for trying to keep my kids from starving!" at the very thought and mention of her children, Sharon felt the thread of what kept her together being pulled apart and tears filling her eyes. "What should have I done? What the fuck should I have done! Let my kids di–" Sharon couldn't finish her sentence, the word caught in her throat. With tears pouring down her face she slammed her palm into the walls of her cube, kicking the base of the glass again and again until her bare foot throbbed. Sharon hated crying in front of others.

"Well, sounds like you probably shouldn't have stolen food, now should ya?" Carl said with his back to her.

"Fuck you!" Sharon screamed and her words were answered with a low, annoying chuckle from Carl. It felt like a circle of hell she found herself in–ghostly gray bodies standing around her in the dark room, staring, judging, watching... No walls to hide behind, her pain, her emotions on display for all to enjoy.

"I told you he was an asshole."

Sharon's thoughts went down a spiral as she went over her final moments with her family over and over, again. The tears flowed continuously as she picked apart her life, dissecting her every failure as a mother. Carl randomly cussed to himself, but the woman remained silently slumped against the wall facing Sharon. Shadows cloaked her expression, but Sharon found her silence sobering. It gave her emotions a direction.

After several minutes passed, she finished the first bottle of water and took a few bites of an apple. It tasted old and slightly mushy but even with the off taste, the sugar cleared Sharon's mind and moved the low drumming headache she had since last night to the back of her head.

"What's your name?" Sharon asked the woman.

"Tonya," she said, clearing her throat.

"Do you know what they're doing with us here? This can't just be a prison."

"I don't know. Carl here thinks they're experimenting on us. Trying to perfect their infection for world domination."

"I didn't fucking say *world domination,* bitch," Carl snapped. "What do you know anyway? You're just a grunt. A coward grunt at that."

Tonya just snickered. "That's right. I forgot, I'm in on it. The world domination."

"I didn't say– god, fucking bitch!" Carl stomped his foot inside his cube like a child.

"Grunt?" Sharon raised an eyebrow. "You're in the army?"

"Corporal Tonya Meyers, U.S. Army."

Sharon was silent for a moment. She felt betrayed. It was a stupid thought, she knew. As if anything she knew was worth being spied upon. Sharon was much more suspicious of the comforting presence Tonya offered. "Don't worry, it doesn't look like I'm getting any special treatment here."

"Why are you here? What are you– what'd you do?"

"Not much different than all you guys," Tonya shrugged. "Carl tried to drive through a military blockade in Nashville and by some miracle didn't get filled full of holes. You tried to steal some food. Me? I tried to leave."

"Leave?"

"She's a deserter. A coward!" Carl stabbed her with his words, trying to wound her from afar.

"Now Carl, that's not nice," was all Tonya said back to him before turning to Sharon. "You been watching the news? You see the kind of shit show that's going on in all the major cities? Yeah, that ain't shit compared to what's going on in Charlotte right now. The day before I tried to run, 237 people were shot and killed–mostly by soldiers and cops. Not saying they're wrong or right, heat of the moment and all," Tonya sat with her knees to her chest as her head lulled against the glass.

"But the fucked up thing is there's no investigation or nothing." Tonya shook her head. "Guy robs a grocery store for food, tries starting a police station on fire, whatever, police show up and end up having to blast the guy, so what, it happens right? But no detectives came out after. No CSI bullshit. After each shooting, they had a dump truck come by and toss the bodies in the back and on to the next one. Can you believe that shit? A fucking dump truck."

"Was Charlotte where the infected were at?" Sharon asked.

"Na, you're thinking of Charleston. They're the ones getting messed up by rabids. But Charlotte was next. Right up the road from it, that's why things were extra fucked there."

Sharon imagined soldiers and police officers shooting rioters and then slinging the bodies into a garbage truck. It was like a black and white documentary of the death camps in World War II come to life. A month ago, it would've been an impossible thought. No one would have believed it if they'd heard the story. Not in the USA

"How'd you get caught?" Sharon asked.

Tonya laughed quietly to herself. "It was stupid. I'm an MP– Military Police, so we were securing the scenes until the fucking trucks arrived to collect the bodies. I had finally had enough of it and took a Humvee that was running outside. I didn't know it was Master Sergeant's or that he was watching the goddamn Humvee from across the street. He radioed others at the checkpoint I drove towards and they snatched me up. Guess I should be happy they didn't put a bullet in my head. Heard they're doing that, too, to deserters up near the front lines. Atlanta and Birmingham, what not."

Sharon finished her apple and rubbed her eyes with her sticky fingers. "I have to get out of here."

"Pff. You and me both," Tonya added.

"Will you two shut the fuck up! There's no getting out of here," Carl sniped. "Even if they aren't experimenting on us, you think the government would let us walk free after all we know?"

"What are you talking about?" Sharon crossed her arms. "I don't know anything, why wouldn't they let us go?"

"You know about this place, and you know the name of the school we're being held at and that the government is experimenting on prisoners against their will. Perfecting their biological weapon," Carl smacked the wall.

"We haven't– they're not– We don't know they're experimenting on anyone," Sharon said.

"Oh yeah? You sign any waivers before they gave you some shots? You get told what's in them? That's what this is right now. Time to cook. They're giving whatever they injected time to eat us from the inside out, and all these glass walls are so they can watch. That care package you're eating, you think it's cause they care about you? For viruses to spread they need live, hydrated hosts. That's all you are to them. Hosts for experiments."

Sharon looked down at her remaining apple and bottle of water and heard her stomach growl. She couldn't deny some of the facts. She had received injections in both her arms and seven vials of her blood had been taken, all without consent.

"He's not wrong, you know," Tonya added, her voice resigned and defeated. "Well, except for all the stupid shit he said."

"Richter & Allen Pharmaceuticals rolled out their goddamn vaccines two weeks before the outbreak, and then one of their office buildings explodes–"

"Yeah, that's the stupid shit I was talking about," Tonya continued. "They're experimenting on us, that's for sure. You don't use these *cubes* and hazmat suits just for housing prisoners. I've seen the jail cells back in Charlotte. They packed those fuckers in like sardines. But this? I bet it's for a cure or something, and not for Carl's conspiracy theory of a master race."

"You're the reason the government gets away with these black flag operations!" Carl shouted. "I look at facts and call it like I see it. Just look. The pharmaceutical companies are profiting like crazy, and congress is destroying the constitution bit by bit all thanks to this super charged rabies virus–" Carl said.

"How can I get out of here," Sharon said to herself more than the others, but it stopped their yelling all the same. Sharon zoned out. Thumbing the small bumps on her shoulder where the injection site was located.

"I wouldn't hold your breath," Tonya said. "And even if you did somehow make it out, you ain't built for this shit. I can tell that just from talkn' to you."

"What does that mean?" Sharon crossed her arms.

"Means you're a fucking pussy," Carl groaned. "Just like the rest of society nowadays. They're all pussies."

Tonya shrugged, "Well... yeah."

Sharon felt a flare of juvenile anger leap inside her as if she was in middle school getting challenged by the school bully during recess. *How am I a pussy? They don't even know me.*

Tonya must have cued in on Sharon's silence because she continued, "You're a mom. You probably live a cushy middle-class life like everyone else. Work in some bullshit office job and binge watch reality TV. It's no big deal, I do the same, really. Minus the kids. But you don't know the world out there, man. Yeah, you got a taste of it and that's what got you here. But you don't know pain, fear, you don't know what it's like to kill... shit, I don't even know that."

Sharon's mind snapped back to her rapist's eyes before she shot him. But this time the man's cries and entreaties didn't phase her. Sharon saw it but didn't fear the memory. The pain the man had caused her still plagued Sharon's body. She felt the wounds that covered her flesh ache with every movement. Imagining the two men's dead bodies rotting on the floor of her house in a congealed puddle of blood made Sharon clench her teeth and almost smile.

I'm alive and they're not. They will never hurt me, again. They will never hurt another woman because of me...

Like calloused skin, there was a toughness in her that wasn't there before. As right as Tonya was about her, Sharon knew she was just as wrong. *I am a killer.*

"...I don't think the government created this, but I don't think it matters anymore," Tonya was saying. "Cause this is it. Zombie apocalypse, nuclear winter, fucking government experiments... pick your way to die or the government sure will." Tonya punched one of her walls near where a blood smear had dried. "The world is over, just watch the news and you'll see. The only people who ain't going to die are the tough motherfuckers. People who aren't wallowing about the past."

Sharon looked down at her hands. Her fingernails were broken and dirt crusted. She rubbed her palms together and felt the combination of fine, coarse dirt with sticky spots of dried apple on her soft skin.

"All you need is a fucking gun to survive," Carl mumbled. "If I had my gun right now, I'd murder every asshole in them damn yellow suits."

"Na, a gun's not enough." Tonya said. "Every asshole in America's got a gun. Hillbillies and gangsters alike, you see them faring well? If you want to survive, you need skills. That's what I've been saying all morning; having a gun and following the laws of the past will get you killed. You need to let that go. You need to change, adapt, become a survivalist. Live off the land, like in the movies. That family you got? Forget 'em. They're gone. How can you help them if you can't help yourself."

"None of us can help ourselves, you dumb bitch," Carl smacked the glass wall again.

Sharon sat in the corner and stared at her hand, making a fist and opening it again. Slowly, without trying, her eyes inched closed, and she felt her breaths become long as the world went black.

"True," Tonya giggled with a darkness in her voice. "We're dead already... we just don't know it, yet."

TWENTY-NINE

Derrick Hart
Chattanooga, TN

Derrick's eyes twitched and cracked open. The film that layered his vision blurred the nurses and doctors that moved around him. The exhaustion that plagued his body was so intense he didn't feel a thing as they lifted his limbs and prodded at his various wounds. He tried to speak but felt the heavy pull of his eyelids closing in.

It had been weeks since Derrick had gotten any real sleep. His mind was beyond taxed and tortured as it recuperated. His mind found rest in the memories of simpler times. When he was just a cop and Alyssa was just his date. The warmth of sleep enveloped his thoughts.

"I don't know if you expect me to get all swoony for a man in uniform on our first date but–"

"Swooning?"

"Swooning."

"Swooning?"

"Yeah," Alyssa said. "Swooning. Like to go head over heels..."

"Okay, first of all," Derrick started. "I don't think anyone has 'swooned' in at least... 300 years. And second, this is not our first date."

Derrick wore his pressed police uniform with his shined 'SWAT' pin above his name tag. His freshly cleaned and waxed police cruiser rolled through the quiet neighborhood of Birmingham during his evening shift. Unlike most work nights, he took the time this afternoon to press, clean, and shine because tonight was, in fact, their first date.

"Oh my god," Alyssa slapped her hands on her thigh in disbelief. "This is so our first date!"

"Prove it."

"Prove it?"

"Prove it."

"You want me to prove that you took me on a ride along as our first date?" Alyssa said, raising her hands. Derrick's radio hadn't made a noise in thirty minutes. He was silently willing for a call to come so he could impress his date or at least keep her awake long enough to consider a second date.

"It's not what you know," Derrick said with a smug and almost caricature-like expression on his face. "It's what you can prove."

"You sound like such a douche cop right now."

"Coffee!" Derrick declared.

"Oh my god..."

"We had coffee together," Derrick shot his hand out. "At the bookstore. We sat with each other and drank coffee. That was a date. Our first date. Which makes this very incredibly boring ride along I talked you into date number two."

Alyssa shook her head, "Umm... Coffee does not count."

"Oh ho ho!" Derrick threw his hands up.

"We *met* while drinking coffee!" Alyssa mimicked Derrick's hands as they turned on a one-way road. "We were sitting at separate tables, paid for our own coffees–"

"Sexist... cough!"

"What was that?"

"Nothing."

"Meeting someone doesn't count as a date. You have to ask the person out for a first date," Alyssa folded her arms, satisfied. "Which for me is a ride along with Officer Hart at night in some sketchy neighborhood."

"Well, if you didn't want to be trapped in a cop car for twelve hours with me you shouldn't have used that joke... gave me the perfect opportunity to spring this on you."

"That joke? ...handcuffs?" Alyssa appeared bewildered. "When I asked if you were a fast handcuffer because I prefer my handcuffs put on slow?" she said deadpan, eyeing Derrick carefully.

"Yeah!" Derrick sighed and made a face in silence as his mind reassessed Alyssa's comment. "You basically were asking to go on a ride alo... Wait, were you talking about sex?" Derrick's eyes went wide.

"Gave you a perfect opening and this is the activity you chose..." Alyssa smirked, holding back a laugh as a red blush filled her cheeks. "I've learned a lot about cops so far on this ride along."

Derrick smacked his forehead, shaking his head in shame.

"Wait," Derrick looked up with a hopeful grin. "How many openings do you typically give a guy?"

Alyssa's jaw dropped. "Oh my god!" she yelled with the slightest hint of indignance and a smile as she smacked his shoulder repeatedly.

"Hey! That's assault– this is assault on an officer, ma'am!"

Derrick pretended to save himself as he laughed. He reached for his set of handcuffs behind his back. "Alright, put your hands behind your back..."

A gunshot jolted Derrick awake from his heavy sleep and thrusted him into the screaming chaos of the hospital. He slapped his chest looking for his rifle and felt pain everywhere. His hand went to his hip where his sidearm once was, but all he felt was the loose cloth of the hospital gown he wore. In the twilight of his groggy sleep, the only thing he could see was a large pool of blood growing across the floor in the hall just outside his room; and the only thing he could hear was Alyssa's jagged screams ripping through the hospital.

THIRTY

Derrick Hart
Chattanooga, TN

Automatic gunfire was a distinguished sound in real life. The explosions leaving the muzzle could be felt in your chest if you were in the vicinity. The concussing gunfire was so loud it felt as though it deafened your thoughts. Derrick could still remember the demonstration for his police academy class years ago.

They had placed an officer's bullet proof vest on a cardboard target and shot five times center mass with a 9mm pistol. Every bullet had been stopped by the vest on impact. There were flattened metal stacks that had smoked when the firearms instructor had used his knife tip to pop them out of the vest. He had repeated the drill with an AR-15 rifle. The image of his instructor pushing five unsharpened pencils through the holes the 5.56 rounds had made in the front and back of the body armor had stuck with him. The lesson? *Don't lose in a fight against a rifle.*

Derrick didn't have to worry about bullets piercing his body armor, though, because Derrick didn't have body armor. Derrick didn't have clothes. Besides the white gown that hung to his knees and was loosely tied behind his back, Derrick was as naked as he could be. *I don't even have freaking underwear.* A brief survey of the room found nothing–no clothes, gun belt, or rifle. The automatic fire continued to rain in the hallway.

He attempted to get out of bed and succeeded only after he pulled the IV from the back of his hand. Derrick felt his heart leap when he saw a figure walk by in a hunched, steady pace while firing his rifle in continuous, short bursts.

Brandon!

Derrick sighed in relief when he recognized Brandon's profile with an outstretched arm executing a firm C-grip on the neck of his rifle. Brandon took cover in the doorway Derrick was standing at, and without looking knew who it was. During a brief lull with whomever he was shooting at down the hall, Brandon spoke without looking at Derrick, "Side arm, right hip."

Derrick nodded and moved behind Brandon and depressed the retention button on his holster and drew the pistol out. It was a Glock 19, the same setup that Derrick had on his own sidearm, only slightly more compact than his Glock 17. "Is it the army?" Derrick asked. His mind was still groggy with sleep as he tried to center himself.

"No," Brandon said. "They pulled up in civilian trucks. I think it's the militia fucks we keep hearing about. Sons of–whatever. A lot of them." Nurses and doctors ran away from the militia's gunfire and ducked into patient rooms across the hall from them.

"Crossing," Derrick said.

"Covering," Brandon replied calmly.

Derrick sprinted across the hallway as a volley of gunfire was shot by Brandon. His gown flapping as he ran, Derrick never felt more vulnerable than in that moment. He hit the room with his gun at low ready, surveying from corner to corner. To his surprise the room was packed. Nearly two dozen nurses and doctors were crammed around the medical equipment with an unconscious Zoe on the bed in the center of the room. She, too, was in a medical gown and had an IV drip hanging on one side. Derrick recognized Eric's hidden face behind Zoe's bed. He wasn't wearing a gown but the pants he was wearing were nurse's scrubs as he coddled his injured leg. Alyssa was on the ground in front of Derrick's feet covered in blood, covered in Jessica's blood.

Zoe's older sister laid in an outstretched position, her body making an extended line as if she had been dragged. There were two bullet wounds in her lower stomach and left shoulder, and a third and final wound on her eyebrow. Alyssa only looked up at Derrick with tearful eyes searching for what to do.

"She was in the hall when they came..." Alyssa cried in a panic. "They shot her– she didn't do anything. She didn't do anything!" Derrick knew the answer before she placed his two fingers on Jessica's neck, searching for a pulse that wasn't there. When Derrick looked into Alyssa's eyes and shook his head, she raised a blood-stained hand to her face as the tears poured.

Everyone flinched when the gunfire erupted again. *Lock it away, Derrick. Focus on the moment.*

Derrick turned and saw Brandon retreating into a room across the hallway as bullets shot at him from both ends. The enemy had surrounded them on both sides of the hallway. Derrick angled toward the left as he made eye contact with Brandon across the hall. They exchanged a single nod, timing their entry into the hallway, firing in the opposite direction simultaneously.

The three men Derrick saw to his left were dressed in a hodgepodge of military surplus store camo and blue jeans. The way they stood clustered together was Derrick's first hint of their skill level. Derrick pushed out with his pistol at low ready and saw the first man's rifle raised at Brandon, not even looking Derrick's way. Derrick shot holes in the man from hip to throat until he fell.

The second and third men were training their hunting rifles on Derrick, but they stood in front of another in a line from Derrick's perspective. Without missing a beat, Derrick moved his aim from the fallen first man to the others and squeezed the trigger. At close range and with the small recoil of the 9mm round, Derrick's bullets struck the second man's throat and smattered three holes in the third man's face.

Derrick slipped one last round down the hallway as he saw a pair of blue jeans scurry in retreat around the corner. Derrick and Brandon both went back into their rooms and exchanged a nod as if to say, 'I'm good'.

Derrick could gauge the seriousness of the threat just like Brandon could. Any idiot with a gun was a threat, but a trained person was dangerous. Derrick read into their untrained stances and poor rifle grips. He recognized the zoomed optics and lack of slings for their rifles for a close quarters fight. *These weren't professionals, they were men who picked a fight at the wrong hospital.*

Brandon pointed down the hallway, held up two fingers, and pointed down. *Two enemies killed.* Derrick did the same but held up three fingers before pointing down.

"Hold fire! Hold yer fire!" a voice called out. "Now let's have a talk, okay? You guys are soldiers, right? United States Army?" The man's accent was thick, southern, and mouthy, but

Derrick couldn't place it. He checked the magazine on his pistol and saw he had less than five rounds left. Brandon saw him do this and without taking his eyes off of his section of the hallway, removed two pistol magazines from his chest rig. One at a time, he tossed them to Derrick who caught them but felt a stinging pull in his left shoulder as he did.

For the first time, Derrick noticed the thick white bandages wrapped around his upper left shoulder and right thigh where he had been shot. The more he thought about it, the more he became aware of the pain. Derrick did a tactical reload on his pistol, seating a fresh magazine in his handgun. He went to put his magazine and a half in his pocket when he realized he was still in a gown. A flushness burned his cheeks when he considered the entire room of nurses and doctors were probably staring his bare ass and more. *Oh well...*

"I understand you're ordered not to talk to us, to trust us," the man continued, "but our fight is not with you. It's with the U.S. Gov'ment. The men in a bunker somewhere in D.C. orderin' the killing of U.S. men and women. Citizens! They're the enemy. Not y'all."

"Then why are you shooting at us?" Derrick yelled back. Brandon shot him a look.

"Son, we've got a lot of wounded and sick to care for, and in the come'n days they're going to be a lot more hurt. I'm sure you know," the man said. "You heard stories in the media of the Sons of Liberty? I'm sure y'all heard we're monsters and all. That's what the media wants you to think. My name is Abraham Moore. I am the leader of all the chapters of the Sons of Liberty. And I'm telling you we mean you no harm. All we want is the doctors and nurses. We won't hurt them. We'd never do that, but we need their help. Send them out to us, and you guys can leave in peace, I give you my word as a Christian soul."

Derrick looked back at the men and women crouched against the walls, the panic clear in their eyes. This was not their world. They hadn't signed up to be hostages. "Give us a minute!" Derrick called out. Brandon was trying to get Derrick's attention, but Derrick held up a finger for him to wait.

Alyssa had pushed back beside Zoe's bed, her blood-covered hands and pants staining the white sheets where she leaned against the bed. Derrick found Nurse Stevens against the far wall between a trash can and a red hazardous materials trash bin. Pulling her up to her feet, he whispered, "Where are you guys parked?" there was a confused expression on her face like she couldn't understand his words. Derrick touched her shoulder, "your cars. Employee parking. Where is it?"

"Oh, um– on– the side of the building, by the ambulance entrance, just to the left there," Nurse Stevens said. *That was right around the corner where I killed the three men.* Derrick gave a curt nod and looked at Zoe. She had IVs in the veins of her foot and was obviously still heavily sedated from whatever they had done to her.

Do we leave her? Abandon her in a hospital alone? Hope that the militia doesn't take her? Would it be worse if she was abandoned, waiting for the infected to come or be taken by these sadistic fucks?

Derrick's eyes fell to Jessica's paling corpse. What little blood was left inside her had leaked out of her wounds and settled at the base of her body. He thought about Jessica giving her life getting Zoe this far. *Jessica would've never let us leave her.* He guided Nurse Stevens over by Zoe and Alyssa. "Get her bed ready to move and get all her IV bags off this thing," Derrick said then held up his hand stopping Nurse Stevens' protests about moving her in this state. "Tell everyone else to get ready to run for their cars."

"When I tell you to Alyssa, you and Eric are going to push this bed down that hall and out the ambulance bay doors. You're not going to stop for anything. Load Zoe up, Brandon and I will be behind you," said Derrick and received a shaky nod from Alyssa.

"Your minute's up," Abraham's voice bellowed down the hall. "What's it gonna be?"

Walking back to the doorway, Derrick locked eyes with an annoyed Brandon. "So, we send out the nurses and doctors, you let us go?" Derrick asked, while signaling to Brandon. Brandon replied with a series of angry shakes of his head before he finally rolled his eyes and agreed to Derrick's plan. Or at least Derrick thought he agreed.

The Army Rangers were taught tactical communication through hand signals, but Derrick didn't know them. While there were a few hand signals he and his SWAT team used, they didn't translate, which meant their entire plan was based upon rudimentary hand signals for shooting, grenades, distraction, and running that a five-year-old could decipher.

"That's right," the man said. "Listen, we got a lot more men. If you don't play ball, we'll come at you. You'll kill more of us, but we'll kill all of you, you hear? No one wants that. One way or 'nother, we're getting those nurses."

Brandon tossed one of his flash-bang grenades from his chest rig carefully to Derrick, which he was barely able to catch using his body with the magazines in his hand. Derrick was forced to abandon his half full magazine on top of a trash can. It killed him to leave bullets behind but with no pockets he couldn't carry two magazines, a pistol, and a flash-bang.

"Soldier!" Abraham's voice was angry now. "I'm about tired of–"

Brandon opened fire down his hallway in a slow but steady spray of bullets. Derrick moved down the opposite way, nearly stepping on the three men he had killed as he hopped over their bodies. His handgun up in his workspace and ready to fire, he angled for a small opening behind the nurse station. As he got behind the counter, a young man with an AR rifle stepped out from the opposing hallway.

Derrick could see the shock in the man's eyes as Derrick shot him in the chest. He hadn't expected Derrick to be so close. Derrick squeezed off one more shot before he saw a line of muzzles pointed his way. He ducked just as the gunfire exploded from the side hallway drowning out the sound of the world. Bullets chewed through computers and plastic files of stacks of paper above Derrick's head. *If they were smart, they'd flank me and kill me now while I'm pinned down.*

"Set!" Derrick shouted. In the shadows behind the counter, Derrick saw the twisted bodies of the two sheriff deputies. They lay collapsed on top of one another with blood soaking through their uniforms from the many bullet holes that peppered their chest. *Sorry, brothers,* Derrick thought. It looked as though from the position of their bodies; the younger deputy died giving first-aid to his partner.

Beside the older deputy, Derrick's gaze followed his pale outstretched hand and saw an army camo duffle bag filled with his green SWAT uniform and duty belt. Propped beside it was his black, Colt AR-15 rifle. Elation exploded in his heart as he grabbed for the rifle and tossed Brandon's pistol and magazine in the bag. He was as happy to hold his rifle as he was to see his clothes. Derrick's ass was growing numb from sitting on the cold tile floor.

There was another lull in the shooting and Brandon yelled back. "Set!" Derrick didn't have enough time to change his clothes, but he did have enough time to confirm there was a full mag in his rifle with one in the chamber. He heard Brandon toss his stun, or flash-bang, grenade just before Derrick ripped the pin free from his and threw it at the intersection of his hallway.

The explosion from the stun grenade shook the floor and concussed Derrick's chest even from behind the counter. Derrick was out from cover and side stepping into the mouth of the aisle as soon as it *boomed*. His thumb remembered the safety on his rifle just as he took the corner and saw the five men clutching their eyes, half of them with their backs exposed as they turned away.

Derrick didn't hesitate.

Right to left, down the line, Derrick let his red dot optic fall on the upper chest of each of them as he strafed from one side to the other and fired killing shots. Bullets pierced their flesh and crumpled them to the floor. Slamming his body against the wall, he did another sweep, shooting the bodies crawling on the ground. An action that would have mortified Derrick last week, now he barely thought twice about.

Hammering his fist into the handicap assist button against the wall, the ambulance bay doors opened to the outside. "Alyssa! Now!" Derrick took a covering position on the side of the hallway where he had just killed the men and saw the flood of doctors and nurses run from the room. Three of them pushed Zoe's bed as Alyssa tried to steer it with Eric hobbling beside her.

Brandon swapped magazines and continued his paced covering fire. The screaming and running alerted the others hiding down the adjoining hallway. More patients and staff took the opportunity to flee as well. Derrick gave a nod of approval to Alyssa and Eric as they wheeled Zoe outside.

A barrage of sporadic gunfire struck several stragglers in the back of the pack. Derrick pressed forward as the last of the civilians ran past him. He had no targets, all he saw was the end of the hallway, but Derrick laid down what covering fire he could so the attackers wouldn't blindly fire from behind their cover. "Move!" Derrick shouted to Brandon.

Brandon chucked another stun grenade down the hallway and ran with Derrick toward the exit. Derrick tried to help one of the shot women to her feet, but Brandon gave Derrick a hard shove on his bare back and sent him toppling forward and barely capable of staying on his feet. Scooping up the duffle bag with his gear, Derrick stumbled outside as Brandon returned fire at the bulk of the militia's force.

The concrete hurt Derrick's bare feet as he stumbled outside. Clusters of rocks and gravel dug into his skin with every step. The hot sun blinded and instantly warmed his sweaty skin. There was an ambulance parked to the right of the door and several cars parked along the back of the lot along a green hill. Most of the cars in the parking lot were reversing in quick succession and accelerating for the exit. Their battered Humvee was backed into one of the ambulance bays. Brandon must have moved it to the nearest door in case they needed a quick getaway.

Alyssa already had it started though the engine sounded as worn as it looked. Derrick went to the rear and saw Eric slumped in the far seat and a sweaty Zoe curled up on the floor in the back. IV bags were tossed across her belly and hundreds of bullet casing cluttered the floorboards around her. Derrick tossed his bag inside and climbed in as Brandon ran behind him. His hands clutched his rifle and another duffel bag that Derrick hadn't seen.

"Here, here!" Derrick shouted. Brandon tossed one of the bags inside at Derrick's feet. Catching Brandon's hand, Derrick pulled him inside as Alyssa lurched forward, nearly spilling all four of them out the open door. Alyssa took a corner leaving the hospital behind them as they fled north.

THIRTY-ONE

Rachel Anderson
Louisville, KY

It was dark outside, Rachel guessed. There were no windows in her room nor were there clocks, so Rachel had no sense of time passing. One of the two corporals who guarded their room caved after two hours of Rachel miming, 'What's the time?' by tapping her wrist. The Corporal, a young man with a skinny, gaunt face approached the glass and held up his watch to Rachel. It was 8:35 pm then and was probably closing in on 10:00 pm by now.

Sixty-two hours left.

Rachel rubbed her hands over her arms. Her skin was raw and red. The afternoon had been spent in decontamination, again. It was similar to the first time they had gone through it in Birmingham, only this time it had lasted five hours instead of forty-five minutes. They had carted her and her three agents into a tiled shower where they were hosed and scrubbed before being loaded into identical but different cubes.

Rachel wondered what her father would do if he knew where she was. He was a soft-spoken man who wasn't known for his outbursts except when it came to Rachel, his only daughter. He had always been protective of Rachel, which was a difficult task for him since she had been a bit of a wild child. Rachel supposed it had become easier once he had become the Vice President and had had an entire detail of secret service agents follow her around. Rachel smirked to herself–*it's probably the reason why he ran for office in the first place.*

She hated this room. She hated the silence. The peacefulness of this solitude was lost in a matter of minutes. When Rachel had been out there in the world, she had the distractions of life to occupy her mind. The fear of the ever approaching rabid and the constant focus of what the next step was to get to safety. There was nothing but her thoughts in this room. Memories of how she had failed. Thoughts that second guessed her actions.

If I would've gone this way instead of that... if we would've stayed there instead of fleeing...

Rachel turned in her bed and saw Sean lying in the bed closest to the window. His eyes were looking at her and bounced away when she looked at him. The room Sean, Allen, and Chris were sharing was slightly larger than Rachel's, but they still had to cram three beds into it. There was a speaker box between the two BSL-4 rooms but it wasn't active.

They shared a look, not taking their eyes off each other for a long moment. Even before the outbreak there was more than one long conversation they had needed to have together. The messy web of feelings and logic. Desire and duty. When you're the daughter of the Vice President, dating an agent on your secret service detail was a complicated manner.

There was a privacy curtain that went around the room. She could have closed it, but Rachel liked being able to look at Sean. And she knew he liked the security of being able to watch over her. Protect her. Their relationship was a thing that should have never begun. It was a forbidden fruit that had made tasting it sweeter. *Things were fine until this fling turned serious. I should have never told him.*

Rachel knew it didn't matter. No matter what she or Sean did, their relationship could have not ended anywhere but where it had. One of the last 'normal' conversations Rachel had before the outbreak was about an hour before news of the infection had broken. Sean had informed her that he was submitting a transfer to leave her protection detail. Fury wasn't an emotion she experienced often but that was what she had felt in that moment. Rachel couldn't understand how the bravest man she knew could also be the biggest coward. Just thinking of the conversation made her blood boil and motivated her to turn on her side, away from Sean.

The front door slid open, and the two guards quickly straightened. Rachel first noticed Major Benning's bald head as he bounced into the room. He activated Rachel's speaker, considered it for a moment, then walked over to the agents' room and activated their speaker as well.

"I um... I have some news I think you all should hear," he said.

"You're letting us out?" Allen's voice echoed through the speakerphone. The men stirred, tossing the covers off them as they sat up.

"No, well, um. Not really, no," Major Benning hesitated. "The President is dead."

Rachel stood up as did Sean, Allen, and Chris while they neared the glass in shock. "What about my dad, is he–"

"What happened?" Chris said.

"Was it rabid? Was it the infection?" Allen asked.

"Vice President Anderson is fine," Benning continued. "He has been sworn in as President of the United States and he has given a national address. I don't have a lot of details. All they said is that President Walker had a heart attack."

The rooms were silent as they all processed the information until Sean broke the silence.

"You need to get her out of here," Sean said. "She is now the First Daughter, and this is not a secure location for her."

"Yes, yes, and Colonel Fields actually did just receive that direct phone call from the *new* Commander of the Joint Chiefs..."

"*New* Commander of the Joint Chiefs?" Allen questioned.

"Yes, it appears, um, Admiral Rotoss has stepped down or– um, General Stockhold is now the Commander of the Joint Chiefs."

Rachel saw Sean and the others exchange a look of uncertainty at the shakeup of personnel. Rachel was still reeling from the idea that her father was the President of the United States. *My father is now responsible for dealing with this mess.*

"Anyways, General Stockhold was in direct contact with Colonel Fields, and he has orders to release the First Daughter and get her back with her father, so..." Benning pressed a series of buttons on Rachel's keypad by the speaker box and her door slid open. "Colonel Fields asked me to come down here and escort you to a helicopter we have waiting for you."

Rachel sighed in relief unable to control the smile that formed on her face as she stepped out of the room to Benning's side

"Right this way, ma'am."

"What about them?"

"Oh, uh– the command was for... they can't release the secret service agents until the full seventy-two hours are up,"

Benning shrugged helplessly. "It's Colonel Fields' decision and the Joint Chiefs specifically asked for you and you only."

Rachel looked back to the glass room that housed her detail and heard Chris' voice first. "Go, we'll be fine. This is our job."

"At least this way you won't be a pain in our asses anymore," Allen smirked as he nodded for her to go.

Sean just stared at Rachel with his silent hard gaze and said, "Go."

"Ma'am, we have to go. The helicopter is waiting."

Major Bennings words sparked a memory in Rachel's mind that almost made her laugh. She saw Officer Derrick Hart's face as he refused to get on the helicopter to safety so he could protect defenseless people. She recalled the faces of her students she had failed when she turned down a helicopter to safety to try and protect them. *You turned down a helicopter for those kids.* Rachel remembered Derrick's last words to her. *Don't you fucking forget that.*

"I'm staying," Rachel said on autopilot.

"What?" Benning furrowed his brow.

"I'm staying," Rachel repeated. "Tell Colonel Fields to get General Stockhold or the President on the phone. Tell them my secret service agents and I are a package deal. All of us go or none of us do."

There was a chorus of protests as her agents went ballistic, but Rachel had made up her mind. She went back into her isolation room as the others tried to convince her otherwise. Maj. Benning had to mute their speaker because the agents' voices were drowning out his words.

"Ma'am, I can't... they're going to make you go– you have to go!"

"Make me?" Rachel snapped. "Unless you find someone willing to physically restrain and carry the President of the United States' daughter kicking and biting out of this room, I'm not leaving. Not until they come with me. Do you understand?"

"I..." Major Benning began to speak but his words were caught in his throat. After a moment of silence, he resigned into pressing a button that closed and sealed Rachel back in her room. Before the Major left, Rachel called after him.

"Before you go, I need you turn on the speaker box between our two rooms. I'd like to hear them tell me how much smarter they think they are than me," Rachel said as she saw the muted faces of Sean, Allen, and Chris yelling amongst themselves.

Major Benning pursed his lips, looking reluctant to obey Rachel's order but he seemed to think otherwise and went over to her speaker box and keyed in a few buttons before turning and leaving the room. Rachel pressed the green button on the speaker and Sean's voice cracked through as he stared at her with his head shaking back and forth. "...you stubborn, stupid..."

"What is wrong with you, woman!" Allen shouted in the background.

"Oh, all of you can fuck off," Rachel yelled back.

THIRTY-TWO

Brandon Armstrong
Louisville, KY

Traveling through Tennessee was the smoothest drive, yet. Brandon had lived in Nashville for three years and Derrick visited often. They knew several side roads and alternative highways to travel north, but as it turned out they didn't need them.

Tennessee Highway Patrol and city police did a better job than Georgia in keeping the interstates clear of non-military personnel. With so many military convoys carrying supplies and men fleeing east and north, Brandon's battered military Humvee did not receive a second look and they were waved onto the isolated I-65.

The drive went so well that Brandon almost thought about stopping at his house in Hendersonville to pick up some of his things–weapons, ammo, new clothes. Derrick and Eric were able to change out of their hospital gowns and back into their clothes during the drive, but everyone at this point was stained with blood and dirt. He decided against it. Brandon's signature on his suicide contract had earned his wife a Yellowband bracelet that had allowed her to travel to her late grandparent's house in Louisville just a few hours north. He could not risk any more detours. Not when he was this close. Brandon drove in silence most of the way with Derrick sitting beside him.

The only sound that was constant in the car were the teary whimpers of Zoe. Her head had been tucked into Alyssa's lap since she had gained consciousness and had been told what happened to her sister. It didn't help that with every passing minute her pain meds wore off, causing her agony.

It had all happened so fast. After one of the doctors had treated Brandon's cuts, he had dozed off in an uncomfortable chair outside Derrick's room. The next moment he had heard gunshots coming from the front door. Brandon had seen dozens of rednecks streaming into the ER.

The memory upset him. So, he didn't think about it. Brandon never understood why people let sad thoughts consume them day in and day out. He had learned early on in life he could ignore pain until he starved it out of his thoughts completely. He assumed all men had this ability to *turn off* certain thoughts that bothered them, but it was Derrick who pointed out, in such a friendly manner, how much of a freak Brandon truly was. That sad thoughts weren't a valve normal people could just turn off so easily.

Perhaps, this ability he had was what made their current world so clear to Brandon, while confounding others. When surrounded by death, those who couldn't help themselves pleaded for others to pity them. Derrick was a sucker for pity. Brandon knew he must find a way to save his friend from himself. To forget his police officer ways and to let go of those who aren't his to protect. Like the nurses back at the hospital.

Or the dying girl in the back seat. He had to understand he was being used before it was too late.

Shit, if he hadn't already been engaged to Alyssa, Brandon would've guessed she was using him too. That heart is going to get him killed.

"Can she not meet us here on the interstate?" Derrick asked.

"Look at the traffic. The crowds out there," Brandon said. "You think she could make it through all that on her own? This place is like a tinderbox waiting to explode."

They had taken a few detours once in Kentucky, but they were able to link up with a convoy of a hundred or so military trucks and Humvees that traveled to Louisville. They were forced to travel at a slower pace because of the convoy, but they had safety in the numbers and disguise to guide them all the way through Louisville and into Indiana if they wanted.

It was a river of people that flowed along the side roads. It was clear that word had spread throughout the day that the Tennessee border had collapsed. Many of those who had trusted the government's message of 'shelter in place,' now took to the streets searching for their own safety. Their exposed skin turned red from the sun and their backs arched from the many miles they had already marched. If Brandon had driven the Humvee into town on his own, he was sure they would have swamped him. Guns and uniforms or not, it didn't matter; it was the convoy that kept them all safe now.

Reluctantly, Brandon scrounged the dash and floorboards of the Humvee searching for the Greenband satellite phone. In all the shooting and chaos of crossing the Tennessee border he had lost track of it.

"Here it–" Brandon found it rolling around by his feet. "Shit."

"What?" Derrick asked.

Brandon held up the Greenband phone and the bottom section where the microphone was located was a tattered mess of wires.

"There goes that," Brandon said, tossing the phone to the floorboards behind him. "Can't even fucking call her."

"The buttons still work," Eric said in the back as he picked up the phone and thumbed a few of buttons. "Screen lights up... Says, 'RTC-2// RADIO,'" Eric furrowed his brow. Alyssa looked over his shoulder and Eric appeared to be enjoying himself, exploring the new piece of technology.

"That's channel two, it's a radio channel," Brandon said with a flash of heat going to his cheeks. His temper might have made him disregard the phone too soon. "It'll pick up other Greenband phones and encrypted military radios in channels in the area. Press the top left–"

"They're talking," Derrick interrupted from the front passenger seat. Eric clicked the volume on the side. They listened for several seconds as different soldiers talked to another about moving units to various bases.

"Charlie 6 to Chalk 2-1, do you copy?" a voice cracked over the Greenband phone.

"Chalk 2-1, go 'head."

"Charlie 6 to 2-1, I need you to relocate your chalk to Cherokee Park. You will coordinate with Captain Gilvers and provide extra security for Swan two while we figure this mess out, over."

"Did he say Swan two?" Derrick asked unsure of himself.

"Yeah, what is it?" Alyssa asked.

"Copy." Chalk two-one replied.

Brandon looked from the road to Derrick who searched his memory. "That's the Vice President's daughter..." Derrick said. "Er... President's daughter, now." Brandon had filled the others in on the news during their drive. The shocking information had little effect on the group's fried nerves.

"How do you know?" Eric asked.

"We did an escort before the infected hit Birmingham, me and..." Derrick looked away and shook his head as if ridding himself of an unpleasant memory. "Rachel Anderson and her three secret service agents– the ones that were still alive. We got her to a chopper and they were ex-filling her to Louisville but that was yesterday. Thought she would be out of here by now."

"Maybe she wanted to slum it like a real person a little while longer before taking Air Force One to eat caviar in some bunker," Brandon growled.

Derrick shrugged watching the road, "she was nice... seemed like a good person."

Brandon glanced behind him at Alyssa who gave a measured look towards Derrick's praise of this rich and powerful woman. There was something strange in her eyes. It wasn't the usual jealousy he had come to expect to see, but an almost pained expression. Brandon hadn't had the time read the signals between Derrick and Alyssa over the long day, but he was beginning to pick up on a strife between the two. By no means was he an expert in feelings, but Brandon had plenty of practice in pissing off Karen to know the feeling when an argument was in the air.

Eric had switched the Greenband phone into satellite mode and with Alyssa's help dialed Karen's number as they entered Louisville.

"Hello?" Karen's voice called from the phone's speaker after a couple of rings.

"Karen, oh my god, its Alyssa, are you okay? We're in Louisville."

"...hello?" Karen repeated with an annoyed song in her voice.

"Karen!" Brandon shouted over his shoulder. "Karen, it's Bran. Can you hear me?"

"Anybody there?" Karen asked.

"Son of a–" Derrick muttered.

"She can't hear us," Alyssa said frustrated.

"No, shit," Brandon scowled.

Eric examined the dangling wires and plastic pieces at the bottom of the phone. "It looks like the phone was shot. Probably damaged the microphone."

They heard the phone disconnect after an exasperated sigh from Karen.

"It doesn't matter. We're going to get Karen," Brandon said.

Derrick took a deep breath and let out a long sigh but said nothing more. He couldn't say anything, and Brandon knew it. Not after everything Brandon had gone through to rescue Derrick's fiancé. It wasn't like Brandon wanted to leave this road either. They had fought so hard to get here. To survive. Brandon and Derrick knew that once they left this convoy to go to his wife, they likely would never be able to get back to it. Not with their Humvee that is.

"How far away is her grandparent's house from the interstate?" Alyssa asked.

"A couple miles," Brandon said. "Maybe a little less."

After a long silence Eric asked, "And she can't, like, meet us in Indiana or something?"

"No." Brandon's voice boomed, ending the conversation. "We're going to have to take the next exit here."

"This isn't going to be pretty," Derrick sighed.

"No, no it is not," Brandon agreed.

"Everybody strap in and hold on," Derrick said over his

shoulder. "Eric, as soon as we stop, you need to toss all of our bags out."

"Okay," Eric said as he pocketed the Greenband radio. Over the last hour, they had Eric and Alyssa top off all of their magazines and pack everything they could into bags to carry with them.

Brandon watched the exit slowly approach. Luckily, there were no concrete barriers. But he could see a Louisville PD patrol car with two police officers down at the base of the exit ramp below. "Here we go," Brandon said.

He veered hard to the right and accelerated down the ramp. Blasting his horn, he alerted the officers that leaned against the patrol car. They looked behind them with enough time to dive to safety as Brandon rammed into the car and sent it in a spin. Tires squealed and skirted across the road, nearly striking a group of civilians trying to pass. The commotion and noise did well to part the crowds for them.

Brandon roared the engine down a side street the police had blocked off. It ran perpendicular to the interstate but not quite the direction they needed to go. Closer was all they could hope for. A group of tired looking police officers tried to wave them down, but Brandon went around them. After about a mile he cut down a street to a one way one lane road blocked with an abandoned car.

"Hold on!" Brandon shouted as he topped fifty mph before ramming the front bumper into the car. Derrick, despite his attempt to brace himself, was flung to the floorboards and quickly scrambled back into his seat. They pushed past the car and drove down the road. They neared the subdivision they were heading for, not far from Bardstown Road but the crowds were so thick–easily in the thousands, perhaps tens of thousands. Brandon punched the horn hard. "Move you bastards!"

A channel opened up enough for Brandon to roar his

Humvee into pushing more cars out of his way, but even still the angry mob closed in on them. They were alone now. When Brandon finally broke past the two vehicles that blocked him, he nearly crushed a man.

"Brandon! Stop– you'll kill them!" Alyssa pointed from behind, as if Brandon couldn't see the bodies he almost hit. Brandon swerved at the last minute and slammed hard into a ditch. They bounced out of it with a thud and the Humvee limped forward, the engine ticking like a time bomb. In all the commotion, they had busted through a house's privacy fence and the Humvee nearly rolled over. With the last of what was left in the engine Brandon rammed through two more privacy fences before the vehicle clunked to a halt and smoke poured from the engine.

"Everybody out!" Brandon shouted. "Derrick on me."

They flung the doors open and with their rifles shouldered, Brandon and Derrick ran to the rear past the others. The mob of exhausted civilians they had nearly run over hopped the ditch and ran for the Humvee–thieves hoping to pick through and steal whatever they could. A few would be more interested in murdering soldiers. Vengeance for the government's handling of the outbreak.

Derrick shouted with his rifle half raised. "Stop! Stop! Show me your hands or we'll–"

Brandon's rifle chugged bullets at the mob's feet. His automatic fire cut sprouts of grass and dirt into the air. The mob stopped in its tracks and dispersed in all directions with panicked screams.

"We've got them all," Alyssa's voice called from behind them. "Where do we go?"

"I got the rear, you take point," Derrick said to his friend.

"Roger, moving."

"Brandon, get Zoe," Alyssa called over her shoulder with

her arms full of two duffel bags. He gave the barely conscious girl in the back of the Humvee a once over as he jogged by and continued on.

"If she can't carry her own weight, then she can stay behind," Brandon said.

"Brandon, you piece of–" Alyssa snapped.

"I've got her," Derrick said, slinging his rifle behind his shoulder as his hands scooped under Zoe's thighs and the small of her back.

They cut through several backyards at a jog and as they put some distance between them and the crowds, Brandon looked back and saw Derrick falling behind as he carried Zoe in his arms. Alyssa, too, was inching back as Eric hobbled at her side. Brandon grumbled to himself as he slowed his pace so as not to lose them.

After another ten minutes of jogging, Brandon turned the corner into the cul de sac leading to Karen's grandparents' home. The old two-story house remained standing with no signs of looting, to Brandon's surprise.

"This– this it?" Alyssa panted, dumping the bags at her feet with her hands on her knees.

"This is it," Brandon said.

Eric mumbled to himself while gripping his wounded thigh, "Thank god."

When the front door opened and Brandon saw Karen come outside, a calmness washed over him. There was a comfort in his wife's familiar presence.

Karen let loose a tiny screech and ran down the porch stairs to hug Brandon. "Oh my god, oh my god! You're ok. Thank god!"

Brandon enjoyed the moment of embrace with his wife. The smell of her perfume. The feel of her long black hair against his cheek. Karen was what Brandon liked to call a *girly-*

girl. So it didn't surprise him to see Karen so dressed up in a short pencil skirt and black top with necklaces. Karen liked her makeup, manicures, and trash magazines, and Brandon liked that she was so cliché.

It made it easy for Brandon to know what to buy her for birthdays and to guess how she spent her time away from him. In today's age where relationship roles were so fluid and modern women liked their man to be more sensitive, Brandon was happy he had found himself a traditional woman. Karen had the same understanding of marriage as him.

"Ugh, ew, you stink, babe," Karen pulled away making a face. She reached to touch Brandon's face. "Oh my god, you're all cut up, baby. And you, is that blood?" Karen stared at Eric's jeans. Karen hugged Alyssa, making sure to keep as much of her body from touching Alyssa's sweaty and bloody clothes. "You must be Eric, hi, I'm Karen. Brandon's wife."

Brandon looked behind them and saw Derrick struggling to walk the final feet around the bend in the road. Drips of sweat poured off his brow onto Zoe's arm and hospital gown. He slowly tried to lower Zoe to her feet without toppling over himself. Everyone moved to help him, even Eric, though it was only two half-hearted limps. Everyone except Brandon. Brandon did a tactical reload on his rifle while the others took Zoe's arms and led her towards the house.

"Come on inside, guys. Y'all look exhausted. Let's get you outta this sun," Karen said.

"Derrick," Brandon said under his breath, just loud enough for Derrick to hear him as he passed. Karen and Alyssa both looked back, noticing them hang back as they guided Zoe inside the house. Derrick looked about as worn down as Brandon felt. His eyes had lost the life in them, they just dragged wherever his head turned. Brandon could not remember the last time he had slept more than a couple minutes.

They both dropped the heavy bags they wore on their shoulders to the front lawn of the house with a thud. Brandon dragged a hand down his chin and circled the stubble. Noticing his bracelet, he decided to ease into the real conversation. "We should probably cut these Greenbands off before we leave here," he said.

Derrick nodded looking down at his own as he regained his breath. "Don't think we can use them anymore?"

"Yeah, cause they worked so great the first time. I think they'll be a liability. People will see them and think we're someone special. Try and kidnap us. Hold us ransom to get across the border... or just cut our hands off to take them... that's what I would do."

Derrick sighed and nodded. "Okay."

"Figure we can stay here for a few hours, rest up..."

Derrick nodded. His gaze resting on the setting sun beyond the next subdivision. They were far enough recessed from the main thoroughfares that the shouts and sporadic shooting in the city were just distant sounds where they stood.

"Look I don't have the energy to argue, but I need you to get on the same page."

"What's that?" Derrick asked.

"You and I both know that girl isn't gonna be up on her feet tomorrow running around. And there's no way we're going anywhere in a car, now that we're in the city."

"Jesus Christ..." was all Derrick said as he turned away. "You've been arguing to get rid of her since this morning; this is just your latest excuse."

"Am I wrong? Tell me I'm missing something."

Derrick stayed quiet for a long moment before speaking again. "Maybe we can stay here a couple days. Rest up, gather supplies–"

"There's no way we're staying here more than a few hours,"

Brandon interrupted. "No way. We'd give up every advantage we've gained. Making it past the military border into the green zone changes nothing. The hot zone is chasing us now. We collapsed the Tennessee border, which was the last one the country had. Just because you don't see hordes of infected running this way, it doesn't mean they aren't. The name of the game is still the same. The person who gets the farthest north and the farthest from people lives the longest, and right now we're in the middle of a million fucking people in Louisville. I'd be surprised if the city makes it through another day."

"You're talking about abandoning an injured fifteen-year-old girl to be raped and killed by looters, or infected by rabid, or just to starve to death."

"We're going to leave her behind plenty of supplies, things we can't take with us. Karen's grandpa's got a .38 revolver somewhere around here with only a few rounds. When the time comes, she can have a quick death. Better than any other death you're putting on her if you take her with us."

Derrick just shook his head for the longest time. Brandon felt Derrick's will start to break as he was beginning to accept the new world order. Brandon thought Derrick held on to his moral standards with pride. They were something he used to make himself feel superior to others. Not like a prick who rubs their money or fancy cars in someone else's face, but it was how he reconciled his life before going to bed. He wasn't a millionaire, he wasn't popular, or a star athlete, but he helped people. He saved girls who needed saving. He was a good guy. A good guy saves helpless kids. A good guy gets his buddy to rescue his fiancé and her little brother. Brandon could see Derrick was finally questioning whether he was the good guy.

Brandon took no pleasure in stripping his friend of his identity. He didn't want to ruin Derrick's moral code, but he had to.

Derrick was his best friend, and his moral code was going to get him killed in this world.

And I'm not going to let that happen.

"I need to get some sleep," Derrick said, his tone suggesting that he knew that Brandon was right.

"Yeah... Yeah, me too. Hungry as fuck, too. I could go for some waffles."

"Hm. Don't even get me started."

They moved slowly toward the stairs to the front porch., lugging their bags behind them. Brandon could smell meat cooking and realized why he was thinking about food.

"You think about your parents at all?" Derrick asked. "Like how they're doing? Where they're at?"

Brandon paused on the first step of the porch. It just occurred to him that up until that moment he hadn't even thought about them. He assumed they were doing fine. They lived in such a small town in Maine he doubted there was any problems, yet. Truth be told, he didn't really care how they were doing. It had been years since he had seen them. "No, not really," he simply answered.

"I remember your mom used to make those monstrous waffles for us for supper when we were kids, remember that?" Derrick smirked.

Brandon nodded. Of course, he remembered them. They were a staple of both of their childhoods. Even before Derrick had entered into foster care, he would eat most of his meals at Brandon's house as a kid.

"Any time your dad was away on business, I'd come over and she'd make them for us– or that summer I stayed with you guys..." Derrick's voice trailed away as sunlight began to make room for the dark. "My, um, my mom... she called like week ago, I think..." Derrick absentmindedly touched his breast pocket searching for his phone that wasn't there. "She left a message apologizing to me, asking forgiveness. I didn't really think about it much at the time. Thought it was just her trying to make herself feel better before the infected hit Birmingham, you know?"

Brandon nodded, "Yeah. Fuck her, she could have asked for forgiveness a year ago. Or ten years ago."

"Yeah... yeah... that's what I thought before all this. I was pissed, you know? Like, I didn't even try to call her back or send her a message– not really. I didn't want to give her that satisfaction." Derrick scrubbed the palm of his hand across his eyes. "But I have been thinking about that message and her, here and there. Since all this shit happened. It's just, I don't know... With everything going on, the constant fighting just to fucking live for five more minutes, only to have someone else try to kill you... makes me wonder..."

"Makes you wonder what?"

"I don't know... Just... what's the point? Why didn't I just forgive her years ago?"

Cause, fuck her. She abandoned you as a kid, you abandoned her as an adult, Brandon thought to himself, but he stayed silent.

"Like what was I holding on to? Why did it matter that I held that over her?" Derrick looked off at the distant intersection. "I don't know... the world ending just puts things into perspective, I guess." Derrick's exhaustion had broken down his emotional walls. Brandon knew because he could feel it wearing on him too. "Like... was it really worth it to be alone now... not to have any family..."

Brandon was silent for a moment as his eyes were lost in a stare. "You remember before you moved in with us, when you used to sneak over when we were kids?"

Derrick smirked and nodded.

"We'd play video games in the dark with the TV muted

and you'd have to hide like every twenty minutes when my parents came downstairs cause we still made too much noise."

"Yeah, I remember," Derrick reminisced. "That time your mom caught us because you were chasing me with that baseball bat cause I beat you in every game that night."

Brandon grinned. "You stayed with us that whole summer before you went to live with your foster parents down the road, but there was something about staying up all night and gaming... I don't know... it was a fun summer."

Derrick nodded and half laughed, "Valhalla waits for no one," he turned, and Brandon saw Derrick holding the pair of Viking dog tags around his neck in his hand.

Brandon shook his head, "you still got that fucking thing?"

"You don't?"

Brandon dug out his matching set of dog tags from under his vest. "C'mon," Brandon nodded to the house. "Let's get some food."

THIRTY-THREE

Derrick Hart
Louisville, KY

The once tidy house instantly became a mess when they entered. The dated living room with wood paneling on the walls and graying couches that stunk of decades of cigarette smoke now had dried crumpled bits of dirt on the floor, messy clothes were tossed in a pile in the corner, and a bag of medical supplies spilled next to the couch where Zoe laid. Alyssa half sat on the floor, feeding the shivering girl toast with butter on it. The bites she took were so small it didn't look like she was eating anything.

Karen came into the room with a bowl of soup that she sat down in front of Alyssa. "Jesus, Derrick, you look like a hot mess, too."

Derrick cracked a smile at Karen. He was glad to see Karen was alright. "I feel like one, too."

"I'd hug you but I think I'd need to shower, again if I did,"

Karen joked, eyeing his distressed uniform. "Go ahead and put your dirty clothes in a pile over there. I'll do a load of laundry tonight, hun."

"We'll wash our uniforms separate," Brandon took his military top off revealing his sweat-soaked undershirt that hugged his athletic torso. "Hose them down with bleach out back and let them dry overnight."

Derrick nodded.

"We're in there," Alyssa said to Derrick, pointing to Karen's grandparent's old room upstairs.

"Oh, um," Karen said, "there are some clothes in the closet. Take what you like."

Eric was in the kitchen receiving passive assistance from Karen while cooking a hodge podge of frozen food in the oven and microwave. Walking by the living room, Derrick paused to kneel beside Alyssa as she brushed Zoe's hair behind her ear. He could see the pain in Zoe's face as she pinched her eyes shut.

"How's she doing?" Derrick asked.

Alyssa only gave Derrick a helpless look and shook her head. Zoe's eyes opened when she heard Derrick's voice. She looked at him, holding his gaze for several seconds. He didn't know what to say. He wondered if she was crying from the pain of surgery or from the loss of her sister.

During the car ride to Louisville, Alyssa, who had been playing mother goose to everyone at the hospital, had updated him on their injuries. They were lucky for the most part. Everyone's wounds were superficial, with the exception of Zoe's. While Derrick and Eric only had tissue and muscle damage that could be treated with stitches and rest, Zoe had had surgery for minor internal bleeding done on her abdomen. A girl in her condition should not have been moved.

What choice did we have?

Derrick touched Zoe's shoulder and gave it a gentle squeeze. "It'll be okay... It's going to be okay..." he told her. "... We're here with you."

Derrick turned to Alyssa, "I think Karen's grandparents may have pain killers here. Probably expired but they might help. Maybe ask her when she comes in?"

Alyssa nodded, "Okay."

"You want me to take over?"

"No, I've got this."

Derrick went upstairs and directly to the bathroom. He showered as carefully as he could so as not to let dirt and debris fall into his open wounds, but truthfully, he was too exhausted to even care. He very nearly fell twice while standing under that hot water, from dozing off. The stitches in his shoulder had ripped open as well and a dribble of blood trickled down his chest.

When he returned to the bedroom, Alyssa sat on the edge of their bed crying silently into her hands. *Sadness was the new normal. The only thing that changes, nowadays, is why you are crying.* The days had blurred together, Derrick barely remembered the facts of each day, let alone the emotions. Happiness seemed like such a foreign concept.

"Oh, um, hey," Alyssa cleared her throat, trying to clean up her face. "Derrick, you're bleeding." Alyssa noticed his busted stitches and went to him, touching his shoulder. He had found an old pair of Brandon's sweatpants to wear but no shirt.

"It's fine, just the stitches broke loose," Derrick mumbled. "Are you okay? I mean– I know you're not okay, but..."

Alyssa gave him a small smile through her sad eyes. The smile stirred a warmth inside him where there was only an icy cold heart, frozen from the reaches of emotions. It was the look he had dreamt of a thousand times in the month they had been apart. Alyssa wrapped her arms around Derrick's neck in a tight embrace and Derrick held her tight to his chest. He breathed in her familiar scent and remembered a previous life they once had together. The normal days of dinner dates with her friends and binge-watching shows covered in blankets at his house.

Alyssa pulled away, swiping at tears from below her eyes and half laughed, "I shouldn't be touching you; you just got all clean."

"I'll survive," Derrick said, sorting through the emotions she had unlocked in him. "Shower's all yours."

Alyssa hesitated, her eyes flickering between Derrick's and his lips for a moment as if she wanted to say something but decided against it. She grabbed a towel from the hall and disappeared in the bathroom. In this intermission of violence they found themselves in, Derrick felt inundated with a spread of emotions. He recalled what it was like to feel again. To care about someone and have them care about you. It was a dangerous feeling.

Every pull of the trigger had walled him off from his feelings a little more. He had compartmentalized away anything that stood between him and survival, but suddenly Alyssa's touch had caused cracks to form in his defenses. Derrick felt the resemblance of love and recalled what happiness looked like. But he also remembered the sound of loss and the pain in his gut as the gaping hole of abandonment opened wider.

Happiness and sadness were different sides of the same coin. He couldn't open himself to one without exposing himself to the other. Life would be simpler if he just walled himself off to all emotions completely, he figured.

...was it really worth it to be alone now... not to have any family...

Derrick shook away his thoughts and went through the drawers until he found a black t-shirt to put on. He brought his uniform and armor out to the back porch where Karen was dousing Brandon's armor in bleach. Derrick, now clean enough, got a proper hug from her before she shewed him away saying she would take care of cleaning it.

Derrick fixed a plate of slices of pineapple pizza, apples, instant mashed potatoes, and burger patties with no buns, for himself and Alyssa. Eric sat in an old red and green striped lazy boy recliner in the living room devouring the concoction of food he had found in the freezer. Exhaustion had won over Zoe who now slept on the couch across from Eric. Derrick checked in with Eric and gave him a pat on his shoulder before going up stairs.

Alyssa and Derrick ate silently, zoned out in their own worlds as they sat on the edge of the bed listening to the occasional *pops* of gunfire outside. Derrick kept his weapons close by in case any of the riots found their way down this subdivision. Alyssa wet hair was pulled back in a ponytail and she wore a snug pair of jeans and a form fitting blue shirt that were Karen's.

"What do you think is next?" Alyssa asked. Her tiredness clung to every word. "I mean, do you think anything will ever be normal, again?"

"I... I don't know," Derrick said, taking a final bite of his apple. "I think we're all going to stuck together for some time, though. Only way to stay safe. Everything that we just went through in the southern states is about to happen in the northern ones now. Everything. We need to stick together– rely on each other, trust one another if we are going to..." Derrick trailed off as he remembered the lie.

"What is it?"

"I think in the morning I'm going to tell Brandon about us. Tell him the truth, I mean."

Alyssa sat her half empty plate on top of Derrick's empty

plate on the nightstand, looking away from him. "Derrick, I'm um– I'm sorry for everything,"

"You don't have to–"

"No, I do. I do. There are a lot of messed up things that have happened these past few days... weeks... We all did things we wouldn't... couldn't imagine ourselves doing..." Alyssa twisted the engagement ring she wore on her left hand back and forth around her ring finger. "I know you lied to your best friend to get him to come get me, and I know that if you hadn't done that my little brother and I... that we'd be dead right now." Alyssa's voice was shaky as she brushed strands of her wet blond hair behind her ear.

Derrick wanted to bring up that it was Brandon who had saved her, but he knew she was still struggling with how he had saved her.

"I just– you shouldn't have been in a position where you had to lie. But I just wanted you to know, everything I said in that message I left you is true. I never should have said no to you when you proposed, it was a stupid gut reaction. I just– you know, freaked out. I was just overwhelmed by it all. Unprepared... when it happened I just saw... The idea of marriage was always scary to me, you know?"

Alyssa twisted the engagement ring from her finger and looked down at it one more time. Wiping away tears with the back of her thumb, Alyssa placed the ring into Derrick's palm with a small sniffle. "Sorry. I just wanted to say thank you for being here with me, now. Not just for keeping me alive, but for *being* here. Your lie about being engaged to me shouldn't have been a lie. I wish... I should've said yes to you."

Alyssa's words moved slowly through Derrick's mind. He stared at the ring as he rolled it between his calloused and blistered thumb and finger. How many times had he fantasized about Alyssa saying those very words to him? He recalled the uncomfortable drive back to Birmingham after their vacation in the mountains, wishing he would die of a heart attack or she would change her mind. Neither had happened and he had known, in the recesses of his thoughts, that she would never change her mind.

That was the worst of the pain. The closer we were to arriving home, the further away she felt.

Derrick thought about the number of times he had nearly been killed in the past days. The gunshot wounds to his shoulder and thigh. The number of people and infected he had shot to get to where he was now. Perry's muddy face came to mind as he realized she had died alone. Infected, covered in dirt, and caked in mud, she had died with her nearest loved one's hundreds of miles away.

Why didn't I forgive her? What was I holding onto? Was it worth being alone?

Alyssa sniffled and cleared her throat, "Derrick say something– anything. You can yell at me or..."

"I don't... I don't know what's going to happen tomorrow. I don't know what's going to happen an hour from now. Truth be told, I don't know how long we'll survive. It may be one day or it may be fifty years..." Derrick's eyes darted away from Alyssa as he realized he was saying too much. "But I do know I want to spend every moment I have in this world with you."

Alyssa smiled with a tremble in her lower lip as she touched his knee. Shaking her head, she said, "I won't ever leave your side. Ever."

Derrick looked down at the ring in his hand as Alyssa's words clicked something in his thoughts. It was like she had spoken a code to unlock a door in his mind he had never knew was locked shut. Derrick asked. "Alyssa... Will you marry me?"

Alyssa's mouth dropped and he here eyebrows went high as she stared at the ring he held back to her. With concern in her eyes, she looked up to Derrick, "are you sure? You don't have to–"

"Neither do you," Derrick gave a small smile. "I'll protect you all the same, you know that. But I still love you like I did a month ago, like I will for the rest of my life."

A smile broke across her lips as she nodded with eager, starry eyes. "Yes, yes, of course I will."

Derrick slid the ring back on her finger. With hands holding each other close, they kissed long, and they kissed deep. His hand cupping her cheek, Derrick held onto the moment, savoring it like it was their last.

THIRTY-FOUR

Sharon Hill
Undisclosed Location

Sharon jolted awake as her box was jostled about. Her mind was fatigued as she tried to recall why she was in a glass box. By the time her memories came back to her, Sharon was being carted down a familiar plastic-coated hallway. She felt such pain radiating from her hips and head, she didn't care where she was being brought as she cleared the crust from the corners of her eyes.

There was no part of her body that didn't either ache from exhaustion or throb from injuries. Whatever healing her body had attempted during the hours she had slept, hadn't been enough. Behind her, Sharon saw more cubes being squeezed out of the classroom doorway. Tonya and Carl were wheeled out along with two other prisoners.

Unsure of what time it was, Sharon couldn't tell if it was dark out because of the plastic covered hallways clogging the windows. She shielded her eyes as she was wheeled past the bright construction light tree and turned down the wide hall for the gymnasium. It was then Sharon had the wherewithal to panic. The large gymnasium floor was empty and dark except for two white, collapsible tables where several doctors sat in a line. The yellow hazmat suits they wore were hunched over laptop and table screens and a single tree of lights illuminated the floor in front of their tables.

Sharon and the others were rolled out of the darkness and stopped in a row before the doctors–animals in their glass cages. The lights shined on Sharon's face. She could barely see the four video cameras on tripods recording them from all four sides. *What is this...*

Sharon went still when she heard the gym doors latch shut as their escorts left the gym. She saw two soldiers, who stood shrouded in darkness, behind the row of doctors. These soldiers appeared different than the others. They wore clear face masks and while their hazmat suits were camo similar to the other soldiers. Sharon saw no patches, American flags, or name tags on their uniforms. Everyone was watching the five caged prisoners in silence. Sharon could hear her heart thudding in her chest as she stood on display.

One of the doctors walked over to Tonya's cube on the far end and read the paper attached at the waist level. "Test site Delta. Trial 00092. Test subject Bravo 4287. Compound series 00148. Inoculation injection eighteen hours and forty-two minutes prior."

The voice sounded familiar. One of the doctors that had been there when Sharon had been brought in. *Dr. Schafer, was it?*

Tonya gave Sharon a worried look. She could see Tonya's face clearly for the first time. It wasn't nearly as hard as her voice made her sound or what Sharon expected a woman soldier to look like. On the contrary, Tonya looked like a high school girl–alone and terrified. Her small nose and wide eyes looked for help that wasn't there.

Sharon looked down at the compartment in front of her own cube and saw an empty glass vial, piece of paper, and a timer. Same as Tonya's. The two soldiers wheeled a metal box to the center of the floor beside Dr. Schafer. It looked like a metallic safe on wheels with a digital read out and number pad. Dr. Schafer punched in a code on the keypad at the top, turned a metal bar counterclockwise, and lifted the lid. He pulled out a silver cylinder with a red cap on one end and walked it back to Tonya slowly. He held it in front of him with two hands and took small steps. Pressing a button on her cube, he placed the cylinder in a cubby and retreated to the foldout table with the rest of the scientists. Everyone, even those in their cubes, stared at Tonya.

"Okay, ma'am," Dr. Ellis said. Her harsh and grating voice instantly recognized by Sharon. She sat at the center of the long foldout table with a tablet propped up and a plastic covered keyboard in front of her. "If you pull open that cubby in front of you, you'll find an injection cylinder. Take off the red cap and press the needle into your upper arm for me, please." Tonya hesitantly opened her side of the cubby and removed the metallic cylinder.

"W-what's in it?" she asked.

Her question was followed by the briefest moment of hesitation, as the doctor had not expected her speaker to be on. "Nothing harmful. Just take off the red cap and inject yourself in the arm; it won't hurt," Dr. Ellis reassured.

Tonya glanced at Sharon again, then stared at the red cap, and shook her head. "I'm not doing it."

Dr. Ellis gave an audible sigh and brushed her hand toward the soldiers standing sentry. One walked in front of Tonya's box and leveled his rifle barrel at her, nonchalantly. Dr. Ellis repeated in a stern voice, "Inject yourself or you will be shot."

Tonya's hands instinctively raised in front of her chest and she stepped back. "Wait, wait... just wait," she said, emotions overcoming her as her hands trembled.

"You have five seconds. We don't have time to discuss. I'm sorry, but this is the way it has to happen." Dr. Ellis continued clicking a key on the keyboard in front of her. "Five.... Four..."

"Wait, you can't do this!" Tonya yelled. Sharon pressed her hands against the glass. Her eyes wide as she wanted to scream at the sight of this madness.

"Three..." at the count of 'three' the soldier fired his rifle once into the high school banner with a growling Panther on it that hung on the wall over Tonya's cube. None of the doctors reacted to the gunshot.

Sharon had collapsed to the ground from the sudden bang and when she stood back up, Tonya had the cylinder in her trembling hand and the red cap removed in the other hand. *No, no, no... don't do it!*

"Two... One..."

Tonya stabbed her left shoulder with the small needle on 'one.' One of the doctors at the end of the table clicked a timer on a handheld stopwatch. Four or Five seconds of still silence filled the air before Tonya was on her knees. She clenched her teeth and groaned, pressing her hands on both sides of her temple. Eight seconds and she started to scream in pain in agony, her vocal cords tearing with every screech. She was on her feet, her eyes wide, as drool and a foamy substance dribbled from her mouth as she let loose a maddening howl.

Sharon covered her mouth to silence her own screams. Dr. Schafer went back over to Tonya's cube and pressed a button that muted Tonya's wretched screams but no one could stop her thumping her face against the glass. He walked around it, observing as Tonya's rabid gaze followed him, banging her fists bloody on the siding. "Blood vessels bursting in the eyes, foaming at the mouth, excess saliva production, extreme perspiration..." he listed off his observations as if it was the most ordinary thing in the world. "There is blood on teeth, face, and hands, likely from self-inflicted wounds..."

"Incubation period?" Dr. Ellis asked as she tapped on her tablet.

The doctor with the stopwatch answered, "four seconds for initial symptoms. seventeen seconds total."

Dr. Ellis shook her head as she continued. "Trial 00092. Test subject Bravo 4287. Compound 00148. Failed. Terminating subject."

Dr. Schafer pressed three buttons on opposite sides of Tonya's cube and a cloud of yellow smoke leaked from the floorboards and enveloped her infected body. Tonya coughed, then vomited a bloody mucus across the front of the glass before falling to the ground with violent tremors. Sharon and the four other caged subjects stared at her shaken body as she went still, and the mucus that oozed out of her eyes, nose, mouth, and ears turned blood red

Dr. Schafer walked in front of Carl's cube, which was next in line and began reading his info. "Test site Delta. Trial 00093. Test subject–"

Sharon started to panic. The prisoners locked in the cubes began to beat on the glass and cried, unheard. They all knew they just watched their fate play out before them. Carl was cursing the doctors before they had finished reading the testing info. The girl between Sharon and Carl was digging at a small vent at the bottom of her cube. Sharon thought she might've found something.

Maybe a way out. Or a weapon?

Sharon dropped to her knees and fiddled with the grate.

The holes were tiny and sharp. The entire base felt like one giant piece of metal. Nothing was loose. There were no weak points.

"Sir," Dr. Ellis said to Carl. Dr. Schafer was walking back to the table after placing the silver cylinder in Carl's cubby. "Pull open that cubby in front of you, there's an injection pen in there. Take off the red cap and inject–"

"Hell fuckn' no!" Carl screamed over her. "I'm not injecting anything! Are you fuckn' retarded?"

"If you don't take the injection, you will be shot," Dr. Ellis repeated much more quickly than before. "You have five seconds."

"Fuck you!" Carl jabbed his finger into the glass. "You fucking touch me and I'll sue the shit out of this place. You will all be in jail! You can't fucking do this– I've got rights you stupid–"

"Five, four, three..." The soldier rushed to fire his warning shot as Dr. Ellis counted much quicker this time.

"Nope, not happening," Carl gave the doctors the middle finger as he leaned back against the glass staring at them in defiance.

"Two, one," Dr. Ellis quickly said, then waved a hand at Dr. Schafer.

"What now, bitch?" Carl taunted as he saw the soldier retreating with his rifle, stinking of false threat. "That's what I fucking thought... coward."

Dr. Schafer carefully and meticulously took the silver cylinder out from the cube, placing it in the storage container. He pressed the combination of three buttons, releasing the yellow smoke.

"Hey! Hey, what the fuck!" Carl panicked, releasing a wet hacking cough. Convulsing, he collapsed to the floor as he choked on his own fluids.

"Trial 00093 incomplete. Compound 00158 requires retesting. Test subject Bravo 4271 terminated." Dr. Schafer moved on to the lady beside Sharon, taking a deep exhausted breath. The kind of sigh a man gave after a long day's work, when all he can think about is getting home and putting his feet up. "Test site Delta. Trial 00094..."

Sharon stared at the young girl beside her who hadn't stopped crying. She didn't look angry or even frightened. Her body was huddled in the back corner and when her tearful eyes raised to meet Sharon's, all she could see was the heartbreak in her expression, the sadness of the moment killing her before the U.S. government could. Dr. Schafer was loading the cylinder into her cube. Sharon put her palm on the glass facing the girl's chest, tears streaming down her cheek.

"Ma'am," Dr. Ellis' harsh voice said. "Pull open that cubby in front of you and there's an injection pen in there. Take off the red cap and inject yourself in the upper arm."

The girl looked back to Sharon, who mouthed, "It's okay, honey. I'm here."

The girl replied with a small, sad nod of her head before turning to the doctors. Tears fell from Sharon's eyes as she thought of Anna and how scared she must be without her mother. The teenaged girl said nothing, but slowly opened the cubby and grabbed the thick injection pen in a trembling hand and popped the red cap off. She stood there for a long minute, waiting in agony for her inevitable end.

"Ma'am, if you don't–" Dr. Ellis started but stopped when the girl quickly stabbed herself in the arm with the cylinder, then, in a flare of anger, threw it at the glass. The scientist started the stopwatch. Sharon counted this time. At the twenty second mark, the young girl was completely gone. She appeared to be screaming as her body collided with the glass, first in one direction, then the other. Her face was strained, full of blood, until the poisonous smoke overtook her. Sharon slid down to the floor and covered her face as she heard Dr. Schafer give his report.

I'm going to die. I'm going to die. I'm–

Even thinking the words felt foreign to her. *Death happened to other people, not me. I won't die. I'm a survivor.* She tried to remember what it felt like to hold her kids and imagined Annabelle's chin in the crook of her neck and Charlie's warm face nuzzled against her side. What she would give to hold them just one more time.

"Test site Delta. Trial 00095," Dr. Schafer read Sharon's information. Sharon looked over to the only other living test subject remaining. He too sat defeated on the ground and rocked repeatedly while holding his knees to his chest. Sharon saw how weak he looked and imagined how powerful the doctors must feel standing over him.

Sharon stood up and wiped the tears from her face. *They're not going to feel powerful when they stand over me. I won't let them.* She pushed her chin high and narrowed her eyes at Dr. Schafer, her jaw clenched. She wanted to show him she wasn't scared, even if it was a lie. "Test subject Bravo 43– um." Dr. Schafer had to pause and glance up at Sharon's glaring eyes that bore into him inches from the glass. "Uh– Bravo 4305. Compound..." Schafer paused, again, and his whole helmet angled to the side as he read. "X-ray-62. Inoculation injection eight hours and seven minutes prior."

"X-ray-62? Where's the protocol on this?" one of the doctors leaned back in his creaking chair.

"There isn't one," Dr. Ellis said as she cupped her helmet. "D.C. sent it for testing with no packet. I have tried to follow up."

There were groans from everyone at the table as Dr. Ellis waved Dr. Schafer to continue.

He went to press a button to turn on Sharon's microphone and saw it was already on. Dr. Schafer quickly shied away from her glare and fetched the cylinder that would infect and kill Sharon. She felt the room closing in on her as he dropped the cylinder into her cubby and walked away. She could taste the death that was only seconds away. It tightened around her heart.

"Ma'am," Dr. Ellis said, swiping on the tablet in front of her. "Pull open the cubby and–"

"Just shut the fuck up," Sharon said as she opened the cubby. She took a deep, shuttering breath while looking down at death and picked up the cylinder. It was heavier than she expected. It seemed like the most existential and shitty question to have to answer.

How do you want to die, Sharon? Either way you're about to die, so if it's less pain you want, fuck them and fuck this test, and skip to the gassing. But the gas is guaranteed to be deadly, whereas injecting myself with this infection gives me a chance, a small chance of survival if it works, right?

"If you don't inject–" Dr. Ellis started but was swiftly interrupted, again.

"I said shut the fuck up. I don't believe in heaven, but you're the only reason I want to believe in hell, you cunt," Sharon snarled at Dr. Ellis.

Sharon popped the red cap off the cylinder and saw the sharp needle pointing at her.

I'm coming home, mom.

Sharon gritted her teeth and took a deep breath before she swung the cylinder down to her arm. An explosion knocked her back against the glass and collapsed her to the floor. Screams filled the gym as gunfire surrounded the school. The two soldiers ran to the gymnasium door. The shooting reached inside the building and bullets shredded the gym door.

THIRTY-FIVE

Sharon Hill
Undisclosed Location

The rapid fire roared so loud that Sharon's chest thumped. She felt as though her heart was going to burst free. It was like nothing she had ever felt. She recalled her late-night adventures as a kid going with her mom to the laundromat down the road. Her mother had always been so good at turning a mundane task like laundry at 1:00 am into a make-believe exploration. Half the time, Sharon would be so tired she'd lay on the warm dryer and fall asleep to the gentle rocking of the machine. That was until a heavy load of sheet made the cheap appliance begin to bounce violently. Sharon would wake to her tiny chin slamming into the top of the dryer and her ears ringing as the world thudded around her. Her mother would then have to swoop Sharon off of the machine and rescue her from the chaotic rattle on the tile floor.

That's what Sharon felt like as the cube's speaker amplified the explosions with crackling distortion. The doctors were on the floor scrambling to hide behind the cubes. As more explosions blew into the brick wall a small hole opened that sent chunks of debris tumbling across the floor. Before the soldiers could reach the exit, the doors swung open, and the gym echoed with gunfire. Bullets cut through the soldiers' and doctors' bodies. Sharon knelt to the ground and covered her head as the glass shards shattered and rained down on her back like razor blades.

The shooting relented inside the gym, but scattered gunfights continued all over the school. Sharon slowly raised her head and heard the glass fall from her hair. She inspected her limbs for any wounds. The amount of adrenaline coursing through her body should have stunted her thoughts. It would have just a few days ago, but she found herself clear headed and looking for escape.

"Look at this," said a man with a southern draw in his voice. "Can we take her?"

Sharon looked up and saw four younger men wearing a mix of camouflage coats and blue jeans staring at her. Their rifles rested casually on their shoulders as they stepped closer to Sharon's dismembered cube. On wobbly knees, Sharon stood up and saw the dead bodies of doctors and soldiers sprawled across the floor. The maze of hallways that fed into the gym echoed with volleys of gunfire. The ongoing shooting played out in the background and didn't seem to worry these men.

"She is kinda cute," a young man with a thick, black beard said as he walked to her and looked down. "What you say, cutie? You want to ride this cowboy?"

The three others laughed as the bearded man reached down to cup Sharon's cheek, his thumb extending toward her lips. Sharon didn't know who these men were or what was going on. But the moment the man's hand touched her, a flare of anger blew inside Sharon, and she swung her fist at his arm. She had forgotten the cylinder she was still clutching in her hand when the needle cut the man's arm.

"Fuck!" the man snapped his hand back and shook it up and down. "Fucking bitch!"

"Oooh, Bobby, she got spirit!" one of the men laughed.

"Yeah, this fucking... this fuck..." Bobby staggered as he clenched his wounded arm. "She... ahnng!" he collapsed to his knees and rolled to his side, wracked in convulsions.

"What's wrong with him?"

"I don't know, hey, Bobby!" his friends neared to check on him, but it was too late. Bobby's screams filled the gym, drowning out the gunshots and the occupants' thoughts. He lunged on the nearest of his friends. One of the men fired his rifle as he retreated, his bullets skipping across the gym floor as the third man was tackled.

Sharon was a little girl, again. She cowered on the floor of her cube and played dead because she did not dare to move. She heard the high-pitched screams as two of the men ran circles in the gym chaotically before sprinting out the doors for the gunfire.

It took time for Sharon to find the courage to open her eyes, but when she did, she saw the carnage of the room for the first time. One of the men wearing camouflage was lying bent backward over a toppled table. Her foot kicked the cylinder that still held the rabid virus away from her as she scooted back from it. Brushing at her arm with her hand, she looked for a puncture mark and she saw none.

Sharon stood and waited for several seconds to confirm she wasn't infected. It took several tries, but she managed to awkwardly climb out from her cube without cutting herself on the jagged edges of glass. The man who was in the cube to Sharon's right laid lifelessly in a pool of his own blood, shot to death when the attack began. A part of Sharon envied him. *His struggle is over. He has nothing to fear. Nothing to run from.*

Sharon went over to one of the soldier's twisted bodies and picked up the machine gun beside him. It was heavy with blood coating the grip. She knew it had ammo in it because it had a clip in the bottom, but beyond that she knew nothing, not even whether the safety was on. Sharon pointed it to the roof, wincing as she held her head to the side, and pulled the trigger. A short three-round burst fired into the ceiling and Sharon jumped when she heard the bullets ricochet. The screeching high-pitched scream that answered her gunshot did not sound human. It sounded like a large predator that had just caught the scent of its prey.

She ran to the opposite side of the gymnasium where the explosion had broken through part of the brick wall and shouldered open a nearby door. The blinding floodlights covered her as the humid night air hit her like a wall. She ran out of its glare and saw she was outside, beneath black sky. The floodlights that had surrounded the school illuminated the tall grass like a football field. Dozens of soldier's bodies littered the field resembling animal carcasses left to rot away. Sharon ran toward the road. She didn't know where it led or where she was going, but she knew it had to be far from this place.

She was halted in her tracks when she saw the door in the corner of the school burst open and fleeing soldiers in army uniforms pour outside. Sharon didn't wait to measure their reaction, nor did she attempt to beg them for help. The moment two of the men looked her way she yanked the trigger of the machine gun in her hands.

Side stepping into a sprint, she felt the gun dance in her hands as it popped bullets at the screaming men. It clicked empty as she was sprinting up the grass fields and into the dark hills that surrounded the school. Sharon tossed the gun behind her and felt her thighs burn from the near vertical incline. Bullets pounded the dirt around her and she saw the soldiers running behind her.

Lost in the pitch-black night and the tall grass, Sharon ran until the lactic acid had paralyzed her quad muscles and dove to the ground near the base of a thin oak tree. The thick weeds were nearly four feet tall and would surely hide her, she hoped.

Sharon held her breath as the footsteps came closer. They were right above her. The set of heavy boots barely made it past her when she heard another set of footsteps running, no, sprinting.

"Oh, god– go, get away," a young soldier heaved with raspy lungs.

The approaching patter of footsteps sounded like they were on all four. The soldier glanced down as he struggled to run and panic filled Sharon as he looked her right in the eyes. It was then as the sweaty soldier kept running that she realized the soldiers weren't chasing her. They were being chased.

The rabid growled and screamed as it scurried through the tall grass. A second soldier, this one heavy-footed in his stomps, barely made it past Sharon when he was tackled.

"No– no, oh god!" his voice broke.

The bodies collapsed in flurry of violent movement only feet from Sharon's face. She couldn't see the soldier through the grass, but she could see the shadowed silhouette of the hunched back of his attacker. She covered her mouth to prevent herself from involuntarily breathing.

"Please– stop, stop! Off! Gah!" the soldier cried. The rabid lifted him up and slammed the soldier back down. Sharon could hear the impact like a sack of meat being beat by a baseball bat.

The rabid bit down on the man's cheek and jerked its head from side to side. The man gargled a scream in agony with scratch at his skin. Wet sounds of meat ripping from bone and blood spilling across the grass was only covered by the useless pounding of the soldier's boots and fists against the earth.

Bullets pattered the dirt and hit the small tree over Sharon's head, and she tucked into a ball. With an animalistic grunt, the rabid lurched off its victim and toward the gunfire, flinging dirt at Sharon as it scurried away. The fear was paralyzing. Sharon's palms were riddled with tremors as they covered her ears. All she could think of was her mother and what she would give to be held by her right now.

You have to move. You have to move. You have to move!

Like a mantra that grew louder inside her, the words coaxed Sharon into raising to her knees. A sudden jolt from the wounded soldier made her drop down to her belly again. The sounds that came from the soldier were distorted and off. His face clearly mutilated and injured badly. But the piercing scream that erupted from him cut into the silence of the hills.

She watched the top of the tall grass whisk violently from side to side. The soldier's fists and legs beat the dirt as he writhed. The few blades of grass that were between the two of them had been flattened leaving only inches of dark space.

Sharon had to run. If he turned to his side, the infected man's eyes would be staring right at Sharon.

Run. Run!

More rabid screams screeched down below and fewer gunshots rang out now. *Run run run*! Her body refused to move. Footsteps surrounded her. Her stomach dropped. She saw her death coming as shadows circled the tall grass above her. She could already hear her screams before she even made a sound.

The fast charge of rabid steps ran up the hill. The other rabids' shrieks caught the attention of the infected soldier beside Sharon and jerked him to his feet. He stomped across Sharon's calf as he ran after the others.

Pain ignited in Sharon's leg, but she didn't make a sound. Clenching her teeth as she twisted weeds from the dirt, she didn't move. Sharon couldn't move. She clutched her hands over her mouth. The only sound in the black night was the ragged screams of the rabid and their hard footsteps as they sprinted through the tall grass circling Sharon like a shark.

THIRTY-SIX

Brandon Armstrong
Louisville, KY

Brandon showered after Alyssa. It was a strange sensation being 'safe' and in a home. Standing under the steaming hot water, Brandon felt the sting of dozens of cuts across his body and face flare when water entered them. More than that, he felt the tension in his hands and chest as he leaned against the shower wall. After so many hours and days of constant combat, peace time was... uncomfortable. It felt as though Brandon had been gripping a power cable with two fists for days, feeling the electricity cut through him. And the moment the electricity stopped assaulting his nerves, all Brandon could think about was when it would start, again.

By the time Brandon came outside, Eric was zoned out in the chair beside Zoe. Eric still held on to the Greenband SAT phone, listening to the encrypted radio and playing with the buttons. Karen beckoned Brandon to the back porch and he followed her out the sliding door. The grass in the small backyard was overgrown and the weeds reached up to the deck top. Brandon saw that half the deck was wet where Karen had sprayed down Derrick and his uniforms and equipment with bleach, scrubbed them with a mop, then hosed them down.

"Brandon, what is going on? Alyssa said that girl on the couch was shot."

"Derrick was, too," Brandon nodded. "Actually, so was I," Brandon looked at his shirt having almost forgotten his grazing wound that the Chattanooga nurses had stitched up.

"What happened? The President's dead. And the Vice President just issued a statement that the infection has been contained, but the news is saying it just had an outbreak in Tennessee."

"It's not contained anymore," Brandon said, but he left out the part that he was the reason it wasn't contained anymore. "The infection is spreading."

"Oh my god, where?" Karen's voice took on a high-pitched tone. Like she had just sat down for mimosas with her girlfriends and wanted the latest gossip.

Brandon sighed, scratching his temple, "Listen, babe, I'll tell you all about it later, but I'm starving and am on the verge of passing out right now."

"Well, there's plenty of food," Karen rolled her eyes impatiently. "That boy you brought cooked about all the frozen food we have."

"I can't believe the food hasn't gone bad, yet," Brandon said. "You haven't had any power outages?"

"No, not yet. I figure we can go to the store tomorrow morning to buy groceries for the next couple weeks. I'll just use my credit card and everyone can pay us back when this is over."

Brandon's face morphed into perplexed confusion as if he was trying to decipher the language his wife spoke.

Brandon simply nodded and moved to the kitchen, figuring it was a conversation for another time. They ate in exhausted silence huddled around the TV, scavenging every bit of food from Karen's kitchen. Before long Eric fell asleep in a lounge chair with his feet up. Paper plates filled with crumbs littered every table.

Brandon finished the last bite of canned ham and he could barely swallow it down to his stuffed stomach. The news jumped back and forth between amateur videos of napalm dropping on Atlanta and President Anderson's address. He was a thin looking man. Meek. His eyes fleeted from side to side with worry behind the thin rimmed glasses he wore.

Say what you want about his predecessor, but President Walker had been a man's man with eyes like a bear. If we weren't fucked before, we are now with this guy.

"Despite the White House's attempt to calm the public," the news report on TV continued. "News of President Walker's untimely death has surged rioting in the major cities. We have reports of major structural fires in Chicago, Detroit–"

Brandon knew tomorrow was going to be tough. The truth was everyday forward would be tougher than the last.

"–and quickly here we want to take time to touch on more domestic terrorist attacks in the Midwest here," the tired looking news broadcaster turned to look into a different camera. A map of the Midwest appeared behind her with speckled red dots in Indiana, Illinois, Kentucky, and Tennessee. "Along with civil unrest, rioting, and several documented cases excessive use of force by police and soldiers, the domestic terrorist group known as 'Sons of Liberty' continue to attack government buildings, military convoys, and now, hospitals. Unconfirmed reports are stating a hospital in Chattanooga, TN was ambushed earlier today killing multiple police officers..."

Karen laid on Brandon's side in the love seat with Brandon's arm around her chest.

"Oh my god, is that what you were telling me about? The hospital?" Karen asked, squeezing his forearm.

"Yup," Brandon's eyes squinted open as he was quickly beginning to doze off. "Yeah."

"That's crazy. Maybe you and Derrick will get a medal or something after this is all done," Karen said.

"Hmm," Brandon hummed as he was beginning to doze off. He knew Karen didn't really understand what was about to happen. No one in the north did. You had to see the infected and the bombs firsthand to understand the world was over. So far, the most inconvenience the outbreak had brought upon Karen was making her vacation in her late grandparent's house for a couple weeks. But unlike every other major city in the U.S., Louisville was the army's central hub, which meant no power outages and nearly unlimited resources to deal with rioters. Brandon knew his wife was in for a steep learning curve in the coming days, but he figured that was a lesson that could wait till tomorrow.

Brandon went rigid with alertness when he heard movement in the house over the murmur of the TV. His hand had made it halfway to his Glock 19 on the table beside the loveseat before he realized it was just Alyssa using the bathroom. Karen and Brandon looked upstairs and watched Alyssa pass by in the shadows as the toilet flushed and pipes drained.

"When did that happen?" Karen whispered after the door to Alyssa and Derrick's room clicked shut, again.

Brandon made a face. "When did what happen? Their engagement?"

Karen's eyes went wide as she repeated too loudly. "Engagement?"

"Yeah. On that camping trip they went on a couple weeks

before all this. They got engaged at Pigeon Forge." Brandon informed an unimpressed Karen.

"Um. Honey, no, they didn't," Karen sat up to face Brandon. "I talked to Alyssa after she got back from Pigeon Forge. She turned him down."

"What?"

"Yeah, like turned down flat. She told me not to tell anyone because she didn't want to embarrass him. But yeah, they basically broke up on that trip," Karen said. She had always loved giving people gossip. There was almost a glow in her voice when she was able to inform people of things they didn't know. "Well, not basically. They did break up."

"They been broken up since before the outbreak?" Brandon asked, feeling heat flood his cheeks and the sting of sweat on the back of his neck.

"Oh yeah, for like a month now. Derrick didn't tell you any of this?"

PART III

Wednesday, May 1st

18 Hours, 47 Minutes Until Calamity Event

"Extinction is the rule. Survival is the Exception."

- Carl Sagan

THIRTY-SEVEN

Derrick Hart
Louisville, KY

Derrick awoke with a full bladder. He palpated his way through the dark hallway on the second floor of the old house to the bathroom. The nightlight casted a red shadow across the porcelain toilet and the gray shower curtain. Groggy and all thumbs, Derrick managed to get down his pants, but he realized he never checked behind the closed shower curtain.

I always check behind the shower curtain—a childhood fear from watching too many horror movies too young. A benefit, at the time, of having no parental supervision, but one that left a scar. He pulled up his pants after peeing and reached for the curtain half-mindedly and froze as he heard breathing from the other side.

His fingers closed around the curtain, jangling the metal rings on the rod, and a growl came from the tub. Derrick's stomach dropped and he felt the sweat building on the back of his neck. He wanted to run, to reach for a gun that wasn't there. He pulled the curtain to the side, revealing the dark figure crouched in the bathtub. Panting. Growling.

The rabid bared its teeth, blood leaking from the sides of its jaw as it stared up at Derrick. It leapt on him, tackling him to the ground. The rabid's fingers dug into his arms; its teeth tore into his neck. The smell of rotting breath bathed his face and Derrick heard his own scream turn rabid.

Derrick jolted awake, his muscles tense. He sucked in hard to clear his stale throat. He was sweating so much that some of Alyssa's hair stuck to his forehead when he separated. His heart rate slowed as he regained his bearings. Patting the mattress behind his legs, he searched for Ginger at his usual spot in his bed. Confusion clogged his mind when he didn't find his dog's heavy body pressed against his thighs, until Derrick remembered the crushing reality. *Ginger's gone.*

Grimacing, Derrick oriented himself to his surroundings.

Karen's parents' house. Second floor bedroom. Room is secure. House is secure.

His hand tapped on the nightstand, checking that his handgun and flashlight were still there before touching his rifle that was propped between the bed and nightstand. His relief was short lived as memories of the day's past rushed to the brim of his mind like the fizz of a badly shaken bottle of soda. It was the memory of Perry's rabid eyes that made Derrick sit up.

You killed her.

There was not a part of his body that did not hurt. The few hours of rest he had seemed to only make his muscles ache worse. The bottom and sides of his feet were covered in Neosporin and bandaged from all the ripped blisters. His body was a checkerboard of bruises with a dozen stitches on various tears in his skin. Through the corner of the window shades, he could see it was still dark outside but birds began to chirp their songs so dawn wasn't far.

Derrick stood with a groan and quietly shuffled to the bathroom. The shower curtain was already open. He eyed the empty tub, remembering his nightmare as he relieved himself then tied the drawstrings on his loose sweatpants. There was a sound downstairs that stood his neck hairs on end. Reflexively, Derrick crouched some as he hid in the shadows of the hallway, trying to identify the sound. The hum of the AC kicking on. The pipes drained into the plumbing. When he heard it again, Derrick relaxed when he realized it was Zoe.

Derrick made his way down the stairs loud enough not to startle Zoe, but quiet enough so others wouldn't wake. A light blue nightlight in the adjoining kitchen sent a cold shade of color on the skinny girl. She was huddled in the corner of the couch, with a pillow held lightly against her wounded belly.

"How do you feel?" Derrick asked and sat on the opposite side of the couch. The black t-shirt he wore was one of Brandon's left in a drawer from a previous visit. It was baggy on Derrick, but it was better than his sweat soaked clothes.

"Hurts," she said barely louder than a whisper. Zoe's teary eyes stared ahead at the coffee table, refusing to look at Derrick. In the reclining chair across the room, Eric was curled in a ball, half snoring, with a white comforter pulled up to his neck.

"Yeah... do you want some more medicine for the pain?"

Zoe shook her head, causing a tear to break loose down her cheek. He rubbed her shoulder to comfort her from a noncommittal distance; Derrick was never good at consoling. He didn't have the first clue as to what the right thing to say was and often chose silence out fear of inevitably saying the wrong thing.

"...alone..." Zoe mumbled.

"What's that?"

Zoe cleared her throat and sniffled, "I'm alone. My whole family is... I'm all alone."

Derrick's half-asleep mind wandered without discipline. *Alone...* He thought about how alone he had felt in the moment after watching the life slip from Perry's body. He thought about his rambling words to Brandon the night before. *Was it really worth it to be alone now? To have no family.* Finally, he thought about his mother, and the last voicemail she had left to him.

Derrick cleared his throat after a moment. "How old are you, again?"

"...fifteen," Zoe answered.

Derrick nodded. He tried to remember what he had been like at fifteen years old. He had been living at his foster home by then, but the place was merely where he'd slept. Between school, track practice after school, working at a landscaping company on the weekends, and hanging out with Brandon, Derrick barely saw his foster parents. That had been fine with Derrick; he was sure they'd only fostered for the monthly state check anyway.

I wasn't a child anymore at fifteen, not after what I went through. Derrick's eyes clicked with recognition as he looked at Zoe cowering in the corner of the couch. *She's not a child anymore either.*

"You know, you and I have something in common," Derrick finally spoke, resigning himself. "I was a little younger than you when I sat in my living room and said the same thing. *I'm all alone.*" Zoe looked up for the first time. Her big, brown eyes staring cautiously at Derrick.

"My um– my dad, passed away from cancer when I was young, like four or five," Derrick continued. "I don't remember much of him... I remember his smell, the cologne he wore to church when he'd hold me sometimes. It was hard when he died, but my mom took it worse. She started to drink to dull the pain, to try and forget."

Zoe winced as she angled her body to face Derrick on the couch as she listened, the distraction from her grief welcome in her expression. It felt strange to speak about his past aloud. Aside from Alyssa, Derrick had never told anyone about his parents. Brandon didn't need to be told; he had been there for it all.

"I didn't notice it for the first few years," Derrick said. "But by the time I was eleven years old, my mom was an alcoholic. She had stopped being a mom for years by that point. She didn't take care of the apartment, she didn't take care of me, and she kind of just stopped talking for a while. For a long while. I didn't have any brothers or sisters so it was just me trying to hold everything together for as long as I could. I'd make the food, help her to bed, throw away empty bottles..." Derrick shook his head as he was lost in his memories. The deafening sound of clinking empty vodka bottles crashing into the dumpster every time he took the trash out.

"I had distractions..." Derrick continued. "I was friends with Brandon since first grade and his house was a couple blocks away from our apartment complex. So I'd spend a lot of nights over there. Typically, it was on nights after I dumped all my mom's alcohol down the drain to avoid her anger tantrums."

Derrick smirked at Zoe but then let out a long sigh before continuing, "one afternoon, I came home from school... I was twelve and my mom wasn't home... I made dinner for us, macaroni and cheese, my specialty, and waited... and waited... Afternoon turned to night and she still wasn't home. Brandon called me on our home phone and asked if I was coming over to spend the night like we had planned. I said, 'no.' Said, 'I have to make sure my mom gets to bed.'"

Derrick smiled and rolled his eyes at the absurdity of his

memories. He could still remember the weight of the heavy chord pulling down the home phone in his small hand. How quiet the apartment was with only him inside it.

"I wouldn't see my mother again for a few years. Not really. Not more than a few minutes here or there," Derrick gave Zoe a sad smile. "My mother was driving when she crossed three lanes of traffic and hit a car head-on. She had, um, she just left the liquor store and the half gallon of vodka she had bought was already half gone."

"Was she okay?" Zoe asked quietly.

"Yeah," Derrick nodded politely. "She had some cuts and bruises but that was all. The other car had two teenagers in the backseat, they were also fine... but their father, who was driving the car, died on impact." Derrick chewed his lip as if he was sealing his mouth from speaking the rest. He omitted the reason his mother had to go to the liquor store that afternoon was the same reason why he had planned on spending the night at Brandon's house.

The night prior Derrick had hit every one of his mother's hiding spots and poured out the nearly a dozen bottles of vodka she had stashed away. Derrick didn't know if he skipped those details for Zoe's sake or his own. He wouldn't admit it, even to himself, but Derrick liked the way Zoe looked up to him. Her eyes marveled at him like he was a superhero. As if she felt safe as long as Derrick was there. It was a lie he didn't want to crush with the truth. It was a mythological version of himself that he could never get back.

Derrick had always dreamt of becoming a police officer. A hero who could stop bad things from happening to good people. Someone who could arrest the drunk driver before she murdered the father of two. He recalled the sharp, stinging smell of the cheap vodka as he emptied the last pint down the drain... His mind wandered to the police officers he abandoned in Birmingham, the soldiers he killed at the Tennessee border, and the look in Perry's eyes as she died.

Derrick knew the truth... he was no hero.

Heroes don't live in this world. Not anymore.

He cleared his throat. "I sat in that apartment for three days waiting for her to come home, but that first night, not long after hanging up the phone with Brandon, I remember sitting there thinking... 'I'm alone now.' I thought she had left. That she was mad at me for– and she had left and gone away. I had no family to call or brothers or sisters to turn to, it was just me, sitting in an apartment alone. But, um, late that night there was a knock on the apartment door."

Zoe clung to every word like they were the last rope keeping her tethered to the world. Her eyebrows high as she waited for the next part of the story.

"It was Brandon," Derrick spoke softly with a reserved smile. "He wasn't supposed to come over, but he did. Told his mom he was spending the night at my apartment that night. For three days I just sat there staring at the door while Brandon sat with me watching TV. When morning came, he skipped school with me so I wouldn't risk missing my mom coming home. My best friend stayed by my side even when he knew his parents would kill him for skipping school." Derrick smirked to himself.

He remembered those days as if it was yesterday. Three days of eating macaroni and cheese and watching reruns of cartoons all day. All the while, Derrick stared at the front door, willing it to open, and his mom to stumble through the door as she always did. It never happened, though. Each day that had passed had eaten away at Derrick's inside. He had managed to stave off crying like a baby in front of his best friend until the last night before Brandon's mom had discovered the two of them.

Brandon had been lounging on the couch. Even at twelve

years old, his long legs and torso nearly stretched from end to end. Derrick had thought he had drifted off to sleep, as he hadn't moved in some time and the TV movie they had been watching in the dark room had played silently. Tears begun to break loose from the corner of Derrick's eyes like they hadn't done in years. The panic seemed to loom over his adolescent frame. The terrifying thought that he would never see his mother, again. When he saw Brandon sit up behind him from the corner of his eye, Derrick scrambled to wipe away his tears with the back of his hand before the inevitable insults would begin to be hurl his way.

Instead, Derrick had felt a tap on his shoulder. Under the light of the TV screen, Brandon held out a hand with a set of dog tags in it. "I'm getting kinda sick of wearing these," Brandon said. "You want them."

Derrick sniffled, staring in shock at the silver necklace piled in his friend's palm. "Are you sure?"

The dog tags had been a prized possession of Brandon's for months then. They had been an exclusive bonus perk that had come with purchasing the deluxe version of their favorite video game, Viking's Slaughter. Brandon had lorded it over Derrick's head all spring break as the thing never seemed to leave his neck.

"Yeah, it's yours," Brandon said, tossing the dog tags in Derrick's lap. In the dark apartment, he fumbled the tags between his skinny fingertips, admiring the two Viking brothers clasping arms and Derrick smiled. Derrick put on the dog tags and never took them off again. By the end of that summer, Derrick had saved up enough money doing yard work around the neighborhood to the same video game and gifted that pair of dog tags to Brandon.

Valhalla waits for no one.

Though years had passed, Derrick still remembered the

comfort he had felt just by having Brandon sit by his side. Scooting closer to Zoe on the couch, Derrick squeezed her shoulder gently. "You can't be alone when you're surrounded by friends," he said.

Tears dripped from her eyes as she released the smallest of stutters reminiscent of her older sister. "B-but I don't have a lot of friends. Jessica was... I've never had a best friend."

"You do now," Derrick said.

Zoe's lips broke into a frown as the weight of the moment became too much of her. A whimper of a cry escaped her lips as her arms parted for a hug. Derrick carefully put his arms around her shoulders and held her as she buried her face in his chest.

Derrick thought of how many people he had killed to get here; how many people he had left to die so that he could live. There was a levity inside him from being finally able to do something right. As he held the young girl in his arms and felt her fingers grip on to him only one thought focused his mind.

I am keeping this girl alive no matter what. No matter what.

"I know you're hurting," Derrick whispered when Zoe finally pulled away, to rub her eyes. "Your heart as much as your wound. But I need you to be strong. Tomorrow is going to be a hard day. It's not fair but I have to ask you to be even tougher than you've been for the last few days. Tougher than me and I'm an old hairy oaf." a crack of a smile came to Zoe's lips as she nodded. "Your sister, Jessica, was one of the bravest people I have ever met. She helped you get this far, but tomorrow it's going to be us counting on you, okay?"

"Okay," Zoe nodded, wiping away her tears. A harden expression already forming on her face. Derrick inched to the edge of the couch as if to stand and Zoe blurted out, "your mom..." then paused as if she reconsidered whatever question she was about to ask.

"Yeah?"

"Do you ever see her? Is she in jail?"

"She, um– she got out of prison when I was in college," Derrick said. "I talk to her on the phone now and again. She doesn't drink anymore. She has a new family now that keeps her busy..." Derrick said. The memories were sharp at the edges, stinging as he grasped at them. "I got the sense when I first started... I think... I think talking to me reminds her of some of the bad parts of her past. She's carried a lot of guilt with her, and I've... I had a lot of anger from when I was in college." Derrick shook his head as he thought about the past few days and how many times he almost died. "It'd be nice to see her again... to give her a hug and tell her..."

Derrick realized he was rambling and quickly shook the thoughts from his head. When Derrick turned, he saw Alyssa standing at the top of the stairs. She wore a polite smile as she looked down on Derrick and he felt a flare of embarrassment.

How much did she hear? What did I just say?

The downstairs bedroom door opened, and Brandon came into the living room wearing jeans and a t-shirt as he rubbed the corner of his eyes. Brandon walked around Derrick to the kitchen, ignoring Derrick's presence and looked out the back window. Derrick could see the pistol in Brandon's five o'clock IWB (In-The-Waistband) holster as he passed.

"Derrick," Brandon said and walked out to the back deck. Derrick knew something was wrong. He gave Zoe an encouraging nod before he followed his best friend outside.

THIRTY-EIGHT

Brandon Armstrong
Louisville, KY

Brandon scanned the top of the privacy fence that encased the backyard. His mind flashed back to Atlanta and him scrambling over the fences as the rabid clawed for him at Alyssa's place. He remembered the fear that had gripped him in the narrow hallway the moment both his weapons had clicked empty.

He didn't feel guilty for shooting Alyssa's parents. Brandon had actually tried to make himself feel bad, at one point, for killing them. *It's what a normal person would do, right? A normal person cries and begs forgiveness from everyone he can.* That's what society expected of cops and soldiers. They were okay with them using their guns to defend their freedom so long as they rack themselves with guilt afterwards. A soldier needed to become an alcoholic or kill themselves after using their weapon and then society might forgive them for defending the country.

Alyssa's parents had a long life and a quick death. I hope I'm lucky enough to have someone to put me down before I die in agony.

Standing at the corner of the deck, his fists gripped the wobbly railing so tightly he thought he thought it might snap in two. Decades of neglect had turned the wood black and gray. Rusted nails sprung out of the warped wood, which made the boards creek and threaten to crack at any moment.

A disaster waiting to happen.

Derrick closed the slider behind him.

"Couldn't sleep worth shit last night," Derrick said. Gunshots popped in the distance as they had throughout the night. Derrick and Brandon didn't even react to them anymore.

"How'd your ex-girlfriend sleep in there?" Brandon asked as calmly as he could manage.

Derrick went still and studied Brandon's face. Though the sun had yet to rise, night was beginning to wane. The cloudy sky turned a bleak gray as the humid air weighed down on them.

Derrick looked down and quietly said, "she slept fine, I think."

"Were you going to tell me?"

Derrick let out a heavy sigh. "Look, I'm sorry I lied. I– it's not like she's some stranger; we are together–"

"She didn't dump you a month ago. She didn't say no when you proposed to her?"

"She did. She was scared. Overwhelmed. She didn't understand."

Brandon's footstep creaked on the bowing wood as he walked to the middle of the deck. A hot anger boiled in his gut. "So, what? Were you on break while she moved to another state? How did Alyssa get to Atlanta from Birmingham? Look me in the eyes and tell me she didn't fall back in love with you just so you could sign a suicide contract for her?"

"It wasn't like that."

"It wasn't– Did you shotgun wedding a marriage certificate just to get your ex-girlfriend to safety, yes or no?" Brandon poked his finger into his palm. Anger flared in his voice.

"She didn't ask me to, I offered–"

"Jesus Christ... You never change."

"Listen, I'm sorry. I fucked up, okay? She and I had a talk last night and we're back together. If it's just the engagement thing that's bothering you, I proposed again last night, and she said yes. She just needed some space–"

"I should've never saved her."

"Dude, what the fuck? I told you–"

"I should've never saved her," Brandon interrupted, repeating it louder, "and I should have never saved you!" Brandon jabbed his finger at Derrick.

Derrick went silent leaving just the chirping of the birds between them.

"What's your fucking deal? You've been on my shit since we left Georgia about saving fucking children. Acting like they're stray cats. There's more to this world than just yourself, you selfish prick."

"No, there's not. Not anymore. Look around you. You hear that gunfire? You think police are responding to that? The only reason we're safe in this house is because you and I make it safe. Without us, they're all as good as dead and you know it. So yeah, I'm all that matters."

"You're freaking unbelievable. Why are we here? We nearly died getting to the middle of this big ass city. We could have been in fucking Canada by now if we hadn't come for your wife."

"Yeah, cause she's my fucking wife! We've made commitments. It's forever. She's not some bitch who'd say anything to survive."

"The hell does that mean?" Derrick stepped closer.

"For a smart guy you're really fucking stupid," Brandon said. "It's simple math. If Alyssa dies. If that other girl fucking dies. If any of them die... you and me live. If you and I die, then they all die. They're not built for this shit. They don't have the skills to survive in this world. None of them should even be alive right now. They're alive because of luck. Because they were lucky enough to know us– or trick you. That's what I'm saying. It's simple fucking math. If you die trying to save this half dead girl or this lying fucking ex of yours, then everyone dies."

Derrick pursed his lips and shook his head in disgust as he backed away from Brandon. "That's not how it is."

"No?"

"No, that's not how it was then and that's not how it is now. How come you didn't think like that when you came back to the army? Huh? Almost no one rejoined last week with the draft when they were recalled, but you went. You didn't have a problem putting your life out there then. Ready to die for other soldiers, for civilians you didn't even know."

"I went because a suicide contract got my wife from Tennessee to Kentucky. And back then we had a chance of beating this thing," Brandon said. "Back then there was more to life than not dying."

"Bullshit. We have a chance at surviving right now! We made it out of Georgia, across the border, through Tennessee... How's this any different than then?"

"Because now only surviving matters!" Brandon felt like he was yelling at a wall. A dumb fucking wall that wouldn't listen. "I came back to the army to kill these fuckers and save some people—namely, my fucking wife, but the minute I found out we're all fucked, I left all that shit behind because it's just about surviving now. There's no more grocery stores, or fucking car dealerships, or funerals. How many times do I have to tell you? There's dead or not dead. You make decisions that keep you alive longer, that's it."

"So that's your fucking problem. You're pissed at me because the world's going to shit and I care about more people than just myself?"

"No, I'm pissed because you fuckn' lied to me, Derrick!" Brandon shoved Derrick, causing him to stumble backward. Derrick clenched his jaw but said nothing as Brandon squared up on him. "The second everything fell apart, Alyssa fucking lied to you saying that she loved you so that you'd risk your life saving her or die trying. She's a bitch for that, but you know what, I don't blame her cause she wants to live. You do what you have to and say what you have to in order to survive. But then you fucking lie to me and get me to go kill myself trying to save that manipulative bitch!"

"Hey!" Derrick shouted.

"Oh, you're in fucking love now, right?" Brandon said with a half-smile. "She saw the light, the error of her ways and wants to *really* get married now? Huh? She was about to get back together with you *just* before the world ended anyway. What a coincidence! She's a fucking crack whore sucking dick to survive! That's it–"

Derrick stepped forward and shoved Brandon hard across his chest. "Shut the fuck up!"

Brandon immediately lunged forward, knocking Derrick's hands to the side.

"Fucking what?!" Brandon screamed. "Do something!" their noses were inches apart. Brandon could see a fire inside Derrick's eyes and hoped he would take a swing at him. The rage he felt spit bile on the back of his throat. He wanted to hurt him. Derrick's nostrils flared with every breath as they stared each other down.

The moment of tension clung to them both, passing when Derrick backed down. Turning away to face the horizon where the first signs of dawn began to break. Brandon took a deep breath. He knew this conversation was pointless. Derrick wasn't going to change. He couldn't. He was as good as dead.

We're all going to die, but I'm not going to let him drag me to an early grave.

"I–" Derrick started but was quickly interrupted.

"Alyssa... Alyssa used your love for her because she doesn't care if you die," Brandon spoke slowly and calmly. "You used our friendship to get me to save her because you don't care if I die."

Brandon could sense Derrick wanting to backtrack, apologize, and mediate a compromise. He knew his friend better than anyone in this world and could read his body language. His shoulders were slumped, and Derrick's hands hung on his hip. Brandon wasn't going to let an apology happen. Derrick was too great of a liability for Brandon. The friendship and history they shared did not compare to risking his own life or Karen's life.

My wife's life...

"You are in charge of nothing now," Brandon continued. "You can fucking leave and take them all with you, I don't care. But if you come with me and Karen, then you do what I say and that's it. If you're so desperate to bring Alyssa and the others along so you can watch them all die up close, then so be it; they're your problem not mine. But if any of them jeopardize my life or Karen's... I'll put a bullet in them. Same for you. We're not friends any more. You understand?"

Derrick stood in silence and crossed his arms. He stared at Brandon and nodded with an iron gaze.

Brandon turned back to go inside and saw Alyssa peering through the glass. Backing away quickly, she retreated into the darkness of the house.

Good. I hope that lying bitch heard every word.

THIRTY-NINE

Sharon Hill
Undisclosed Location

The break of the morning light woke Sharon from her sleep. Her first instinct was to jump up to her haunches and smack at her face and exposed skin to kill all the bugs that had crawled on her in the night. The heavy air was thick with the buzz of insects and the busy flapping of birds. It took a moment for her to remember the previous night. The memory brought her down to the ground again, surveying just above the tips of the tall grass for threats.

She had remained awake most of the night, frozen in place and afraid that the wrong move, the slightest twitch would draw the attention of the swarm of infected persons buzzing around the fields. The rabid had screeched, searching the area for an hour after the militia had fled in their pickup trucks.

Sharon started walking along the side of the road, sticking to the grassy shoulder because it was easier on her bare feet than the gravel covered concrete. Her body still ached. She figured it had been seven hours since the infected had run off in different directions. Enough time had passed that she hoped they were long gone.

The roads were empty for the most part. There were a few abandoned vehicles but they all seemed to have been out of gasoline. In the trunk of one of the unlocked cars, Sharon found a warm, half empty bottle of soda. She had never been a big soda drinker, but she forced herself to down it in one gulp. The sound her stomach made in reply was not a happy one. According to the sun's position, she walked south along the road in the hopes of finding a vehicle to return to her family. But the road winded back and forth so much she didn't really know where it led, much less where she was in relation to where she had left her family. But she had learned from her previous mistake. She first needed to find food and water and then look for her family. *And clothes...* Sharon looked down at her dirty and grass-stained nurse scrubs that barely stayed on her.

After two hours of walking and scrounging through abandoned vehicles for supplies, Sharon had made her way to the nearest town. Junction City. She had spent most of last night trying to imagine what David and the kids were doing. *Had they found shelter? Did someone give them water?* He was more diplomatic than Sharon. David was able to talk to someone for hours on end even when there was nothing to talk about. She often marveled at his desire to talk to strangers. She'd often think, maybe if she stayed near him long enough, she would start to care about others as much as he did. However, it never seemed to rub off on her. *They're fine. They are fine. David will take care of the kids.*

Junction City was more of a small town than a city. It had several small subdivisions separated by fields of green weeds and tall trees. As she finally made it to the first subdivision, she realized it how quiet it was. It was like a scene out of a horror movie. There were no cars on the road, no people outside, and no sound coming from any of the houses, but the sun was shining as if it was just another beautiful morning. The first few houses had 'no trespassing' signs; Sharon didn't like the look of them. The front porches were cluttered with items and unkempt. Cobb webs and spider webs plagued the entry way to the house with lots of.

She smelled it before she turned around the corner. And when she saw it her body froze. A corpse, or what was left of a corpse, had been dragged across two lawns leaving a long red smear over the bright green grass, and a large chunk of meat was left on the side of the road. *The rabids had already been here.*

Sharon panicked, feeling exposed. She stood in the middle of the road with open fields and houses on all sides. Too many people could see her from too many places. She ran to the nearest house. It was a two-story ranch style house. The front porch was cluttered with three bags of trash and six pairs of shoes, some of which were kids' shoes. *That was good, right?* She knocked on the door as calmly as she could and waited. *Nothing.*

"Hello? Is anyone there?" she knocked, again. "Umm... I'm not infected or anything. My name's Sharon Hill. I got separated from my husband and two kids..." Sharon rolled her eyes as she remembered telling the convenience store owner the same things. *Look how well that worked out for you.* Sharon ran her hands through her hair and tried to look through the windows. It was dark inside. No light, no movement. She tried the door. *Locked.* She went around the back to find that door locked as well. There wasn't a car in the driveway. The grass was overgrown.

They must've left a while ago, maybe days ago. Most of the back window was covered with a curtain but she could see the silhouette of the kitchen through a small gap. A large can of of food on top of the fridge stood out, inviting her. Sharon chewed her lip. She went down to the backyard and found a pile of large rocks twice the size of her hands. She grabbed two of them and went back. She thought if she broke the glass near the doorknob, she could reach in and unlock the door. She tapped the two rocks together in her hand and took a deep breath. "Jesus Christ, Sharon..." *First robbing a gas station, now breaking into a house... is this the new norm?*

Sharon stood back and threw the first rock that smashed a hole in the window, sending the rock tumbling across the hardwood floor into the dark recesses of the house. With the second rock, she knocked out the remaining glass to make the hole bigger when a noise came from inside the house. She paused, leaning against the hole. She stayed there for a while before straightening and continuing to smash out the small fragments of remaining glass. The shot was the last thing she heard before a bullet struck her straight in the chest.

FORTY

Derrick Hart
Louisville, KY

Derrick went through the drawers and closet of the bedroom looking for anything worth taking. He was normally very careful about asking permission before going through other's things but the thought of talking to Karen or Brandon turned his stomach. Derrick had stormed upstairs after Brandon and he had their bout.

The house slowly woke. Karen made coffee in the kitchen while Alyssa took a shower. Derrick could tell by the sound of the water hitting the tub that she wasn't in the shower, but it was clear she was avoiding Derrick after overhearing Brandon's words.

Fuck him. Brandon's a prick. He's always been a prick. That will never change.

...But is he wrong?

Derrick recalled the burn of rage in Brandon's eyes.

Brandon had a temper. As kids they would wrestle in Brandon's basement when his parents were away. On the rare occasions Derrick would get the upper hand over the taller and stronger Brandon, the playful fight would quickly turn into a real fight that ended in bloody noses and fat lips. It was times like those that having a drunk as a parent was a bonus. There were no prying questions into suspect injuries when he returned home.

The possibility of leaving Brandon and Karen behind crossed Derrick's mind. The scenario played out in his head and every outcome ended disastrously. Derrick had barely made it out of Birmingham alive and that was when he only had himself to take care of. Police officers were trained to operate in pairs. Two officers could handle any conceivable situation, but a lone officer survived on borrowed time. Luck could only keep a man alive so long. A solo officer could only face one direction at a time.

No matter what my back is exposed.

Thoughtlessly, Derrick thumbed the dog tags beneath his shirt. Realizing what he was doing, Derrick clenched the tags in his fist as his grip grew tighter by the moment until he felt the metal start to bend. The worst part, of course, was Brandon was right to an extent. Brandon was always right in some twisted unemotional, pragmatic way. That's why Derrick hated arguing with him even when he knew he was right. They couldn't split up. If what they'd faced in the past days was a measure of things to come, Derrick and Brandon needed each other to survive.

Derrick's backpack was loaded with a change of clothes, ammo, canned food, and a few medical supplies. He topped it off with warm bottles of water that were collecting cobwebs in the garage. Derrick zipped up the front of his damp uniform and laid out his body armor, gun belt, and rifle on the bed.

They decided last night to reuse their uniforms as the police and military insignias may still give them an advantage.

Alyssa returned to their room having avoided Derrick most of the morning.

She sat on the edge of the bed as if she might run out again at any moment. Derrick walked around the foot of the bed and saw her thumbing something between her fingers. It was the engagement ring. Derrick sighed and sat silently beside her.

"Are you mad at me?" Alyssa asked in almost a whisper. "Do you– do you hate me?"

"No, of course not. Why would..." Derrick's words trailed off as he chewed his lip. Alyssa turned to Derrick, analyzing his silence. It was easy for Derrick to remain silent. It was a gift or a curse from growing up as a lonely child of a drunk. Little things bothered him like anyone else, but they were easy to ignore when there never was anyone to complain to.

"If you..." Alyssa started, unsure of herself. "If you want– just say it. Please, just say what you're thinking."

Derrick hesitated. But when he looked at Alyssa, the words fell free of his mouth before he even thought them. "Why did you come back?"

Alyssa's eyes narrowed as she shook her head. "I told you. I was scared and overwhelmed–"

"You told me why you said no to getting married," Derrick said. "Why you left... but why'd you come back?"

Alyssa went still and the silence filled the room. It was an obtuse silence. The kind that hung in the air and made its presence known. The cop in him saw something in her body language he hadn't before. Her shoulders slumped, her eyes looked away, and her breathing changed. It was slower. The tiny muscles of her face that worked so hard to mask her emotions relaxed.

She is resigning herself. She's letting her guard down.

"That's not your question," Alyssa mumbled. "You don't want to know why I came back; you want to know if I only came back just to use you, and–"

"I don't care if you used me," he blurted out. Derrick was nearly as surprised as Alyssa was at the revelation. "I really don't. Brandon kept saying that like it was news to me, but I've been chased by rabid and shot at and... this is survival. You do what you need to in order to survive, I get that. I want you to be able to rely on me, but... but can I rely on you? Can I trust you? If we ever get to safety, wherever that is, would you still want to be with me?"

Alyssa shook her head as she pinched the engagement ring between her thumb and forefinger. A smile came over her lips as she spoke. "One of the most frustrating things about our relationship was when we argued, that handful of the times that we did, you'd never yell at me. Sounds so stupid saying it, but God, the number of times I just wanted you to yell out what you were thinking rather than just change the subject... Maybe I'm guilty of keeping quiet, too. Jesus... the things we worry about even during the end of the world..."

Alyssa let out a long sight before she continued. "When you proposed, all I could think about was everything I would miss out on if I said, *yes. I* never imagined becoming a housewife or a stay-at-home mom and whether that's what you wanted or not, that's all I could see looking at this ring." Alyssa smiled down at the ring with a brightness in her eyes that quickly disappeared. "The second I said 'no' I was regretting it, but the only thing I thought would be worse than just saying *no,* was playing games with you. I broke up with you thinking it would be just a break, in my head. That either we'd get back together and be stronger for it or we wouldn't, but at least I wasn't playing with your emotions. When the outbreak happened, I knew if I tried to get back together with you—I knew what it would look like. Well, you know what it looks like... Everyone does... The only difference is I don't care what it looks like anymore."

"Eric was shot. Jessica– a seventeen-year-old girl, was murdered. My parents..." Alyssa took a deep breath and released it slowly as if she was walling away her emotions before they could drown her. "That phone call. The message I left you... That was manipulative. I meant every word I said, but I-I was scared and would have said anything. The truth is I wanted to get back together with you the moment I broke up with you. But the outbreak... I just stopped caring about the stupid shit I shouldn't have cared about before... I don't care what it looks like to other people, I don't care about appearances, I don't care about anything besides what you and I think."

Derrick nodded. He knew what she meant, of course. The outbreak was a single line of demarcation in everyone's lives. A before and after when people realized their life, their dreams, and their future would never be the same. That the person they once knew themselves to be—the businessman, the mother, teacher, traveler, entertainer—that person was no more. Death would soon claim most people away and for the few who survived, it would be because they chose to survive. Because they chose to leave who they were and what they cared about behind to become who they needed to be. What this new world demanded.

The safety of these walls would soon be left behind for the chaos of the world outside. Sneering at the thought of Brandon's insults, Derrick was done apologizing for his moral code. He was sick of the self-doubt. No longer would he be a victim of Brandon's or this world's bullying to break him to his lowest self. His heart knew what was right and what was wrong. And Derrick's heart knew Alyssa was right.

Closing his palm over Alyssa's gently, he pinched the ring between their hands as he surprised her with a tender kiss. His lips lingered on hers for a moment before the shock subsided and Alyssa hooked her other hand around the back of his neck, kissing him back with a passion that had been restrained for far too long. Squeezing the diamond ring between their palms, Derrick felt Alyssa's love in her embrace.

Derrick broke from the kiss with his cheek still pressed to her's. "I love you," he whispered.

"I love you so much," Alyssa whispered back before she kissed him deeply.

The bright morning sun broke through the bedroom windows as the day had begun. Finishing gathering their things, Derrick snapped his gun belt on and Alyssa helped him slide his heavy ballistic armor vest over his shoulders. The armor and his uniform were covered in soured browns of dirt staining the fabric that was grayed from the bleach. Derrick belted his armor straps tight to his body.

"You ready?" he asked.

Alyssa surveyed the room for her their things. "I think so."

Derrick watched her be the good house guest she was and begin to straighten the sheets and make the bed.

"Lyss..." he smirked.

"Hm?" Alyssa looked up at Derrick watching her as he slung his rifle over his shoulder. She glanced down and he could see the recognition in her eyes that they were never coming back to this house again. "Oh..." Alyssa dropped the comforter in a messy ball on the bed and laughed at herself.

"I mean, not that I mind watching you do you womanly duties..." Derrick joked, turning to the door.

"Shut up," Alyssa restrained her smile.

"I get it," Derrick shrugged. "It's in your DNA. You see a messy bed, dirty dishes– you're just compelled to clean them."

Alyssa grabbed her own backpack and tossed it over her shoulder as she smacked Derrick's butt with the palm of her hand as they both laughed walking out of the bedroom into the hallway.

The group gathered in the living room. Each of them placed their full backpacks around the coffee table. Karen was in the kitchen, wiping down the counters and taking the trash out to the dumpster.

"Karen, leave it. Come on," Brandon said, entering the room. Derrick stole a smirk and a wink in Alyssa's direction who only shook her head, rolling her eyes.

Brandon's digital camouflage uniform was worn out with frayed edges on the sleeves. They had enough extra ammunition to top off all of Brandon's and Derrick's magazines and spare rounds to put in the backpacks. The tension was noticeable as soon as Karen entered the room. She went to Brandon's side of the coffee table while Alyssa stood beside Derrick opposite them.

The battle lines are drawn.

Eric sat on the couch beside Zoe, their eyes darting between the two couples.

"I still don't see why we can't just stay here a few more days," Karen said. "You said the army is bombing the infected in the south, right? Maybe that'll stop them."

"It won't. Nothing can stop them at this point," Brandon said, unfolding his crinkled map on top of the coffee table. "The only way to survive is to get farther north, faster than the infected and find somewhere remote to hunker down. A small town, low population, with lots of natural resources to sustain us."

Eric leaned forward as if to speak, but Brandon stopped him with a raised hand.

"Eric, I swear to god, if you say something about a gun store one more time..." Brandon warned. Eric closed his mouth and slouched back into the couch in a pouting silence.

"Well, where then?" Karen asked, crossing her arms. "If here's not safe, where is?"

"What about Michigan?" Alyssa said, tapping the state on the map. "It's not terribly far and we'd have the great lakes on all sides."

Brandon glared at Alyssa as if he was offended by her even speaking, let alone touching his map. "No," was all Brandon said at first, but when Alyssa began to counter, he cut across her. "It's too obvious a choice. Every gun nut within five-hundred miles will be heading there. Besides, we need to stay near water. We're going to be on foot most of the time."

"On foot?" Karen repeated.

"The roads are going to be jammed with cars," Alyssa's eyes flicked to and from Karen. "Then what about Maine? You two are from there, right? You know the area and it can't get more remote than that."

"Maybe, but it might be too far north come winter," Brandon said to himself more than others.

"Winter?" Alyssa repeated.

"Babe, today's May 1st," Karen said with an obvious grin. "Look outside, there's a heat wave."

Brandon's eyes lifted to Derrick's for the first time before moving to others. "Listen, I need you all to hear me right now, because apparently I haven't been clear enough before... Make no mistake this country is collapsing. Right now, states are being held together by local police and abandoned military units cut off from the reality of the situation. But soon, without transportation and government oversight, food shortages will happen, hospitals will be overrun, the remaining police and soldiers will disband, and then the infected will come. We're not looking for a place to go camping for the weekend. We're looking for a place to survive."

Brandon's words were an icy reality to everyone, and even Derrick, who knew all of this, felt a queasy twist in his gut.

"For how long?" Eric asked.

"For as long as it takes," Brandon said and pointed to the right of Louisville on the map. "We'll cross the border today into Indiana. We'll follow the Ohio river north to West Virginia or Pennsylvania. They both have a dense countryside and relatively low populations as long as we steer clear of the cities."

"They're not going to let us out of Louisville." Karen shook her head, her hand motioning to the TV. "The military is adamant to shelter in place; they're not letting anyone cross into Indiana."

"Louisville was made the major military hub for coordinating and supplying the southern fronts," Brandon said. "The military will have plenty of people to man the border here in the city but not in other parts of the state. We'll push north into Louisville since we're already here, but head east before reaching downtown. Once we're ten miles or so east of Louisville, the military presence should be low to nonexistent by night. We'll sneak across some bridge, find a boat, shit, we can swim for all I care."

"I don't think Zoe is in any condition to swim," Karen said, sitting on the arm of the couch and rubbing Zoe's back. Zoe had showered while everyone packed this morning. She wore a change of Karen's clothes that was too short and too big for her, but she made it work. They had found a bottle of expired Vicodin pills left over from one of Karen's Grandpa's surgeries and planned to parcel them out throughout the day. Zoe had a broken look on her face, but the pills must have dulled the pain because she sat up right for the first time.

Brandon's eyes reactively bounced to Derrick then quickly

looked away as if he was anticipating the fight before he spoke. "Zoe's not coming."

"What?" Alyssa snapped.

"What do you mean?" Karen added.

Zoe's eyes went wide as she looked at Derrick who gave a silent nod of reassurance.

"She's in no shape to travel," Brandon continued. "It would only be torture to bring her along. We'll leave food and water behind when we go. Lock all the doors. When she's feeling better, she can go find help." Brandon's lie was so transparent, he didn't even try to hide the disbelief in his own words.

Karen squared off with her husband. "She's a child. We can't abandon a child by herself."

"What do you mean 'find help?' You just said nothing's stopping the infection," Alyssa yelled. "Food shortages, hospitals falling apart, but Zoe's just supposed to *find help?*"

Derrick had his rifle slung casually across his chest, his arms resting on the buttstock as he stared at Brandon while he fought battles on multiple fronts.

"Who knows," Brandon glared at Alyssa. "Maybe she'll get lucky and get engaged to a Louisville SWAT officer..."

"Fuck you," Alyssa cursed.

"Hey!" Karen yelled, wagging her finger at Alyssa. "You wouldn't be here without Brandon!"

"Maybe my parents would if it wasn't for him!" Alyssa snapped. Karen recoiled as confusion formed on her brow. Obviously, it was one of the stories Brandon had neglected to tell his wife. "Yeah, ask him–"

"The point is," Brandon said, "Zoe can't travel which means–"

"I can travel," Zoe said, her voice louder than any of them had heard till now. It seemed to have even startled her. "I'm–I'm strong enough to go."

Derrick gave her a smile.

Brandon rubbed his brow with an agitated sigh. "Look she can barely walk, and we have twenty miles to go today, so–"

"We've got my grandpa's old moped in the garage," Karen said. "She can ride on that while we walk."

"Eric can ride with her since he has his leg injury," Alyssa added. "He's driven a moped before, all Zoe would need to do is hold on."

"Got to be fucking kidding me..." Brandon mumbled to himself as he rubbed his face.

"Baby, we have to try," Karen said to Brandon. "We can't leave a kid behind."

Brandon's eyes wandered before they found Derrick. They glared at one another for a minute but Derrick refused to say a word. "Are you happy now?" Brandon said with a toxic look in his eyes.

"Brandon," Karen pulled his arm, but his eyes stayed on Derrick.

"Huh? I bet your–" Brandon continued as he wallowed in Derrick's smug silence. Derrick knew he could soften Brandon's defeat by apologizing or simply speaking, but instead he chose to stay quiet because he knew it would bother his old friend the most.

"Brandon, stop. Stop!" Karen pulled Brandon's gaze down to her's. "Brandon..."

"–just in. Breaking news out of Chattanooga, Tennessee," the news anchor's voice on the TV came into focus as everyone turned to watch it. "This is just coming in. Amateur footage that has been sent to one of our affiliates and um–" the angle of the broadcaster cut to a shaky video of small children crawling around in a messy living room carpet full of toys and coloring books. A voice in the background called out for someone to get away from the windows. The camera panned up to the window and focused on a group of five people on top of a single person struggling on the grass. They were swinging their fists down and biting the crying man who began to scream the familiar maddening scream.

"Um– I'm sorry about that, I didn't realize how troubling the footage would be," the broadcaster cleared his throat and adjusted in his seat as the video quickly cut away. "We have yet to receive confirmation from the White House, but it appears the Rhabdo-11 virus may be in Tennessee. Again, this has not been confirmed."

Brandon sighed, rolling his eyes, then looking over the others. "We leave in two minutes."

FORTY-ONE

Sharon Hill
Junction City, KY

If it wasn't for the agonizing pain that radiated from her chest, Sharon would have thought she was already dead. Perhaps only seconds had passed as she writhed on the ground, but they felt like hours, making her wish she was dead. Breath escaped her. No matter how much she gasped or how wide she opened her mouth, air refused to fill her lungs. It felt as though a thousand tiny chasms of fire and blades had opened in her chest. Bottomless pits that leaked every breath of air before it could reach her lungs.

Her hands touched at her burning chest then scraped at her throat as if there was a rope tied around her neck that needed to be ripped free. Sharon's vision darkened and the edges became hazy. The tunnel consumed her vision until she was nearly unconscious. Then, as if a straw had been forced down Sharon's throat, she felt the trickle of air pass down her throat.

The trickle turned into gulps. Her voice was ragged as she groaned and felt a steady stream of oxygen find its way into her lungs.

"–now!" a man's voice came into focus. "Your last warning."

Turned over on her side, the pain from her chest came into focus. She started to grab her chest as she cried but that seemed to only make the pain flare up. Her eyes focused through the tears and saw a figure standing through the window inside the house.

He's just looking at me. Why isn't he helping? I've been shot. Call the police– call an ambulance!

Then she saw the barrel of the long black and brown shotgun pointed at her through the broken wood and glass. The pain grew smaller in Sharon's mind. It still hurt but she realized she wasn't dead. Not yet.

"Ten, nine, eight, seven..." The man started counting and Sharon was already scrambling to her feet as she pieced it all together. It was instinct. Her mind flashed back to when she was a little girl and refused to go to bed when an African Cats special was on National Geographic late at night. She and her mother would laugh and negotiate over how late she would stay up and usually came to an agreement after much giggling. On rare occasions her mom would be especially irritable, and Sharon would push her luck for more time. When her mom had started counting, she had known the games were done with. She would never reach *one* because Sharon was already booking it for her bedroom by seven. She didn't know what would happen if her mother got to *zero*, but she knew it would be bad—just like now.

"...five, four, three..."

Sharon managed to get to her feet but tumbled down the stairs, falling chest first into the grass. "Ahh!" she cried and struggled back to her feet. She ran around the house falling into the siding and trees as she ran across the street. Everything her chest touched got streaked in red. Running between houses and around fences, she didn't stop to look behind her, but she heard other sounds now. Distant ones.

Screams.

Muffled popping sounds.

Sharon didn't stop. If she did, she wouldn't have the strength to move again. She'd lie where she was and bleed out.

I've been shot. I've been shot. I've been fucking shot!

Sharon didn't understand how she was still alive, much less how she was running. Her thoughts immediately jumped to all the movies she'd seen of people falling to the ground instantly after being shot and dying. In the stomach, in the head, in the chest... she knew you died when shot in those places on TV.

Why the fuck did they shoot me? They could've yelled or said something! I would have left. She wanted to call the police on them. They needed to be punished. Something needed to be done. *I was shot!* The farther she jogged the more alone she felt. The ties that bound her, and everyone else, to society were gone. Without friends or family by her side, Sharon was not part of a community. No structure existed to protect her. She was alone.

Footsteps alerted her to slow as she jogged between two houses, but it was the snarling, panting, and high-pitched growls that made her stop. She fell against the side of the nearest house as she heard the screams getting closer from the other side of the house. Sharon knew those sounds. She had heard them scream as they ran circles around her last night. With a jolt of panic in her veins, Sharon ducked behind an AC unit on the ground beside the house. The burst of pain that filled her chest was intense, but the fear of the rabid was worse. The footsteps stomped into the alley between the houses.

Sharon covered her mouth to keep from screaming. There were two rabids. Male. Their clothes were torn and their skin glistened from the thick layer of sweat that dripped from them. Sharon could do nothing but pinch her eyes shut like a frightened child waiting for the ghost to find her and pounce on her. Sharon kept her eyes closed for a time after their grunts were behind her. They had run by her; in the direction she'd come from. Where she had been shot. *The noise. The sound.* Sharon pieced together last night with what she had just seen demonstrated. *That's what they were doing last night. Running in circles, they were looking for a new sound to go after.*

Sharon looked down at her wounds for the first time. The purple nursing gown she wore clung to her chest sticking to the red blood stains and dirt. It was an oblong of tiny cuts in her skin. The shotgun blast had chewed small bites out of her breasts, chest, and right upper arm. Drops of blood oozed from the dozen or more wounds. Sharon's hand trembled as she peered beneath her shirt.

I can't keep doing this. I can't... I don't know if I can keep going...

There was a clearing of grass behind the house with a single shed in the backyard. She stumbled towards it figuring at the very least it was four walls she could sit inside. The shed was mostly covered in brown rotting wood with only a few boards still having chipped red paint on it. Instinctively, she kept her distance from the open door of the shed and side stepped around it, peering inside. It was empty except for a workbench and a wall of dusty black and rusty tools.

Stepping inside, she closed door as best she could but there was no latch, so the door hung open by a crack. Her head throbbed and she felt dizzy, but she was breathing fine and moving okay. Slumping down in an old wooden stool, she figured she wasn't going to die from her wounds. There was nowhere near as much blood coming from her as the two men she had killed.

You're not going to die, you're not going to die. You're not going to die...

Though part of her envied the thought of death. The finality of it. The release of fear and the discovery of new pains and horrors around each corner. Every moment since this outbreak began, something bad had happened to her, each worse than the last. *Haven't you had enough?*

"Okay, Sharon. Think..." She whispered to herself. Her lower lip quivered as she fought to keep from breaking into tears. Taking a deep breath, she exhaled slowly. "Think. Think, bitch, think... What... what do I do now?" she looked around the shed. She knew she needed to bandage and clean her wounds, but she also needed food and water. *I need a gun and shelter. I need a car. I need to find my fucking children!*

Overwhelmed and hurting, Sharon smacked an empty gas can off the workbench in a fury and heard it clatter into several loose tools.

"Shit!" she winced from the pain in her shoulder. "Okay... okay... prioritize, Sharon."

The shed looked as though it had been years since anyone had been inside. Spider webs covered everything that dirt didn't. There was a white box in the back of the shelf that looked the size of an old first-aid kit. She gritted her teeth as she reached for it but froze still when she heard the footsteps.

She moved to the corner of the shed as the running feet thumped nearer on the grass. She imagined another man running from the house with a shotgun in his hand to pick up where the last hillbilly left off. She lowered to her haunches and inched her head out the door to look. He stopped not far from the shed. The man wore dirty blue jeans and no shirt. Dirt covered his backside. It wasn't until the man turned that

Sharon saw the flow of blood that poured from the man's mutilated face onto his chest. His eyes were bloodshot and wild.

Sharon jumped back, hoping she hadn't been spotted. He was infected. His eyes were wide with a maddening eagerness. Deep scratches gored his arms and chest. Chunks of meat hung from where his face used to be. Sharon didn't dare look again. She could feel him standing there on the other side of the shed wall.

She held her breath and closed her eyes trying to calm herself but opened them again when the darkness only made her panic more. She stared at the opening of the shed and imagined seeing the rabid's head, then body appear in the doorway. She could already see the excitement in its eyes before it lunged on her and could hear its vicious crazed growls as it tore her apart. Sharon exhaled through her mouth as silently as she could, but nearly screamed when she heard the rabid yell. It was sharp and forced Sharon to clap her hands over her ears.

Just as Sharon felt sure she was going to be mauled, it ran. Away from her toward the house on the other side of the field. Once it had disappeared around the house, Sharon gently put her left hand on her chest as if to calm her erratic beating heart.

If he had come in here, I would be dead... no, if it came in here, I would be rabid.

Sharon would have crawled into the corner and covered her face while screaming as it mutilated her, she imagined. She was defenseless. *Prioritize...* Sharon looked up at the wall of tools and worked herself to her feet. There wasn't much she recognized. Different kinds of old hand saws and other farming equipment that was either too big for her or too small to be useful. If she was going to stay here or go anywhere, water, food, or first-aid weren't going to be the priority. A weapon was number one. Beside the worktable was a tarp that covered several pieces of wood. She pulled the tarp to the side and found a thin metal pipe that stood about as tall as her leg.

She picked it up and brushed off the cobwebs. It was heavier than she thought. Solid and difficult to lift. She needed two hands to pick it up and winced as the pain flashed in her chest. Sharon looked out the door when she heard a noise. It was distant. The screams outside carried with the wind. They came from the front of the house where the rabid had disappeared. Something about the screams brought her outside. It wasn't the sound of the rabid. She had to hear better. It was a human cry. She stepped closer to the noise. It was... it was a child, a young boy's voice.

Sharon's feet ran before her mind could stop her. The image in her head was of Charlie alone in the road crying for his mother. Screaming for her. She nearly dropped the metal pipe because it hurt her wounds so much as it bounced in her grip. *It can't be Charlie. How could it be? But what if it was?*

As she circled the house, the young boy's voice was now getting hoarse from the high-pitched wailing.

"Charlie!" Sharon yelled as she rounded the front of the house.

The pitch of the screeching heightened when it became aware of Sharon's presence. His strides were short and skin pale as he bounded for Sharon. Her concerned expression quickly soured when she saw the mess of blood across the boy's face. *No...* and the bloodshot eyes. *He looks only ten. He can't be...*

"No..." Sharon stumbled backward as the boy ran between parked cars in the driveway, his tiny voice screaming loudly. Then she saw the others behind the boy. Three of them. Adults. One female and two males, one of whom was the same shirtless rabid from the shed. "Oh no, no!"

Sharon turned and ran at such a pace her feet nearly

tripped over themselves. From one house to the next she dove between parked cars and the garages, pounding on the garage doors as she ran. "Help! Please, help me!" Sharon's voice was hoarse and ragged as the rabid gained on her, their feet pounding the earth with a purpose as they neared.

Sharon threw the pipe behind her and it clattered at the feet of the rabid boy. "Stop! Stop it, go away!" Sharon yelled. Her legs burned and gave out as she ran across the street. Her lungs gasped for air that wasn't there. Backtracking, Sharon crawled in the middle of the street as the rabid ran on the pavement, ready to dive on her.

The gunfire that cracked over her body sounded distant and faded as if she wore earmuffs. Her vision was veiled as she saw the rabids chewed to pieces by the gunfire in a haze. The last thing she heard before passing out was the long southern drawl of an older man.

"Gawddammit, Baron. Is she one of them or not?"

FORTY-TWO

Sharon Hill
Junction City, KY

The pickup truck rattled with every grassy bump they drove across. It was the gentle rocking that soothed Sharon awake. She felt a déjà vu as she feigned unconsciousness, trying to gather information about where she was.

The young man in the driver's seat was called Robert. He looked to be in his mid-twenties with a defined jaw. He wore a dark, flannel button-up shirt that closely matched his father's attire. His father was an older man with long gray hair and a beard. Sharon eyed the two men's rifles that rested on the floorboards by their legs. They were out of reach to Sharon and she couldn't help but stare at the black barrels that casually leaned in her direction.

"Na, tell Tommy to turn them around," the gray-haired man was pointing at the CB radio. "If Abraham ain't answering the radio then we're heading back home. We already got all the supplies that we can haul anyway."

"What about Kings, pa?" Robert asked. "We don't have any. Besides Amber, that's it, but she's barely more than a midwife."

"Abraham is in charge of Kings," the father quietened his boy with a wave of his hand. "Once we have the time, we'll meet with Abraham and get some Kings. Until then, there ain't no reason for us to be risking–"

Robert stole another look at Sharon and caught her with her eyes half open. "Hey– hey pa, she's awake." Sharon scrambled to a seated position as the old man turned in his seat. He had defined creases in his face that showed a man in his fifties, at least, but he had surprisingly warm eyes.

"Well, hello there, miss. Whoa, don't be alarmed. We are of the friendly sort. My name is Wesley Montgomery. This here is my boy, Robert Montgomery," Wesley said. His voice was so light and joyful it reminded her of a sweet old grandpa.

Wincing at the pain in her chest, Sharon touched at her wounds and was surprised to feel the cloth of an old gray hoodie that had been used to cover her wounds and the torn-up scrubs.

"Careful now," Wesley continued. "Looks like you took a good shot of rock salt there to the chest. Must've picked a fight with the wrong farmer somewheres. It ain't lethal but wooo, it burns, I can attest to that." Wesley chuckled to himself. "I hope you don't mind, my boy Robert here put the hoodie on you to help cover your lady bits."

Sharon's eyes caught Robert's in the rearview mirror. He reached over his shoulder with a sealed bottle of water in his hand. "Are you thirsty?" Robert's voice had a similar accent as his father, but it was flattened and less noticeable. Sharon took the bottle of water and cracked it open and drank half it in under two seconds.

"You can slow down, dear. You poor thing. We got plenty of water to go around," Wesley said. Sharon tried to take smaller sips, but she was parched and couldn't help but guzzle the water. Once the water filled her stomach, she was able to take in her surroundings more clearly. Robert was following behind two other pickup trucks that bounced along the grass field they were driving across. She looked behind them and saw eight more jeeps and trucks following them with men sitting in the bed of several of the trucks.

"What's your name, hun?" Wesley asked.

"Sharon Hill," she said. "Where are you guys taking me?"

"Nice to make your acquaintance, Sharon," Wesley chuckled, shaking his head. "We're not *taking* you nowhere. You don't have to be frightened, child. We have a tight-knit community up here in Northern Kentucky. Buncha' families who take care of another, that's where we are headed. We heard your cries on our way and saw you being chased by them rabid. We couldn't just leave you there on the road, now could we?"

Sharon felt herself being lulled into comfort for the first time in days. It was a disgusting mix of feelings that plagued her. Nothing made her want to run more than the sight of men sitting over her with guns. The simple sight made her anxious and a part of her mind screamed at her to rip the door open and runaway. But another part of her recalled that every instinct she'd had since leaving her home had been wrong. Police had kidnapped her, soldiers had experimented on her, she had been chased by rabid, and shot by strangers. As much as she hated being around these guns, every moment she had spent without a weapon had been a terror.

Am I safe? What do these men want? What are they after?

"Are you a nurse?" Robert asked, filling the silence.

"No," Sharon shook her head.

Wesley clicked the side of his mouth as if to say, *aww shucks.* "We just thought because of your clothes maybe you were."

"Can I go?" Sharon blurted out. Her words came out carefully, she didn't want to make it sound as if she was kidnapped because then maybe it would be true. "I mean, thank you. Thank you for saving me but am I– can you let me out?"

Robert looked to Wesley who nodded for him to stop. Robert put it in park and picked up the CB radio mic, "Tommy, hold up now."

"10-4," a voice said back and the truck ahead of them halted.

Sharon opened the door and stepped out into the tall weeds. Her legs hurt from the soreness, her back ached, and she felt blisters on the bottom of her bare feet. She looked back inside the truck and saw Wesley talking with Robert, ignoring her completely.

"Which way is the nearest town or city?" Sharon asked not even seeing a road to guide her.

"Well, Junction city is where we came from," Wesley shrugged. "That'd be the closest about five miles that way. Otherwise, you got about a twenty-five-mile hike south as the crow flies to Moreland."

Sharon did all she could do to keep from breaking down in tears. She was stuck between decisions she hated. Every choice she had made thus far had only made her life worse and now she thought she was about to do it again. Looking to the sun that was directly above her she didn't even know which way was south. She remembered walking down the road in Tennessee and the helplessness she felt at not knowing what to do. The thirst, the hunger.

"Miss," Wesley said. "I don't recommend you being off on

your own, but we ain't gunna stop you. There's bad folk and them rabid running all over the place up here. But if you wish to part ways, well, we'll be on our way then."

Sharon bit her lower lip to stop it from trembling as she tried to speak. She knew the childlike tears would burst before the words even left her lips, but she had to ask. "Could you take me to the Tennessee border?" Sharon's voice shook as the first of many tears spilled from her eyes. "My family... my children are there... just north of Knoxville..."

Wesley looked down at his lap as he pulled on his beard. "Ma'am, I'm sorry but we're not going that way."

"Please..." Sharon cried. She knew how pathetic she had become. Helpless. Her tough outer core was stripped away leaving her bare and exposed.

Robert opened his door and got out of the front seat. He was tall and he kept his distance as he spoke softly. "I'm sorry, Sharon. I'm so sorry about this whole mess that's happening. I don't know what's happened to you but I know no one should have to go through it. We can't go get your kids now, today, but maybe later, tomorrow, sometime. All I do know is that if we leave you here, sure is shootin' you're gonna die. Then, who's that gonna help?"

Sharon cried silently burying her face in her palms. After a moment passed without words, Sharon reached for the back door with heavy limbs and slowly crawled back inside. Her stomach ached. She would puke if she had anything in it and her eyes continued to tear up as she felt the distance growing between her and her children. Robert closed the door carefully and got back inside the driver's seat.

"Pa, hey, pa," the radio speaker called.

Wesley keyed the CB mic. "Go ahead, Baron, what you got?"

"Switch up channels," Baron radioed. "Abraham's tryin ta get you."

Wesley turned the knob on the old radio box and keyed his mic. "Wesley to Abraham, you on here?"

"Abraham to Wesley, it's good hearing your voice, Wes. You doing okay? Your boy Baron caught us up." Sharon had to strain to understand Abraham's words through his thick, southern accent.

"We're good, we suffered some losses at the school, but we got what we needed. How about y'all?"

There was a long pause before Abraham responded. "We. um... well, we suffered a lot of losses too, you can say. Couple of soldiers surprised us in Chattanooga yesterday. Todd, Jeff, Matt, Andrews, and more, all gone."

"Jesus, pa," Robert whispered to Wesley who only shook his head in disbelief.

"Lord rest their souls," Wesley radioed back.

"Amen, partner," Abraham said back. "Look, I have a crappy assignment for ya. How are you looking on supplies?"

"Supplies are real good," Wesley replied. "We have a couple of Jacks and a Queen, but that's all. What about y'all?"

"We don't have any Kings, Wes. Not one. They all escaped from Chattanooga and every other team has been a bust looking for them. We've got no Kings and no Aces to trade."

"Shit," Wesley cursed to himself before putting the mic back to his mouth. "How about Queens?"

"Plenty of Queens, but that don't do us no good without Kings."

"You think the Kings are all gone?"

"Negative. They just been moved," the radio crackled. "We've questioned several people and they all say the same. All the Kings in the area been moved to a central location, and you're not gonna like it."

"Don't tell me," Wesley said.

"Yup. They said they're split between Military Command and General hospital," Abraham said.

"This is a big ask, Wes, but you know how important they are for us– for our future," Abraham sighed. "You don't need any heroics. Just in and out with as many as you can get. Can you do it?"

Wesley sighed as he stared at the dash of the truck for a long minute. "We'll do it."

"Thank you, Wes," Abraham said. "Every chapter is gonna be in your debt. And that's a good thing for you guys. You know that right?"

"I hear you," Wesley said. "We'll let you know when it's done. Wesley Chapter out."

"You sure about this, Pa?" Robert asked as Wesley turned the knob on the radio again.

"We'll have a look. If we can do it, we'll do it," Wesley said.

Sharon's focus on this strange conversation had succeeded in distracting her from her tears. Tucked in the corner of the truck she listened intently at what was said but understood very little.

Wesley keyed the mic and one by one each of the ten other vehicles of their convoy responded that they were listening. "Boys, I know we were hoping to spend tonight in our own beds for a change, but I spoke to Abraham, and something's come up. None of the other chapters of the Sons of Liberty have any Kings. Y'all know this is all for nothing if we don't have any Kings. So the men, women, and children of the future are turning to us for help today, right now. And we won't turn our backs on them. Sons of Liberty, we're going to Louisville."

FORTY-THREE

Rachel Anderson
Louisville, KY

"You should be resting," Sean said, guessing it was still nighttime. With no windows in their room to see outside or clocks on the wall, it was easy to lose track of time in the quarantine cells.

"So should you. Are they?"

"Loud and louder?" Sean looked over his shoulder. "Allen with his wheezing snores that he denies he does."

"Thank God I got my own cell, or I'd probably smother him in his sleep," Rachel snickered and felt her heart flutter when she saw Sean's smile. A man as serious as Sean was tough to be around, but when he let his guard down and let you *inside*, it felt like a special occasion.

Sean let the silence linger for a moment. He leaned against the glass partition that stood between him and her. His eyes lowered before he changed the conversation. "What you did was really stupid, you know..."

"How come when a woman does something brave she's called stupid, but if a man does the same thing everyone can't shut up about how courageous he is?" Rachel raised an eyebrow.

"You have any idea how many times you've called me an idiot over the past two weeks?"

Rachel rolled her eyes, "touché."

The room was dark. She had drawn her curtain across the front of the glass where the two guards stood. There was something unnerving about trying to sleep with people leering at you. Not that she was able to sleep anyway. For hours, she had tossed in her hospital bed unable to close her eyes without recalling the horrors that now lived in the recesses of her mind. Rachel told herself that she would forget them with time. Trying to convince herself to not let the feeling of hopelessness consume her whenever there was silence, she repeated the police officer's words to herself. *You turned down a helicopter for those kids, don't you fucking forget that.*

It was a comfort to have seen Sean move the curtain to the side and go stand by the speaker box between the two rooms. With her blanket wrapped around her shoulders she had tiptoed over to the speaker and pressed the green button to talk to him.

"Rachel, what you did was really brave," Sean continued. "After what you went through the past few weeks, no one can deny your courage–"

"Don't patronize me."

"I'm not," Sean said. "You should hear Chris talk about you, even Allen. They respect you. Think of you as one of the guys– one of the team. Which is saying a lot. A lot of people out there like to think they'd risk their lives for others but when the time comes, most don't. You have on multiple occasions... But you have to get that soldier's attention. And when he turns on your mic, tell him you changed your mind. Tell them to put you on the first chopper out of here before it's too late."

Rachel mulled over his words. They felt hypocritical and sexist at best. But her expectations of Sean were hypocritical as well. In the modern world, pre-outbreak, of short attention spans and a selfie obsessed generation, Sean stood the test of time as a traditionalist. *Old fashioned,* Sean would characterize himself. Not in beliefs, per se, but in behavior for sure. In the first days of his assignment to her detail it had annoyed her to no end. Reminded Rachel of her dad.

Hold the door for a woman, don't spit in front of a woman, don't curse in front of a lady.

The list went on for things Sean felt a woman should be protected from and Rachel couldn't stand being treated as the delicate flower he pretended she was.

"There's nothing delicate about you, Rach," Sean had said one night before she went into her apartment for the night. She had blown up at him for his *sexist* treatment of her. It had caught her off guard because Sean had been the only secret service agent to always call her 'ma'am' and never by her name. "A lady can curse in front of whoever she wants," Sean had said, "but only a true gentleman waits for her permission before doing so." Rachel had furrowed her brow as she had hung in the doorway of her apartment. Half in the hallway, half in the dark entrance, struggling to find something to snap at him for.

Sean had softened his expression with a light shrug of his shoulders and a small smile. "I was taught my behavior is a measure of who I am, and not a reflection of what I think of you... Sorry if that bothers you... Goodnight, *ma'am,"* Sean had emphasized *ma'am* with a playful grin before he dismissed himself down the hall to the elevator.

That was the first night Rachel had lay awake in her bed attempting to understand her new, but simple secret service agent. With a new perspective of his behavior, the *old-fashioned* sense about him became fascinating to Rachel overnight. His concern for her was not a belief of her feebleness, but was a cornerstone of his character, she'd understood. *That's the kind of man he is.*

"Would you?" she asked, searching Sean's expression through the glass. "Get in a helicopter and abandon me, Chris, Allen– everyone you fought with and helped keep you alive the past weeks?"

Sean looked down as he scratched his thumb on the glass wall. He murmured something so softly that the speaker didn't pick it up.

"What'd you say? I couldn't–"

Sean looked up and repeated his words slightly louder. "I would if I was pregnant."

Rachel went still as she searched every inch of Sean's expression for anything she could pounce on. The slightest judgement in the corner of his mouth. An edge of condescension or superiority in his eyes, anything that she could use as a reason to rip into him. Instead, she saw something she had never seen in him. Vulnerability. His usually hard-set and focused eyes were wide and glassy, his eyebrows open as he looked beseechingly at her.

"Funny, how that matters now but it didn't seem to matter before," Rachel said, looking away.

"It always mattered."

"No, it didn't. Not to you. Not the morning after I told you, it didn't. Remember? Before the festival that morning?" Rachel's voice was louder than she intended as the burst of anger seemed to come from nowhere. The argument they should have had two weeks ago had boiled and stewed inside her far too long.

Sean nodded and chewed on the corner of his lip. "I know I didn't handle it right... but it mattered even then. I was– I was selfish, I was a coward. I only thought about me and justified my actions as being best for you. I'm sorry."

Rachel fumed and looked away as she let out an exasperated sigh. It was probably the most annoying quality of Sean... his ability to apologize and mean it. It was impossible to have a good fight with someone who wouldn't swing back, and Rachel had much more shouting she wanted to do. "How would you leaving my detail, leaving me after getting me pregnant be best for me?"

Sean raised an eye to Rachel as if to ask if she was serious, "come on, Rachel."

"What?"

"You know the news channels would have a field day with you and your dad," Sean shook his head. "Vice President's daughter pregnant after sleeping with *black* rookie secret service agent... you'd be swamped by reporters."

Rachel pursed her lips as she stewed on his words. She wished it wasn't true, but she knew it was, but she didn't care about any of that. She had dealt with shitty reporters and paparazzies for years now.

"I was... scared. I was... I was ashamed," Sean crossed his arms uncomfortably as he checked to make sure Allen and Chris were still asleep.

"Ashamed? Ashamed of being with me?" Rachel's eyes narrowed. "So, you were okay sleeping with me but only in secret?"

"Rachel," Sean sighed and looked up, as if talking about himself required focus and was equally exhausting. "You have to go back, before the infection spread, back to when I was just a rookie secret service agent on your detail and the world was normal. If our relationship was discovered then, I would have been fired on the spot for cause. This job was all I had, and it wasn't like you were pushing for us to go public at the time, either. I would have never gotten another job in this field." Sean rubbed at his left wrist. It was bare, devoid of the gold watch that used to be there until a few days ago. "My father is the only family I have left. We're not close, I mean, he's– he's got some issues but... the one thing he talks about, the one thing he's proud of is my job. It's the only thing we talk about when I call... I couldn't imagine him hearing I was fired in the news or having to tell him myself... I was ashamed."

Rachel felt the twist of angst inside her as her hand pressed her palm against the glass without thought. Sean took a long breath and did the same with his palm. Rachel had never heard Sean speak about his father or anyone in his family for that matter. "He's in Texas? Your dad?"

"Yeah."

"Have you– when was the last time you talked to him?"

Sean flinched as he spoke. "Christmas, I think."

Rachel nodded.

"Listen, I was wrong before but I'm right now," Sean said. "You need to get to your father. If not for yourself, for your... for our baby... Allen, Chris, and I will be right behind you."

"You don't even believe that," Rachel shook her head. "I don't care what you say, I'm not leaving you guys. Allen and Chris both have families in Washington D.C. that are waiting for them. Now, do you think they have a better or worse chance to get to their family if they're by the President's daughter's side?" Rachel cocked her head to the side. Sean was silent in response. "That's the end of the discussion as far as I'm concerned." Rachel started to go back to her bed but stopped and said, "Oh, and in the event the pee stick thing I took is right and I am pregnant, there's not a chance in hell I'm raising this child without a father. So you might want to start getting your shit together."

Rachel half smiled at Sean as she pressed the green button silencing any response before returning to her bed. Curling beneath the covers, she lay on her side and slowly closed her eyes to the sight of Sean watching over her.

FORTY-FOUR

Derrick Hart
Louisville, KY

"Fucking pig!"

The voice was barely audible over the thousand different conversations going on at once. Derrick trailed behind Alyssa, with Eric and Zoe on the moped in front of her. He had to put his hand on Alyssa's back to motivate her to keep walking as she turned toward the man shouting looking for a fight. It was nothing new to Derrick.

Bardstown Road, which was a main vein that traveled through Louisville, was a mix of a block party and a mass migration of people. Every house and storefront that lined the street had hundreds of people gathered outside or crammed in the air conditioning inside. They drank beer and did shots while dozens of speaker systems thumped with music. The locals were using the procession of southerners migrating through their city as entertainment not unlike a parade for Louisville to enjoy.

It had taken Derrick and his companions all day to walk into downtown through the thick crowds. The moped might have given the doped-up Zoe rest from having to walk, but it did no favors while maneuvering through the masses of people. Derrick was glad Brandon was at the front and far from him; he would be losing his mind at the slow trot they paced at. Only Karen's periodic whispers in his ear were keeping him calm at this point, Derrick bet.

The people who filled the cracks between and around the gridlocked traffic of abandoned cars had seen a long grueling road to get to where they were now—couples with sunburnt faces and backpacks wearing them down; families carting exhausted children; flushed faces and jittery eyes of the ones alone among tens of thousands of strangers, each one struggled to keep moving forward. One thing that Derrick noticed was there were no elderly people in the procession. The oldest seemed to be in their late forties or maybe early fifties. And they were all relatively in shape.

One of the fathers on the opposite end of the street looked over and saw Derrick peering in his direction. He smiled and nodded as if they had just caught eyes on their lunch break at a restaurant. The middle-aged man's hand rested on a young boy's shoulder who walked beside him. Derrick gave a small nod in return and turned his attention back to his lane. *Getting here was only the first bottleneck.* If Brandon was right, in the following days, what little government structures and social contracts remained, would disappear. The next bottleneck for survivors would be the fighters.

Those who can take what they need and defend what they have.

Derrick's eyes fell to Zoe's skinny hunched body as she

leaned on Eric's back. They moved at ant-speed through the crowded streets; Eric had to walk the moped with his feet to keep it from toppling over.

"Hey, man... I said, hey man. I'm talkn to you."

Eric eyed the man for a brief second and looked away quickly.

"What? Whatchu looking at? Am I not good enough to talk to?"

Derrick eyed the beer bottle the tatted man stole sips out of as he struggled to get Eric's attention. "Hey, o'er here, scared little bitch."

"Leave me alone," Eric muttered.

"Oh, he talks!" the tatted man laughed and gestured to his friends who started infiltrating their group. Derrick counted at least three men with beer bottles in hand. He did a once over the men. *Late twenties, tattoos, skinny, no sign of guns in their waistbands...* None of them seemed to be the most reasonable people. "Come on, man, step off with your lady, let me test out your ride. I said, step off."

The tatted man grabbed Eric's right throttle nearly sending him and Zoe stuttering onto the ground.

"Hey!" Alyssa yelled.

"Back off, now." Derrick stepped forward. The tatted man's eyes sparked when he looked behind and saw Derrick's police uniform. A habit of the past, Derrick figured. Months ago, the police uniform meant *run* to troublemakers. Now it was but a shadow of itself. The man's eyes set, and his jagged toothed smile returned.

"Or what officer? You gonna shoot me?"

Derrick's grip tightened on his rifle, but he kept it low and tucked against his body.

"Hands up, don't shoot," one of the men mocked from the background.

Alyssa shoved the man backward. "I'll fucking shoot you!"

"Let's go, Eric, come on. Keep moving," Derrick said, trying to ignore the loudmouth and guided Alyssa and Eric ahead. Eric righted the moped, but the man stepped in front, putting his hand on the ride. The crowd parted as more eyes paused to watch the standoff.

"Where's your back up, officer?" The man was slurring his words now. Derrick saw his right-hand slip toward his waistband. It was a common enough motion for those who wore baggy pants or felt the need to constantly grab their crotch. It was Derrick's job to quickly determine that was his purpose or if he was reaching for a weapon. "All by yourself, officer"

Before Derrick could raise his rifle, a flat black object smashed into the man's cheek sending him crumbling to the ground. Brandon put one leg over him so he straddled the tatted man as he reeled on the asphalt. Blood trickled from a bloody wound on his brow and dropped to the center of his confused and dazed face. Derrick looked back at the tatted man's friends to make sure they hadn't moved. They hadn't—either because they couldn't see through the crowd or they didn't want to come near the soldier standing over their friend. Brandon stuck the barrel of his M4 rifle between the man's lips and pushed it deep enough into his mouth to make him gag.

"Want to ask me if I'm gonna shoot you?" Bandon said over the man's hacking. Brandon glared at Derrick, then stepped back to the front of the group as they continued to walk. Derrick stared at the back of Brandon's head as he followed and imagined throttling his own rifle into the back of it.

Alyssa's fingers slipped into Derrick's clenched fist and relaxed him instantly, as if she knew his thoughts. Derrick gently squeezed her hand and she smiled, kissing his knuckle. Derrick hadn't spoken to Brandon all day, not since early this morning despite Alyssa and Karen both taking turns at convincing them to reconcile. It didn't take long for the two girls to hash things out. Alyssa and Karen always had a relationship that was fraught with drama. They had strong opinions and differed in ideas on almost everything. They were used to entering and exiting arguments like a revolving door.

When they were a half mile from downtown Louisville, Brandon took a right turn down a side road headed east. They were now walking against foot traffic, which made it more difficult for everyone, especially Eric and Zoe. The old moped puttered as he revved the engine at one or two miles an hour. They spent much of the afternoon walking east to get to the outskirts of town, only to see a wall of fifteen-foot chain link fences up ahead.

"What the fuck?" Brandon said as Derrick maneuvered to stand beside him. They backtracked a block to see where the fence ended, but there was no end in sight. There was a line of soldiers on the opposite side of the fence, spread out every thirty yards. Brandon hopped up on a car hood to get a better view.

"Well?" Derrick asked. Brandon only replied with a shake of his head.

"Hey, Corporal." Brandon hopped down and approached the fence, waving at the nearest soldier. He was a skinny boy with a pointed chin and a hooked nose. "Corporal, how far does this go? Corporal!"

The Corporal ignored Brandon, which sent him into a flare of rage. "Hey!" Brandon smacked the fence and then pretended to climb it, a half-hearted attempt since the top of the fence was lined with concertina wire.

"Hey! Back off from the fence!" the Corporal shouted as he approached Brandon with his rifle raised.

Brandon hopped off the fence with his arms raised to his sides. "Hey, I'm Sergeant Armstrong, Army Rangers. I'm on assignment to get these civilians into Indiana. I need you to get us through." Derrick absent mindedly rubbed his right wrist where his Greenband was once cinched. They had cut their Greenbands off this morning, but they would really come in handy right now.

"Yeah, you and every other deserter," the Corporal said.

"The fuck you say to me, Corporal?" Brandon pressed his face into the fence as he yelled.

"Back away from the fence, Sarge. There are tons of you guys trying to sneak by and around us for the past week. Why d'you think we put the fence up in the first place?" the Corporal said, the barrel of his rifle switching between Brandon and Derrick, who was now standing beside Brandon.

"Whoa, easy," Derrick said with his hands raised. "How far back does the fence go? Just tell us that... come on, man; We're from Atlanta... Sooner or later it'll be you on this side of the fence."

The Corporal eyed Derrick with contempt and curiosity before he answered, "fifteen miles back. And they ain't going to let you go around either. Must be thousands trying to sneak around Louisville. Now backoff!"

"Fuck!" Brandon shouted as he stomped away with his hands clutching the top of his sweaty head. Alyssa had led the others to a shaded stoop across the street and concealed themselves while they took a water break. "A whole fucking day wasted!"

Brandon kicked a dent into a parked car as people steered clear of his hostility. "Fifteen miles back," Derrick repeated. "Would send us right back the way we came. Maybe by midnight we'd be back at Karen's grandparent's place. If we kept walking, we'd see the end of the fence by dawn."

"At the pace we're going we'd be lucky to..." Brandon

trailed off as he studied the fence. "What if we fought our way through? We'd have to take out, what three, four guys max?"

It bothered Derrick that he considered it. That in this world they navigated, a possibility would always be to kill whoever stood in their way. Even if that person was a police officer or a soldier. "You see how well fortified the army is here?" Derrick said. "They're not exactly stretched thin. We start a gunfight, and they'll have a roving patrol on us in minutes. Besides, how would we get past the fence without bolt cutters and–"

"Okay, okay! Fuck," Brandon growled as he paced.

Derrick looked at the gray and black buildings that reached into the sky of downtown Louisville ahead of them. "What if we push on. Keep heading downtown," Derrick thought out loud.

Brandon shook his head. "There's got to be fifty thousand people crammed in there, at least."

"I know, we use that."

Brandon thought about it, working the problem. "Like the Tennessee border."

"We get close to the river or bridge or one of the fences and use the grenades to blast a hole through. Drive the crowd through to create another total loss scenario. Use it for cover to get through."

Brandon considered it for a minute before adjusting the sling on his M4 rifle. "It's either that or we spend a day walking back the way we just fucking came, so I guess it's an easy choice."

"Agreed." Derrick looked back at Alyssa across the street. "This is going to be a shit show, you know, right?"

"What part of this week hasn't been?"

FORTY-FIVE

Sharon Hill
Louisville, KY

"Steady... steady..." Wesley said as softly as he could in the truck's CB radio. Robert and Baron stood in the bed of two separate trucks ahead of the truck that Wesley and Sharon sat in. Wesley had taken his son's place in the driver's seat, while Sharon had moved up front to the passenger seat.

The road was blocked with abandoned cars all the way up to the privacy fence of a house that they had hid their trucks behind. Robert and Baron, Wesley's two sons, had their hunting rifles resting on the roof of the pickup truck, peering just above the fence.

"These two guards hold the key to Louisville, and they don't even know it," Wesley whispered to Sharon, while pointing ahead, as if his voice would spook the prey. "The government set up their cities the same across the country. They leave all the streets to fend for themselves but secure a handful of thoroughfares north and south and east and west through town so the military can still move around."

Sharon listened intently to Wesley, but her eyes darted back to the old purple Toyota Corolla behind them. In the rearview mirror, she could see the sweaty brow and terrified eyes of the young man gripping the steering wheel. *Please don't honk. Just sit there. Don't do it.*

After the last time the purple Corolla honked, Wesley cursed to himself and gave the order to his men to execute the young driver if he honked again. Sharon felt a tightness in her chest as she worried for the sharp *honk* was going to come any minute.

"Set," Robert's crackled voice came through the radio.

It had taken the Sons of Liberty over six hours to drive eighty miles north-west to Louisville. A dozen times they'd had to pause at blocked roads to clear the way using a tow truck in their convoy. Warning shots had been commonplace as crowds of exhausted and starving people had neared their vehicles. Sharon had stayed in the air-conditioned truck and watched the gaunt and sweaty faces of families pass, remembering the hopelessness that was her family just yesterday. It was the Sons of Liberty's numbers that gave them strength. They traveled in tight lines and stopped in small groups. Dozens of men, all armed with military assault rifles guarding their trucks.

Once they'd neared the city, their convoy had taken a road to the right, devoid of pedestrians. The trail of pedestrians was on the most direct path of least resistance to downtown Louisville while the Sons of Liberty roared their engines up a steep incline veering to the right.

"No way we can make it there before dark," Baron had radioed his father. "Took us six hours just ta get here, pa."

"Cool your jets, boy, and keep your dawg dang voice down, will ya?"

At the top of the hill there had been a blocked intersection of abandoned cars that had been sitting baking in the sun. The tow truck had slowly backed into place to make room for them to get through. Baron was a young boy who looked barely twenty years old. Unlike his older brother, Baron had a country way about him. He had a shaved head, spoke in a thick accent, and constantly had a full lip of chewing tobacco tucked under his wet lip.

Baron leaned on the passenger door as spoke to his father through the open window. Sharon had seen the bulge of dip in the wet corner of his lip that made her sneer. Baron stuck his bald, sunburnt scalp inside the open window so he could leer at Sharon. Robert studied the map as the two wreckers had gone to work, dragging the cars out of the way. "There's a subdivision up ahead and past that is the entrance ramp."

Wesley had nodded and winced when he'd heard the screeching sound of metal as the smashed bumpers had dragged against another. "Is Tommy back, yet?"

Baron had leaned back and looked past the cars. "Not yet." Baron had smiled a brown-stained teethy grin at Sharon. "You comfy back there? You know, I got more room in my truck if you wanna come back to mine."

"I'm fine here," Sharon had said glaring back at the boy.

"Leave her alone, Baron, she been through 'nough," Robert had said.

"Oh, big Robbie is protecting his piece of tail," Baron had gritted his teeth as he'd spat a black wad on the ground beside him. "I'm just bein' friendly." Baron had popped his head inside the window and reached out a hand to squeeze Sharon's knee. She'd pushed away and Wesley had finally spoken up, shoving his son.

"Dammit, Bare!" Wesley had warned. "You getn' your dip all over here!"

"Sorry, pa," Baron had backed away with his hands up. "I was just messn–"

"I don't care, go n' get gone," Wesley had shooed him away and gone back to looking at the map. Baron had let loose an annoyed growl as he'd walked away and kicked at the dirt. Sharon had kept her eyes on the young man as he'd yelled at the others standing around. She knew men like this all too well. There wasn't anyone more dangerous, she'd thought, than a selfish child in a man's body.

"Sometimes I wonder if I whooped that boy enough," Wesley had said to himself.

"Pa, Tommy's coming." Robert had said, angling his head to see better. Tommy was a scrawny eighteen-year-old boy with shaggy blond hair who had run through the opening to the intersection as the last abandoned car had been dragged away.

The boy was out of breath when he'd got to Robert's window. "Well?" Robert had asked.

Tommy had taken a deep breath. "It– it's... just like– just like you said." Tommy had pointed back the way he came. "There's a subdivision up ahead n' just past there is an entrance ramp. They got two cops at the mouth of it... but other than that... nuthin."

Wearing a grin, Wesley had smacked Robert's arm with the map folded. "We're in business. Good work, boy."

"Thanks– thank you, sir," Tommy had smiled. "It's crazy. They got these giant walls up around the road with barbed wires on top so no one can get to the road. But there ain't no one around there. They all walking on the roads downhill, I think."

"That's how we're getting to the hospital tonight. We take out those cops guarding the entrance ramp. That gives us a direct route to Louisville General Hospital. No crowds. Nothin. We'll be halfway home by midnight tonight."

When their convoy had crossed the intersection, so had a purple Toyota Corolla that had been hiding with the abandoned cars. It had started following them at a safe distance. The driver must have come up this way not long before the Sons of Liberty had but probably hadn't possessed the means to get through on his own. They had allowed it to follow for the time being, like a stray dog begging for scraps. They didn't care about one civilian following at a distance, as long as he kept quiet and didn't interfere.

"Steady..." Wesley whispered. "If we bungle this up, than this whole day long trip has been a waste."

From the passenger seat, Sharon could only see the back of Robert and Baron as they aimed their hunting rifles over the rotting privacy fence at their unsuspecting targets. The rest of them stood outside their trucks with their weapons clenched in their fists, prepared to act if something went wrong—for a fire fight to break out and bullets to fly. Sharon imagined the two officers standing at the entrance ramp, exhausted just doing their jobs.

Sharon had resigned to herself hours ago. She coiled into herself in the truck and tried not to think about anything. The two gunshots happened so close to one another, it sounded like an echo. Robert's low-toned voice cracked through the radio as he looked over his shoulder. "Two hits. We're good to go," he said.

The trucks moved, making room for the flat back tow truck to reverse through the privacy fence. It splintered and flattened the already warped wood straight to the entrance ramp. Robert and Baron hopped in the bed of the truck as they passed by. The wrecker easily shoved the patrol car that sat sideways blocking the entrance ramp. Sharon tried not to look, but she couldn't help it—the splatter of blood and slumped over bodies. The tow truck remained behind, blocking the road after allowing the convoy of trucks to enter the open interstate.

"Hey, we got a straggler," Baron hollered. Wesley led the way onto I-64 E and checked his driver's side mirror. The purple Toyota Corolla that had impatiently followed them sped by the convoy of trucks along the interstate.

"You want me to pop him?" Baron yelled over the whipping wind. Sharon anxiously turned in her seat and Wesley saw the concern in her eyes. Baron kneeled in position, shouldering his rifle.

Wesley sneered then shouted out his window. "Na, let him go. No shooting. We don't want no noise now. Besides," Wesley grinned at Sharon and gave her a wink, "we're protectors of the civilians."

Sharon watched the purple car accelerate past them into the heart of Louisville.

FORTY-SIX

Derrick Hart
Louisville, KY

"Hey! Back off, you– hey!"

"Get off, get off! Just leave it, Eric!"

"Zoe, come here," Alyssa pulled Zoe from her haunches. Her delicate body folded as the toppled moped was ripped from underneath her. Keeping his rifle tucked to his chest with one hand, Derrick's other arm wrapped around Eric's waist and yanked him away. The hot-blooded men fought over the now half broken moped, snatching it left to right as rearview mirrors and plastic pieces were ripped off. A young man wearing a blue surgical mask saw Eric's backpack abandoned by his feet and seized upon it. Derrick grabbed it with one hand at the same time. The man's eyes narrowed at Derrick, doubling down on his attempt to steal. Derrick didn't waste a second before connecting his fist in the center of the thief's face, toppling him backwards.

Derrick grabbed the scruff of Alyssa's shirt. She still held Zoe to her chest. He shoved them both in the direction he pushed Eric. It was a wall of bodies. They pushed through as Derrick tried to put distance between the boiling crowd of shouting and sweaty bodies and themselves. Brandon appeared in the crowd using his rifle to make room for them.

"Go! Go! Go!" Brandon yelled as Derrick passed.

Derrick saw Karen hiding behind Brandon and scooped her up in his wake to follow in the same direction. Brandon took the rear as Derrick led them to a nearby intersection that had a small amount of room to breathe. There was a narrow concrete set of stairs with a black metal railing that took them to a building door. Immediately, they all dropped their heavy backpacks in a circle on the stairs. Derrick tried the door handle, but it was locked. The brown door was covered in chaotic lines of days old white and black spray paint. Eric had a scuffed-up shirt and a small dab of blood dripping from his nose. Karen was starting to look the way everyone else felt. Her eyes were wide and her hands jittery.

"What was that? Why did they– they can't just do that!" Karen shouted. "We have to call the police; they can't just steal my grandparent's moped like that!"

Brandon came out of the crowd exchanging cuss words with a woman jabbing her finger at him. He stepped past them on the stairs and tried the door handle as well to no avail. Kicking the door, he smiled maniacally at Derrick as if to say, *well this is fucking great*. They had entered the downtown portion of Louisville and immediately felt the heat rise from all the bodies crammed together. Even now as Derrick looked over the street of people that were funneled into narrow four and three lane streets, the scene was claustrophobic. A sea of sweaty faces shoulder to shoulder, shuffling down a maze of roads between the buildings.

Derrick shared a look with Alyssa as he rubbed her back and tried to reassure her before the doubt in her eyes consumed them both. Zoe sat on the concrete steps with her shoulder resting against the railing.

"Zoe, you alright there?" Derrick asked leaning over and feeling the soreness throttle his shoulder wound and aching back. Zoe nodded with a strained face. Derrick could see the pain she tried to hide through pursed lips. He touched her back as Alyssa knelt down and gave her water. The moped was a lost cause; Derrick should have known. He was amazed it got them this far.

Derrick stepped beside Brandon as they looked over the mass of people being slowly herded in one direction. From their slight elevation on the stairs the sea of bodies didn't look human, instead resembled an industrial farm filled with millions of cows all being funneled into the slaughterhouse.

"Should we turn back? Try and find a way around?" Derrick asked.

Brandon laughed, his voice barely loud enough to be heard over the thousands shouting. "We're way past that. We'd be fighting the entire city if go against the crowd. We're committed now. The only way is forward."

"Well... this fucking sucks." Derrick lifted his heavy armor a few inches to air out the heat from his sweat-soaked chest. "We left the south when we did to avoid being in this exact position."

"We have a state and a half between us and the infected, I say that's better than we were." Brandon's eyes shot down at Zoe as she sipped water. Derrick couldn't think of anything to say that wouldn't descend the conversation into sniping and arguments, so he remained silent. Brandon pulled out a folded map from his pocket and looked it over.

"Hey, Derrick," Eric said. He was holding the neck of his

shirt to his bloody nose. "I'm sorry I lost the moped; those guys came out of nowhere. I tried to stop them but–"

"It's alright, it's not your fault," Derrick tapped Eric's shoulder. He had to yell over the increasing volume of the crowd. "I should've gotten you guys off that thing as soon as we got downtown. You did good."

Derrick saw Eric's eyes light up briefly from his praise. Derrick hadn't thought much about Eric these past days, but he couldn't imagine what he was going through. Him and Zoe. To be at that age and have your parents killed in front of you. All Derrick could think about was how well they were handling it and how messed up they would be if they survived to adulthood. *If they survived...*

"I'm going to need your help tonight," Derrick spoke in Eric's ear. "How's your leg doing?"

"It's okay– a little sore but I can push through it," Eric said proudly.

"Good," Derrick nodded down toward Zoe. "She's going to be hurting when we start moving again. I need you to keep by her, okay? Keep an eye on her."

Eric beamed as he nodded. "You got it; I'll protect her."

Derrick tapped his shoulder again before sitting on the step beside Zoe. Karen and Alyssa appeared to be arguing again, about what, Derrick couldn't guess.

"How you feeling?" Derrick asked. Zoe's cheeks were flush and she had a buildup of sweat on her brow. He hoped it was from the hot sun and not an infection or, God forbid, internal bleeding.

"I'm– I'm fine," Zoe mumbled as her hand pressed on her wounded belly.

Derrick nodded. "You're doing better than me. My arm is on fire, and my back feels like it's about to fall off, and my feet– if my feet don't fall off, I think I might just chop those suckers off, they hurt so bad." Derrick said with his legs extended and his boots shaking back and forth.

Zoe gave a meek smile and looked up at Derrick.

"Being tough isn't about ignoring pain, er, pretending it doesn't exist," Derrick said. "It's okay to be in pain. Tough just means you don't let your pain control you."

Zoe nodded to herself before mumbling. "My stomach hurts. And I'm– I'm kinda dizzy."

"I want you to keep drinking," Derrick spoke, leaning over to her ear. "Finish off that bottle of water. Eric said he's hurting, too. His leg is bothering him. Think maybe you can keep an eye on him? Just stay close to him. Make sure he keeps up?"

Zoe nodded, her eyes hardening with a purpose.

Derrick considered it for a moment then shifted his weight where he sat and removed a tan pocketknife that was clipped to his front pocket. He held it casually in front of them and flipped the blade open. "Have you ever had a knife before?"

Zoe shook her head but stared at the worn and abused grip of the tactical pocketknife.

"I've had this since I was a rookie. I actually got it as a graduation gift from the academy. It's no toy, so be careful with it." Derrick took a moment to show Zoe how it locked open and where the thumb release was to collapse the blade. Closing the blade, he tucked it inside Zoe's boot, clipping the belt loop on the inside. "Does it hurt there?"

Zoe shook her head, again. "No, I don't even feel it."

"Good. You can be our secret weapon, then," Derrick winked. "Keep it safe for me, okay?"

"Okay." Zoe's eyes lit up with excitement as she took the knife out of her boot and turned it in her hand.

The crowd surged as people pushed on another like a never ending mosh pit. Derrick had to shove one stumbling man back into the crowd who nearly fell on Zoe. "Hey, hey..." Derrick said, grabbing Alyssa's forearm gently to get her attention from her heated conversation with Karen. "Can you give Zoe another Vicodin?"

Alyssa's eyes softened. "We gave her the last one this afternoon when we stopped. We're out of pain meds."

"Shit," Derrick whispered. "Just some aspirin then."

Alyssa made a face that said what Derrick thought. *Aspirin isn't going to do a thing for her,* but Alyssa nodded and reached in her backpack.

"There's nowhere to go back to." Brandon's voice barely reached them over the loud crowd. Derrick saw him arguing with Karen at the top of the stairs. *We're falling apart at the seams,* Derrick thought. He looked at the graying daylight between the buildings. It will be night in a matter of an hour. He knew they must be free of these crowds by nightfall, or they would be as good as dead.

All it would take is one idiot with a gun to trigger a stampede.

"Everyone up, we're moving!" Brandon snapped as Karen shook her head, pouting in the corner with her arms crossed. "As the crow flies, we're no more than a mile or two from the bridge to Indiana. We stay tight, stay to one side of the crowd, and follow until we find a way to the bridge or water. We're swimming or crossing tonight, no matter what."

Derrick adjusted the single point sling he had on his rifle. "There's police and soldiers everywhere and they're not fucking around. We start shooting in the crowd, they aren't going to care about your uniform or my police patches on my uniform. They'll gun us down on the spot."

"No shit," Brandon said, putting on his backpack.

Derrick held up his palms peacefully. "I just want to be sure we don't do anything rash or hot headed. We didn't survive crossing the Tennessee border just to be killed crossing into Indiana."

Brandon towered over Derrick. His eyes still frenzied from arguing with his wife. "*You* didn't survive the Tennessee border. *I* saved you. We're crossing into Indiana tonight. We move forward, no matter what."

Derrick pursed his lips and took a deep breath to try and steady his anger. Staring at the graffitied door he felt Alyssa come to his side and take his hand in her hand. Derrick smiled and took a deep breath.

"I'll take rear guard this time," Brandon said at the foot of the stairs. "Derrick, you take point. Everyone else stay between us. Keep it tight. Nut to butt. Karen you're in front of me."

Derrick sighed as he walked down the stairs. "Alyssa behind me. Then Zoe and Eric. Don't let anyone get between us."

Derrick gave Alyssa's hand one final squeeze before letting it go. Her eyes were full of a nervous fear that they all felt—a dysfunctional family about to go to war. This battlefield was different though—thousands of innocent families and children interspersed with hundreds of desperate and volatile men and women. Derrick glanced at the faded Birmingham Police patch on his shoulder.

Remember. You're not the police anymore,

Derrick waded into the crowd and was immediately struck by an unintended shoulder blade to the jaw. Bodies thrusted every which way into him as he struggled to find a relatively calmer path along the right side of the crowd. Alyssa's voice cursed behind him and Derrick looked over his shoulder to see her gripping the top strap of his backpack and managing to stay close.

After putting several yards behind them, the crowd simmered down to a slow but loud moving procession of crammed bodies. With people pressing on all sides, Derrick found a bigger man, wide and tall with a thick neck, to stay behind like a lumbering blocker heading for the end zone. It took a half hour of walking to get around the block to see the first indication of where they were being led. A large sign hung between two buildings over a blocked street and had an arrow pointing in the direction they walked and read:

'FEMA SHELTER AHEAD. FOOD AND WATER AVAILABLE. REMAIN ORDERLY'

Derrick peered over the five-foot concrete barrier that blocked the streets they couldn't turn down as they followed the sign and saw the hundreds of soldiers lounging against the building. The streets were empty behind the blockade except for a few military vehicles and police cruisers. It looked as though the army had most of downtown sectioned off from civilians.

It was another half hour of baby stepping with the crowd before everything changed. Though the sun had fallen behind the tall buildings that encased them, the temperature had not. Body odor radiated from all sides and hung in the heavy air. The buildings wouldn't allow a breeze to touch the crowds. Derrick felt sweat run down his brow to the bridge of his nose. He wiped it with the back of his hand and heard chanting growing louder with each step forward.

"Fuck the police! Fuck the police! Fuck the police!" the voices shouted.

Unlike the rest of downtown, at this turn in the intersection, the people weren't moving. The stayed cluttered throughout the road, most concentrated around an entrance ramp to a blocked interstate that crisscrossed overhead. Two lines of soldiers and Louisville police officers in riot gear stood sentry behind two sideways police cars that blocked the entrance ramp. Derrick could tell they were nervous from their furtive movements as they played with their rifles and constantly touched their radio mics. They didn't have shields and batons, but rifles and duty pistols.

Their only option to respond to any aggression is with death.

Derrick recalled being told days ago that Birmingham PD was to shoot, rather than arrest, by order of the United States President and Governor. He remembered the bile in his throat at such an alien and disgusting notion. Now, having not killed one civilian as a police officer, he had lost count of how many people he had killed to save himself and loved ones.

"Fuck the police! Fuck the–" The chanting grew louder and consumed them as they neared the intersection. Near the front of the crowd closest to the entrance ramp, the angry mob lifted a young man up in the air. At first Derrick thought he was crowd surfing like this was a rock concert on a Saturday night, but then he quickly saw the lifeless fall and twist of his head and limbs; noticed the fresh blood that dripped from his body down to the hands carrying him. *He was shot. He was killed by soldiers or law enforcement.* Another young man's lifeless body was raised high by the crowd.

"Stay close!" Derrick shouted to Alyssa who tightened her grip on his backpack. Alyssa's hair was sweaty and frizzed while her face was stressed beyond exhaustion. The buildings that surrounded them showed signs of looting. Trinket shops and bars with smashed windows and spray-painted doors.

"Watch out," Derrick commanded as he shouldered through a stagnant group that refused to move. "Step aside!"

"Fuck you, pig!" a young woman cussed at him. Derrick

didn't engage as the woman moved out of the way. *Great fucking idea, wearing my goddamn police uniform.*

"Clear the area!" Derrick shouted. "Move!" his words were drowned out by the deafening yells.

"Fuck the U.S! Fuck the police! Fuck the U.S! Fuck the police!" the chants rose until every person stopped to express their rage—weeks of pent-up fury at the government for allowing this infection to happen; bombing their own country; refusing to protect their cities; gunning down citizens. This moment became an outlet for the thousands of enraged and terrified people.

Derrick pushed past a scrawny man swinging from the side of a light pole.

The air they breathed was hot and reeked of bad breath. Bodies began to smash into him as a fight broke out in the center of the street. People screamed as they fell like dominos to the ground.

"Go!" Brandon's shout was barely audible from behind. "Derrick. Go! Move!" Brandon yelled.

"–police! Fuck the U.S.!"

"Shit!" Derrick cursed. "Move now! Out the way!" Derrick pounded through the crowd as he stumbled over several people. He saw a store front across the crowd of pumping fists and raced for it. A place they could regroup.

"Piece of shit!" voices snarled at him as he pushed by.

"Motherfucker!"

"I'll kill you, bitch!"

"Fuck the U.S.! Fuck the police! Fuck–"

Halfway down the block Derrick felt a grazing strike to his jaw from a man to his left. With a quick jab, Derrick struck the man's throat and grabbed his lapel, tossing him to the asphalt before he could catch his breath.

"Move! Police! Get out of the way!" Derrick turned back to

see Alyssa clinging to Zoe's hand as she struggled to keep up. Derrick pressed forward, grabbing a hold of Alyssa's arm. "Stay with me! Stay–"

"Derrick, watch ou–" Alyssa screamed with wide eyes.

Derrick turned forward with only enough time to see the strike swing down. The large, jagged rock clenched in the man's fist struck Derrick on his temple, sending him crumbling to the pavement. Darkness engulfed his vision as a thousand feet consumed his vision.

FORTY-SEVEN

Brandon Armstrong
Louisville, KY

"Don't shove me, bitch!"

"Fuck you, you chicken shit!"

Brandon felt the man's hot breath and spittle cover the side of his neck and flared in anger. Brandon didn't have the temperament for this shit.

"Fuck me? Fuck you, motherfucker!" Brandon shouted using his broad shoulders and elbows to check every person who lunged at him. Brandon had a trail of people he was still fighting with that reached back half a block. Karen's annoyed pull on his chest rig was what kept him moving on from one fight to the next.

Brandon's eyes found Karen as she yelled with her hands around her mouth. Something had happened but the barrage of shoulders and heads obscured Brandon's sight. Eric and Zoe were thrusted back violently into Karen's panicked arms as fights sprouted throughout the crowd. Derrick and Alyssa had disappeared and in their place a void was created in the mob. Dozens of people circled around something laying on the street below.

"Son of a bitch!" Brandon shouted as the realization hit him.

Brandon clamped one arm over his rifle and held his wife's belt tight with the other hand as he bulldozed into the people. He let go of Karen when he saw Alyssa trying to cover Derrick's unconscious body with her's as a dozen feet swung, kicked, and stomped at him like a piñata beaten to the ground. Brandon drew his side arm and fired five rounds into the air. The shock and piercing sound it made stunned the crowd long enough for Brandon to pull Alyssa to her feet.

Eric and Zoe moved to help Alyssa drag Derrick's limp body next to the closest door as the crowd's rage peaked. Brandon grabbed Derrick's heavy vest with one hand while pointing his pistol at anyone who lunged too close. His rifle bounced off his knees as he moved. They made it to a stoop with a few people standing on the stairs above the crowd. Brandon didn't even look them in the eyes before elbowing them over the hand railing.

With three hard kicks, he broke open the heavy wooden door, revealing dark stairs that led to the second floor. Karen and the others managed to drag Derrick's body up to the first landing when a man threw a brick that brushed past Brandon's face. Another man with long hair and a wiry body charged up the stoop towards Brandon with a brick in each hand. Brandon fired a three-round burst into the man's chest, crumbling him to the pavement and the crowd erupted.

The angry mob was split between helping the wounded attacker and wanting to charge inside after Brandon. Brandon slammed the damaged door shut. He fired five more rounds into the door to make them think twice about pursuing him. They quickly carried Derrick to the second floor. The apartment they went inside was some kind of loft, a small studio above the business center below. Whoever lived there seemed to have been smart enough to leave days ago.

"Eric, here, grab this," Brandon said as they took hold of a loveseat and brought it to the top of the stairs. With a final jostle, the couch tumbled and flipped down the stairs until it lodged against the door. Brandon looked around the room and pointed out a few other things for Eric to toss down the stairs.

Derrick had a nasty gash in his hairline that leaked blood down the side of his face. "Is he alive?" Brandon asked over Zoe's shoulder, who despite her pale complexion, was helping clean and dress the wound.

Alyssa glared back at Brandon. "Yes, he's alive!" she snapped, as if the mere question of doubt could kill him. Alyssa had a bruised welt forming on her cheek as well and more on her arms from protecting him.

Brandon sighed in relief, "I was just asking."

He was surprised that Alyssa had protected Derrick like that in the street.

Didn't think the selfish bitch had it in her.

The windows above the one remaining couch that Derrick was laid on overlooked the city streets. It was like an ant farm with the ants crawling and turning on each other. Brandon could see the entire street they had crossed to get here. People packed the street as far as he could see. The interstates ran above ground through downtown Louisville creating overpasses for the streets below. The lines of soldiers and Louisville police still blocked the entrance ramp to the interstate, though the crowd was beginning to shake the cars that blocked the ramp.

A banging on the door made everyone jump and even caused Derrick to stir to consciousness. Eric had just finished tossing a table down the stairs. "Eric, watch that door. Let me know if they start to get it open," Brandon said.

"There's no way they're getting it open," Eric replied.

"Just watch the damn door," Brandon growled. Eric shrugged, annoyed, but kept an eye on it nonetheless.

"What happened?" Derrick mumbled from the couch.

"You lost a fight with a rock," Alyssa sniffled through a smile. She had a visible sigh of relief at watching Derrick sit up.

"Your face... are you okay?" Derrick sat up as he touched Alyssa's bruised cheek.

Alyssa smiled and took his hand from her bruised cheek. "You should see yours." Alyssa pointed to his now bandaged head as Zoe wrapped gauze around his forehead. Derrick adjusted the rifle strap that pulled at his throat and looked over at Zoe who kneeled beside him. "What do you think? Am I still beautiful?"

Karen took Brandon's arm and walked him to the opposite corner of the room. Everyone was coated in a film of sweat and stained clothes. Their bodies radiated heat like each one of them were just plucked from the oven.

"What is it? Are you okay?" Brandon asked when he saw tears appearing in Karen's eyes. Brandon did a once over her body looking for injuries or bleeds but saw none.

"You– did you... is that guy dead?" Karen asked, hesitantly.

"Which guy?" Brandon asked, oblivious.

"Which guy?" Karen's face in disbelief. "Brandon, you shot that man downstairs."

"Oh," Brandon shrugged and shook his head. "I don't know, maybe."

"We– we have to call someone. The police or army. We need to tell them it was self-defense– that it wasn't your fault," Karen stuttered as her eyes danced back and forth. "Before the people lie and say... and say you started it or–"

"Karen..." Brandon whispered. He had to fight not to roll his eyes or sound too callous about shooting the man. He couldn't deal with another stupid fucking argument right now. He wanted to say something along the lines of *fuck him* and move on but knew that wouldn't do with his wife.

"No, no, I'm not letting them try and make you out to be the bad guy." tears now streamed down Karen's cheeks. "This place– this, this fucking city tried to kill you. Kill us! Where is the army? Where is the police!? Why is everyone just letting this happen?"

The other occupants stopped their conversation as they looked at Karen. Brandon guided Karen over toward the bathroom and hugged her. He felt her fingers dig into the small of his back and shoulder as she pressed her face into his chest. "Listen to me," Brandon whispered to his wife as he pulled away and looked down into her watery eyes, his calloused palms gently cupping her cheeks. "I'm going to be fine and you're going to be fine. No one's taking me away. The shooting isn't even on the army's radar, okay? Trust me. I promise you. I'm not going to let anyone hurt you. I'm going to get us out of here, okay?"

Karen's lower lip trembled before she bit it. She let out a long breath and shook her head. "I can't lose you. Promise me that nothing will happen to you either. You can't leave me."

Brandon smiled and nodded. "Nothing will happen to me, I promise. We're not going to die, not today. Not any time soon, alright?"

"Okay," Karen took a deep breath. "And we're never fucking coming back to Louisville."

Derrick had gotten to his feet, his fingers palpating the tenderness of his latest wound.

"You good?" Brandon asked.

"Think so," Derrick said. "Lost my damn backpack."

He might be an asshole, but he's one tough motherfucker.

"Price of doing business," Brandon looked out the bathroom window and saw it fed to a fire escape into a side alley that was also full of people. "We can't stay here long,"

"Maybe for a bit?" Eric suggested.

"Might be good," Alyssa agreed. "Rest... come up with a plan."

"Maybe wait till night or morning even," Karen said.

"We can find somewhere else to rest and make a plan," Brandon said. "This place is going to shit. We're a mile or less from Indiana, we need to push through."

Derrick nodded and touched the small of Alyssa's back to get her attention. "He's righ–"

"Car..." Zoe's broken voice caught their attention. Brandon and Derrick moved to see out the windows. A purple older model Toyota honked as it sped down the entrance ramp. The car veered left then right. The soldiers were so preoccupied with the rioting crowd they barely had time to turn and dive out of the way of the car speeding down the interstate. The purple Toyota Corolla smashed into the corner of one of the cop cars blocking the entrance ramp, then plowed into the crowd of people. Screams and panic reverberated through the block as the civilians didn't have a chance to get out of the way as it ran over dozens of innocents.

"Oh my god..." Alyssa whispered as she cupped her mouth.

The sedan made it fifteen yards down the street before the crowd succeeded in stopping its carnage. The protestors that had tried to flee before turned on the driver and swarmed the car. Hundreds of people who could reach the vehicle, smashed the windows and shook the vehicle as they reached for the perpetrator inside.

"This could be good," Brandon scratched his chin. "A good

distraction." Brandon was back in battle mode. His mind working the problem and thinking through the solution.

If we can get down the fire escape, we can get to the interstate on ramp.

"Look, its perfect," Brandon pointed to the dozens of people mobbing the soldiers to run up the entrance ramp. "The car just gave us our exit. We just–"

"Brandon..." Derrick's voice trailed off. Brandon looked back at the car that was being torn apart. The driver was ripped out from the car. He screamed and reached desperately for it like the car was his child and it was being taken from him. *Maybe his child was still in the car?* His attackers tore apart the seat cushions and covers while a few of them went over to the trunk and popped it open.

The creature lunged out on the first person there. It's wrists and feet were bound in a blood-soaked rope. Brandon couldn't tell if it was male or female; there was too much blood but judging from its size it definitely was a child. The rabid adolescent latched on to a woman's face as its teeth tore a chunk free from her cheek. It screamed a chalky ragged scream and let go to fall on top of a man, pulling him down to the asphalt. "Infected..." Brandon whispered to himself.

The woman clutched her face and writhed in pain as blood poured down her face and those around her rushed to help her not knowing what was coming next. The woman's screams turned a maddening pitch and echoed off the Louisville buildings—vicious and rabid.

"It's here," Derrick gasped.

FORTY-EIGHT

Derrick Hart

Louisville, KY

"Oh my god! They're killing each–" Karen screamed.

"Oh no, no, no..."

Derrick was still dizzy from his head wound when the infected began to attack and turn the crowd, their number gained exponentially on the uninfected. He blinked, hoping this was just a nightmare.

This can't be real.

"Fuck! Let's move, let's move!" Brandon ran to the bathroom in the back and used the butt of his gun to smash out the glass. "Come on, Karen."

"Wait! Wait!" Derrick held up his hand as he stared out the window.

"Are you serious?" Brandon hollered. "We're going now, come on!"

"Brandon, look out the window we can't go now, we'll be dead in seconds!" Derrick said.

"What are you talking about?" Brandon stormed back over to the window. The streets were darkening with streetlights clicking on to illuminate the carnage below. The masses of panicked faces looked like a wave pool of smashed bodies. Tens of thousands of people all clamored over one another to get to safety that didn't exist. The rabid disappeared in the masses. Civilians running were sucked under the crowd, never to be seen again. For every person a rabid attacked five more fell to the ground to get trampled to death.

"There's no room to move down there," the crowd had chased the police and soldiers onto the entrance ramp where hundreds fled. "Best case, we lose track of each other running on top of people's backs. Worst case, we all get sucked under and trampled to death. We won't be able to track where the infected are until they're right on top of us. We have to wait, man."

Brandon paced back and forth in the living room for a moment with his rifle clenched in his fist. "Shit!"

"Look, look..." Derrick's mind fought the headache that stung his mind as he worked the problem. "This is ground zero for the infection, which means this will be the first place that clears of infected. I've seen it before." Derrick pointed to the people fleeing up the interstate and the infected giving chase. "Civilians will run away from here and the infected will follow. When it clears then we'll move."

"Everyone hydrate and get ready to move," Brandon announced. "Check each other for open wounds. Crazy glue and duct tape them if you find any."

"They're– they're killing each other! Oh my god... oh my..." Karen screamed, covering her mouth. The final layers of comfort and security that Karen had viewed this outbreak through so far were finally being stripped away. Only a thin pane of glass stood between her and the horrors below.

Alyssa looked below at the growing pile of bloodied bodies then back at Derrick.

"We're just going to wait?" Alyssa whispered to Derrick. Brandon pulled a tearful Karen away from the windows and tried to calm her down.

"A few minutes. What other option is there?" Derrick said.

"Maybe we can stay here longer? The night at least? It's already getting dark," Eric said.

"We're not staying the night," Brandon butted in, Karen still in his arms. "This place is about to become like Atlanta... only a thousand times worse, because there's a thousand times more people on the streets. Who knows? They could have a bomber en route to level this city as we speak. If we want to live longer than a night, we need to get to the north of the city now. Before everyone's infected."

"We'll wait for a clearing and go out the fire escape," Derrick nodded. "We can use the infected as cover to cross the bridge into Indiana..."

"Maybe even find a goddamn Humvee," Brandon said looking out the bathroom window. They froze when the loud tornado alarm sounded off and echoed through the streets, an eerie sound that made Derrick's heart thump in his chest harder.

Alyssa was on the verge of a breakdown herself. Derrick felt her hands trembling. "Hey, hey..." Derrick said.

"I don't want– I can't," Alyssa whispered as she held back tears. "I can't do this, again. Derrick–" Her quick, shallow breaths were nearing hyperventilation. Derrick could see her reliving Atlanta all over again. The fear and panic were thick in her voice just like it was in the voicemail she had left. "Listen, we don't have to go we can stay– we can just stay here, I–"

Derrick's mind was flung back to the roll call room as he listened to the sobbing young officer crying for his mother. There was something primal about the fear the rabid elicited. A man with a gun trying to kill you was terrifying. But the rabid were monsters, as if plucked from a child's nightmare. They didn't feel pain. They didn't grow tired. They were single minded and vicious like no creature this planet had ever seen before. Derrick remembered Officer Perry pulling the terrified officer in for a hug, steadying him.

"Shh shh... It's okay, just breathe... breathe..." Derrick whispered into Alyssa's ear as he hugged her tightly. His mind was awash with the lies and harsh truths of the past few days. He thought of Rachel Anderson, the Vice President's daughter, telling him and Perry to get on the chopper with them. The look in Perry's eyes as she had regarded Derrick.

The life he could have saved just by getting on the helicopter with her.

"Listen to me," Derrick said sternly but with soft eyes. "You're not going to die. I'm not going to let one fucking thing happen to you guys out there. But we have to go," Derrick said focusing his gaze on her. He took her jittery hands in his as her breathing calmed. "I'm going to kill every fucking thing that comes near us. But we have to go, okay? I'm not going to lose you again."

Alyssa nodded through pursed lips as she swiped at her eyes. "Okay," she said. Her voice breaking as she mouthed, "I love you."

Kissing her forehead, Derrick whispered, "I love you."

The streets below were rife with screeching and howling. The infected chased people in every direction leaving a long stretch of ground that was layered with trampled and beaten bodies. Rabid leapt on top of the crowds clawing through them. Every bite, each scratch they inflicted on a person led to a rise in their numbers. Zoe was lost in a trance observing the violence below. Derrick thought for a moment to tell her not to watch but he couldn't. *She is going to be walking over those bodies in a moment. She needs to be prepared.* Derrick squeezed her hand, letting her know he was there. Her sunken eyes didn't look as though she had the energy to even stay standing.

"Are you ready to be tough?" Derrick asked.

"I am tough."

"I know you are."

Distant pops sounded off from another side of the city, followed by others. The infection was spreading.

"There's a clearing down below," Brandon said as he thumbed bullets into a pistol magazine. Palming the magazine into his pistol, he completed a press check to confirm a round in the chamber before re-holstering it. "It's time."

Derrick looked back over the nervous faces of the others, who all looked to him and Brandon. "We stay together, move as a unit, and we'll stay alive. We're going to make it– all of us," Derrick lied. "Let's go."

FORTY-NINE

Sharon Hill
Louisville, KY

Sharon could see the nervous fretting in Tommy's movements. He sat in the driver's seat of the pickup with his rifle clenched in his palms. He was just a boy, after all, as evident from the patches of stubble on his chin where he had tried to grow a beard.

This teenage boy wasn't meant to be watching Sharon in the middle of this chaos. He was supposed to be playing video games and texting girls. The mass of civilians must have overrun a blockade at one of the entrance ramps to the interstate, because hundreds of people flooded the overpass. The people smacked the side of the vehicle and shook the door handles as they passed, begging to get inside, before they cut their losses and continued running.

"We should go down below, drive down there," Sharon

said. The tornado siren made Sharon the most anxious. Its waning warning permeated the entire city.

"No. We're supposed to s-stay here, in case things go bad," Tommy stuttered as another person smacked the window.

Part of Sharon wanted to toss Tommy out of his seat and drive away as fast as she could, but she doubted she had the strength. "Things are bad, look around. Look down below. Look how many people ran into the hospital–"

"Shut up!" Tommy snapped as he hit his rifle against the steering wheel. "I'm in charge here, I'm in– you... Stop talking and just wait."

He sounded like the teenager he was. Wesley had taken all the men into the hospital with him, expecting a fight. The interstate passed by the front entrance of Louisville General Hospital. Wesley had spied dozens of soldiers along with armored trucks guarding the hospital. Sharon had stayed behind but she'd heard the Sons of Liberty argue on their radio.

"It's too heavily guarded."

"Don't be a pussy, we have the high ground."

"No way. Reinforcements will swamp us up here."

Wesley had been in the middle of arguing with Baron, his hotheaded younger son when luck had turned in their favor and chaos had broken out among the soldiers. A sudden jolt had gone through the soldiers guarding the door. They'd turned at one another, exchanging shouts as they'd turned up the volume on their radios. Wesley's eyes had lit up as if God had sent him a personal message when every one of the soldiers had moved in a frenzy into a Humvee and hauled at a high rate of speed towards downtown.

The assault had been over even before the Sons of Liberty had charged down the ramp at the few remaining police officers. With sheer force and surprise, Wesley had been able to radio back and confirm they had made entry into the hospital without suffering a single loss. That was nearly ten minutes ago. A thousand people had flooded the interstate since then. Something was happening in Louisville right now.

One of the passersbys smashed a brick into the windshield that sent a crack through the glass, large enough to get Tommy moving. The skinny boy yanked on the gear shift and put the truck in drive. They lurched forward and drove against the crowd down the overpass entrance ramp across the street from the hospital. The truck rocked back and forth as he ran over the bodies of executed police officers, which made Sharon grimace.

"What the fuck, man? What are you doing down here?" a burly man in a red flannel shirt asked Tommy as they parked the truck beside the dozen others. He had a shotgun held a little too casually in their direction.

"It's fucked up there. We were getn swamped!"

The man sighed and pointed to the hospital. "Go find Wesley or one of his boys, then." Sharon was already jogging past them.

I need to get a gun or something. If I can find a weapon, I won't need to rely on these guys anymore. Maybe I can steal one of their trucks?

Sharon froze in the entryway of the ER lobby. The wall behind the front desk, once smooth, was now peppered with hundreds of bullet holes. The dead were sprawled across the floor and hung over rows of gray chairs—men mostly, but a few women, as well; patients, police officers, soldiers running for cover, their blood streaming down the tile floor. Even Tommy seemed to have been taken back for a moment by the bloodbath.

No guns. They've already stripped them of their weapons.

"C-come on," Tommy directed Sharon and they walked through a set of doors into the emergency room. For a second,

Sharon even considered trying to disarm Tommy, but she wasn't sure enough in her ability to do so.

"Please! Just– just let us go!"

"I'm doing what you say. I'm doing–"

"Get your hands off me!"

The voices cluttered the hallway as smaller groups of nurses and doctors were herded together at the far end of the hall. Sharon followed Tommy's forceful nudges despite the twisting in her stomach. Her situation was worsening by the moment as she felt less and less like a guest and more like a captive being marched under guard. They stepped between two dead police officers who lay half on top of each other in the center aisle. *Guns were missing.*

"Twenty-five, twenty-six– Tommy? What the hell?" Baron scowled, in the midst of taking a head count. Baron's finger dangled in the air before him like he was at a restaurant getting the total size of his dinner party. But really, he was counting the number of terrified women he had lined against the hallway wall.

"Baron, um– the overpass is overrun with people." Tommy spoke, staring down at his feet. "They– the people bum rushed us up there."

Baron groaned and rolled his eyes. "Man, now you made me mess my count. Just go watch the front with George."

Sharon's eyes clung to a scared looking Hispanic woman who had someone else's blood splattered on the front of her nurse scrubs. Her hands shook in front of her belly. Without a sound, the nurse's big round eyes begged for Sharon's help. Sharon didn't much like Tommy, but she knew she didn't want to be in the same group as these women, whatever they were being herded together for.

Mouthing an apology to the young nurse, Sharon stepped away, following Tommy back the way they came until a swift tug at her arm sent a surge of pain to the rock salt wounds on her chest and stopped her in her tracks.

"Whoa now, little lady, where do you think you're goin?" Baron asked, his lips wet from the dribble of his tobacco chew.

"I– Wesley," Sharon tried to sound calm as she was pulled off balance back to the other women.

"See, my father put me in charge down here while he's havin a look upstairs," Baron said, eyeing Sharon like she was an animal. Baron's eyes sized up her worth by the body part. "Why don't you join the other lovely ladies."

"I will not–" Sharon tried to fight off the boy, but he easily shoved her to her knees into the hallway full of nurses. The Hispanic nurse helped Sharon to her feet and pulled Sharon slightly behind her.

"Gawddangit. What was I on, Bill?" Baron closed his eyes trying to remember.

"Twenty-six, I think."

"Ahh... works fer me. Twenty-six, twenty-seven..." Sharon's eyes bounced between the five men surrounding her and the other women. Their rifles were all pointed at the women as they eyed them like a prize waiting to be won. Sharon had made many mistakes today, but she was realizing the worst of them now. She was just another face to be counted. She was a prisoner, again.

"Thirty-three. Radio up to my dad that we got thirty-three queens down here," Baron said with a crooked smile. "Looks like most of them are kings, too. It's gonna get crowded back home."

Sharon realized then what they were doing. She knew why they were there, and what they were after. The Sons of Liberty were stocking their shelter with supplies. They were preparing for the end of the world. They came to Louisville to kidnap doctors, nurses... and women.

FIFTY

Rachel Anderson
Louisville, KY

The sirens had been wailing for twenty minutes now. It was the kind of city wide siren that was sounded in the event of a tornado. The glass walls muted the sound, but the alarm continued its lament and sent a panic through Rachel's chest. She didn't know what it meant but what scared her the worst was that the two guards who stood watch, didn't seem to know either.

They had not activated the speaker so Rachel could not hear their words, but their worried looks were enough to make her sweat. Her feet paced about in her glass cell as she chewed her thumb nail. The men constantly looked out the large double doors to see if anyone was coming or if there was news about the sirens.

Could the infected have reached Louisville already?

"Make sure you got everything on you that you need—

boots, clothes..." Sean said to her as Allen and Chris were lacing up their boots.

"You know, we're not getting out of here unless someone lets us out," Rachel said, even as she put on her boots.

"Yeah, but when that happens, I don't want to wait for you to put your socks on," Sean said, giving her a look.

"Grab your MREs and bottles of water," Rachel said.

"We don't have any bags to put them in," Chris said over Sean's shoulder.

"Use your pillowcases," Rachel suggested.

Chris shrugged, having not thought of it. Allen grabbed his pillow. "Good ideas like that is why she gets away with being a stubborn SOB."

Rachel had put on her camo pants, t-shirt, and combat boots and filled her pillowcase with the four bottles of water and two MREs she had left. There was nothing even remotely close to a weapon she could find in the room, otherwise she would have grabbed that too. One of their two guards had disappeared out of the room and the second looked close to following. He was a young boy with chubby cheeks and shifty eyes.

Pounding on the glass until her knuckles were red, Rachel tried desperately to get the boy's attention. To get him to at least turn on the speaker so she could talk to him. "Come on, turn on the radio. Just talk to me!" Rachel yelled uselessly at the thick glass. The boy looked at her for the briefest of moments and her eyes widened with hope as she smiled and waved him over. He took a step in her direction then stopped and in a sharp turn, ran out the double doors.

"No, no!" Rachel yelled.

"Come back, you piece of shit!" Allen's voice crackled through the speaker.

They stood there silently for a minute. The four of them

staring at the double unmanned double doors as the ominous sirens continued to wale. *What if this is it? What if the infection's here and everyone runs away? Is this how we die? Left to starve in a damned glass cage?*

The double doors slammed open in a fury as men flooded the room. Their forest green uniforms were wrinkled and dirty, but Rachel could clearly see the American flag patches on their shoulders. Their beards were thick, and eyes focused over their weapons as they cleared the room. The lead soldier shoved the chubby face guard who had just attempted to flee minutes ago towards Rachel's glass door. The guard, with shaky hands, keyed in the code and the glass door slid open.

"Get her secret service detail out, now!" the scruffy faced soldier ordered the guard then turned to Rachel. "Rachel Anderson?

Rachel nodded in excitement. "Yes, yes!"

"Ma'am, I'm Lt. Miles, U.S. Special Forces," he grabbed her right arm and using a small electronic tablet the size of a phone, scanned the barcode on her Greenband bracelet. Satisfied with what he saw he nodded. "We're tasked to extract you and your three body men to the bunker. Will you come with us?"

"Yes! Thank you," was all Rachel managed to say as emotion overcame her. Lt. Miles was an older man with a gray stubble in his thick five o'clock shadow. His face was creased and aged in the way that seasoned soldiers often looked after the stress of combat. His tall athletic frame gave him an imposing presence when Rachel stood beside him.

Sean, Chris, and Allen came out of their cell and the Special Forces soldier released the guard's collar and let him run out the double doors. Lt. Miles removed a satellite phone from his cargo pocket. The phone had worn green electrical tape wrapped around the base of it and a number written on the back in white lettering. Lt. Miles dialed a number, presumably the one on the back of the phone. "Sir, this is Lt. Miles reporting, package is secure. I repeat, package is secure. We are still on the ground proceeding with the extraction. Yes, sir." Lt. Miles nodded and hung up his phone, grumbling to himself.

"Ma'am, gentlemen," Lt. Miles said, tossing the phone back in his pocket. "The rabid are loose in this city. We've got a helicopter on the other side of Cherokee Park to get us out of here, but there's a lot of unknowns between there and here."

Three of the Special Forces soldiers drew handguns and handed them to the secret service agents.

"About fuckin' time," Allen griped, taking one of the pistols.

One of the soldiers murmured to Chris, "watch your muzzle control."

"I need you all to move fast, stay close, and do as we say, understood?" Lt. Miles said.

Rachel's eyes met with Sean's. With the glass wall no longer separating them, she longed to touch him. She wanted to hug him, to kiss him after all the angst and uncertainty she had felt, but she knew it wouldn't help Sean. She owed it to him, to Sean's father, to keep their relationship secret as long as they could.

"Understood," Rachel said.

When they ran out of the trailer into the open green fields, chaos didn't begin to describe the crisis the world was in. Soldiers sprinted between trailers and ran for vehicles passing by. Gunshots went off like fireworks as they cracked and boomed. Panicked shouts of leaderless men filled the grassy fields. The army had set up a large maze of white trailers and green tents that filled the Louisville Cherokee Park and extended into the streets and surrounding buildings. Rachel had no bearing on where they ran; she just followed.

"Stay close." Lt. Miles let one of his men lead the way as he jogged to Rachel's side with Sean following closely behind. There was a calm order in how she watched the soldiers move, jogging through the grass. Rachel didn't know much about the military, but she knew enough to be glad the Special Forces soldiers were on her side and not against her.

"Did my father send you? Is he at the White House?" Rachel asked as they trotted ahead.

"The President's fine," Lt. Miles reassured. "He's not in the White House, they moved him to Mount Weather."

"C.O.G.?" Sean asked.

"Yeah," Lt. Miles nodded.

"What's... What's Mount Weather?" Rachel asked.

"Continuity of government protocol," Sean said. "Long term bunker designed to preserve the continuation of government during a catastrophic event."

A scream cut through the chaos stopping Rachel and her protective detail in their tracks. They knew the sound they heard. Rachel's mind reeled as it was brought back to the chase in Miami. Her sweat glands went into overdrive as she began to panic from hearing that tearing screech.

Two rabid leapt from between an aisle of tents onto the lead soldier's backside. The soldier writhed and shook, but the rabid's teeth already was tearing flesh from the soldier's scalp. The Special Forces soldiers opened fire, peppering the rabid's back with bullet holes. Hands pushed on Rachel's back as the soldiers bolted by their own man who lay shot to death along with the rabid. The soldier had an intentional looking gunshot wound placed to the side of his head. Rachel imagined it was an unspoken rule among these men. Put an infected soldier down before he turns. *Shoot me before I turn.* Rachel hoped Sean would do the same for her.

Rachel heard the helicopter before she saw it. Her escorts

popped controlled bursts in opposing directions at ancillary rabid approaching them as they neared the roar of rotary blades.

"Up here," Lt. Miles pointed to the left. They sprinted around a series of tents and saw a clearing with a helicopter idling on the ground. The pilot was out of the cockpit hollering at the dozens of soldiers and doctors who had crammed onto the bed of the chopper. They screamed in desperation, shaking their heads as they refused to get off the chopper.

Lt. Miles held up his hand, "stand by," he said to Rachel and her agents then ran ahead with his men. The Spec. Ops. soldiers trained their rifles on those who attempted to steal their transport. There was a tense standoff as soldiers on the choppers defied their orders, nervously shifting their own rifles in their hands. Sean took hold of Rachel's wrist and pulled her back as Allen and Chris moved shoulder to shoulder in front of her.

Automatic gunfire exploded, but not from the direction of the helicopter. Rachel didn't know where to take cover. The bullets snapped by her head and thudded into the dirt by her feet as she felt Sean jerk her arm to the side and covered her body with his. The Special Forces soldiers pivoted as the bullets fired on them ripped through the tent behind them. Holes pierced the tent as men screamed for help and rabids' screams answered their cries.

Lt. Miles and his men fired over Rachel's head and Sean pulled her under his broad shoulders. Their bullets pelted holes in the tent flapping in the wind, but their gunfire adjusted when the infected sprinted around the tent. Rachel covered her ears as Sean fired from his knelt position into a rabid's chest that was scurrying for them. The muted explosions of gunfire echoed through her cupped ears as Rachel turned and saw the hysterical faces of the soldiers in the chopper as one of them dove into the cockpit. With terror flooding his eyes, a young man pulled on the throttle of the helicopter despite the pilot's attempts to stop him. Lifting the chopper into the air a dozen feet before the chopper began to tilt on its axis.

"Look out– oh god!" Rachel yelled but her voice was lost in the automatic gunfire and the roar of the rotary blades that came crashing down. She braced as the nose of the helicopter came barreling down on them. The tail of the helicopter summersaulted overhead, flipping the chopper upside down before crashing down on top of them.

FIFTY-ONE

Brandon Armstrong

Louisville, KY

Brandon jumped the remaining few feet from the rusty fire escape. A few stragglers had found the alley and ran past him with wide fearful eyes while thousands followed the herd running up and down the main road. The brick alley walls were black with mold and chipped red spray paint. The air was rich with the stench of weeks old rotting garbage. The rest of his party dropped down behind him with Zoe yelping as she hit the ground. Alyssa and Karen rushed to her side. Derrick was the last one to hop off the fire escape.

"Moving," Brandon said, even toned, over his shoulder. His rifle was held at the low ready as he jogged on light knees.

At this mouth of the alley that fed into the street, it was impossible not to pause and gasp at the massacre before them. The road was littered with hundreds of bodies as far as the eyes could see. The blood-stained pavement was alive with groans and small movements of the half dead. The trampled and broken bodies left behind to bleed out.

"Jesus Chri–" Karen said in a daze.

A rabid with ragged hair and torn clothes raised its head over the broken-down purple car in the middle of the road. Its eyes were wide with red blotting out the whites. It erupted in an ear-splitting screech and clamored over the hood of the car for their group. The rabid tripped over a dead body and scurried on all four of its limbs.

"Shoot– shoot it!" Karen screamed.

Brandon squeezed the trigger five times in quick succession. The gunfire pounded the rabid's chest rolling it to its side. Brandon lowered his rifle to the top of the infected's head and placed the final shot into his skull. As if the gunshots were a declaration of war against the rabid, vicious screams from every direction cried out, filling the street. Karen sank to a squat as she covered her ears.

"Contact, rear!" Derrick's voice called out before Brandon heard Derrick open fire. Four infected tumbled out of a storefront to Brandon's left, and more figures sprinted from the opposite side of the road.

"Run, run! Up the entrance ramp, go!" Brandon shouted as he moved to the center of the road. Alyssa pulled Karen to her feet and led the others for the overpass. Brandon fired at the four infected who were closest. He tried to wound and slow them down; they were too close to kill them all in one go. The first two were smaller and thinner. Brandon's 5.56 bullets broke their femurs and smashed into their hips.

Brandon shuffled backwards and changed targets as quickly as he could. The other two were half naked and bulkier in their build, the fat on their shirtless bodies jiggled as they leapt for Brandon's rifle. The sound of their ragged breaths heaving for him was drowned out by the sound of Derrick's rifle firing in rapid succession. Bullets smattered into the infected's face and chest dropping them to ground. Brandon looked up and saw Derrick waiting for him, laying down covering fire from the bottom of the entrance ramp.

Brandon ran between bodies as Derrick snapped bullets at infected that chased him. When he reached Derrick, they took turns completing tactical reloads on their rifles, smacking a fresh magazine into the mag-well while jogging up the overpass where Karen and the others waited. The road began to clear of dead bodies as they topped the interstate. Alyssa checked Zoe's stomach. "She tore a stitch," Alyssa said as Derrick approached. He patted Zoe's shoulder, "We'll deal with it later, come on."

They kept a steady jog on the interstate toward the bridge to Indiana. Hundreds of civilians ran with them. A few had pistols but most carried luggage or children as everyone made a desperate sprint to leave the city.

Screams amassed in the streets below as the city devolved into chaos. Brandon looked over the side of the overpass at the city streets and saw rabid leaping onto victims and chasing others from one building to the next. 100,000 people ran on survival instincts they had never used before in their lives.

"Help hel– get away!" a woman cried.

"Contact, left," Derrick said casually, as if he was giving directions to a restaurant.

Brandon turned to an exit ramp they were passing and saw a skinny woman with short black hair and glasses running frantically as three rabid bounded after her. *Damn, woman's leading them right to us.*

The crowd they ran with began to panic and parted, running from the girl like she was a leper. Brandon and Derrick took up positions on either side of the ramp with their rifle sighted. Their loud rifle reports silenced the panicked civilians as their overlapping fields of fire chewed the three rabid to pieces before they could summit the overpass.

"Oh god... oh god..." the skinny girl with thick-rimmed glasses gasped for air at the top of the interstate and went to touch Brandon's arm. "Thank... thank you..."

Brandon moved away before she could, "Derrick, on me."

He took point, leaving the woman and running ahead as Derrick fell in behind their group.

"Hey... hey wait!" the girl in glasses called out. When they didn't, the girl began to jog behind them. Brandon noticed more civilians now taking note of Brandon and Derrick. They eyed Brandon's camo tactical vest and Derrick's SWAT uniform. Families and small groups of civilians slowed and maneuvered themselves into their wake, running behind Derrick at the rear.

Parasites, Brandon thought. *Civilians with no weapons and parents carrying small children who offer no benefit but will shadow us for protection.* Brandon let them. They would be a good distraction for the rabid until they crossed the border. *We can't be far from Indiana.*

"I– I can see the bridge!" Alyssa called out. The interstate curved in such a way they he could see the arching metal support beams and the tethered suspension cables of the bridge over the Ohio river. It was still a distance away but its sight ignited a jolt of energy inside him.

The crowd parted in front of Brandon to let civilians running the opposite way through. They weren't infected, but they were coming at them. A dozen at first. Then fifty or so. Soon, more were running towards them than with them. Their shoulders thudded into Brandon as they sprinted frantically by.

"Why are they running?" Derrick's voice called from behind as they slowed.

"Hey– hey," Brandon stopped a bearded man, catching his arm. "Where are you going? Why–"

"Run– run, they're coming!" the man shouted as he tore away from Brandon's grip and kept running.

"The rabid? How many!" Brandon called after the man.

Brandon heard the thunderous roar before he saw them. There were too many damn people in the way to see. He slowed to a trot and the others came to his side.

"Run, run!" a woman shouted as she passed.

"Wha-what's that soun–" Eric gasped.

An explosion shook the interstate violently, rocking everyone off their feet. The world rattled even on his knees, but Brandon managed to look up to see smoke filling the sky where the bridge once sat. "No..." Brandon whispered as the trembling road steadied and Brandon could see a huge section of the bridge was demolished and crumbled in a pile of metal and concrete on the water below.

"They... did they just..." Derrick said, exasperated as he and all the civilians stood frozen in the moment.

The rattle of large caliber fire deafened Brandon's ears. Fifteen civilians in front of Brandon yelped and fell to the ground as bullets ripped holes in their bodies.

A wall of four Humvees idled at a slow pace in their direction. The .50 Cal Barrett machine gun turrets sprayed into the crowd of runners ripping limbs free with their gunfire. There was a procession of infantry columned in between the Humvees, numbered in the hundreds.

"Oh, fuck! Derrick!" Brandon screamed but the ringing in his ears half muted the world and his voice. Brandon lay down firing, emptying his magazine at the soldiers and armored vehicles before falling back, running as bullets thudded the pavement at his feet.

"Brandon, they're killing–" Derrick panted. "They're killing everyone!"

The turrets of the Humvees poured rounds into the backs

of the crowd indiscriminately. Men, women, and children were torn apart as they sprinted around the bend in the interstate.

Alyssa pulled Zoe to the ground and scooted to the side of the interstate where nearly a hundred civilians ducked beneath the concrete barrier on the side.

"Derrick!" Brandon yelled and took cover with the others. Derrick and Brandon pushed between civilians cowering on their knees. Karen lay almost flat beside Eric as bullets whistled and snapped overhead.

Brandon reloaded as he glanced overhead at the approaching convoy coming around the bend in the road. It was only a matter of moments before the convoy took the bend in the road and had a clear shot on everyone who was hiding.

"You take right, I got the left," Brandon glanced to Derrick who nodded.

With a nod of Brandon's head, they both popped up and opened fire on the convoy. Their bullets peppered the windshields of the Humvees, made the gunners take cover, and dropped two of the soldiers in front, halting their advancement. They took cover as the return fire pounded the concrete they hid behind. Reloading his magazine, Brandon saw Derrick shouting something to Alyssa and the civilians hiding around him.

Derrick nodded removed his last two stun grenades from his vest and motioned to Brandon to give covering firing on his mark.

Brandon nodded, "on you."

Derrick took a deep breath and shook his head with a small smirk in the corner of his mouth as if to say, *this is fucking stupid.* When the chorus of gunfire slowed, as many of the shooters had to reload, Derrick pulled the pins off the two stun grenades and threw them one at a time in front of the Humvees.

"Run! Go now!" Derrick yelled to the civilians, not waiting for the explosions. With darkness almost upon them, the stun grenades ignited a blinding flash that disoriented the unsuspecting soldiers. Brandon stood, providing covering fire as Derrick got their group and the rest of the civilians running for the nearest exit ramp. Brandon clicked empty just as Derrick came to his side.

"Move! I got you!" Derrick shouted and Brandon ran for the exit ramp he saw Karen run down. He heard Derrick's covering fire answered with the booming roar of the .50 Cal returning fire.

FIFTY-TWO

Sharon Hill
Louisville, KY

"I don't care! Show me a body or show me another queen!" Baron booted a small trash can that bounced and tumbled down the hallway. "She was right here a minute ago!"

Sharon didn't flinch but she didn't look in Baron's direction either. She didn't want to draw any attention to herself. The nurse to her right moved closer to Sharon so that their arms brushed together—an obvious intrusion into her personal space by a stranger that Sharon would have shied away from any other time, but Sharon knew what this stranger was doing, and she pressed her arm back into the nurse's arm just as hard.

The collection of doctors, nurses, and women that Baron had gathered together had been marched into a 'Family Only' waiting area inside the emergency room. The room was crowded with the forty plus people they had filed inside but it was big enough for everyone to keep to themselves. There were twenty or so chairs on one side of the room and in the corner where Sharon stood there were a few couches around a simple coffee table with colorful blocks, coloring books, and cabinets filled with more distractions one could push into their child's hands while a father or mother struggled to survive in the ER outside. The walls and the door were all large panes of glass that made the room feel more like a window cage at the zoo. The Sons of Liberty leering at them through the windows didn't help. The men gripped their shotguns and rifles as they stared deadpan at the women who paced inside their cage.

A group of nurses had collected in front of Sharon and conversed in low voices.

"What's happening out there?"

"Do you think the police are coming?"

"Police? We have every doctor and trauma nurse in the tri-state area in this hospital."

"They gonna send the marines to kill these white trash assholes."

Sharon wasn't so sure. The scene outside was one of chaos with thousands of people storming the interstates. If the military retreated then they were on their own, but if the infection had made it to downtown Louisville there was no telling what the government would do. Sharon knew firsthand just how ruthless the government was behind closed doors. She didn't trust a cop or soldier any more than she trusted the Sons of Liberty. Sharon's mind cycled through every zombie and apocalypse movie she had ever seen and the gruesome acts the military would do in the name of the greater good. While the thought of the army dropping nuclear bombs on cities seemed far-fetched, Sharon did question if the next soldiers to come through the hospital doors would shoot only the Sons of Liberty or everyone indiscriminately.

"You, come here," Baron opened the door and curled his

finger at a gray-haired man who wore a white coat that had managed to retain its ironing and pristine quality. "Dr... Dr. Belfort. Buddy, tell me again what you said before."

Dr. Belfort looked nervously around the room. When his eyes paused in Sharon's direction, she and the other nurses froze, and Sharon felt her stomach drop.

"Hey! Focus. Don't make me think yur playn' games with me," Baron pointed at the doctor's wincing face.

"I'm– I'm not! I swear," Dr. Belfort said through squinted eyes with his hands up. "I just said that– that there was another police officer here– a woman. She– she was here when you– you came through. Hiding behind that– that counter in the front." Dr. Belfort hand shook as he pointed past Baron as if he thought Baron would cut his arm off at any moment.

"So, you saw this lady cop alive by the front door when we were already here? You see her go? You think she left?" Baron glared up at the tall doctor.

"I– I don't know... could be?" he shook his head. "Probably."

Baron grumbled to himself. Spitting a gob of chew on the floor, he rubbed the top of his bald head several times as if organizing hair that wasn't there. Keying his radio, he paced back and forth, "Baron to Tommy... Baron to Tommy, answer your mic!"

"Tommy here, go ahead," the young voice crackled back through the radio.

"You see anybody leave out that way?" Baron asked.

"No, no one," Tommy replied. "But um. There's– somethings happening out here. I think I should come inside."

"Fuckin' pussies, I swear–"

"Baron, Baron!" an older man wearing a half-buttoned up red and black flannel shirt ran into the room. "You got to get your dad, somethings going on out there– outside. I think they're losing the city."

"What?" Baron started to leave the room when he stopped and pointed back at the men in the far corner of the room. "Hey, get these men with the others and take this Doctor Belfort and find this goddamn woman cop. I want her dead before she starts fucking with our shit."

Baron went down the hallway one way while two guards took the dozen or so men that were in the room down the opposite way of the hospital. Sharon eyed the last remaining guard who sat spinning in a chair across the hall. His hunting rifle rested across his lap as he switched directions to spin like a child who was bored and waiting for his mother to finish shopping.

Sharon nudged the nurse beside her. She was a bit heavier and was the same nurse she had seen before with dried blood on the front of her scrubs. She looked in her early twenties with her black hair pulled back in a bun. The nurse glanced out of the side of her eye at Sharon.

Sharon whispered to her without moving her shoulders, so her body stayed blocking the cabinet they stood in front of. "What's your name?"

"Martinez," the nurse whispered back.

"Martinez, are you able to get another set of scrubs?" Sharon asked.

Martinez looked down at the blood stain on her shirt and furrowed her brow. "Yes, but they won't fit me."

Sharon shook her head. "They're not for you."

A few seconds passed before Martinez nodded in understanding. She tugged on the back of a woman's sleeve who stood in front of them. The woman turned around with a bothered look on her face as if the discussion she was having with her coworkers had a sign posted somewhere stating, 'Do Not Disturb.' She looked at Martinez and immediately eyed Sharon sidled beside her as an intruder. An inferior among nurses and doctors.

"What is it?" she asked Martinez.

"Stephanie, can I use your zip-up?" Martinez asked.

Stephanie's eyes dropped to the blood on Martinez's stomach and back to Sharon for a measured look. Stephanie wore light purple scrubs like the other nurses, but she also wore a black zip-up spring coat personalized with Louisville General Hospital on the back and her name printed on the left breast pocket. "No, I don't want any blood on it and besides– um... I don't think it will fit on you, sorry. It's not–"

"It's not for her," Sharon whispered glaring at Stephanie.

Stephanie crossed her arms and popped her hip to the side as she shifted to face Sharon. "And who are you?" the other nurses in Stephanie's *clique* turned to face them, their eyes already expressing the battle lines that had been formed.

"I'm Sharon, I–"

"*Sharon*, what are you doing here?" Stephanie asked. "I saw you talking to that bald guy out in the hall. Are you with these guys?"

"You're one of them?" another nurse the others called Jessica asked with revulsion in her voice.

Sharon felt a mounting anger boiling inside her, her mind flashing back to every fight she had been involved in high school and middle school. "No," Sharon spoke carefully so as not to overreact. "These guys found me on the side of the road and kidnapped me before coming here," Sharon lied.

"Mmmhmm," Stephanie raised an eyebrow as if she just heard the most absurd lie of her life. "Just like that, it's that easy to kidnap you?"

"Yeah, you didn't put up a fight or anything?" Jessica

added. It was becoming clear that Jessica was Stephanie's number two.

"Did you, bitch?" Sharon ignited before she had a chance to think it through. A few more nurses turned their eyes to their corner and Stephanie squared off with Sharon. The tension mounted until Martinez intervened.

"Okay, okay... relax guys," Martinez whispered and pushed between them as she tapped Stephanie's shoulder to walk behind her. "Just– look in the cabinet a second, Stephanie."

Stephanie wore a look of confusion as Sharon and Martinez moved in front of her, giving her room to open the large cabinet. Stephanie opened the door and quickly shut it, her body going rigid as she froze.

"Are you kidding me?" Stephanie whispered with an edge to her voice. Her eyes bounced to the guard who still spun in his chair. "Are you kidding me?"

"No, Stephanie, we really need your help," Martinez said. "Will you give us your coat?"

"I'm not giving you my coat. It has my name on it. If I get caught they'll know I was involved," Stephanie said pointing to her embroidered name on her zip-up. Jessica and the two other nurses nearby grew increasingly interested in what they were talking about and they moved closer.

Sharon pulled down the zipper on Stephanie's coat and opened it to see her scrubs.

"Hey," Stephanie snapped as she pulled away from Sharon and clutched the collar of her coat as if it was the only thing shielding her naked body.

"Then give us your scrubs," Sharon whispered sternly. "Your name's not on them."

"Oh, yeah, leaving me half naked with just a zip-up?" Stephanie scowled. "And what? You want me to strip right in front of our creepy fucking captors?"

"Have your gang make a wall shoulder to shoulder so they don't see," Sharon replied, but Stephanie was already sneering at Sharon's *gang* comment.

"Stephanie..." Martinez interrupted and held her eye for a moment. "This is life or death."

Stephanie released an excessive sigh and whispered to Jessica and the two other nurses who wore a confused look but did as she asked. Between Stephanie's friends, Sharon, and Martinez they formed a human wall on two sides of the corner of the room while Stephanie sunk down to her haunches and removed her coat and pulled off her scrub top exposing her light blue bra. She quickly slipped the coat back on and zipped up like a turtleneck before smacking the scrubs into Sharon's hand.

"Everyone stay where you are," Sharon whispered, giving one last look at their guard who was staring at the ceiling as he tilted backward in his chair.

Sharon carefully opened the cabinet creating a slice of light inside the dark storage area that would normally house jackets, board games, and stuffed animals but today hid a person. The light cut across her black uniform and reflected off her metallic metropolitan police badge. The female officer's eyes had the same jittery panic Sharon saw when she and Martinez had first been brought into the room.

Sharon looked over her shoulder one last time before whispering to the officer. "Take off your uniform. Put this on. You can step out if you hurry. Stay low." Sharon handed her the scrubs top and backed away from the cabinet. There was a pause where the officer had to make fast calculations on how best to stay alive. Carefully, she climbed out of the cabinet in a crouch.

The officer's name tag read, 'V. Richards'. She had long blond hair pulled back in a ponytail with colorful tattoos covering her left arm down to her wrist—red dragons that looped around rainbow fish. With delicate features, she was young looking.

Richards slid her uniform, bullet proof vest, and undershirt off and quickly slipped into the scrubs, which were a bit tight on her athletic frame. Sharon reached down and grabbed her vest and put it in the cabinet and whispered, "Boots, too." Richards eyed Sharon for a moment then relented and removed her black military boots to put in the cabinet as well. She still had black pants on, but they were easier to explain than combat boots.

Sharon did one last sweeping look around the room and let out a sigh of relief, satisfied they hadn't attracted any unwanted attention from any of the other women. Martinez and Stephanie glanced back as Richards finished putting her uniform in the cabinet before taking a deep breath and standing up slowly. Richards gave a small appreciative smile to Sharon who returned it with a nod.

It was then Sharon saw the dozen Sons of Liberty who stood outside the windows including Wesley who stared directly at Richards with narrowed eyes. Wesley combed his fingers through his long gray beard for several seconds before jabbing his finger out at Richards and hollering to his men, "What is she doing in there? Bring her here!" his gravel voice boomed through the glass walls.

FIFTY-THREE

Derrick Hart
Louisville, KY

Derrick's adrenaline surged, nearly blinding him with jittery panic as he sprinted with his empty rifle clutched in his hands. The pain from his collection of injuries didn't even register while the bullets snapped and whipped by his head. The convoy of soldiers cashed him with speed.

I think I pissed them off!

"Down here!" Brandon waved Derrick down the exit ramp while covering him. Zoe and Eric limped slowly at the back of the pack of people who fled into downtown Louisville. The streets were alive with movement. Screams for help and panicked cries were blotted out by rabid screeches. Infected mobs scrambled to every sound heard and any movement seen. They lunged upon survivors like lions on a gazelle.

Reloading his rifle, Derrick's mind was still focused on the army shooting at his ass when a pack of rabids took notice of

Alyssa and Zoe and veered up the exit ramp for them. Zoe screamed and cut to the left in front of Derrick. There were four of them.

Alyssa pushed the others over the concrete wall along the side of the ramp as they tumbled to the grassy hill along the entrance ramp, Derrick relaxed his shoulder with one focused exhale, raised his rifle, and went to work. Three shots into the first one's chest. Five at the second, but most missed. Brandon opened fire while side stepping toward Derrick. Together their bullets hit the remaining rabid bodies enough to slow them and drop them eventually.

Their collective gunfire caught the attention of infected throughout the city block.

"Oh, shit," Derrick panicked as he saw dozens of heads turn his direct from down the road before them.

"Go, go!" Brandon shoved Derrick's arm. A hundred infected stormed towards the mouth of the entrance ramp. Reaching the concrete siding of the entrance ramp, Derrick's inner monologue told him to go out fighting as running was hopeless. *Death has come.*

It was the familiar thumping gunfire that saved Derrick and Brandon's ass. The military convoy had reached the top of the entrance ramp and opened fire below. The crowd of rabid quickly angled their attention to the louder noise and the bigger target. The Humvees and soldiers scrambled to get into a firing line.

Derrick rolled over the gritty concrete siding of the overpass with clenched eyes and gnashed teeth as the stream of rabid brushed past his backside, ignoring his presence for the thundering .50 cal turrets. Rolling over to the grassy embankment, Derrick fell beside Brandon. Using each other, they pulled another to their feet and ran into the street where the others waited.

"Can you believe that just fucking happened!" Brandon shouted.

Derrick panted as he stumbled into point for the group, "on me."

They ran past a skinny rabid child gnawing upon a dead woman's neck. They stared but didn't engage. Over his shoulder, Derrick saw the wave of infected overpowering the soldiers on top of the overpass. One of the turret gunners fired rounds into his own men as rabid climbed up its hood and chased the shooter down into the gunner port hole.

Thousands ran frantically in every direction. Families pounded on gated store fronts. Groups kicked at doors and smashed windows only to be tackled by infected from behind as they climbed inside. Derrick turned down an alleyway that was darker than he realized and the others followed. Daylight had disappeared. The graying light left in the sky was barely enough to see in front of them as they ran.

"Graahhh!!" the rabids' screams echoed violently off the brick walls, skirting Derrick to a halt.

"Wait wait– help us! Help!" a young man shouted. Running from the alley, the wide-eyed man and his wife clench two young children in their arms. Derrick back tracked out of the alley with them as he saw galloping figures scurrying, bouncing from side to side against the brick walls towards them.

"Get– back up! Back up!" Derrick stuttered as he pressed Alyssa back.

"Contact rear!" Brandon shouted as he fired on a pack of rabid that ran from where they had come from. Derrick's trembling hands fumbled with the light switch, accidentally clicking on strobe mode as he saw the blood-stained skin of five half-naked figures leaping for him.

He jerked his trigger back barely able to aim until his rifle was empty. Slinging his rifle, he drew his pistol and emptied it into the remaining two infected who fell at his feet. Derrick slammed a fresh magazine into his side arm and turned to the rear beside Brandon. Terrified civilians pulled their loved ones behind Derrick and Brandon as they sighted their targets and dropped the pack of rabid giving chase. Squeezing his Glock 17 trigger in fast but smooth succession, Derrick's 9mm rounds peppered the last rabid's face.

Brandon and Derrick noticed the group that had amassed behind them. Sweaty, exhausted faces of young men, women, and children being dragged by their parents. Dozens of civilians who were unprotected and terrified chose to stay behind these two men rather than running into the unknown.

"Derrick!" Alyssa from up ahead. Derrick and Brandon quickly caught up with them as they reloaded their weapons. Their new shadow of a dozen strangers followed in their wake of safety. Zoe was straggling at the back of the group behind the hobbling Eric. Even Karen was limping now as she trailed behind her husband.

Derrick saw the blood stain on Zoe's shirt spreading on her side and sticking to her body. Alyssa gave him a brief worried look like she already knew what he was thinking. Zoe could barely walk at this point.

Brandon tried to lead them down a side street but cursed as infected spilled from that intersection.

"H-help us!" the pleading scream from behind was cut short by the rabid that lunged on one of the civilians that followed them. Packs of rabid exploded from the window of a building they passed and landed on the backs of unsuspecting survivors. Derrick fired on two infected that were closest, which sent three more infected barreling his way.

Brandon pivoted and fired low on them, shattering their kneecaps and femurs with his bullets. Every civilian that followed was tackled to the ground by rabid as they scattered in a panic. More infected homed in on their gunfire and leapt off of the interstate overpass above. Their bodies smacking the pavement hard at Brandon's feet.

"Shi– go, go!" was all Derrick could gasp as he pulled Alyssa away from a rabid body that nearly fell on top of her. It was Brandon's words that blinded Derrick's mind at that moment. *'But you and I? We don't die– not at first. We fight just long enough so you get to watch Alyssa get torn apart. Then I'll get a front row seat to watch my wife get ripped apart. Then you and I will die after watching everyone else go.'* More and more his words were becoming a prophecy as the dark streets became darker and the swarm of infected were everywhere.

The intersection up ahead was walled off on two sides by a military blockade. The top of the ten-foot walls were thick with concertina wires leaving no chance of scaling. That hadn't stopped three dead men—stacked and intertwined in the razor wire at the top corner of the wall. Their bodies were drained of blood, painting a section of the wall red. Their limp bodies gave Derrick an idea that Brandon picked up on.

Derrick fired sporadically into the legs and hips of the nearest infected. They stumbled and fell into one another as they clawed at the dirty cement, aggressing to their dying breath. Brandon stopped to stand under the bodies atop the wall and without giving Karen time to protest, grabbed at her waist and thighs, lifting her up.

"No, no, I– Brandon!" Karen struggled not wanting to touch the ripped open bodies that still dripped blood.

"Up! Up! Up!" was all Brandon shouted as he grunted and pushed her, forcing her to roll over the body and drop over to the other side.

"Go go!" Derrick yelled to the others as he planted his feet and pivoted to give them cover. Switching targets, Derrick fired in every direction in controlled bursts. Bullets thudding against blood-soaked chests and stretched faces. Brandon and Alyssa hoisted Eric over the wall, then Zoe who made a gut-wrenching scream as she went over.

"Derrick, come on!" Alyssa called out as she went over the wall. Derrick shot his rifle dry and emptied his handgun before running back to Brandon. Derrick pushed his foot into Brandon's cupped his hands and pushed for the top of the wall.

The rabid were a sea of arms and faces. They mashed together as they closed in on Brandon's back. Squishing the dead body beneath him, Derrick turned around as Brandon leapt up and grabbed a hold of one of the dead bodies, pulling himself up. Derrick grabbed Brandon's backpack, shirt, belt, anything he could, as he saw the infected latch onto one of Brandon's boots.

"Gahhg!" Brandon hollered. Keeping his grip on Brandon's thigh, Derrick leant backward, and they fell messily together on the other side of the wall.

The ten-foot fall to the asphalt knocked the wind out of Derrick. The hands that grabbed at his back made Derrick explode in adrenaline. Drawing his tanto knife from his vest he rolled around, grabbing the throat of his attacker with his knife at the ready.

"Stop!" Alyssa shrieked. Derrick immediately relaxed his hold on her and allowed himself to breathe. Brandon groaned as he stayed on his hands and knees. Brandon had fallen on his head and was struggling to stay conscious, swaying back and forth.

"They're coming," Karen screamed. "Brandon, they're coming!"

Derrick staggered to his feet. His heart thumping in his chest as he leaned on Alyssa, the searing pain in his wounded shoulder beyond agony. The rabid were fewer compared to the other side of the wall, but the infected still covered the road. A police SUV with smashed windows and blood-covered seats was crashed into the side of a building with its hood caved in. Figures, a dozen at first, then more, ran out from the cover of darkness getting exposed under the streetlights. They ran on all fours and sprinted at an erratic pace. Brandon raised to a knee as he drew his pistol and fired.

Derrick's eyes wandered to Alyssa. She pulled at Zoe's shoulders who had stopped trying to get to her feet. She was a bundle of pale limbs laying in the road. *This is it. This is where we die...* Derrick thought as Alyssa looked at him. *This is where I watch her die.*

"Here, up here!" a voice shouted over Brandon's gunfire. Eric had climbed on top of the wrecked SUV. The building it was crashed into was an open level parking garage. Standing on the vehicle roof, Eric was able to reach the second story of the concrete ledge and pull himself inside. Derrick threw Zoe over his shoulder with Alyssa's help, ignoring Zoe's screams, and followed.

Brandon climbed onto the SUV hood as the infected rammed face first into its side. Brandon reloaded his side arm and fired on the infected. Alyssa pulled Zoe into the parking garage. Brandon and Derrick struggled with all their might to pull themselves inside as the number of infected below grew from dozens to hundreds as more flooded in from around the street corner.

FIFTY-FOUR

Brandon Armstrong
Louisville, KY

They lay on the rough concrete, gasping for air that never seemed to be enough. Brandon's lungs burned like every breath whispered fire through them and his muscles stung as if they were bathed in battery acid. The second story of the parking garage was empty, from what he could see. The growls and screams of rabid running on the streets below echoed inside the open garage building. Eric and Alyssa were the first to their feet.

"Derrick, did they get you? Are you okay?" Alyssa said hovering over him. Derrick couldn't talk so he nodded instead as he turned over on the concrete. Karen hopped on one foot over to Zoe who laid curled in the corner.

"I'm, um, okay... okay..." Alyssa paced and looked around the parking garage with jittery eyes. "Eric and I will check downstairs. Make sure there's no other way in here."

Brandon saw Alyssa's hands trembling wildly as she and Eric went limping down the parking ramp to the first floor. Derrick sat back against a concrete pillar and slowly reloaded his rifle with numb fingers.

"How many... How many mags you got left?" Brandon asked between breaths.

Derrick looked down at his chest rig and patted at his waist. "One more after this. You?"

Brandon shook his head. "I'm out."

Derrick nodded and pulled the last rifle magazine from his chest rig pouch and slid it on the concrete ground to Brandon. Brandon loaded that magazine into his rifle and threw his pack off his shoulders. "We're done. It's– we're done." Brandon chose his words carefully as he eyed his wife trying to pour water into Zoe's pursed lips.

"What do you mean?" Derrick asked.

"I mean we'll make our stand here," Brandon panted and nodded his head toward the upper floors of the parking garage. "Use the top floor as a fallback position."

Derrick eyed Zoe and Karen as he struggled to his feet, then walked to the dark corner of the parking garage and Brandon followed. The city streets were alive with screams and gunfire. They drowned everything else out.

The exact same story from Atlanta and Birmingham three days ago... the exact same story that will be told in Indianapolis, Philadelphia, New York City... the entire country soon.

"We can't stay here," Derrick whispered to Brandon. Brandon could see a mix of dirt and blood smeared on Derrick's face. The bandage Alyssa had wrapped around his forehead had fallen off already revealing the blood-soaked hair on one side.

"No shit," Brandon spat.

"If we stay here, we'll die," Derrick said. "The infected will be ten times the number they are now in a couple hours. They'll find and kill us. Or just surround us and we'll die of thirst."

"Like I said, no shit," Brandon snarled. "What choice do we have? You got a SWAT team to extract us? You see a helicopter coming for us? No, we walk outside we're just two assholes with a handful of bullets. We'll all be dead in seconds. We stay here at least we'll live an hour or two longer. Easy math. I choose the way that gives us the most time to live."

"And I say I'd rather die going for a chance at living than staying here to die for sure."

"Too bad you're not making decisions anymore!" Brandon shouted as he walked past him.

Brandon felt his cheeks redden with heat at Derrick's defiance. He needed room to breathe. He needed space.

A screech cut into Brandon's eardrums as it echoed between the concrete walls. Karen was scurrying on her butt backwards away from Zoe's trembling body. Hands clamored over the ledge of the concrete wall followed by a partially scalped head and shattered face of a rabid pulling itself into the garage. Its face was so mangled Brandon couldn't guess if it was a male or female. Derrick and Brandon both managed to put four bullets in its chest before it fell beside Zoe. Derrick finished it off with a headshot as it reached for her.

"No, no– I'm not– I won't go! I won't–" Karen cried as Brandon pulled her to her feet. Her fingers dug into Brandon's arm like tiny vice grips. "I can't go out there. I can't go out there. I can't go out there!"

Brandon had to cover her mouth to muffle her screams, but the damage was already done. Derrick's eyes told the whole story when he peered over the edge.

Derrick backed away quietly. Eric and Alyssa rounded the corner after checking the lower levels and Derrick held a finger to his lips to keep them silent. The other rabid hadn't figured out how to climb up on the crashed car to get inside, yet. Any extra noise could be the difference in motivating them. Brandon helped walk his wife up to the third level and the others followed. Karen pulled at Brandon's vest with trembling hands like she was trying to climb on top of him. It was like a mental seal had been broken and the terror had seeped into Karen's bones. *She knows...*

He had done his best to keep it from her for as long as he could. Any husband would have. It was a man's duty to protect his wife. Even if that meant protecting her from the hard truth. *She knows now, though... we're all going to die.*

They passed rows of Louisville Metro Police cruisers parked on the ramp leading up to the third floor. Abandoned vehicles that were left behind in the chaos of the outbreak. Brandon brought Karen to a bench beside the elevators and sat her down. The look in her eyes was broken at best. Tears streamed down her cheeks as she held herself. "I can't do this... I... I want to go home... I want to go home..." Karen's words only sent her down a spiral panic that Brandon had to head off.

He clutched her into a tight hug, his fingers feeling her soft hair as he whispered, "It's going to be okay," he said. "It's going to be okay. I'm here. I'm here."

Derrick set Zoe's body down on the cold concrete floor beside Karen. Brandon saw Zoe's eyes lolling from side to side as sweat trickled down her brow. Eric sat beside her holding her hand.

"I'm um..." Alyssa paced with a hand on her brow. "I'm going to see if any of the cars have keys in them." Derrick nodded as he knelt over Zoe. Alyssa seemed to be the only person alert at that moment. Perhaps, she still thought they had a chance to survive. Maybe Alyssa sensed the fight leaving Derrick and Brandon and was doing her best keep it together. It didn't matter. The bridges were blown. They weren't driving out of this city.

"We're not. Fucking. Leaving. This. Parking garage," Brandon repeated with eyes on Derrick. Derrick could only reply with an exhausted sigh and a shake of his head.

"Um, guys?" Eric said. "Someone's radioing on this thing."

His hand held up the battered satellite radio with pieces dangling free and green electrical tape frayed and ripping at its base.

The speaker cracked and the static became louder before the hints of a voice broke through.

"This– opy?" it was a male voice, but it was drowned out by the static and gunfire in the background. "This is Agent Sean Williams I'm with the protection detail for the President of the United States' daughter, does anyone copy? This... requesting backup from any police or military units in the area!"

Brandon eyed Derrick who stepped closer to the radio, a look of wonder and disbelief in his eyes. "I know that voice– I know him."

FIFTY-FIVE

Rachel Anderson
Louisville, KY

"Sean! Sean! G–get up!" Rachel screamed over Sean's unconscious body. Her eyes fluttered to Allen. He wore a wide-eyed look with a gaping mouth. The life having drained from the bottle size chunk of metal that had impaled his chest. Tears filled her eyes as she shook Sean's body. Every slap on Sean's limp face he didn't respond to sent a jolt of fear down her spine. *Is he dead?* "No, no, wake up!"

Sean gasped, sucking down air as his eyes fluttered open to the world. The groans of soldiers with broken limbs spread across were mixed with the screams of the rabid that circled them like flies. Chris had escaped the chopper crash unscathed. In the time it took Rachel to regain her bearings, Chris emptied his pistol into an infected that charged at them.

Clutching a bleeding gash at the back of his skull, Sean got to his knees before he dry-heaved on the muddy patch of grass between him and Rachel. Rachel rubbed his back while looking for their Special Forces escort only to find dead bodies and chopper wreckage where they once stood.

"We gotta go– we gotta go right fucking now!" Chris shouted over Rachel's shoulder.

"Allen?" Sean groaned as he struggled to his feet.

"He's gone," Rachel said coldly. Her heart toughened by the thought of their impending death. "Come on, on your feet," she ordered Sean as she struggled to pull on his arm.

"We need to get out of here!" Chris yelled in a panic. Rachel shook her head as she tried to think. Chris snatched a rifle from one of the fallen soldiers and fired on infected converging from every direction. *The sound of the crash brought them here– running is not safe right now.*

"Take Sean," Rachel said to Chris, nodding to a large white trailer with an ajar door. "Get him inside there."

"Rachel– you have to–" Chris tried to argue but Rachel wasn't listening. She handed the still dazed Sean over to Chris and ran back at the pile of bodies beside the smoldering wreckage. She saw uniforms and faces she didn't recognize. Young and old. Some were still alive, though they were missing an arm or had a leg bent backward. A gruesome scene that would have given her pause weeks ago but barely registered as she looked for him.

She found Lt. Miles beside the tail rotor that had been broken free from the destroyed chopper. His face was blood stained and pale like the rest of the dead around her. Tapping at his thigh, she ripped open his cargo pocket, and grabbed the satellite phone she had seen him use in his pocket. She ran for the trailer. Darkness had fallen on the park. The screams were getting louder and more plentiful than the sound of gunshots. Slamming inside the dark trailer, Rachel panted as she fell against the far wall. Chris slammed the door shut locking it with a flimsy latch that couldn't possibly stop a child.

"Shit... shit, shit!" Chris paced by the door. Sean sat in one of the two chairs in the trailer and held a bloody towel to the back of his head. "Allen's gone? You're sure?"

Rachel nodded and hid her eyes as she caught her breath. Chris clenched his teeth as he gripped the rifle tighter as if he was choking it. "We have to get out of here," Rachel finally said.

"Do you think they're sending another helicopter?" Chris asked. "Jesus, I can't believe that helicopter crashed like that!"

"They probably don't even know the first one crashed," Sean added.

Rachel held up the satellite phone in her hand. Its green tape squished and peeling at the bottom. She started dialing the number written on its back as the other two realized what it was.

"Thank god," Chris sighed but jumped instantly when a rabid slammed into the side of the trailer causing a loud thud.

"They're not going to send another chopper," Sean said as he stood, testing his legs on his own. "Not here. It's too hot. Too many infected."

"Shhh!" Rachel shushed them both as she put the phone to her ear. It rang for an unnerving amount of time before someone picked up.

"This is Sneed," a tired and already annoyed voice of an older man answered.

"I'm– This is Rachel Anderson the daughter of–"

"Ms. Anderson... this is Todd Sneed, White House Chief of Staff. Where is Lt. Miles?"

"Dead, they're all dead. The helicopter they came in crashed. It's just me and Chris and Sean– my secret service agents," Rachel said. She combed through her mind of the array of people she had met that surrounded her father's political career for someone named Todd Sneed, but she could not put a face to the name. "I-I need to talk to my dad."

There was a long sigh on the other end of the phone. "I'm sorry, Ms. Anderson, that's not possible. The President's in the situation room right now, he can't–"

"Get me my fucking Dad right now!" Rachel's voice snapped as she stomped her foot in a rage.

"Give me the phone. Give it to me," Sean walked over and pulled the phone from her ear with little resistance as Rachel continued to curse to herself. "Sir, this Agent Sean Williams with the Secret Service. Myself and one other agent are all that remain of Rachel Anderson's detail. We are trapped in a trailer near the LZ in Cherokee Park. There are infected swarming the location. If the President wants his daughter to live we need help, sir... okay... okay..."

"He told us to standby," Sean said, checking to see if the back of his head had stopped bleeding.

"Great," Chris rolled his eyes. "We're in a warzone and they put us on hold."

"How many bullets you got left?" Sean asked as he put the phone on speaker and set it on the desk between them.

"Not enough," Chris said.

Rachel pointed to the front door. "There are tons of rifles in the grass; all the soldiers' bodies have weapons, ammo, their vests..."

Sean nodded but she felt his stare lingered too long at her and she questioned the callousness of her statement. Chris peaked out the window again and shook his head as he muttered about how many infected there were. "I think there's a parking lot over there. Humvees, SUVs... maybe one of them has keys in it?"

"That's a big maybe," Sean sighed, staring at the satellite

phone that was still silent. "Okay, what else, what else. Weapons, ammo, vehicle, maybe..."

Rachel looked around the room as she chewed on her thumbnail. Clipboards and tac boards covered most of the wall with flight manifests and schedules. In the far corner was a city map of Louisville with highlighted roads downtown to and from Cherokee Park. Untacking the map, she pulled it from the board and placed it on the desk beside the phone. Sean nodded at her as if to say *smart thinking*.

There was a rustling on the satellite phone before a new voice sounded. A younger man said, "Agent Williams?"

"Go ahead," Sean spoke down into the phone.

"This is Lt. Commander Jason Greene. I work with the National Security Advisor and the Joint Chiefs of Staff. I understand it's just you and another agent. We've got your location. Are there any other military or law enforcement assets that can assist you?"

Sean looked to Chris who stood by the window and shook his head. "No, it's falling apart down here."

"Yeah, yeah... we're monitoring the situation now," Lt. Com. Greene sighed. "What's your capabilities? Are you armed? Are you mobile?"

"We've got access to small arms and vehicles, I think," Sean said.

"Okay, Agent Williams, we've rerouted a Tier One team to your location. They are hooking up with an Apache escort to Louisville, but Cherokee Park is too hot for an extract. They're thirty-four minutes out right now."

"Thirty-four minutes?" Chris looked back incredulously.

"Where do you need us to be?" Sean asked, turning the paper map so he could see it.

"Slugger's Stadium," Lt. Commander Greene sighed. "It's a baseball field. It's not ideal but it's the only place clear of infected and drone footage is showing the roads relatively clear if you take eastern parkway to I-65 N."

Sean followed Rachel's finger along the route to Slugger Stadium. Sean shook his head. "There's got to be another pickup site. Some place on the outskirts of the city."

"Sir, there's plenty of places on the outskirts of town but every road there has collapsed or is blocked. You won't be able to drive out of town. This is the best option for success–"

There was a rustling on the phone and Todd Sneed's voice came back on the line. "Those are your orders, Agent Williams. This is not a debate."

"Yes, sir," Sean straightened and gave Rachel a look that was void of hope.

"Two things," Greene said, taking back the phone. "At the top of the phone you're on there's a button labelled, 'RTC-2// RADIO.' Press that and you can switch the phone to an encrypted radio channel. There might be military or law enforcement assets on the ground that can help you get to the stadium. Put out the call for backup, do you understand?

"Yes, sir," Sean said as he located the button.

"Keep the satellite phone with you at all times. It has a GPS locator in it so we know where you are. Good luck, son."

FIFTY-SIX

Sharon Hill
Louisville, KY

Sharon's heart clenched in her chest like the cold grip of death was squeezing it. Wesley's finger pointing in their direction was a death sentence, at least for one of them. Richards cowered in the back, retreating to the cabinet as all the eyes in the room turned toward her. *Did they recognize her as the police officer? Even without her uniform?* Three of the Sons barged into the room. They were the muscle of the group. Each cleared six feet and weighed well over 300 lbs.

I've done it. I've killed her. Sharon's apologetic eyes shifted to Richards. *I should have just left her in the cabinet. She would've lived– she would have lived longer.*

The men shoved past Martinez, nearly toppling her over and surrounded Sharon. To her surprise the first man grabbed Sharon's arm and guided her toward the door. The other two didn't even seem to notice Richards except for a lingering leer at the revealing cleavage from her ill fitted shirt. Sharon made it a point not to look back at Richards so as not to draw more attention to her as the three men marched Sharon out of the waiting room.

"There she is..." Wesley sang with his soured accent. "I'm sorry, ma'am, you weren't meant to be put in with the rest of the herd. Why don't you have a seat back here while we finish discussin' a thang or two, hm?" Wesley gestured toward the chair one of his men twirled in. He quickly leapt out to make room for Sharon.

Baron glared at Sharon. His yellow teeth were visible beneath his snarling lip. Baron's brother, Robert, picked up on Sharon's uneasiness and smacked his brother's arm breaking his stare.

"Now, things have changed, that for dang sure," Wesley said to the group of men. *These eight men must be the decision makers of this chapter of the Sons of Liberty.* "If them rabid runnen' wild here in the city and the people packing up on the interstate, I'd say it changes a lot."

"Wes, we can't stay here. Have you lost it?" said a barrel-chested man wearing a blue flannel shirt stretched across his gut. "We all agreed to come here for the meds and doctors and what not, but we were supposed to be back home by tonight."

"We don't have an exfil route, Mike," Robert said pointing to a crinkled map on the nurse desk between them. "I hear ya, Mike. We all do. We all want to go home, none of us signed up to be stuck in the middle of gosh dang Louisville for all this, but you got to listen to my Pa. If we get on the road right now, we'll be overrun by the people or the infected and it's already darkening out. All that risk just to get home sooner. It's too much, not enough good."

"Don't make no sense, Mike," Baron agreed. Sharon watched how the others responded and listened to Robert. He was Wesley's eldest son but still just a young man in his twenties. Yet, it was clear he had the respect of this group. Sharon's eyes looked to the nurses staring at her through the glass walls. Their eyes shifted as Stephanie, the queen bee, plotted and whispered to the others. No doubt about Sharon. *The longer I spend with the men, the more alienated I become by the women.*

"Now I'm not saying we camp out here for weeks, but there's worse places to hold up a night or two. I already got some of the boys goin' around locking emergency doors and pulling down gates, setn' up a perimeter," Wesley reasoned with the men. "Just long enough for the government to be ran out of here and them to abandon this city like they done the rest the country. Y'all see this is the last straw. They ain't got no force or wall between here and Chicago, New York City, or D.C...." Wesley chuckled to himself. "You want to see a shit show, pardon me, ma'am, just wait till this rabid hit them cities."

"Copy!" the crackle of the radio blared startling Sharon and every Son of Liberty gathered around the map. "–oes anyone copy this?" the radio boomed, again, and men looked around the room for the source of the sound.

Baron saw the odd-looking radio on the hip of a dead soldier behind the nurse's station. He quickly bolted around the table and grabbed it like a child finding a lost toy. "This is what I was tellin' ya about Pa," Baron said with an excited grin.

"This is the protection detail for the President of the United States' daughter. Does anyone copy? ... protection... any police or army units in the area, please respond," the radio continued to chirp.

"Look! You see here? Green tape, it's just what that Army Lieutenant was sayin. That one from that last raid we done." Baron shook the radio from side to side for all to see.

"This is Agent Williams with the secret service, protection

detail for the First Daughter, does anyone copy? Any units in the Louisville area?"

"Can I respond, Pa?" Baron said, nearly hopping up and down in excitement. "Maybe the President is here, too. Maybe we can get us some Aces!"

"Well, what the hell you gone say?" Wesley chuckled.

"Bare, put that down already," Robert sighed, rubbing his temple. "The President's not here. The President of the United States won't be walking around Louisville."

The radio went silent for several seconds and Baron was visibly upset as he started to pace with the radio in hand. "Come on, talk!" Baron shook the radio like a loose battery was the issue.

"Is somebody there?" a new voice crackled through the radio. A woman's voice. She sounded young. Her voice was strong but with a desperate edge. "This– this is Rachel Anderson. I'm the daughter of the President of the United States. I've got two guys with me—two secret service agents... if anyone can hear this, we need help."

The room shifted as everyone looked to Wesley who scratched his beard. Baron jumped up and down, unable to handle the surge of energy. "Oooooo! I told you! I told you it was!"

"It's the President's daughter, not the President," Robert corrected.

"Who cares?" Baron grinned. "Her– him. They the same really. She's even better."

"You think that's really her?" Mike asked. The excitement in the group heightened and Sharon struggled to understand why.

It was like they were all starstruck. They were acting like fanboys wanting an autograph, only I doubt it's an autograph they're after.

"I am Rachel Anderson. We have multiple helicopters coming to get us. We need escort," she said.

"Baron, key up and pretend to be one of the army," Wesley leaned forward.

Sharon could see Baron's eyes go blank as he depressed the mic and brought the radio to his mouth. "I-I am the army... Kentucky army–"

"Good lord, Bare," Robert rubbed his hand across his face in dismay.

"Gawddangit, Baron," Wesley smacked the desk. "Give that radio over ta Robert."

"No, Pa!" Baron whined, but Robert snatched the radio from his hand like an older brother would.

"Hello? Hello? Is someone there?" Rachel yelled through the radio.

Robert sighed and cleared his throat before keying the radio. "This... is Sergeant Mitchell with the army. Is someone looking for assistance?" his voice was deeper and much of his Kentucky drawl was missing as he spoke.

"Yes. Yes!" Rachel yelled. "This is Rachel Anderson. I'm with two agents. We're leaving Cherokee Park right now. It's overrun. The military base is overrun with infected. We need escort to the baseball field, the Louisville baseball field. Slugger's Stadium. We have helicopters coming for us; they can take you too."

Robert nodded as the others looked at the map for their route. "Yes ma'am, we can help you. And what road are you on right now?"

"We– we're gonna take eastern parkway to... to 65 N."

Robert pointed to their route on the map. "Okay, and do you just have the two agents with you?"

"Yes, we had more but they're gone. It's just us three. Where are you guys? Are you coming to help?"

Wesley snapped his fingers at one of his men and circled his finger in the air. Mike and two other men ran off toward the front lobby. "Yes, we're going to help, ma'am," Robert radioed. "Now what kind of weapons do you guys have?"

"What kind of–" Rachel's voice was interrupted by a man's voice on her end.

"Stop– wait," the radio went silent.

"Ma'am?" Robert tried again. "Ma'am what's your position right now?"

The radio stopped responding and finally Robert tossed it on the counter like he just slam dunked a basketball. "Alright, good work, son!" Wesley clapped Robert on the shoulder. They all stood congratulating each other as if it was some achievement and Sharon still didn't understand.

"I could have done that," Baron announced. "I found the radio."

"Baron, 'nough," Wesley said. "Alright, I already sent Mike to ready the men. I want three trucks to meet them on the road. Right here," Wesley pointed at the map. "That's where we take them. No dilly dally'ian, just kill the men, get the girl, and get back here, you hear?"

"This is good enough for the risk," Baron elbowed the man beside him. "I got this Pa, don't worry, I'll get her."

"No, son, I need you here. Robert, I want you to lead on this," Wesley said, and Robert nodded.

"What! But pa–" Baron protested.

"I don't want to hear it, Baron, ya damn hot head," Wesley snapped. "Now go and take them girls with the rest of them. I got Tommy watching them up there. Then I want you to get on the horn and call our Command and tell em' we got plenty of Queens, plenty of Kings, and are going after a bonafide Ace!" the boys around the map slapped the table and hooted and hollered in celebration. Wesley looked up at Robert and grabbed his son's shoulder. "Rob, I need you to take her alive. We get this harlot alive then we are untouchable by the government as long as we keep her so, you hear?"

Robert nodded and pushed away for the door, but his father stopped him one last time. "And son..." Wesley eyed Robert, his voice taking a cold turn. "If you can't take her alive, you don't let them feds leave this earth alive."

"Yes, Pa," Robert said as he shouldered his rifle and stormed out of the ER with a stern look on his face.

"That's my boy..." Wesley said to the others.

"Come on, lady," Baron grouched, poking Sharon. "Let's go!"

The women from the waiting room were collected and escorted under guard to the bank of elevators around the corner. "Up!" the men shouted. Sharon saw Martinez walking behind Richards whose black pants and bare feet stood out like a sore thumb amid the line of nurses in scrubs. Thankfully, most of the men seemed easily distracted by the other things the nurses possessed and not their clothes.

"No, not her," Wesley waved to Baron. "You can take Sharon to room 203 upstairs. She'll be more comfortable there. I'm using that as my temporary quarters." Wesley smirked and winked at Sharon.

Richards glanced from the floor in Sharon's direction as she walked by and Sharon felt the spike of panic inside her. Sharon bolted upright. "I– I'd rather go with them, the other women," Sharon said, looking at Wesley whose grin soured into a grimace. "I... I'd feel more comfortable going with them."

The stare-off between the two of them silenced the chuckling men until the beep of the elevator could be heard around the corner.

"Very well then, ma'am. If you want to be one of the herd.

Go join the herd," Wesley said, motioning for her to join the others at the elevator shaft.

Sharon walked beside Richards and Martinez as Baron made room on the elevator. His body pressed into Sharon's side. She felt his leer and the stench of his body odor mixed with the foul musk of tobacco on his lips. As the elevator whisked them away, Sharon couldn't help but worry what fate awaited her at the end of this elevator ride.

FIFTY-SEVEN

Derrick Hart
Louisville, KY

"Okay, and do you just have the two agents with you?" the southern voice questioned.

"Yes, we had more but they're gone. It's just us three. Where are you guys? Are you coming to help?" Rachel's voice replied. Derrick and the others were huddled around the damaged satellite phone lying on the cement between them.

"Yes, we're going to help, ma'am. Now what kind of weapons do you guys have?"

Derrick shook his head as he chewed on his thumbnail. *Don't tell him, Rachel...*

"What kind of–" Rachel's voice was interrupted by another man's voice on her end of the radio. *Sean's voice,* Derrick thought.

"Stop– Wait," the radio went silent.

"Ma'am?" the southerner persisted. "Ma'am what's your position right now?"

Derrick's eyes held Brandon's for a long second after the last transmission went silent. His mind worked the information just like Brandon, but judging by Brandon's expression, he was sure they were coming to a different conclusion.

"They have a helicopter coming," Karen said. "They can rescue us. Can– can you radio them? Tell them that we have kids with us. That we're soldiers and cops and–" Brandon stood up and paced while scratching the stubble on his chin, clearly ignoring his wife. Karen recognized this and snatched up the radio. She held the radio to her mouth. "Hello, hello? Can you hear me?"

"It doesn't transmit anymore," Alyssa said, her hand resting on Zoe's trembling back. "We can listen but can't tal–"

"Well, come on!" Karen said, shooting to her feet. "We– we have to get to them. They have to get us out of here. We have to get out of here!" her voice broke as it turned manic, and her hands formed trembling fists. "We can't just– they're going to leave without us!"

"Alyssa, you said there are keys in that Suburban?" Brandon said, pointing at the black undercover police Suburban with blacked out tinted windows.

"Yeah, it's got someone's things in the back, too," Alyssa said. "A gun and clips its looks like."

"They said they're sending a couple of trucks after her," Brandon thought out loud.

"Those guys didn't sound like soldiers to me," Derrick added.

"Me neither, but it doesn't matter. If they're not military, they'll be all the easier to kill," Brandon said. "We stand a chance if there's more ammo in the suburban."

"What?" Derrick rose to his feet, but Brandon was already taking charge.

"Eric, start that car, make sure it runs," Brandon pointed. "Karen, get our bags and start loading them in the back. Empty out everything in my bag except the grenades we have left. Alyssa–"

"Brandon, wait– what are you talking about?" Derrick held up his hand close to Brandon's chest to halt him.

"We take out those two trucks and there's only a couple secret service agents protecting the President's daughter," Brandon said. "You said you know them, right? Even better. If we get their guard down, kill the agents, and she's ours."

"Brandon, what the hell are you talking about?" Alyssa snapped.

"They're not going to let us on the choppers because we've got fucking women and children," Brandon spoke as if it should be obvious to everyone. "The military is killing everything that moves in the streets. We have one shot, one chance at getting out of this city. If we take the President's daughter hostage, we'll get the choppers to pick us up and drop us off somewhere north of here. Once we're in Indiana or Ohio, we'll let her go."

Derrick exchanged a look of desperation with Alyssa. *Has it really come to this?*

"Look– they said their extract is at the Slugger's baseball field?" Brandon continued. "That's right up the road. They'll pass by us in what? Ten minutes. We'll be in a perfect position to ambush–"

"Brandon..." Derrick said but was quickly ignored.

"Alyssa, get in the car– we don't have much–"

"Brandon, stop, we can't–" Derrick spoke sternly but was cut off by the more authoritative voice.

"Shut up, Derrick!" Brandon snatched Derrick up by a fistful of his collar. Derrick saw fire blazing in Brandon's eyes as he stared down at Derrick. "You're not fucking in charge here. You don't have a say! You don't have a vote! So, either get in the car or stay fucking here with your goddamn *wife!*" Brandon gnashed his teeth as he shoved Derrick backward, roughly.

Derrick's nostrils flared as he felt heat burn his cheeks. His fists clenched. He wanted to hit Brandon. The rage had been simmering all day and now it was nearly blinding. He just wanted it done. But it would be absurd. To waste any amount of time fighting with each other seemed asinine. But the alternative to fighting was compliance. Whether he stood by while Brandon murdered secret service agents in order to kidnap a young woman, or if he actively participated, it did not matter. His guilt in the crime would be the same.

Taking a step back Derrick disengaged and felt his clenched fists loosen, though the bile splashing in the back of his throat told him the fire still boiled inside him. He walked toward the Suburban without another word. Images of his rifle reticle bouncing over Sean's chest as he killed him flashed in his mind. Of Rachel screaming and pulling away in terror as Derrick and Brandon hauled her into their car.

We'd have to bind her wrists and ankles to control her. Maybe tape her mouth to keep her from screaming.

Alyssa heaved as she tried to lift Zoe to her feet but all she got in return was a sickening groan. "Karen, help me with Zoe. Grab her feet. Come on."

Karen limped over to Zoe. "Come on, hun."

"No, leave her," Brandon waved for Zoe to be put back down. "Come on, let's go."

"The hell do you mean?" Alyssa asked.

"Bran..." Karen said.

"Now! The girl stays here, she'll be safe. She's not coming with us. Let's go," Brandon stomped over to Karen whose convictions faded under Brandon's commanding voice. He walked her over to the SUV. She put up little resistance but huffed enough to make sure the others knew her dismay.

"We're not leaving her!" Alyssa snapped as she tried to lift Zoe again. This time she got Zoe halfway up before her pale legs gave out. Brandon stormed back over to Alyssa and tried to escort her to the car the same way he did his wife, but Alyssa shoved him away. "Get your fucking hands off me!"

"Get in the car now!" Brandon's voice boomed as he towered over Alyssa. "Someone's going to waste seconds trying to save a dead girl out there and get me killed! I'm done playing nice. I'm not dying for someone else's problem!"

"Get out of my face!" Alyssa went to punch Brandon in the cheek, but it turned into a long push across his face. Brandon slung his rifle behind his back and was in the process of maneuvering Alyssa's arms down into a pseudo bear hug body lock when Derrick pushed Brandon to the side.

Brandon's eyes ignited as he walked back toward Zoe.

"We're not doing this!" Derrick shouted as he pointed down at Zoe. "We don't leave people!"

"You fucking psycho," Alyssa yelled over Derrick's shoulder. "We're not going to let you leave–"

"Fuck this," Brandon murmured to himself as he drew his side arm, leveled his pistol at Zoe's head as she looked at him doe eyed.

"No!" Derrick shouted.

Brandon pulled the trigger.

FIFTY-EIGHT

Derrick Hart
Louisville, KY

A high-pitched scream pierced the air before the parking garage echoed with the gunshot. Derrick leapt forward and snatched the handgun as he fired. The two of them spun as they both squeezed at the pistol in Brandon's hand. Derrick peeled back Brandon's fingers while they shoved the muzzle in each other's direction.

Brandon's free hand swung to Derrick's face. He pushed his thumb into Derrick's eye and shoved his nose up and backwards. Derrick's eye throbbed and he heard a *pop* in his nose as his head twisted backward and he nearly lost his balance, but his hands never left Brandon's pistol. Twisting on the rear sight and pushing with his other hand at the barrel, he sent the handgun tumbling across the concrete floor of the garage.

Derrick immediately felt Brandon's large, strong hands close around his face and throat. Brandon's fingers clawed at his cheek and strangled his throat. With a twist of his hips, Derrick smashed his forearm across the top of Brandon's wrists and separated his arms long enough to get his sight and breath back. Derrick's straight cross struck flush into Brandon's jaw followed by another punch that stammered Brandon backwards a step.

Brandon's guard came up, blocking Derrick's last punch. Derrick didn't even see the strike that thudded him in the temple. The pain stung and rocked him. Derrick's arms raised to his face, blocking Brandon's next strike as the two gripped each other's vests, pushing and shoving one another off balance.

Hands grabbed at them both, but they were too gentle to stop this fight. Their bodies violently whipped about knocking the interferers away as their slung rifles battered against another. Derrick grunted and gnashed his teeth as he tried to destabilize Brandon, but Brandon's height and strength worked in his favor. Derrick yanked on the neck of Brandon's vest as he slammed his knee into Brandon's gut. He felt his second knee strike penetrate deep and buckle Brandon. Derrick went for another knee but with a hard twist, Derrick's feet left the ground as Brandon swept him onto his back.

Air emptied from Derrick's lungs and the world faded into gray from the hard impact on the cement. Brandon straddled Derrick's hips and everything slowed as Derrick saw Brandon's fist falling down at him at half speed. The punch stung his cheek beneath his eye but the hit sped up his world in an instant. Brandon snarled as he swung with all the strength.

He's angry. He's not thinking. He's over committed.

At the last second Derrick parried the second punch across his body and with a buck of his hips, Derrick rolled Brandon on to his back. Slamming his elbow down across Brandon's face, Derrick felt the hard impact and knew immediately he had hurt him.

Groaning with blood leaking from his mouth, Brandon

palmed the grip of his rifle, still slung across his chest and began to turn the barrel in Derrick's direction. Derrick dove his body across the side of the M4 carbine as Derrick drew his Glock from his holster.

Brandon ripped Derrick back by his hair, trying to make room for his rifle, but it was too long and cumbersome for this messy fight. Pivoting, Derrick punched his handgun out, pressing the muzzle into Brandon's cheek below his eye socket.

Brandon's lips moved. That was when Derrick realized he wasn't hearing anything.

"Shoot! Fuckin' shoot!" Brandon snarled with spit flying from his clenched teeth. The sounds of the world came into focus. The sound of women shouting in the background and the rabid outside the garage hit Derrick all at once. The world moved in fast forward as Brandon tried to stand.

"Shoot–" Brandon yelled as he rose up still trying to aim his rifle. "Shoot me you cowar–"

Derrick swung the butt of his pistol down and smashed it into Brandon's cheek. Grabbing the barrel of Brandon's rifle, he jerked it to the side and pistol-whipped Brandon again in the jaw. And again, until the strength and fight left Brandon's body.

Tugging hard on the rifle still slung over Brandon's shoulder, Derrick ripped the weapon free from over his head and tossed it to the floor behind the Suburban. Brandon's eyes fluttered as he struggled to stay conscious, a welt forming under his eye. Derrick panted as he turned to find Karen's arms wrapped around Eric, and Alyssa standing in front of both of them with a look of terror frozen on their faces.

In a panic, Derrick looked to see Zoe's body lying where they had left it. Holstering his pistol, he released a sigh of relief when he saw her chest rise and fall. She looked up at him with pain in her determined eyes but no gunshot wound from Brandon's weapon.

Alyssa looked upon Derrick with almost fear in her eyes, like she was unable to believe the aggression he had within him. Brandon groaned as he covered his face with one hand and spat blood beside him.

"We're not killing her..." Derrick shouted at Brandon after a moment. "You're not fucking killing her! Do you see– do you see yourself? Can you live with yourself after killing a kid?"

Derrick swiped blood from his lower lip with the back of his hand. He shook his head, looking around the garage floor. He searched for an answer that wasn't there. "I... I don't know what's right and what's wrong anymore, Bran. I don't...

Brandon moved so slowly and in a daze, Derrick questioned if Brandon could even hear him at that moment.

"What I know is that we made it this far because of you, that's what I know." Derrick looked at Brandon who slowly rose to a seated position. "The Tennessee border; the fuckn' hospital. You pushed us through it, I know that," Derrick panted with his hands on his knees. Blood dripped from his lip, and he could feel his racing pulse strain in the back of his skull. "But kill or be killed is one thing. This... murdering people in cold blood, kidnapping a woman, murdering a child who's slowing you down?"

Brandon twitched and looked up at Derrick while sucking in deep breaths.

"There's got to be more... There's got to be more... You're right," Derrick took a knee in front of his friend. "Everyone knows you're right, Brandon, no one here disagrees with you. Killing off the weak links will make us live longer," Derrick shrugged. "Zoe's sick, Eric and Karen have got a limp, let's kill them all, right?"

Brandon glared silently at Derrick as he coddled his cheek.

"You've been walking around here thinking that you're the only one who saw it. Like you're the only one who knows the way forward. We know what to do to live the longest, we just can't live with ourselves if we did it. That's what *you* don't understand. It's not fucking weakness to not choose the easy path to survive. It's just that I know the difference between living a life and just being alive."

Derrick saw the defiance in Brandon's eyes like a teenager refusing to heed their parent's words. "Fine. You can leave, Brandon. If that's what you want. Alyssa, you gonna let him kill Zoe?"

"No," Alyssa said.

"Eric, how about you?" Derrick asked.

"No," he muttered.

"Karen?"

There was a pause from beside the SUV, but her meek voice answered. "No."

"If you leave, you'll make it farther on your own; you'll live longer on your own. But you're not killing the girl. You're not taking the car. I won't let you kidnap Rachel ... We have one chance to get out of the city tonight– And it lies with helping the President's daughter get to the helicopter... I know her. She'll get us out of the city..." Derrick looked at the blood-stained ground between them and whispered, "there's got to be more to life than just being alive, man. I'm– I'm not killing a kid. And I won't let you do that to yourself, either."

Brandon groaned as he looked down at his chest and refused to answer. There was an exhaustion in his childhood friend that Derrick had never seen before. A defeat that permeated Brandon's convictions.

Derrick shook his head incredulously and spat out a gob of blood. The shine of metal caught Derrick's eyes on the concrete beside him. Derrick's dog tags still hung from his neck but during their fight Brandon's had been ripped free. He recognized the etchings of two Viking soldiers, locking arms.

Derrick snatched Brandon's set of tags from the ground and clapped it against Brandon's body armor on his chest. "Are you with me?" Derrick asked.

Brandon groaned but pulled himself up to a knee.

"Are you with me, Brandon?" Derrick repeated.

Clasping Derrick's hand, Brandon rose to his feet with a groan and took the tags from his friend. His eyes found Derrick's for the first time, and he nodded. "I'm with you."

FIFTY-NINE

Rachel Anderson
Louisville, KY

The police cruiser jerked and juddered hard as Sean drove them over a curb and back down. The tight turn around the roadblock of abandoned police cars was followed by a hard fall that sent Rachel sliding in the backseat of the caged-in section of the car. She realized as soon as she sat in the back of the police cruiser that she had never been in the back of a cop car. The seats were hard plastic, and her legs were cramped by the divider that held her in the rear of the vehicle. The police cruiser was the only vehicle Rachel had found unlocked with keys in the ignition, oddly enough.

Sean was not enthused by their vehicle when he ran to it after having scavenged all the weapons and gear he could carry. He would have preferred a Humvee or some monstrous armored vehicle to drive them to the baseball stadium, but instead they were left with a Ford Taurus.

"You okay back there?" Chris asked over his shoulder.

"No," Rachel half joked as she pressed her hands and feet against the door and plastic divider in front of her to keep from sliding around.

"Put on your seat belt," Sean said with a glance in the rearview mirror.

"Why don't you focus on not driving like a psycho," Rachel said. "I'll take care of myself."

The bullet proof vest Rachel swam inside of didn't even come close to fitting. She tried fussing with the straps but even at the tightest setting there was enough room to fit two of her in the vest. Sean and Chris had both scavenged a vest and rifle for themselves as well. There had been only one rabid wandering the crash site they'd had to shoot to get to the gear, but that had been one burst of gunfire too many. The screams that had followed had been immense and all-surrounding. It had made finding the running police cruiser even more important.

"You got that satellite phone still?" Sean yelled back to Rachel.

Rachel smacked her cargo pocket on her thigh and felt it there. "Yeah."

Sean cursed as he sped around groups of survivors. He dodged them as best as he could and cussed at the ones he clipped with his mirror for trying to hop on their car.

"Out of the way!" Chris shouted and waved his hand from the front passenger seat at the pair of men who tried to dive in front of their car to stop them. Everyone was in survival mode. People who had never been in a fight in their life were now at war. Nothing was more terrifying than being hunted and chased by a creature with no mercy.

More than a few attempted to leap on the side of their police cruiser and every one of them was sucked under the tires and run over. The rabid lunged too. Their faces smashed into the glass and streaked blood down the side before tumbling to the asphalt. For every group of survivors they passed, there was a trail of rabid sprinting. The red eyes, strained faces, and howls identified them. Entering I-65, they rammed into an orange and white roadblock sign, splintering wood pieces across the street.

The sun had set which left the ominous gray of night to lurk over them. Despite her resolve to harden her fortitude under pressure rather than break, the looming night cut streaks of fear straight through Rachel's tough exterior. The thought of being stranded in the city at night with the rabid hunting them was unbearable. *I'm not going to turn into one of those things.* Her grip tightened on the rifle Sean had handed her. *I'll end it before I let myself become rabid.*

The interstate that cut through downtown was littered with the dead and soon there were no more people running. It was only the rabid. "Jesus, they are everywhere," Chris hollered as dozens of rabid abandoned their kills and sprinted after their cruiser as they sped by.

"I know," Sean replied.

"There!" Chris said, pointing out herds of infected that lunged for them. Like dogs leaping after a moving vehicle. "Oh, shit, there's another!"

"Chris stop talking!" Rachel shouted as she braced herself in the backseat while Sean zig-zagged through the bodies. Their police cruiser screeched as it crushed a stack of three corpses and went up an entrance ramp. Rachel's eyes went wide when truck headlights clicked on in front of them. The truck's engine roared as its front end lurched forward with a trajectory to T-bone their police cruiser.

"Sean, Sean!" Rachel squinted and clenched, steadying herself for impact as she saw the fast approaching front grill of the truck.

Sean cut hard to the side and accelerated at the last moment. The headlights disappeared as the truck clipped their rear end, spinning the cruiser to the side. Rachel's butt slid across the back seat as she slammed into the opposite door. Sean accelerated, not allowing them to stop for a moment as he regained control of the car.

Glancing at Sean, Rachel silently clipped on her seat belt and looked behind them. There were three pairs of headlights that pursued them. Pickup trucks with men clinging to the bed. "Who are they?" Rachel yelled.

"Why the fuck did they–" Chris' question was cut off by the burst of gunfire that exploded their rear windshield.

"They're shooting at us!" Rachel shouted.

"Rachel, get down!" Sean shouted, then pushed Chris toward the window. "Shoot, shoot, shoot!"

Rachel slammed her head down on the seat as more bullets pounded the rear bumper. She felt one of the bullets pierce the back seat and snap over her shoulder as Sean drove wildly, trying to avoid the gunfire.

With the rifle in his left hand, Chris awkwardly shot out the passenger window, but nearly fell out as Sean swerved to avoid a rabid that dove on their hood. Rachel's mind was in a panic. Every time she tried to stick her head up to try and shoot back, bullets riddled the back of their car. All the violence of the world felt like it was crashing down on her. Pieces of glass pelted her face, and she watched the bullet holes speckle the backseat, just waiting for the surge of pain from the random shot that would pierce her skull.

Rachel's trembling hand gripped the satellite phone in her pocket. Depressing the radio button, she shouted into it trying to make herself heard over the whipping wind and the roar of Chris' gunfire. "They're– they're shooting at us! Stop– stop! They're gonna kill us!"

The front windshield that already had bullet holes punched through the center of it crunched into a spiderweb of cracks as two rabid bodies flipped over the hood and smashed into it. Sean managed to keep his composure despite Rachel and Chris' screams as he skidded down the road, nearing the exit onto the city streets.

Chris reloaded his rifle, looking over his shoulder. "Shit, there's a fourth car back there, an SUV!"

Rachel peaked out the back window and saw a black SUV with the red and blue lights flashing in the windshield coming up behind the three pickup trucks.

"It's a cop car," Rachel yelled. "Are they with us?"

SIXTY

Derrick Hart
Louisville, KY

Derrick veered the steering wheel from side to side.

"Watch the curb. Watch the–" Brandon shouted from the front passenger seat. The SUV nearly lifted onto two tires when they turned another corner.

"Fucking shit!" Eric yelled from the back row of the SUV. He had stayed with Zoe and Karen in the rear trying to keep Zoe stable and still. It had been difficult getting her into the vehicle. No matter how little she was moved, she winced and groaned in pain. Derrick didn't think they could move her again. Running was out of the question. Either this plan was going to work, or this girl was going to die.

If we don't save Rachel, we're all dead.

"Careful!" Alyssa yelled. Derrick could hear the roar of the engines echoing between the buildings up ahead along with the automatic gunfire. The sound beckoned every rabid in the city.

Brandon stuffed a stack of full rifle magazines into his chest rig pockets and shouldered his M4. The back of the undercover police Suburban they had acquired held the gear for a Louisville SWAT officer along with his rifle and ammo. Derrick and Brandon had split the magazines and given the extra loaded rifle to Alyssa who sat behind Derrick.

The satellite phone that rolled about in the cupholder between them crackled alive. "They're– they're shooting at us! Stop– stop!" Rachel's voice was strained.

"Fuck!" Derrick swerved around an abandoned Humvee covered in blood and cut the corner sharply almost causing himself to fly out of the seat. When they straightened out, they saw several taillights up ahead.

"There," Alyssa pointed between Brandon and Derrick.

"They're gonna kill us!" Rachel's voice crackled over the radio.

"Hold on," Derrick said. Three older model pickup trucks chased after a bullet riddled police cruiser. Its bumper dragged on the concrete sending bright sparks in the air as the trucks took turns taking pot shots at the cruiser in bursts of automatic gunfire. They were ahead by twenty yards; the men in the bed of the trucks hadn't noticed them, yet. Brandon went silent as a cold, hard expression came over his face. He turned around, put one knee on the seat and rolled down his window letting the wind snap inside.

Derrick sped alongside the pickup truck in the rear, so Brandon had a direct view of the tattered vehicle. Its old, maroon color hid the rust along the siding. His focus on the truck, Derrick didn't see a rabid lunge at his vehicle until its long torso smacked the front bumper, then rag dolled over their roof. The loud tumbling sound the rabid's body made caused the driver and three men in the bed of the pickup truck to finally notice their SUV pulled beside them.

There was flash of shock in their eyes for a moment before the gunfire roared. Brandon poured heavy automatic fire on them. They never had a chance.

Half hung out the window, Brandon emptied his magazine into the windshield of the truck, eating a hole out of the glass. Bullets chewed blood out of the driver's chest and face. The vehicle jerked left then right out of control causing the three men in the cab to cling to whatever they could before being violently ejected into the air when the truck smashed into a telephone pole and rolled.

"Fuck you." Brandon growled to himself. He sat back in his seat before the airborne men struck the pavement. Flicking the empty magazine to the floorboard, he slapped a fresh magazine in his rifle and released the bolt catch.

Derrick tried to think how to communicate 'friendly' to Rachel and her agents in the lead police cruiser given they couldn't radio her. Looking down at the familiar center console of the police SUV he drove, Derrick flipped the switch to the right, turning on the red and blue emergency lights.

Bullets speckled against their windshield and Derrick flinched low instinctually. The second pickup truck had seen what Brandon had done. It was a beige clunker with a brown stripe along the side. The lone man in the bed of the truck sat on his butt attempting to stay in the vehicle as it shook from side to side. His AK-47 jumped from his hands with every burst of fire as the man could barely keep two hands on the rifle with the erratic driving. Derrick switched to the right side of the truck to avoid the bullets, but Brandon screamed at Derrick to switch back to give him an angle.

Alyssa fired a handful of rounds out her window, but the returned shots pounded the side of her door prompting Derrick to slam on the brakes. Rachel's SUV took a hard curve and the two pickups followed downtown. Derrick mounted a curb to avoid the thicket of rabids trailing the roaring pickup trucks, then gassed the engine to catch up.

Brandon connected the seatbelt behind him and locked it taut so the belt wouldn't extend any farther. Wrapping his left forearm around the loop, he pushed outside his open window, again half hanging outside. Firing in short three-round bursts, he pelted the rear of the pickup truck as Derrick approached. Derrick found the tempo Brandon fired at and steadied his steering wheel before his final burst. Blood splattered across the back of the pickup truck as the lone gunman collapsed to his side, wounded, before being jostled out of the truck bed.

A pack of rabid dove from an alleyway they passed and quickly seized upon the wounded man. One of their heads smashed against the SUV's side as Derrick gritted his teeth and roared the engine for the beige pickup truck in the rear.

"Oh my god," Karen yelled as the SUV shook from the masses of rabid that dove into its side. "There's so many!"

"Hang on," Derrick called out as he accelerated, prompting Brandon to tuck back inside the vehicle. Roaring his engine beside the rear axle of the beige pickup truck, Derrick saw the panicked glances rearward from the driver. With his front tires almost parallel with the truck's rear tires, Derrick accelerated, swerving into its side.

Alyssa screamed as the two vehicles collided and the metal screeched against metal. Even Brandon cursed and braced against the front dash. For Derrick it was just another day at work. The PIT maneuver worked flawlessly. Ramming the truck's rear end off center, the beige truck driver over corrected and steered his front end into side of a brick wall.

"Goddamn, Derrick," Brandon said looking in his side mirror then back at Derrick. Derrick smirked, glancing back at Brandon. *One truck left...*

Derrick startled when one of the rabids dove at their side

and was able to cling to his sideview mirror. It smashed its face and large forehead into the window repeatedly. By the fifth crash of its face against the glass, the window began to crack. Jerking left to right in fast motions, Derrick loosened the rabid's grip on the car and sent it tumbling to the road behind them.

"Derrick!" Brandon shouted tucking into his seatbelt.

"Watch out!" Alyssa added.

The police cruiser he and the final pickup truck were pursuing braked hard. The truck swerved around the police cruiser at the last second, but Derrick didn't have enough time to react. He felt the twist in his gut as his breath got caught in the back of his throat. At full speed they approached the police cruiser's white rear bumper. Derrick swerved hard to the right, as their tires squealed. Brandon was thrown at Derrick despite his grip on the seat belt.

There was a moment of weightlessness. It was a suspended moment of surreal peace before the catastrophic crash. The world went sideways as their vehicle rolled in the center of the city streets.

SIXTY-ONE

Rachel Anderson
Louisville, KY

"Shit!" Sean smacked the steering wheel as he accelerated.

"They were helping us!" Rachel shouted. The black SUV that had taken out two of the pickup trucks had rolled onto its roof. It was an unintended consequence of Sean's plan to get the final truck ahead of them by braking. It worked. The light blue pickup that had a half dozen threats in it had zig-zagged around their police cruiser and disappeared around the corner, but the cost was that their altruistic allies' SUV was wrecked on its roof.

"Stop– stop! Sean, stop the car!" Rachel yelled as she jerked the door handles uselessly in the back of the police cruiser. Sean was accelerating past the SUV ignoring Rachel's plight.

"We can't help them," Chris yelled back at Rachel. "We'll die!"

"They didn't have to help us! We said on the radio we'd help them– That's what we said!" Rachel snapped. She could see a foot smash through the tinted glass window of the SUV as they passed. Its blue and red police lights still flashing in the windows.

"I'm not– no," Rachel said. Her mind flashed back to her students and all that's happened in the days since then. *You can't save everyone.* She recalled the words that the police officer said to her in, what felt like, a lifetime ago now. *You turned down a helicopter for those kids, because that's who you are.* Her hand reached out her broken window, palming the side of the door until she found the door handle.

"Rachel– stop! The baby!" Sean yelled back at her, stomping on the brakes.

"I'm not leaving them!" Rachel's door popped open, and with her rifle tucked to her chest, she fell out of the slowing car. Thumping the pavement, she landed butt first on the road, she let out a short yelp before rolling to her feet. Limping into run, she raced for the upside-down SUV.

SIXTY-TWO

Derrick Hart
Louisville, KY

Through the murky haze that clouded his sight, Derrick saw the inside of the SUV in mysterious shapes that didn't make sense. Bags hung upside down by their straps and backs of chairs were pointed in odd directions. Shattered glass and limbs stuck out from the seats in the back. By the time Derrick realized the SUV rolled upside down, the infecteds' scream registered in his concussed mind.

Derrick stomped his foot through the driver's side window, breaking the glass on the third kick. "Alys..." Derrick mouthed the name and tasted blood. *I bit my tongue.* "Alyssa."

"I'm– I'm stuck," she replied through a strained voice. Derrick focused and saw she and the others hung from their seatbelts.

"Hold on," Derrick scooted his legs out the window. "Try and get free." Derrick grunted as he felt a new stinging pain in his ribcage that wasn't there before the wreck. Brandon was face down in the ceiling's upholstery and wasn't moving. "Brandon... Brandon!" Derrick yelled then pulled at his limp shoulder. Brandon turned over like dead weight coursing panic through Derrick's veins.

Gunfire cracked outside.

With a sudden pull on Derrick's ankles, that hung outside the SUV, he was dragged out of the window of the car with a jarring force. Derrick kicked his heels free as he turned to his back like an awkward tortoise, ready to defend himself from the rabid only to see a broad-shouldered man with a familiar face.

"Friendly, friendly, frie–" Sean hollered with his hands raised. Recognition sprouted across Derrick's face as it did on Sean's.

"Derrick?" Rachel blurted out, confused. She stood over him to his side, the muzzle of her rifle pointed uncomfortably close to him.

Derrick shook the surprise of the moment from his head and thumbed back to the SUV. "I got people inside."

"Get 'em out, we'll cover you!" Sean shouted and took position. Rachel and her other body man, Chris, formed a protective wall around Derrick as he dove back inside. *They came back for us– they came back.* Derrick felt a burst of hope grow inside him. *This is happening. I can save them.*

Inside the SUV, Brandon had roused from unconsciousness, but he moved slowly and with great confusion. "Come on, Bran. We gotta go, brother," Derrick groaned through pained breaths as he snagged the strap of his rifle. The scream that arose from the back was piercing, and the words were thick with pain and difficult to understand. Alyssa had managed to get herself free from her seatbelt and was in the back row, clinging to the limp and bloodied body of her little brother. His torso half-dangled out of the shattered glass window beside him. His eyes hung open as his graying skin underscored his shell of a body left behind.

"No, no, no! Eric, wake up!" Alyssa heaved as the tears were pinched from her eyes and she gasped for breath. Her hands touched the mortal wound on his forehead but pulled away instantly when she felt the lifeless corpse that once was her teenage brother. The metal debris that had penetrated his forehead had killed him quickly.

We get to watch everyone else die... Brandon's prediction is coming to fruition.

"Alyssa, Alyssa!" Derrick failed to get her attention as fear mounted inside him. Brandon scrambled out his own window. After jimmying her seatbelt, Karen fell down hard on the roof as gunfire erupted outside the vehicle. "Karen, grab her. Grab Alyssa. Get her– Karen!"

Panic was imprinted on Karen's face as she ignored Derrick's words completely. With crazed, wide eyes and trembling hands she crawled quickly out of the nearest shattered window. Oblivious to everything except self-preservation. The staccato of gunshots outside grew as he tossed his rifle out the window and edged to the back of the vehicle.

Zoe was sagging from her seat, the seatbelt preventing her from dropping to the floor. Derrick drew the tanto blade from his vest and cut the belt. He was so exhausted; he didn't even try to catch her when she fell. The teenage girl curled to her side and let out a long groan of pain. *Pain is good. Means she's still alive.*

"Derrick!" Brandon's voice cut through the gunfire. Derrick shoved Zoe out the window and snatched Alyssa by her waist, dragging her out with him. She didn't fight but she didn't help either. Alyssa's body was limp with defeat as she sobbed over the loss of her entire family.

She's given up...

Derrick saw the disheartened faces casted in shadows by the streetlight. Sean, Chris, and Brandon fired at the approaching rabid down the road. They picked them off before they could form a pack too large, but more streamed their way with every gunshot.

"Alyssa– Alyssa!" Derrick shook her until her shattered eyes looked into his. Derrick's rough, dirt covered palms cupped her tender cheeks. "I'm sorry, I'm so sorry, but I need you right now. Do you hear me? I need you."

Alyssa's blank eyes blinked as an alertness appeared in her expression.

"We have to go!" Brandon yelled.

"Hey, hey! Are you with me?" Derrick asked as another burst of gunfire exploded over his shoulder.

Tears rained from her eyes as Alyssa shot a worried look at the rabid scrambling towards them, "I'm– I'm with you!"

Brandon stepped forward and blasted four rounds into the nearest rabid's head before it could reach them. Sean and Rachel carried Zoe to the bullet riddled police cruiser. Its engine sounded as if it could stall at any moment. Brandon tossed Derrick his rifle causing him to wince when he caught it. The searing pain in his ribs pushed tears from the corner of Derrick's eyes as he slid the sling over his arm and neck.

"You good?" Brandon asked.

Derrick took a shallow breath and felt a stabbing pain. "I'm–"

"Look out!" Chris shouted.

The roar of a stressed pickup truck engine filled the street followed by the beam of its headlights barreling towards Rachel. *The last of the trucks that was after Rachel.* Half-naked bodies cluttered the hood and bed of the truck as it shook left then right. The vehicle looked diseased. Like the dozen rabid clinging on to its side were pus ridden boils on a patient's skin.

A symptom of the underlying condition killing its host. Rachel and Sean snatched Zoe away from the police car before the truck plowed into its side.

Their police cruiser flipped onto its side. Infected bodies launched across the road while others continued to clamor inside the cab after the driver. Smoke bellowed from the hood of the truck as more rabid approached.

"Shit– go, just go!" Brandon shouted for the others to run ahead. Chris scooped up Zoe and Sean grabbed Rachel's wrist before taking off in a sprint.

"Get them out of here," Derrick said to Alyssa who followed Karen and ran ahead with the others as Derrick covered them. Derrick snapped rounds from his rifle into the thighs and hips of the rabids clamoring to their feet, dropping them to a crawl. Brandon chugged bursts of gunfire into the cab of the totaled truck where bloodied rabid tousled like panicked spiders trying to scurry out of their den. Derrick smacked Brandon's shoulder signaling him to move.

Brandon limped to catch up to Derrick, who himself grunted with every step. Rachel and Sean ran down the center of the road firing at the infected popping out from each corner they approached, while Chris struggled to keep up Zoe draped over his shoulder. Brandon glanced behind him and groaned a labored breath. "Fuck."

Pivoting, he fired his magazine dry prompting Derrick to turn around and cover Brandon's reload. Exhausted and gasping for air, Derrick's reticle bounced across the nearest rabid and snapped rounds in the chest and stomach.

"Loading," Derrick croaked, ejecting his rifle magazine only to find his ammo pouch was empty. Derrick saw the figures cluttering the street blocks behind them. The streetlight illuminated them sprinting toward the living. Derrick slung his rifle and drew his Glock.

"Up," Brandon panted. With his collection of injuries, Brandon struggled to keep pace with Derrick. The tall, athletic man that Brandon was, had been battered, broken, and exhausted to the point where he could barely jog at the back of the group.

"Hurry, come on!" Alyssa shouted ahead as the distance between Derrick, Brandon, and the rest of the group grew.

"Come– come on," Derrick pulled on Brandon's shoulder as he gasped with cotton mouth. Dehydrated and sweat pouring down his flush cheeks, Derrick had trouble focusing. They hobbled up the road like broken men. They took turns falling into each other's shoulders to steady themselves.

Infected seemed to sprint out from every alley and side road ahead of them. Rachel and Sean fired in rapid succession until one of them tossed their empty rifle to the ground. Moments later the other did as well.

This is it...

Derrick saw the terror in Alyssa's eyes as she stole a look back at him over her shoulder.

We don't die– not at first... We're trained... Derrick exchanged a knowing look with Brandon. The magazine pouches on their chest rigs were empty. Brandon fired his rifle sparingly at a rabid that swiped at their heels. Treating each bullet as if it were their last, because it was about to be.

We fight just long enough so you get to watch Alyssa get torn apart.

Derrick was on his last magazine for his handgun. It was a horrendous and surreal thought, but Derrick found himself wondering if he should save the bullets for themselves. He nearly dry heaved stomach acid as he ran from the consideration that he should just shooting his friends and loved ones in the back of the head right now. *Would it not be a better death?*

The black building channeled them up a steepening hill

into downtown Louisville. The skyscrapers were speckled with random office lights on along its side and distant faces inside the offices looking down on them.

This is it. This is where we die...

"I-I can't, I can't," succumbing to sharp incline of the road, Karen had fallen behind and collapsed at Brandon's feet. "Please, just– I can't do this!"

Karen cried a defeated wail as she clutched her right leg. The nearest pack of infected that trailed them screamed in a frenzy at her mental break. Brandon panicked, lifting Karen up by her lifeless arms. "Karen– Karen, get up!" Brandon shouted. "Fucking get up!"

With unsteady hands, Derrick sighted the rabid with his pistol and fired a single shot at a time. He struck its shoulder, its other shoulder, then the third shot sent a bullet into the rabid's cheek, dropping it. Two more rabid females scurried on mangled legs and injured arms like animals to Derrick's blind side. Derrick had time to get his front sight on the first's rabid's gaunt jaw and snap two rounds into its head, but it was Brandon's rifle rounds that stopped the second rabid and saved Derrick's thigh from being bitten.

"We got to go! We got to go, right fucking now!" Derrick hollered at Brandon who struggled to get Karen to her feet. Alyssa had run back for them and dragged Karen, who hobbled on one leg towards the others. Sean had led the others to a small convenience store and was prying the large pieces of plywood from one of its windows. Rabid screams could be heard far and near throughout the city. The streetlights shone on the streams of rabid running in their location from as far as the eye could see.

"Get them out of here!" Brandon jabbed his finger at Karen and Alyssa. "I'll cover."

Derrick ran to Brandon's wife and scooped her up in a half

carry-half dragging motion as he and Alyssa pulled her onto the sidewalk. Sean had managed to open a hole wide enough in one of the smashed windows and broken plywood sheeting to squeeze Rachel and the others inside.

"Run, run!" Rachel shouted from the mouth of the store.

"Get in here!" Chris ordered as he pulled Rachel back inside. Derrick reached the entrance just as a pack of rabid rounded the corner of the store. He dropped Karen like a piece of luggage as he fired into the wide bodied rabid's chest and face, crumbling him hard to the ground.

Alyssa dragged Karen inside the store and a rabid chased them inside. Derrick's mind flashed back to the gun range days ago and the single rabid that infected all those civilians in the trailer. Diving for the rabid inside the store, Derrick snatched the back of its shirt in a desperate attempt to stop it.

The rabid stretched the shirt and the fabric tore as it dragged Derrick inside the room. In the pitch black store the rabid ripped free of its shirt as it bounded across the tile floor for Alyssa who crab walked backwards in a panic to get away.

"N-no!" Derrick hollered.

His trigger pulls were fast and his aim erratic as his bullets pounded up the rabid's back. His pistol locked back empty as the rabid slowed but didn't stop. It was Chris who grabbed the stool from behind the cash register and smashed it down on the rabid's head, allowing Rachel to pull Alyssa out of the way. Blood loss quickly slowed the rabid as Chris continued to beat it until it finally stopped moving.

The last pops of gunfire boomed outside. Derrick raced to the carved out hole in the plywood and saw Brandon dropping rabid with close range head shots from his handgun. His gunfire drew the converging rabids' attention away from the store they hid inside.

"Brandon, run!" Derrick shouted, double checking his rifle

and handgun were out of ammo. Brandon emptied his pistol into a rabid as he side stepped and turned to flee but was tackled by a lone rabid that scurried from the shadows behind him.

"No, no, no..." Derrick gasped.

From the flat of his back, Brandon used the side of his rifle to hold the near naked rabid at bay, its grip wrapped around Brandon's shoulders like a giant squid with its long, muscular limbs.

"Shit!" Derrick moved to climb out of the store when Alyssa pulled at his shoulder.

"Don't," Rachel said.

"Derrick, no– We'll die if we try..." Alyssa cried as she pulled his gaze to her's. "I can't lose you."

"Chris, find something to block the hole in the window with," Sean ordered. Chris and Sean moved to secure the store.

"W-where's Brandon?" Karen mumbled in a daze from where she sat on the floor beside Zoe's body.

Looking back, Derrick saw the lean rabid bash Brandon into the concrete before forcing its wide jaws down onto Brandon's shoulder. Shaking its head back and forth, the rabid tore into him as he screamed.

Derrick's stomach twisted with a familiar pull. Clenching his fist, Derrick turned his back on Brandon. He could not bear to watch his best friend die.

SIXTY-THREE

Brandon Armstrong
Louisville, KY

"Fuck. Off!" Brandon gritted his teeth as he rolled his whole body to the side, and with a violent twist, smashed his shoulder, with the rabid's jaw still attached to it, into the asphalt. He felt a spike of pain from the hit that hurt worse than the bite. But the rabid's jaw was knocked loose and Brandon was able to get the flat of his rifle across the rabid's chest. The rabid's teeth must not have pierced through his shirt and body armor strap because he wasn't infected, yet.

Come on, mother fucker! I'm not fucking dead, yet.

The rabid gargled a scream as it rained down hammer fists on Brandon. The vicious strikes pounded Brandon's body and the side of his rifle defending his face. The infected had long locks of black hair that curtained its face as it roared a wretched scream, its horrid breath suffocating Brandon.

"Is that all you got!" Brandon snarled through clenched teeth.

A long swooping hammer fist arched over the top of Brandon's rifle and smashed across his jaw. Instantly, Brandon's vision tunneled. His arms went weak, and his body crumpled as the rabid closed on him. Brandon watched the black gaping hole between the rabid's foul jaws widen, consuming his sight, before it snapped closed on his face.

The only sound that pierced over the rabid's growl was the desperate scream that Alyssa made. "Derrick, don't!" she pleaded.

An elbow rammed Brandon's side violently, and he was roughly clobbered onto his stomach. He tried to get to his knees and fell over from the whiplash. Brandon shook his head free of the dizziness he felt, clamored to his knees, and saw Derrick entangled with the wiry rabid on top of him. The rabid's hands swung down madly into Derrick's defenseless face as he tried to hold it at bay. The rabid's long black hair shook from side to side as it pummeled Derrick's nose and jaw with furious strikes until instantly, it stopped. The rabid's arms and legs went limp and collapsed on Derrick.

Derrick heaved and rolled the rabid's body off of him and withdrew his tanto knife from the rabid's throat as he rose to his knees. Squinting through the blood, Derrick's gaze rose from his hands to Brandon.

Brandon's best friend was unrecognizable. His shirt, hands, and face were drenched in the rabid's crimson blood. The deranged image contrasted sharply with the man Brandon knew. The police officer who saved helpless children. The guy who wrestled with his dog for hours at the park. The innocent boy Brandon used to play with every day after school.

Standing, Derrick dropped the wet knife and Brandon saw

the whites of his eyes. His red, sticky hand rose to the pair of dog tags that dangled from his neck. Derrick clenched them in his fist as his eyes met Brandon's for a fleeting moment.

"Derrick..." Brandon mumbled, but it was too late. He was already running.

Derrick sprinted as fast as he could away from Brandon and towards cluster of infected that poured into the road from surrounding streets. He only made it a few steps before collapsing hard to the asphalt.

"Nooo!" Alyssa's voice broke. Someone was holding her back inside the store as she pulled to get outside.

Derrick's fingers raked his scalp as his knees locked out, driving his face into the ground. Brandon could barely stand, let alone walk. His rifle was empty as was his pistol. All Brandon could do was gnash his teeth as he watched the infection take hold of his friend.

Derrick slammed his forehead on the asphalt and rolled stiff limbed to his back.

"Goddammit, Derrick," Brandon whispered.

Derrick jolted to his feet with a maddening shriek and rounded on Brandon. Veins throbbed across his forehead and neck as he sprinted. The bloody chain of tags bounced off his chest with every step. Brandon removed his set of matching dog tags from his cargo pocket and wrapped the chain around his fist with one hand, while he drew out his Ka-Bar knife from his chest rig with his other.

"*Valhalla waits for no one,*" Brandon nodded at the tags clenched in his fist accepting the same fate as his approaching brother's. "*Valhalla waits for no one,* brother."

His hand tightening on the grip of his knife, Brandon's eyes locked on Derrick's and the hundred more rabid that ran behind his infected friend.

Then the black sky erupted.

Brandon watched Derrick's infected body be decimated by large, rapid fire projectiles that rained from a hovering helicopter overhead. Ducking instinctively, Brandon dove as missiles strafed the skyline exploding the road around him.

SIXTY-FOUR

Rachel Anderson
Louisville, KY

Sean's arm looped around Rachel's waist and brought her down to the ground as bullets rained on the street outside. Chunks of concrete were spat into the air. The ground rumbled and shook Rachel and the others while missiles exploded pillows of fire and smoke into the air.

The only protection she felt were Sean's arms and legs wrapped tightly around her backside. His palm gently, but firmly pressed along the front of her belly, shielding her from spits of debris that shot inside the store. It felt like the world had come crashing down on them. That the world was ending as the explosions shook the earth beneath them. Rachel grasped Sean's hand and squeezed it tightly and he squeezed her back.

Seconds that felt like hours passed and the explosions gave way to bursts of machine gun fire. When the shooting slowed to a stop, Rachel unclenched her eyes. She coughed to clear the blockage in her throat from the aerosolized concrete. A fog of smoke filled the store. The whipping rotary blades from the two choppers that circled overhead stirred up more smoke as they surveyed the area.

One of the two helicopters lowered in the cleared intersection while the second rose up higher above the city streets. Sean stood beside Chris and stepped through the hole in the broken plywood, exiting their refuge.

As the smoke cleared, Rachel searched for any remains of Derrick's body in the eerily quiet sprawl of destruction, but only saw a small crater where she had last seen him. Sorrow and disbelief cluttered her mind as Rachel's nerves were burned to exhaustion.

The helicopter's blades slowed and quieted as a tight group of soldiers disembarked. The dust in the air was ablaze from the streetlights as the soldiers created a perimeter. "Hands on your head! I said, hands on your fucking head!" two soldiers advanced toward Sean and Chris with rifles trained on them.

They complied as they were pushed out into the street. "Secret Service! We're secret service!" Chris shouted. "Rachel Anderson is inside. She's the President's–"

"Shut up!"

The soldiers separated and one group ventured into the store, barking orders with their rifle raised. "Everyone on your feet, now! Let's move, outside!"

The soldiers donned in black body armor and black gas masks with wide, black bug eyes. They didn't look like any U.S. soldier Rachel had ever seen before. Rachel and Alyssa helped the nearly unconscious Zoe to her feet.

"Hey! What's wrong with her? Is she sick? Is she infected?" a soldier boomed.

"No, no!" Alyssa replied forcefully with tears in her voice. "She was shot. She– She was shot."

Sean and Chris knelt in the street with their wrists and ankles bound by white plastic zip ties. Two soldiers roughly dragged a battered and barely conscious Brandon, also zip tied, beside Sean. The man looked to be in a daze, lost in his swamp of thoughts. By the time Rachel realized the others were bound in zip ties, she felt the plastic cinched around her wrists behind her back.

"Hey– wait, stop!" Rachel snapped as she was forced to her knees.

"Quiet!" a taller soldier warned her with a dip of his muzzle.

"Blake, stand fast."

Blake lowered his rifle. Hidden under his black uniform and mask, Blake towered over the others with his broad shoulders. There were six soldiers total and five of them made their rounds, patting down and grabbing at each of their bodies, searching for weapons. Sean was on his knees beside Rachel, his eyes not leaving her's the entire time.

This doesn't feel like a rescue.

"We secure?" the soldier who appeared to be in charge asked his men.

"We're good. Seven survivors, four females."

The leader keyed a small radio attached to his chest rig and looked up at the chopper circling overhead. "Overwatch, give me a sit-rep."

Touching the area of his mask where his ear would be, he nodded and replied, "Copy," pointing at the group of women huddled together, he told his men, "Three minutes. Check them," the leader said. The five soldiers went down the line of women and asked them their names.

"Karen. Are you going to help us?" Karen asked.

The soldier didn't bother to reply and moved to Alyssa and then to Zoe.

"What's your name?"

When Zoe didn't respond, the soldier kicked her thigh making her yelp. "I said, what's your name?"

"Hey!" Alyssa snapped, her lower lip trembling. "Her name's Zoe and she's fifteen years old."

When Rachel identified herself by name, the leader gave Blake a nod to begin confirmation. Blake found the Greenband satellite phone in Rachel's pocket and showed it to the other soldiers, "she's got the GPS, too."

Pocketing the Greenband phone, Blake removed a small tablet strapped to the back of his body armor. He held three of her fingers down on the screen of the device until a light flashed green.

Rachel studied the looming soldier's uniform as Blake performed a retinal scan on her with the same device. The black uniform had no name tags or rank insignias. The shoulders of his uniform didn't hold a patch that identified what branch of the military he served.

The lead soldier appeared to stare at Brandon who leered back at him with cold eyes.

"You're... you're not military," Brandon said. "That Blackhawk is..." Brandon nudged his head toward the helicopter that had the American flag along its side. "That Apache overhead is... who are you?"

The leader stepped toward him. "Lieutenant Gavon Reins, U.S. Navy." Gavon studied Brandon's skeptical expression. Gavon ported his rifle to reveal a Greenband bracelet on his right wrist. He tapped the metallic green with a single finger. "Re-enlisted. And you?"

"Sergeant Brandon Armstrong. Rangers..." Brandon said.

"Gavon," Blake said, holding up the device in his hands. "I've got her. Fingerprint and retina both are a match for Rachel Anderson."

Gavon nodded and looked at his watch. "Get the girl on board."

Rachel turned to Sean in a panic. "Wait!" Rachel said but Brandon interrupted her.

"Lieutenant Reins," Brandon spoke forcefully enough to stop the commotion and get the soldier's attention. "I am an Army Ranger. My friend..." Brandon looked away for a moment. "My friend, Derrick Hart, a Birmingham SWAT officer—we fought to get these women, these children to safety; we fought, and my friend died protecting the President's daughter so she could be rescued. None of us are infected. Take us with you. At least get us out of the city." Brandon's hard-set eyes stared at the black reflective eyes of Gavon's mask.

"It's true," Rachel said. She was on her knees being held up by Blake. "These two men are my secret service agents, assigned to me. Chris Carroll and Sean Williams. They got me from Florida to here and these people kept us alive until you came. I'm the President's daughter and I'm telling you; we need to get all of these people to safety. Let go– You have to take them all!"

Rachel summoned every bit of will power left inside her to sound and look authoritative. The rising speed of helicopter blades made the dread surge inside her. She was willing to crawl across the debris to fall at the Lieutenant's feet to beg for the others' life. The thought of being whisked away to some bunker, safe from the collapsing world while leaving Sean here to... she couldn't do it. *I'm not leaving him. I won't.*

After a protracted pause, Gavon turned his head to Rachel and nodded. "Yes, ma'am."

The knots in Rachel's gut seemed to loosen all at once as a wave of relief overcame her. Even as Blake tried to help her to her feet, Rachel's elation mixed with a sudden onset of exhaustion made her knees give way.

"Okay, you ready to get your friends loaded up?" Lt. Gavon Reins asked as he stepped to Rachel's barely vertical body. She nodded with tears streaming down her cheeks.

Gavon grabbed a fist full of her hair with such force, he nearly toppled her. Rachel screamed as he wretched her hair from side to side, but her voice was drowned out by the helicopter blades gaining speed.

"Hey– Fuck you!" Sean shouted from the ground.

Gavon looked over Rachel's shoulder at the pilot of the Blackhawk. Blake must have caught Gavon's line of thought and shuffled over so his broad shoulders hid his commander's actions from the Air Force pilot. Rachel felt her hair being ripped out by the clumps as Gavon straightened her with one hand.

"You know why I fucking hated the Navy?" Gavon said. His mask filtered voice was low and guttural, like a growl. "I've seen the men behind the curtain and just how pathetic the fucks are who're giving these orders. *President's Daughter?* Where is that rank in my chain of command, hm? You think you can tell me what to do, little girl? Do you feel in control now? Do you want to give me an order?" Rachel felt the cold metal press into her belly then saw the barrel of the pistol he pointed at her stomach as he cranked her head back, ripping another scream from her.

"I could waste you right here and tell your daddy you were infected," Gavon growled. "I could tell him that I put a bullet in you myself, and I bet he'd thank me. You want that? Huh?" Gavon shoved Rachel backward into Blake's arms. Keying his radio, he spoke to overwatch as he holstered his pistol. "Copy, we're wheels up in thirty seconds."

Cocking his mask to the side, Gavon turned his head down to her exposed cleavage from her shirt that was stretched thin over the curves of her body. "Remember this moment, girl," he said. "This is the new world, and in this world the President doesn't control shit. I do. You don't breathe without my permission. Every coward that is alive right now is so because men like me allowed them to live."

"Let's go!" Blake yelled as another soldier grabbed hold of Rachel's shoulders.

"What about them?" a soldier asked, pointing his rifle at Brandon who fumed silently on his knees.

"Don't waste the ammo," Gavon shook his head. "Leave them for the rabid."

"No!" Rachel screamed as her feet left the ground. She kicked at the air while Blake and another soldier dragged her by her hips toward the chopper. "Sean! Sean! Take them! Just take the Secret Serv– Sean!"

Rachel writhed and shook, trying to free her shoulders to no avail. Sean stared at her with acceptance in his eyes. He looked at her desperately. He saw her like this was the last time he would see her.

"–him. Just take him! Sean no, please! Just take Sean!" the soldiers climbed onto the belly of the Blackhawk and lugged Rachel across the cool, dirty floor of the chopper. The helicopter was waned a high-pitched tone as it reached max power. The chopper lifted from the ground and Rachel couldn't even hear herself scream, "no, no! I love you, Sean– don't go!"

Wednesday, May 1st

1 Hour, 48 Minutes Until Calamity Event

SIXTY-FIVE

Brandon Armstrong
Louisville, KY

"Gah– Dammit!" Brandon growled as he flexed his arms. "Come on!" he jerked his arms back and forth. The zip cuffs dug and sawed into his bleeding wrists as he tried to pull free.

The sound of the helicopter's propeller faded in the distance leaving an eerie silence in the annihilated streets of downtown Louisville. The cluster of 70mm rockets fired from the Apache chopper had caused a partial collapse of a five-story building. The charred road, covered in chunks of debris and obliterated bodies, looked like a wasteland from a dystopian movie. The 30mm casings that littered the road caught the glint of the streetlights that still stood.

The only sound Brandon could hear now were the cries of the girls—Karen's above all others. It was his job to protect her.

And I failed her...

Brandon heard her shallow breaths and her childlike whimpers.

"Anyone see a knife– anything?" Brandon grunted. "Hey, anything jagged? Anything sharp?" Brandon looked over at Sean who had already given up. He only stared at the ground where his head rested.

"Shit!" almost in reply to Brandon's curse another groan came from the nearest dilapidated building. Everyone went quiet and watched as a figure squirmed out from a pile of bodies, its hands and feet crunched over shattered glass. The rabid crawled in the shadows for a long moment before a streetlight touched its mangled face and damaged limbs.

The rabid appeared barely human with half its scalp obliterated and one of its kneecaps dislodged. It was dazed, probably from the blood loss, but still croaked a wretched screech.

"Shit," Brandon said under his breath.

"No, no, no!" Karen cried as she wormed away from the rabid. Alyssa barely moved and Zoe was kicking so much one of her boots had come off. There were more sounds coming from the distance. Growls. Screams. Footsteps. Every rabid across the city that had heard the explosions and the choppers would be sprinting their way.

The desperation could be heard in the quickening of everyone's movement. Brandon knew they were dead. He had known this moment was coming from the start of the fight in Atlanta. They were dead men walking; it was just a matter of when they would stop walking. Brandon only wished it was a bullet to the head and not the slow, torturous death that crawled towards them.

"Brandon! Brandon, do something!" Karen squealed like he had never heard before. It was a guttural terror in her voice as the rabid with flesh hanging free from its cheek snapped its jaws and dragged nearer.

"Oh– oh god– shit, get back!" Chris shouted as the rabid neared his feet where he lay hobbled. "N-no go– go away!"

"Hey, you piece of shit!" Sean yelled trying to get the rabid's attention. Pulling at his ties, Chris rocked back and forth helplessly. He stomped his heels out uselessly at the rabid's chest but it caught hold of his boots.

"No, geh– please don't– help!" Chris wormed to his side. The last strips of resilient toughness were stripped away from his voice as the reality of death sunk into his core like everyone else's.

The panic in Chris' voice was replaced by a bellowing pain as the rabid bit into his thigh ripping side to side. Ignited in a frenzy, the rabid dove on to Chris' chest. Its teeth dug into the fleshy portion of his cheek, ripping skin away as Chris flexed against the binds on his wrists. No one spoke as Chris' body arched and his agonizing scream turned a maddening pitch before the rabid slammed its jaws onto Chris' exposed jugular. Tearing into the meaty portion of his throat, Blood poured from the wound as the life left Chris' body.

"Oh my god," Alyssa panicked. "Oh my god!"

"Brandon, do something!" Karen begged as the rabid began to move again. Karen's body was the next one in its path.

Brandon looked at Karen's shadowed as she struggled to worm away. "I'm sorry, Karen, I'm so fuckin–" But before he could finish a figure stood over her. A second figure she hadn't realized was there.

"Hey, you son of–" Brandon started before a glimmer of light cut across Zoe's pale face. "Zoe?"

She stepped over Karen and stumbled. Her arms and legs were free of her ties. "Zoe," Brandon said in astonishment. She held a khaki colored pocketknife loosely in her hand. She fell down gripping her stomach while trying to bend over behind

Brandon. The rabid scurried closer, angling for Karen. "Hurry up!"

Zoe slashed at the zip ties on Brandon's wrists, but it was too late. The rabid was already on top of Karen. It grabbed Karen's ankle with an outstretched arm as she twisted in its grasp and cried. It pulled its lips apart revealing blood-stained teeth and bent over to bite her ankle.

"Stop– No, get away!" Karen screamed.

Brandon flexed his arms with all his might and felt the ties break free as Zoe cut them. With his ankles still bound, he leaped onto Karen protecting her with his body. He slammed his boots down on the rabid's face and heard a crunch. He struck the rabid with his heels again, forcing its hand from his wife.

Brandon snatched the knife from Zoe's hand. Driving his knees down on the rabid's back, he pressed its face into the concrete with one hand, then with an arching swing, he hammered the tip of the knife into the back of the rabid's skull.

He didn't have time to catch his breath. Brandon could hear the commotion coming from all directions now. Glass breaking. Objects being toppled over. Brandon cut his ankles free then went around cutting the others' ties.

"Look at me," Alyssa said to Zoe, cupping her cheeks. Zoe had collapsed into a ball of limbs where Brandon had once lain. "Look at me, honey..." Brandon looked down at Derrick's khaki pocketknife he held in his hand.

"Brandon, they're coming." Karen tugged at his shirt as she pointed downhill at a lone rabid running for them, still a distance away.

"And there," Alyssa said pointing to their side where a handful roamed.

"They're this way, too," Sean spoke quietly as he looked behind them.

Brandon looked for an exit but with every second that passed, more rabid joined the fray. Scurrying bodies that galloped on all fours going in and out of the black night as they ran under the streetlights, converging on their position.

Then, like a series of light switches turning off, the city was plunged into total darkness. The checkerboard of comforting lights that lit up the skyscrapers overhead, blinked off, giving way to a permanent wall of looming gray buildings. The low hum of electricity that Brandon had come to be so accustomed to hearing was gone. Every streetlamp and traffic light clicked to darkness, Brandon saw nothing, but in the true silence of the night he heard everything.

Karen screamed but all Brandon could do was hold her. *At least I can hold her.*

"Move! Move, this way!" Sean's voice hollered a direction of travel as he began to move. "Follow my voice, over here!"

Karen immediately limped his way and Brandon followed.

"Brandon!" Alyssa heaved as she tried to pick up Zoe. Gritting his teeth, Brandon squeezed the grip of the khaki knife in his palm before sliding it in his pocket. With Alyssa's help, he heaved a dead limbed Zoe onto his shoulder.

"Hurry!" Karen shouted to them from where they ran up the road.

Stumbling, Brandon limped behind Alyssa as they ran blind to the world. Someone fell. Then another tripped. Debris and bodies littered the road. Brandon kicked over a hollow metal box of some kind, the sound of it hitting the pavement echoed and rattled across the street. Screeches adjusted their sprint to home in on their location. Thousands of rabid sounded off from the city as they closed in on them.

"There, there! Up there!" Karen directed the group to the lone building that still had lights on in one of the top stories. The building was one of the taller ones and was only a half a block away. Sean ran ahead and using a rock he could barely lift, smashed the glass door to the building. When the giant pane of glass came crashing down on the fourth strike, the high-pitched screams ignited only feet behind Brandon.

"Oh god oh–" Karen repeated as they tumbled inside. Sean led them to a side door from the lobby with a red emergency sign over it that read 'Stairs.'

Gritting his teeth as the weight of Zoe bore down on him, Brandon leapt inside the stairwell as the brush of fingertips scraped at his back. Sean slammed the door for the stairwell shut behind him. The door rattled and shook as the bodies piled against the other side, barging to get through.

The stairwell had small emergency lights above the door that gave enough illumination to show a red shadow of their sweaty faces. Sean looked around the room and took a head count as Brandon sat Zoe down on the floor. Alyssa sat beside her checking the girl's pulse. They had no water or food, nor did they have any guns or ammo. Only the clothes on their back and this khaki knife.

The thudding door seemed to give a little bit more with every hit that jarred the room into action.

"We have to go upstairs," Brandon panted.

"How far?" Alyssa asked.

"As far as we can go," Brandon said. Karen, a jittery mess of fear, was already limping up a flight of stairs.

"Kare– wait for us, we don't know what's up there," Brandon warned.

Sean nodded, "I'll take lead." he quickly bounded up the stairs with his long legs and athletic frame.

"Zoe, honey, come on. With me." Alyssa encouraged Zoe to move toward the stairs but instead her body slowly slumped to the side in the fetal position. "Zoe– no, get up. Honey..."

"I... can't... go without... leave me," Zoe mumbled, barely conscious.

Alyssa looked up at Brandon. With his hands on his hips, Brandon's gaze lingered on Alyssa. He felt the wound of Derrick's death sting him all over again as he clenched his teeth and looked away to keep the tears from falling.

"God damn you, Derrick..." Brandon whispered.

Brandon bent over and, gritting his teeth, he hoisted Zoe up with one hand under her thighs and another under her backside. "Come on," Brandon grunted. "Derrick didn't keep you alive this long just for you to die here." Alyssa sniffled and cupped her hand over her mouth as she watched Brandon shoulder Zoe's weight up the first steps.

Alyssa pressed on the small of Brandon's back for the first several flights of stairs to give him support. Zoe groaned as he switched her position and draped her over his arms for the next several flights of stairs. Brandon felt his legs tremble with each step as he leaned against the wall.

They had marched up eleven stories and every part of Brandon's body was either numb or searing in pain like it was being held under a blow torch. Through gnashing teeth, Brandon managed to will himself to the eleventh floor before his trembling thighs gave out.

"Give her here," a voice surprised him from overhead. Brandon looked up and saw Sean standing beside him. The others all took the moment as a break, a chance to catch their breath as they sprawled against the stairwell railing. Sean took Zoe and hefted her onto his shoulder with ease. Brandon's legs shook as he pushed himself up. Alyssa checked on Zoe to make sure she was still breathing and had a pulse. Brandon felt a wet spot on his shirt where her stomach wound had bled through. A loud thud echoed from the basement floor and screams filled the stairwell.

"They're in! They're inside," Karen said in a panic already running up the next set of stairs on her hands and knees.

"Go," Sean said to Brandon who took point. With the last jolt of adrenaline spiking in his system, Brandon ran up the stairs passing the others. The screams filled the stairwell and became louder than Brandon's thoughts. He checked doors on each level only to find them locked. Sprinting up three flights of stairs, Brandon slowed as he stomped five more.

"Brandon, wait for– I can't!" Karen said.

It was when they made it to the nineteenth floor, the stairwell door exploded open without warning. It was like a mouse trap had sprung. A young man with blond shaggy hair held a rifle in twitchy hands with the barrel pointed Brandon's way.

"Hey! H-hey, what are you doing here?" the boy shouted.

Brandon huffed labored breaths as he leaned against the metal railing. He was so tired that the boy's presence didn't even register as a threat. The boy appeared to be as young as eighteen years old, but the uncertainty in his eyes and his frightened demeanor convinced Brandon he was no soldier. Just a lanky boy who happened to have a rifle. Alyssa was the next to summit on the nineteenth floor, then Karen who crawled up on her hands and knees.

"Stop or st– Go back down there! Down the stairs! I'll kill y'all, I fuckn' swear!" the boy warned. Alyssa and Karen tried to raise their hands but couldn't, even they seemed barely phased by the gun stuck in their faces.

"We can't, man," Brandon said, sucking down a deep breath. "You hear that? The screams. That's rabid coming up the stairs. They'll be here–"

"I don't care!" the boy shouted with more authority to his voice. His feet stepped toward Brandon who rested his hands on his wobbly knees. "Move downstairs, now! Or I'll throw–"

The boy jabbed the barrel of his rifle into Brandon's arm

and Brandon snapped. Smacking the barrel to the side, Brandon yanked the boy toward him by the neck of his shirt. Brandon smashed his forehead into the young man's nose. While he reeled from the pain, Brandon cupped the back of the boy's neck and slammed his face into the metal stairwell railing again and again. By the time Brandon grabbed the boy's belt buckle and tossed him over the railing, the young man wasn't even conscious.

The doorway the gunman had come from remained open and was now populated with several faces curiously peering at them. Electricity was on at this floor. It was then Brandon wished he had the wherewithal to snatch the rifle from the boy before tossing him over the railing with it. Though, the faces that looked his way didn't appear to be enemies. The lights on this hospital floor shined on an open room filled with dozens of women. Most were dressed in scrubs.

SIXTY-SIX

SHARON HILL
Louisville, KY

TOMMY'S EYES shot to the stairwell door as did the eyes of the growing number of women huddled near Sharon. Martinez along with four of her coworkers, also nurses, gathered in a waiting area near the stairwell.

The clatter became louder as footsteps echoed and stormed upwards to their floor. Martinez and her friends stared at the door the same way Tommy did, as if it was a jack in the box toy and an explosion could burst from it at any moment. Tommy leveled his machine gun at the door, his weight shifted, and feet pattered like a child holding in his urine.

Sharon sat on the first in a series of empty ICU beds that were along the windows overlooking the city. Victoria Richards, the Louisville police officer Sharon had helped to disguise as a nurse, approached Sharon from behind and grabbed her wrist gently. Sharon looked at the young woman who nodded her head backwards to signal a retreat. Quietly, Sharon stood and backed away with Victoria by her side.

"If they start shooting," Victoria whispered to Sharon. "Duck behind that pillar."

She nodded to a thick, concrete pillar that was beside the nurse's station behind them. Sharon looked at Martinez's hopeful face and realized then that Victoria and the others believed those charging up the stairwell were marines coming to rescue them from the clutches of these terrorists. They like everyone else in this room hadn't considered that something much worse was fast approaching, because no one here had seen the infected. None of the nurses or doctors had felt the desperation of walking along the interstate like Sharon had.

After Baron had left them under the guard of Tommy, Stephanie had separated to the opposite end of the ICU they were secured in. Her groupies had gone with her, shooting nasty looks at Sharon. Their opinion of her clearly already poisoned by whatever Stephanie had whispered in their ears. Martinez had found a clean pair of scrubs for herself and better fitting scrubs for Victoria's athletic body.

"Thanks," Victoria had said after changing into her new scrubs, and nodded appreciatively to Sharon. "For everything."

Sharon had nodded back and checked to make sure Tommy wasn't listening to them. "Are there any guns on this floor? Other police left?"

"Are more police officers coming to help us?" Martinez had blurted out, wide eyed.

Victoria had only shaken her head silently to both their questions, dousing their hope in cold water. It was then the power had clicked off to the city. The hospital had gone dark for several seconds before the hum of emergency power had clicked on. Martinez and Victoria had seemed to stay close to Sharon's side. The pseudo leadership role she had was picked up on by others as well. More than a few other nurses had seemed to gravitate towards wherever Sharon had stood. Perhaps they thought she was special in the eyes of their captors, and they'd be safer by her side than elsewhere.

No one is safe anymore.

"Brandon, wait for– I can't!" the voice called just outside the door. Tommy panicked and approached the door.

"Wai– Tommy!" Sharon called out but the headstrong boy pressed the metal bar along the door and flung it open.

"Hey! H-hey, what are you doing here?" Tommy's voice cracked as he saw the group of strangers in the dimly lit stairwell. From the corner of the door, Sharon could see the man nearest to Tommy. He was rugged looking, in a dirty and worn-out sort of way.

"Stop or st– Go back down there! Down the stairs! I'll kill y'all, I fuckn' swear!"

"We can't, man," the man said through a labored breath. "You hear that? The screams. That's rabid pounding up the stairs. They'll be here–"

A few of the nurses perked up and went to the doorway at the news of rabid. Sharon felt her heart thumping in her chest. She recalled laying in the dirt, hiding in the Kentucky tall grass as rabid circled around her.

We are trapped on top of this building. If they get into this enclosed room.

"Move downstairs, now! Or I'll throw–"

Tommy was yanked so violently, Sharon flinched even from yards away. In shock of the moment, Sharon watched the boy seeming to shrink in the man's grip as he handled him. The smallest pained, whimper escaped Tommy's lips as his face was smashed into the metal railing repeatedly before being tossed over it, falling down the stairwell.

Sharon drew closer to the doorway, thinking that she could

perhaps dive and close the door, locking it before the man could do the same to her. But then her eyes met the shadows where the man's eyes would be. His cold stare was paralyzing as he glared down at her. Two women were close to collapsing as they panted and gripped their thighs at the top of the stairs. Victoria inched ahead of Sharon. Sharon glanced down at Victoria's hand and saw she had swiped a scalpel at some point and now held the thin blade tight in her fist hidden behind her thigh.

Without drawing attention to it, Sharon put her hand on Victoria's thigh giving her pause. When she looked at her, Sharon only shook her head. Sharon didn't know anything about Victoria other than her being a police officer, but from what she saw of this man, he was larger and capable of violence that she didn't think the officer could match.

Another man almost fell as he pounded up the final steps with the young girl in his arms. Through shallow breaths, he quickly glanced between Sharon, Martinez, and the other nurses behind her.

"They're– they're coming," the sweaty, young man said. "Five flights down... they're coming up." his eyes turned to the nurses as he stepped toward them. "Can– can you help her?" he asked, offering the unconscious girl to them. The girl was ghostly white, and her shirt had bled through from an unseen wound.

Instinctively, Martinez stepped forward following her nursing instincts to start assessing the teenage girl, but Sharon stopped her by putting a hand on her shoulder.

"Wait," Sharon said. "Was she bit? Is she infected?"

The dark-skinned man holding her looked down at the girl's bloody belly as if he hadn't even considered the possibility until that moment.

"No," one of the women on the floor answered. "No, no,

she was shot. Her name's Zoe– she's just a child and she was shot yesterday. Please– Please, help us. My name's Karen and– and we– we don't have any weapons. Please..."

Sharon stepped forward carefully and lifted Zoe's shirt to see the small broken stitched wound that leaked crimson blood from it. There was a crash below as bodies slammed into walls and the screams of the infected howled closer.

"Okay, come on," Sharon nodded at Martinez, giving the go ahead.

"Oh, god, thank you!" Karen cried from her knees. The man carried Zoe inside and the others followed. Sharon felt as though she was letting war refugees into her camp. All of them were soaked in sweat and covered in dirt. The worst of them was the last through the door. The tall man grunted through gnashed teeth as he straightened. One of his arms was slick with blood from a wound she couldn't see.

He stepped inside and eyed the Intensive Care Unit of the hospital. There were a dozen mirror image hospital beds and equipment set up along the windows that overlooked downtown Louisville. On the opposite side of the room, where most of the other women were, there was a nurse's station and a waiting room with couches and TVs.

"What's your name?" the man asked.

"Sharon. Sharon Hill."

"Hill? Help me move these couches," he said, already lifting one side of a loveseat. He only used one arm as the other looked injured and he barely could walk as his feet shuffled along. Sharon lifted the other end, and they walked the gray couch over to the stairwell.

"You a soldier?" Sharon asked, eyeing his uniform as she backed down the hallway.

"Army Ranger," he winced in pain. "Stairs."

"What's– your name?" Sharon adjusted her grip on the couch with her knee.

"Brandon," he said. "Set it down there."

Sharon placed the couch in front of the stairs and Brandon pushed it down with the heel of his boot. It tumbled and slid until it jammed between the wall and the railing. Sharon looked down and saw through the glow of the emergency lighting hundreds of infected charging up the stairs.

"Oh my god," Sharon mouthed as a spark of fear tightened on her spine.

"Come on," Brandon went back inside. "Some of you grab those beds there and wheel them downstairs." Brandon pointed at a group of nurses near the door. The nurses hesitated at first but the shrieks of the infected got them moving. By the time the first of the rabid made it to the nineteenth floor, a mound of patient beds, couches, and office chairs had been tossed into the corner of the stairs clogging the way.

They didn't wait to see if it would stop them. Once the first rabid screeched and clawed at the fabric of the couch, Brandon and Sharon hustled inside and locked the door shut.

Pressing her hands to her temples, Sharon tried to focus. Her house, her family, and life before—it felt like it was buried by a decade of awful memories. She had taken small steps to survive every minute of every day, but now after a thousand steps she stood a lifetime apart from her family.

Keep it together. Put it in its place. Do what you have to in order to survive now. You'll get your family tomorrow.

Sharon looked at the newcomers—the two women who huddled together in the dark corner of the room crying, the two men with eyes lost in stares at nothing, filled with defeat. They, like everyone else, struggled to process what was happening. How the lives they had built over the past decades crumbled to pieces so easily over the course of a few days.

"Get me a bag of O-neg and let's get her down the hall to imaging for a CT-scan," one of the doctor's voices cut through the rest. The young girl, Zoe, was wheeled down the hall in a hospital bed surrounded by Martinez and two other nurses. Karen stayed behind but the other woman with blond hair and faded tattoos across her arm and chest followed the nurses who carted Zoe away.

Another nurse came around and handed bottled water to everyone. Sharon took her bottle of water and offered it to Brandon. His iron jaw was clenched while his watery eyes stared at nothing on the empty floor in front of him. Brandon was preoccupied with a metal necklace of some kind in his hands. Two metal plates dangled from one end. Sharon thought the necklace was a military thing.

Dog tags?

Sniffling, Brandon put the necklace on over his head and took the water. He guzzled half the bottle without a word. "Is it just you guys? Are you all nurses and doctors?" Brandon asked.

"Most of them are," Sharon said.

Brandon nodded as he surveyed the room. "Most of them," Brandon noted the distinction from herself. "Who are you?"

"I'm..." Sharon hesitated to answer. *What am I? A wife? Homemaker? ...Mother?* "I was taken. Out on the road by the Sons of Liberty."

"That who that guy was? Militia?" Brandon asked, finishing off the rest of the bottle of water and tossing it. "Are there more on this floor?"

Sharon shook her head. "Not here. Downstairs in the ER, I think." Brandon's shoulders relax at the news. His eyes looked like he was searching for the next fight. "Are there more soldiers out there? Is there going to be a rescue?"

Brandon's eyes met hers for the first time as he looked down at Sharon. His focus was severe, and his eyes were that of a man twice his age. The women who weren't working on Zoe congregated around the nurse's station and listened to Sharon's conversation. Brandon only responded with a curt shake of his head.

Sharon sighed, confirming what she already suspected.

Brandon went back to being disinterested as he looked out the window. It was an eerie sight overlooking an unpowered city. A dozen dark buildings without a single window lit up. Beyond it was the murky black of the Ohio river that snaked between Louisville and Indiana.

Sharon looked down at the streets. In the darkness, even the asphalt looked like water. *We are surrounded. Isolated. Alone.* It was a haunting thought that struck her. As if a moment of clarity had opened in her consciousness and she understood something that had buzzed in the back of her mind all day.

I'm not leaving this building tonight. I'm not leaving this city. I'm not... I'm not going to find my family.

"Oh my–" Stephanie gasped. "Is that a plane?"

The others joined her as they moved in front of the windows. Brandon, who was crouched over Karen who cried on the floor, was beside Sharon in two strides. Sharon looked but saw nothing. She cupped her hands to the glass around her eyes and then it appeared. With no light emanating from the city and with a full moon, the plane came into focus. It was black and appeared to be escorted by two other jets that followed on its side as they flew in an arch over the Indiana side of the Ohio river.

Karen stood and tucked beside Brandon in a familiar way. Sharon glanced over as Brandon put his arm around Karen's shoulder and hugged her tight to his chest.

"Did you see that?" Victoria asked.

"It just dropped something," someone else added.

"Look over there, there's another plane."

Brandon turned to Karen, cupping her cheek. "Look at me, look at me... I love–"

There was no explosion. Not at first.

Across the river the blinding flash of light ignited and consumed the entire sky. Sharon pinched her eyes shut hard and tried to look away but even with her eyes shut, she could still see. Her hands covered her face and the hot flash of light acted like an X-ray machine, revealing the small knuckle bones in her hands and fingers. The bright light consumed the city before the rumble shook the ground and turned violent.

The pulse of the explosion struck Sharon like a car wreck. She heard the windows shatter into a million pieces, before she felt the splinters dig into her skin as she was knocked off her feet. The deafening crack was the last thing she heard before she felt the whipping wind filled with heat wash over her skin.

Sharon screamed with the others but the roar of the blast sucked their voices from their lungs. Curled in the fetal position, her son's giggling face flashed before her eyes. The warm feel of Annabelle's face pressed against her chest. The smile of Sharon's mother as she peaked underneath the sheet of Sharon's living room fort after a long day's work.

I'm coming home, mom, Sharon thought as she embraced the end.

Wednesday, May 1st

00 Hour, 00 Minutes Until Calamity Event

EPILOGUE

Brandon Armstrong
Louisville, KY

Brandon's eyes opened to a cloud of dust hovering over him and the sound of someone coughing. Everything hurt. He could smell aerosolized concrete. He gasped as he breathed some into his lungs before hacking it up in a wet cough. He couldn't move his legs or maybe he just couldn't feel them. Pushing himself to his knees, he heard the sound of concrete chunks falling off an edge and remembered he was on a top floor of a building.

Blood trickled down his head from an unknown wound. Digging through the upturned beds, drywall, and ceiling tiles, he found Karen shaking beside him as she covered her face. He tried to speak to her, but the words escaped him. He couldn't focus and she wouldn't look up. *She's alive...* He told himself. That was enough. *She's alive...*

Brandon's legs didn't hold his weight at first. He had to take support of a nearby metal piece jutting out of the wall. The floor was a mess of broken glass pieces and overturned furniture. Unabated by windows, the wind whipped in and out of the nineteenth floor of the hospital with alarming force.

Brandon saw others scattered throughout the floor, coughing as they slowly stirred from the floor. The sound of the howling wind turned his attention to the city skyline and showed a sight so terrifying and awe striking, he refused to believe it was real. Stretched across the Indiana side of the border was a sea of fire that burned the ground red even in the middle of the night. Brandon stared speechless at the silhouette of the large, gray mushroom cloud that bloomed in the sky before him, blocking the full moon.

The massive cloud ignited in a blaze with leaps of flames and sparks of lightning. It created a wall of fire between Louisville and the rest of the country. Brandon fell back down to his hands and knees as his legs went weak with disbelief. His stomach turned upside down as he stared at the rubble covered floor, worried he might dry heave what little fluid that remained inside him. Brandon's eyes went in and out of focus as he steadied himself. His eyes centered on the dog tags that swung from his neck beneath his face.

Valhalla waits for no one...

There was hoarse coughing followed by a woman's familiar voice. "Is... is anybody there? Is anybody alive?" Sharon called out between ragged breaths.

"I'm..." Brandon rasped, "I'm alive."

JOIN SAM WINTER'S NEWSLETTER

Book one of the Calamity Series is over

but the story continues in Confliction, Book two.

Read the last chapter ever written of Officer Derrick Hart by joining Sam Winter's Newsletter now!

www.samwinterbooks.com/newsletter

The exclusive bonus chapter will be emailed to you in your welcome email. Unsubscribe at any time.

CONFLICTION

Calamity Series, Book Two

The President of the United States is rushed to an underground bunker as the rabies variant infection devours the nation he swore to protect. The nation is in chaos as millions are slaughtered in Florida. The Chief of Staff must try and stop the spread of this infectious disease while secretly orchestrating Continuity of Government protocols. Should the worst happen, the United States must prevail at all costs.

Meanwhile, Brandon and the survivors in Louisville must navigate the rubble that remains of the city as the infected flood the streets.

The F.B.I. task force investigating this calamity must find answers quickly as the nations of the world reel from the collapse of the United States. *How could this happen? Was this a terrorist attack? An accidental spill at a pharmaceutical company? Who is responsible for the greatest loss of life event in the history of human kind?*

ALSO BY SAM WINTER

www.samwinterbooks.com

Calamity Series

Calamity

Confliction

Fallen City Series

Fallen City

Before The Darkness

After The Light

ABOUT THE AUTHOR

Sam Winter is an American author who writes fiction. Calamity is a post-apocalyptic, horror novel and Sam's debut series that reimagines the collapse of modern society from the very first minutes of disaster.

When he's not writing, Sam enjoys mixed martial arts, binge watching epic shows online, & exploring the world one country at a time. Sam currently resides in Tennessee with his dog and cat.

www.samwinterbooks.com

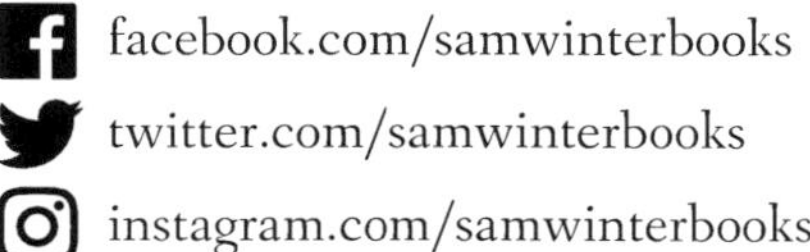

facebook.com/samwinterbooks
twitter.com/samwinterbooks
instagram.com/samwinterbooks
patreon.com/Samwinterbooks

Made in the USA
Middletown, DE
18 July 2021

44399149R00352